Whalesong

Stoney Compton

Nazca Press

Whalesong

Stoney Compton

This edition published by Nazca Press
A division of Misti Media LLC
Available in both Paperback and eBook Editions
1 2 3 4 5 6 7 8 9 10
Copyright © 2012 this edition © 2024 by Stoney Compton
Cover art by Tadd Galusha — http://www.taddgalusha.com
Cover Design by Stoney Compton
Cover Copyright © 2024 Stoney Compton and Nazca Press
Paperback ISBN: 9781963479553
Hardback ISBN: 9781963479584
eBook ISBN: 9781963479546

Dedication

For Robert Silverberg and Karen Haber
Thank you both for all that you do...
And
Researchers and Protectors of Cetaceans Worldwide

Acknowlegements

A shorter version of Book One was my first professional story published in *UNIVERSE 1*, (Bantam Books, 1990), edited by Robert Silverberg and Karen Haber, for which they have my eternal gratitude.

For this edition, **Whalesong** has been re-edited, and some portions modified. The Prologue has been restored (cut by a former editor, I was never convinced it should have been deleted), and small discrepancies have been rectified.

Thank you for reading my work.

Stoney Compton
Farmington
New Mexico
September 2024

CONTENTS

Book One

PROLOG

WHEN THE WELDING FLARE WINKED OUT everything in Alison's vision went black while the bubbleport compensated. By the time the port cleared, the welder was already reeling herself back to the maintenance hatch.

Good, she thought, *the main array can function again.*

As the suited figure entered the hatch below the supervisor's bubble, Alison's gaze shifted to the slice of earth hanging at the bottom limit of her view. Clouds covered the planet.

Although she wondered what a cloud felt like, Earth seemed oppressive. It dominated her life and the community, yet in all her thirty-three years she had never walked on it. Most of *Firm Resolve's* population was native to the forty-year-old station.

Even so, they all knew the station owed much to that fat old lady down there, which is why the space-born provided eyes and ears for the groundhogs; until three days ago.

Last Wednesday freak clusters of small asteroids smashed the three widely spaced communications and radar arrays at the extreme end of the blue web. For 72 long, sightless hours, the station hung without sensors or communications. Being electronically deaf gave Alison goosebumps.

The airlock icon on the screen synapsed from red to green. Carol, the shift welder, was inside and safe.

"Power up," she said tightly into the microphone attached to her shift-boss harness. "Don't fry her gonads. Just boost it easy."

Harri's "Yus, bawz!" made her grin as she watched the three monitors come to life. Pixels bloomed and danced hesitantly across enhancement screens. Numbers and images jumped around — and made ridiculous readings.

"We got all our wires in the right place, Harri?"

"Cubed, A-one. My board is green. You should be getting exact readings and holos up there."

The comm link with the other stations suddenly trilled the emergency code. Alison stared at the screen and her eyes widened as facts surged through her brain.

Holy Mary, Mother of God! Can this be true? Her heart lurched for a nanosecond as it flooded with adrenaline. Instantly her mind surged as close to lightspeed as possible.

She slapped open the comm switch. "Why didn't someone else see this before now!" she screamed, fisting the red panic button. The Alert klaxon screamed at maximum decibels. "Are all the other stations *asleep*?"

"*Resolve!*" a hurried voice shrilled over the comm net. "This is *New Hebron*. You must launch your nukes *now*!"

"Launch yours, too!" she screamed, slashing across the comm switch and cutting off the other stations.

Harri thoughtfully rubbed the bristles on his jaw. They were coming in white on his black skin now, and he wasn't sure he liked that. "What's cookin', mama?" he asked quietly.

"We got the biggest fukkin' asteroid in history running right down our throats! That's what!" she said jerkily.

"Changing screens," he said in his official voice.

"You're relieved," Conners called from the back of the pod.

Harri tapped the Command Display key. "Still a thousand klicks out..." his eyes raced across the screen. He always put his mind in neutral during emergencies — his reactions worked better that way. It still took him a few seconds to really absorb the numbers that finally steadied into flashing red. "Naw, it can't be *that* big!"

"We gotta nuke this one," Alison said in her hardest voice. "I invoke the charter and take full command. Weapons officer, arm 'em all."

"Thirty-six missiles armed — all carry a full case," he replied.

"I know what megatonnage we're talking about here, Hafid. Don't try to second-guess me again!" she snarled.

"Yes, *sir*," he snapped back.

"Launch! Launch every fukkin' one of them!"

At the extreme end of the red web pinpoints of light flared and dwindled into the flat black background, mixing with the resident stars.

"Hafid, how long 'till impact?"

"On your screen," he said with a quaver while his fingers blurred over the pads.

"Seventy-two, seventy-one, seventy," Alison said in a small voice.

"This shit is getting *scary*," Harri whispered.

Alison tapped, and the collision warble pulsated through the network of structures making up her station. She was *Pure Resolve's* shift captain because she could handle the job. But this! *Nobody* could handle this!

"Thirty-two, thirty-one, thirty…"

Anxiety levels surged throughout the station. The damage control crew squirmed into atmosphere suits, and grabbed ESA paks.

Nuclear blossoms erupted 897 kilometers from the station as missiles met the asteroid. The flares coalesced and grew to a monstrous size. The port dimmed to black and flickered redly as the compensators ate themselves trying to cope with the impossible.

"It broke up! A lot of it's gone!" Hafid shouted happily.

"We still got three good-sized moons in different trajectories! Damn this slow son-of-a-bitch!" She pounded on the console.

The trajectories winked on. She jabbed the animation pad. A meter-wide holo of Earth popped into being, turning slowly above the projector.

The four stations appeared as solitary tangles of colored threads equidistant around the planet. *Firm Resolve*, coded yellow, hung closest to the sudden on-rushing threat from deep space.

A red dotted line shot out of the mottled holographic explosion and traced a curve over and down past Earth. A near miss.

A second red line spiraled past *New Hebron*, coded green in the image, passing through Earth's atmosphere over the South Pacific off the coast of South America.

"Ohmigawd," Harri whispered reverently.

A final blood-red line pulsed across the holo erased *Pure Resolve* and impacted the Middle East.

A shocked buzz went through the command center.

"Allah Akbar!" Hafid sang out.

Alison stared out the port and saw death rolling across the stars to her. *At least it'll be quick*, she thought and held her breath.

The massive asteroid smashed into the station at the speed of forty-two thousand kilometers per hour, shattering the fragile tethers of metal gossamer containing its life. As the station impacted across the face of the huge, pitted space traveler, the soft human bodies didn't have time to perish in the vacuum before the space rock atomized them. Their remains adhered to the surface and were cremated in the incandescent journey down through the atmosphere — home to mother.

The death and destruction of the station didn't slow the gigantic object as much as the computers had predicted. It smashed flaming into Syria 3.479 seconds earlier than the atomized machine's final postulation.

Twenty Years Later

Solomon Manaluk edged through the blowing snow; his eyes squeezed nearly shut above his face mask against the barrage of icy crystals. Dark gray clouds scudded ceaselessly overhead, unseen and ignored. He hated to look at the sky, because he could remember when it was blue, and the clouds were white.

Before the stars fell, he thought.

Solomon concentrated on finding meat, his family needed food. His hunting partners, Jimmie Quaasaq and Dominik Pitsook were out here with him. Jimmie was off to his left and Dominik ranged off to his right.

They hunted together because after the stars fell the long storms came and limited visibility for months at a time. Animals had a way of evading a single hunter, but the three of them usually brought something back to their homes on the ice-encrusted coast of the Chukchi Sea. A lot of the People had left after the stars fell, saying it was too hard to live at Point Hope.

Solomon couldn't leave. His father and grandfather were both buried in the cemetery. Martha didn't want to leave either.

The thought of his wife depressed him even further. He thought he had avoided laughing with her during the times she could quicken. But she had borne him a second son.

In other times and other circumstances this would have been a thing to brag about. But he already had a son. Nicholas was a strong healthy two-year-old who displayed alert, quick responses to everything around him. He would be a good hunter, perhaps even an umialik if the sea ever thawed.

But Noah, Martha's name for their second child, was the opposite of his brother: puny, hairless, sickly, always fussing and whining. They hadn't had a decent night's sleep since he was born two months ago.

It didn't take no genius to see that the child was doomed. The quicker it was put out naked on the ice with its mouth packed with snow, the better. But Martha didn't see it that way, and Solomon had another mouth to feed.

Something dark moved ahead of him. He pushed two fingers and his thumb out of his right mitten and grasped the end of the arrow he carried next to the bow in his left hand. Without taking his eyes off the dark quarry, he nocked the arrow, then slowly moved the bow up so he could fire quickly if needed.

It wasn't a large animal, and it wasn't healthy. It staggered as he watched, and it should have been aware of his presence even though he was downwind. He saw a quick flash of fur, and he realized it was a wolf. Solomon was an excellent shot. The arrow found the base of the skull and the wolf collapsed without a quiver. The hunter trudged up to the kill.

"I took you without pain and you will feed me and my family. I honor your inua and thank you for your meat and your hide. Please quickly come back to this world."

The words came effortlessly, a part of the People's tradition as old as the race. Every kill, no matter how big or small, must be thanked with respect.

Solomon wondered if Jimmie or Dominik had found anything. If not, he would have to share his kill with them. He knelt and saw the wolf was old and emaciated.

"Ain't gonna be much meat on you, but it'll all be welcome."

A whistle off to his left told him that Jimmie was finished hunting, whether he had taken anything or not. It seemed to Solomon that Jimmie was losing his energy. Not that long ago Jimmie could go for most of a day on a handful of food.

Solomon reached inside his parka and found the old whistle on its lanyard around his neck. He blew two, quick blasts and put it back against his skin where it would stay warm for further use.

A shape materialized out of the blowing snow. Dominik hurried up to him. He carried two Arctic hares and Solomon immediately felt better.

"What you got there?" Dominik said, bending over the wolf.

"Oldest damn wolf I ever saw," Solomon said with a quick grin. "But we'll eat him anyways."

They waited for Jimmie for another couple of minutes.

"Y'think he got lost?" Dominik asked.

Solomon pulled out his whistle and blew it twice. They waited for what seemed a long time and still saw no sign of Jimmie. Solomon pulled a cord from a pocket and tied the wolf's feet together and hefted it over his left shoulder.

While he worked, Dominik tied both hares to his belt. As one both men carefully positioned arrows so they could shoot in as little time as possible. They slowly moved in the direction where Jimmie's whistle had last sounded.

Without words they moved apart until they could only see the other's shape in the constant snowstorm. Jimmie couldn't have been too far away.

Dominik's bow came up and Solomon snapped his into firing position.

What does he see? He peered ahead and saw something move. It was a lot bigger than Jimmie, and Solomon felt his guts go watery. He forced himself to keep moving.

"Nanook!" he exclaimed despite not meaning to make a sound.

The polar bear heard him and rose to its full height, almost half-again taller than the men. Solomon pulled his arrow back as far as he could and put it into the huge chest.

Two arrows hit the bear a split second apart. The bear bellowed in pain, then went down on all fours to charge them. It went for Dominik. Solomon buried another arrow in its side just behind the front shoulder. He grabbed another arrow.

The bear stumbled and fell on its face, sliding close to the feet of a terrified Dominik who looked like he thought he was about to die. Despite the withering snow-laden wind, Solomon was sweating. He decided to start breathing again.

"You okay, Dominik?" he asked as he walked over to the bear.

In answer, Dominik abruptly dropped to his butt in the snow. His small frame shook, and Solomon knew it wasn't from the cold.

"Good shot," Dominik rasped. "I thought I was dead."

"You'd have made the same shot if it had charged me."

"Sure as hell woulda tried," Dominik said with a crooked grin.

Neither man touched Nanook. Solomon glanced over to a smaller form on the snow-blown ice.

"We'd best see to Jimmie."

Their friend sprawled where he had died, and snow already drifted over him.

"Nanook surprised him," Dominik said.

"Yeah. I bet Jimmie didn't know what hit him."

"You want me to go for the sled?"

Solomon looked at his smaller friend. "Naw, I'll get it. You keep your eyes open. Nanook might have a partner."

"This time of year? They're usually solitary until—"

"That was in the old days, Dominik. Lots of things have changed."

"Yeah. Well, don't get lost."

Solomon trudged back to the village of Point Hope, doing his best to follow his inner compass. He wondered who would feed Jimmie's widow after she had eaten Jimmie's share. For a moment, he pondered taking her as a second wife. Then he shook his head and laughed out loud.

"As if one wife ain't enough trouble!" But the thought flashed through his mind that if it had been Dominik who had died out there, taking Anna Pitsook as a second wife would have been something he might consider, no matter what Martha said about it.

The sky abruptly lightened above him, and he stared up in surprise. The cloud cover had lifted; for a moment, he could see the outline of the sun. Then the lower clouds closed in again with a new blast of blowing snow.

However, Solomon clung to the brief elation. He wondered if it were a sign, but a sign of what? He quickened his steps toward Point Hope.

Three Years Later

Three year old Noah Manaluk struggled with his brother, Nicholas, for possession of the toy sled. Noah, still frail, small, and weak, proved no match for the robust older boy. Nicholas jerked the sled from Noah's hands and knocked him to the floor of the cramped kitchen.

Noah knew that if he cried his father would yell at him in a most un-Inuit manner. So he merely pushed himself against the wall and lay on the floor, guardedly watching the others.

Solomon Manaluk sat at the kitchen table and stared at his youngest son with hot, liquid eyes. "He'll never be a hunter, Martha. Nobody will say nothing if we put him out on the ice." Solomon shivered in the close, moist heat of the room and drank tea from the cup clutched in his trembling hands.

Martha moved her short, stout form between her husband and youngest son. "You're gonna have to put me out there with him." Her voice held no threat, only promise. "Then who's gonna take care of you and Nicholas, Anna Pitsook?"

Nicholas noisily pushed the toy sled across the worn wood floor. "Hup, dogs! Gotta get me a caribou!"

"Now there's the son of a hunter." Solomon smiled at his firstborn. "There's someone worth the meat they eat."

"You ain't brought much meat in lately," Martha said.

"I'm sick, woman. What do you expect?"

"Stop sticking your troubles on Noah! It ain't fair. He's doing the best he can, just like you."

Solomon surged to his feet, knocking his chair over with a crash. The noise hit Noah like a physical blow. He flinched, suppressing the instant urge to hide.

"I'm just a little under the weather," Solomon said with a sneer, pointing at Noah. "But he's worthless."

Martha picked up the chair and held it in her strong hands. "You go to bed now," she told her husband, "...before I do something to you with this chair."

Anger blazed impotently in Solomon's eyes. For the past week, his strength had melted like spring ice in the old days. He shuffled toward the small bedroom, speaking over his shoulder, "Don't you go givin' him any of the good meat!"

"How 'bout that seal you're so afraid of?" she sneered.

Solomon stopped and fixed his feverish gaze on his wife. "That seal is *wrong*. You shouldn't even feed it to the dogs."

She squared her jaw. "Strange things have happened since the stars fell. This seal ain't so different than lots of other things."

"I told you before," he said, "it showed me where it was! I didn't find *it*. It found *me*." He shook his head and turned toward the bedroom. "You do what you want. I got nothing to do with it."

Martha went to Noah and scooped him into her arms, hugging him tight to her ample breasts. "Not everyone is a hunter," she whispered into his ear as she nuzzled his cheek. "There are other things a man can do."

He furtively looked over his mother's shoulder, making sure his father had gone, before allowing himself a slight smile. "What can I do, Momma?"

She looked away from his face, and let her gaze travel around the small house. "Let's go see about that kairalayrak your father won't eat."

Noah wondered if she knew the young ringed seal glowed in the dark. He had peered at it earlier in the evening when the cold storeroom already lay deep in darkness. Not that it ever got truly light in the windowless shed.

Nicholas stabbed a carved ivory caribou with his toy spear. "I take you for meat. I will honor your inua."

Martha carried Noah through the white, frozen night to the shed. "Eee, I remember when I was a little girl, and my mother kept our food in a fridge."

"Could you walk in it, like the shed?" he asked. He felt her smile.

"No, 'course not. There's an old one out back of the shed, that metal box your father uses to smoke fish. That used to be a fridge."

"It's cold now, momma. Why don't you put food in it?"

"It's the wrong kind of cold. The shed is better."

"How did it get the right kind of cold?"

"With electricity, and that's all gone, like gasoline, and motors, n'stuff. Been gone a long time before you were born." She pushed the shed door open and caught her breath. "The seal looks like it's got electricity!"

"Did the fridge glow too?"

"No," Martha said absently as she put him down. She reached

into the small pouch tied to her waist and took out her ulu. The keen, triangular blade with a rounded cutting edge briefly caught the seal's glow as she knelt and butchered the animal with quick, sure strokes.

"Why is papa so mad at me allatime?"

"He's not mad at you. He's just worried about things."

"What things, momma?"

"He's worried the sun ain't gonna come back. He's worried the animals are going to die out or go away. He's been worried ever since the stars fell out of the sky."

Noah could only remember dark, gray sky. "What's a star?"

"One day soon I'll show you. The clouds are thinnin' out more and more. I saw a star through a thin part, I know I did." Martha sliced raw seal liver and sniffed it before giving him a piece. "Eat this, it will make you strong."

Noah obediently popped the meat into his mouth and chewed quickly. He liked raw liver better than anything else. The heavy flavor of bloody organ meat swam through his senses and streamed into his head, making him dizzy.

A surge of joy coursed through his mind, startling him. He stumbled and caught himself on his mother's shoulder, pushing her left hand under the quickly moving ulu.

"Aii! Now look what you've done! I've cut myself." She dropped the knife; blood flowed from the cut that had bisected the back of her hand. She grabbed her wrist with her other hand, squeezing hard to stop the bleeding.

Her barely contained panic leapt from her and lanced through Noah, frightening him. The joy winked out.

"I'm sorry, Momma! I didn't mean to do it." Tears streaked his face and he wanted her to not be so afraid.

"Gotta get your father," she said, lurching to her feet and hurrying into the night. Her panic faded with her. Dimly he felt his father's agitation at yet another frightening thing.

Noah ignored his family. He ate the rest of the seal liver, and it was good. He suddenly felt as if he were looking at himself for the first time and seeing much more than a small boy. But then, there were many things he didn't understand.

CHAPTER 1

SEVENTEEN YEARS LATER

THE POD OF LEVIATHANS MOVED NORTH, great muscles tirelessly undulating to the DNA command of unknown generations. The Humpback whale population knew increase over past seasons. Rarely solitary, they formed pods of varying numbers directed by the whim of nature.

Many cycles of the warm eye ago, the long-teeth suffered calamity. Their numbers dwindled. This spared the pod much of the tearing death.

Because of their scarcity, the long-teeth no longer hunted the Cea across the far reaches of their liquid universe. Only near the edges of the world did they lurk. But even there, any threat from them usually proved minimal.

Thinker followed the great bull, Palff, along with the rest of the Humpback pod. As the others sang back and forth, he would prod their minds, hoping to find what he had shared with his mother, but none responded.

For many cycles of the cold eye, he believed they ignored him as they had ignored the painful death of his mother. While he had vividly felt the agony caused by her rapidly wasting organs, the others remained oblivious and unmoved.

His mother's death inundated him with new emotions and awareness: relief, peace, sorrow, and abject loneliness. No longer did he belong with anyone. None cared if he lived or died.

Thinker tried to nurse from the other females, but all pushed him away. In desperation, he had copied the feeding actions of the others. He stayed in the middle of the great circle of thindrink expelled from the blowholes of several in the pod. They all followed just below the curved wall of gas as it rose toward the top of the world.

Suddenly he sensed the multitude of frantic sustenance panicking in the bubble net and abruptly felt compelled to open his wide maw and engulf as many of the creatures as possible. Of its own volition, his tongue pushed the mass of water through the fibrous baleen filters ringing his mouth in layers. The rapidly expiring sustenance then became easy to swallow and he felt revived and exhilarated.

Although ignored, he was not driven from the pod. Therefore, he prospered over the long migrations from the place where water-becomes-rock to the warm place of little food and much mating. He observed everything around him and remembered all. Slowly he became aware that he was not only unlike the others, but separate and apart in his world.

He moved with them, fed with them, but did not sing or mate although he experienced those urges. Now Palff led them toward the cold water where sustenance teemed.

Some of their songs told of death from long-teeth many migrations ago. But more recent songs told the top of the world had turned to rock much closer to the old mating places than ever before in memory. All revolved around the great loss.

His mother had tried to explain the great loss, but cetacean vocabulary could not contain the concept. The thing he most vividly remembered was one of the last things she told him; we suffered much but gained more.

He followed the pod and slowly prospered, not understanding so incredibly much but learning more and more as the Humpbacks followed Palff north. Excitement grew in Thinker the closer they came to the frigid world. He wondered at this alien reaction since there was nothing in his current existence to match the feeling.

He realized he had much to learn.

In two cycles of the warm eye, he had grown into a young adult. Thinker knew the middle of the pod offered maximum safety from the toothed-ones in their world, and from the long-teeth that waited above.

As the Cea moved through the vast reaches of a mostly pacific ocean, Thinker's mind turned over the imponderables that tormented him while the bull Cea sang the migration song.

The racial history of the Cea lived in their songs.

Events considered out of the ordinary by their author evoked new compositions. Songs that lifted above the average were repeated by others and sometimes were embellished in agreement or counterpoint. Repeated songs usually represented an event common to the memory of the entire pod.

After a time, other events would be added to the growing medley. Each existed as a separate statement, but part of the greater paean. Some lasted many generations after their creator's final dive.

Thinker comprehended more than even the most complex songs revealed. He searched for reason in a universe of liquid geometry and wordless melody, but it eluded him.

He continued his search as the pod moved north into waters growing colder and colder, and closer to the remaining long-teeth.

CHAPTER 2

Noah's mother lay wheezing on her deathbed. He sat next to her, feeling every twinge, pain, and new fear as her body slowly but resolutely shut down. He had learned much in the past seventeen years, but he had not puzzled out how to rebuild organs to grant longer life to anything, especially a human.

His fear measured close to hers. She feared death. He feared life without her.

All his life, she had been there to deal with the others on his behalf. He remembered the day in his eighth summer, half a mile from the village when he had sat on a hummock and pictured an Arctic hare in his mind. Concentrating on the image, he pushed his mind as if avoiding rocks from his peers.

Come to me. Come to me, he thought.

Movement caught his eye and he looked up at the hare hopping down the hill towards him. More movement. More hares. Soon there were nine trembling animals fanned out before him within a hundred paces.

Pain! Shock! Suddenly one leaped into the air and came down thrashing with an arrow through its neck. The rest of the rabbits scattered into the landscape. Two boys rushed up to Noah.

"How'd you do that?" the larger boy demanded. "Can you do it again?"

"I, I am not sure how I did it," Noah said. "Maybe I will try again later."

The boys grabbed their prize and ran off toward the village.

Noah allowed himself to shudder. He had vividly felt the arrow pierce the hare's neck, as he'd been in the hare's mind when it was struck. He hadn't been able to get out before it died.

He knew the village would be apprised of his new power within minutes. Point Hope wasn't a large place, and everyone appreciated something new to talk about. They would want him to do it again, and again, and again.

Not three weeks later, as he studied the intricate construction of sphagnum moss, a rock came out of nowhere and glanced off the side of Noah's head. The rock stunned him, erased his control, and made his mind feel like mush. Balance fled as he fell to the tundra. He retched from the pain and humiliation as distant laughter echoed in his ears. They had already learned they could not catch him unaware if they were close.

And the thoughts he had heard over the years still swirled in his head.

He's a runt.

What good is he?

Where's his hair?

I always feel mean toward him.

He can't even hit a target with a bow, let alone hunt animals!

I suspect he can't even make good babies.

Some of the voices in his head had been there for over a decade, yet the attitudes toward him had not changed. The words and thoughts caught in his mind like fishhooks, replete with pain.

There were a few good memories.

"Noah," Alexi Tuktoolik called. "Which direction d'ya think one should go to find game?"

They were both thirteen that year. Noah liked Alexi, who had never thrown a rock or felt ugly about him. So, he thought about caribou and let his mind sniff mental wind. Nothing close enough to… there! But it wasn't caribou. His eyes narrowed. xxxxx

"Go that way, I think." He pointed. "I feel—" he checked himself before going on. "It may be that musk oxen are over the second line of hills."

"Musk oxen!" Alexi's grin displayed strong teeth. "I hope your feelings are good, Noah. Thank you." He hurried away to find his hunting partners.

Noah watched men depart with spears, bows, and arrows. One carried a priceless rifle that would be used only if the prey threatened a hunter's life.

This is good, he thought. Alexi would make meat today and he wouldn't forget who told him where to look. Tonight, his mother, brother, and he would eat fresh musk oxen steak.

It pleased him to know that he brought in more meat than did his muscular, physically adept brother.

A few years after that they made Noah shaman by acclamation. That memory still gave him pride.

A week after the traditional hunt of a sixteen-year-old with his uncle, he sat in the men's house as his uncle told the men of the village, "When I asked him where we should look for oogruk, he told me to follow. He led me many miles out to where the ice finally thins to water. There was a seal hole there." His uncle took a deep breath, a sign of having reached the important part of his story. "And as Noah stood there, the oogruk came shooting out of the water and landed on its sunning shelf! Noah rushed forward and killed it with one thrust from his kakivak!"

Noah watched his uncle look around at the other men in the kashgee. They in turn regarded the hunter — knowing he would not say these unlikely things if they were not true. Then they turned as one and stared at Noah. An important thing had happened, and it was fitting to discuss it on this day and in this manner.

This was the final and most important day of the Bladder Feast. The hunters who had killed sea mammals over the past year had carefully inflated and painted each creature's bladder. For that was where the animal's inua, or spirit essence, lived.

After sweat bath purification in the kashgee, the men performed the final ritual of the Bladder Feast. They deflated the bladders and returned them to the sea, pushing them under the ice so their inuas would return to their home. The deflated bladders would then become other sea mammals for the People to consume.

"This one is a shaman, surely," Uncle said through the steam.

"How is one to know?" a hunter asked. "Who among us can remember the last true shaman?"

"My grandfather's brother told me there was such a one here when he was a small boy," a second man said. "But the gusiks had already sent their doctors to us. The old ways began to die when they made little gusik doctors out of our young men."

Steam wrapped about the men. All went quiet save for appreciative grunts as pores cleansed themselves and heat penetrated to the marrow.

"We need one who can speak with the inua of our new-but-old world," Uncle said. "That one," he pointed to Noah "...can speak easily with the animal spirits. He can summon the beasts and make them understand they are needed for the People to continue living."

The senior hunter moved toward the door to leave. He stared into the steam where Noah sat. "These things are true. Let us regard him as a special one. Even if there is none to train him, what have we to lose?" The pervading silence indicated agreement.

So Noah enjoyed more courtesy than normal, as well as respect and fear for his powers. He was a man. Almost...

His body changed and he felt physical frustrations previously absent or merely hinted at. He became increasingly aware of the emotional states of his parents. Solomon's vitality decreased markedly month by month which frightened and angered him.

In response, Solomon exaggerated his lusts and vitality to fit what he remembered in his youth. When Solomon initiated "laughter" with Martha, he radiated anxiety, forced lust, and fear. Compliant as always, Martha enjoyed the encounters, even the ones that failed.

Noah felt it all and would become aroused to the point he would have to leave the house. He yearned for a female to respond to him as Martha did to Solomon. He watched the few girls his age, but none seemed aware of him other than as a joke.

Solomon's health abruptly plummeted over the space of a week. Martha approached her son.

"Your father is very ill. Can you help him?"

"How, mother? What would you have me do?"

"Make his pain stop."

"I'll see what I can do for him."

Knowing that his father not only didn't believe in his abilities but also had sneered at them in the past, Noah did not approach him directly. He sat in the tiny kitchen where he had spent his childhood in fear and went into his father's mind to find the source of that fear. He found things much worse than he'd expected.

Solomon knew there was something wrong, because his headache continued to intensify, and it seemed his heart rattled rather than beat. But he didn't trust his son and would not ask him for help. Solomon knew there was nobody else who could do anything, which is why he was so terrified.

Even though the People called him "shaman," Noah knew little about how the human body worked. He wasn't sure how to look inside a person. Despite that, he focused on his father's debilitating headache and realized he could see his father's brain.

A tide of emotions swept over him, awe, curiosity, fear, and superiority. Had he always been able to do this? He set those feelings aside and did his best to try and help his father. He wasn't sure what to look for, but he focused closely and imagined himself walking across the pink surface of his father's brain, jumping lightly over the fissures and bends.

A large, boulder-like form jutted from the surface and pressed against the hundreds of veins two and three deep lining the skull. The mass didn't seem to fit the rest of the innerscape; it glistened oily white as it pulsed at a slower rhythm than the surrounding veins.

Noah didn't know what to do, let alone how to do it. Solomon's pain increased and Noah realized the white mass grew larger as he watched. He imagined he carried a tiny harpoon and stepped up next to the mound and stabbed it.

Instantly, blood inundated him like water from a broken ice dam. Solomon's pain vanished as he collapsed back on his bed. The blood filled the skull around the brain and rapidly increased pressure on it.

The pressure continued to grow as his father's brain slowly shut down. Noah frantically searched for a solution but didn't understand what needed to be done. In awful solitude, Solomon Manaluk died as his son helplessly watched.

Noah pulled his focus from his dying father's head. With tears running down his cheeks, he stared at his mother.

"His pain is gone, but so is he."

"I thought that might happen," she whispered. "Thank you for trying." She went in to tend to her husband.

Noah couldn't decide if he had killed his father or not. The fact he did not mourn the man's death didn't help his mental confusion. Nicholas grieved and lamented his father's passing, but Noah detected a degree of smugness in Nicholas because he knew that he was now the head of the family.

Noah's attraction to the village girls continued to grow.

At eighteen, the soft beauty of Flora smote him. She was somewhat larger than him, but who wasn't? He followed and watched her while she did women's work. His heart pounded with love and desire.

She saw him and giggled, more in embarrassment than any other reason. Still, she did not reject him out of hand. This gave Noah hope.

Others saw him and told her father, Old Nathan, of the shaman's attention. Old Nathan had many children and grandchildren and he loved all of them, but Flora was his youngest daughter, and therefore extra special to him.

He made a point to be near the shaman the next day.

"The People say you watch my daughter as a man watches a woman," the old man said.

Summer warmed the tundra and short-lived wildflowers nodded and bowed in the constant scented breeze. Bright blue again filled most of the sky.

"Your daughter pleases my eye and warms my heart. I would speak to you about marriage," Noah replied, smiling inside.

Old Nathan looked down at the diminutive boy with pity in his eyes. With steel in his voice he said, "Perhaps when you grow into a man."

Instantly perceiving the cold distance in Old Nathan's mind, Noah's eyes flooded with tears, and he fled to the sanctuary of his mother's kitchen. After a time, he again watched from the shadows, but he never spoke as a suitor again.

Thereafter, Noah lived in his mother's house. She constantly tried to integrate her strange son more fully into the close-knit fabric of village life. But his peculiarities created a stark contrast to the rest of the village and most people felt unsettled in his presence.

She also arranged his services as a shaman. Some, mainly those who had criticized her son in the past, paid more than others for his services. But once agreement was reached, she would tell her son what he must do.

When the wife of the junior umialik fell ill, the shaman was requested.

"Go make the umialik's wife well," she told him. "Her inua is not strong. She needs your help."

As Noah edged into the umialik's house the stricken woman's mother and sister looked up from the bedside and hope filled their eyes. The wooden-faced husband watched the shaman carefully as if memorizing his every movement.

Noah looked down at the woman's sweating face, glassy eyes, and trembling limbs. Her tortured breathing seemed unnaturally loud. Uneasily, he felt death shadowing the room and the woman's total surrender to it.

Quickly he probed her being, seeking leverage against extinction. He found nothing. Her inua lacked strength.

She not only accepted death; she welcomed it. She was tired of the constant work required of the wife of an umialik. For years her joints had ached like those of a woman twice her age.

She lost her only child to the wasting disease. Even though her husband was young and an umialik, sex with him was not as enjoyable as it had been with others. Death seemed inviting, a release of her inua so she could start over in another life.

With the death of his father fresh in his mind, he did not try to mentally adjust or manipulate any portion of the woman, but he admitted to himself that he had no idea what to do for her in either direction.

Noah found it impossible to convey her feelings to her husband without becoming offensive. Nothing he could do or say would change the outcome of this situation.

Without once visibly touching her he turned to the man and said, "I am sorry, but your wife is dying. There is nothing I can do."

The two women began wailing. Noah left the grief-stricken whaling captain without comfort or further apology, ashamed of his incapacity.

The umialik instantly hated Noah, seeing only a shaman who had refused to extend his much-demonstrated powers. Being a shaman was a double-edged knife. After all, they usually buried their mistakes.

The captain spoke with malice to the other villagers and found ready listeners.

Soon Noah came close to starvation. No longer did fresh fish appear in the passageway between his door and living space by those wishing him well. The People no longer gifted him portions of fresh seal or walrus. The People did not speak to him when he passed.

Feeling the People's anger, he began to hate the People.

As the People shunned him, he pushed the game away. Hunters came back to the village empty-handed. The snowshoe hares eluded the snares, seals ceased appearing at breathing-holes in the ice if men waited, and the caribou took a different route. Even Nanook, the fearsomely respected polar bear, could not be found.

When hunters from Sheshalik visited and found the People of the village near starvation. They gaped in amazement.

"Game is more plentiful than ever," the hunters said. "The sun again reflects on the water. Have you offended an inua?"

The People reconsidered events of the past few months and decided that Noah had been wronged. The senior whaling captain, Nicholas Manaluk, accompanied by the widowed junior umialik, as well as the oldest trapper in the village, sat outside Noah's house and called for him to come out.

"Noah Manaluk, we would speak with you," Nicholas called to his brother.

Noah's bald head gleamed moon-like in the shadowed opening as he pulled back his door.

"Do you wish to speak with the shaman, or kill him?"

"We wish to speak with you, Shaman," the trapper answered.

"I bring you food, though I have but little," the junior umialik said as he pushed a bowl of rancid blubber toward Noah.

Noah stepped out and sat on the ground in front of his door. "I would offer tea, but I have none," he said.

"We thank the Shaman for his thought," Nicholas said evenly. "But all we ask is that the shaman help us find meat. Since the, ah, misunderstanding," he stopped and cleared his throat, "hunting and fishing has brought us very little game. We now realize we have wronged our shaman. We ask his pardon."

As the other two nodded their agreement to the umialik's words, Noah realized this was a very hard thing for his brother to do. The ingrained antipathy for his older sibling lessened a bit.

"The shaman holds no grudges," Noah said, though it was not so. "I would be happy to use my gifts for the People." His eyes squinted in the warm summer sun, and his voice fell. "But I thought I was not needed."

"The People starve," the old trapper said flatly. "Our lives are in the shaman's hands. If the shaman would speak to the animals and ask them to return, he will be given a hunter's share."

"Caribou are moving this way. They walk on this side of the Kukpuk." Noah nodded toward the river, flowing in a wide bend around the village before finding the ocean. He looked at his brother. "It would be good to put out nets at the mouth of the river, as the whitefish are many."

Respect returned. People were careful not to offend him. He perceived their efforts and retreated from the everyday life of the village.

No matter their attitude, he was lonely.

The awful day came when his mother's now-frail body could bear no more. Her decline worsened as he watched. Carefully he probed her being and could find nothing broken or damaged; her body had worn out.

He spent hours by her side, remembering past events and conversations. Her ever-present protection had given him the chance to flourish mentally if not physically.

His mother gasped, bringing him back to the awful present. She muttered something.

Noah bent close and put his ear to her mouth.

"Water . . ."

He quickly filled the cracked glass container from the bucket of drinking water and held it gently to her lips. She drank, and the ghost of a smile creased her lips. She eased back into her fading mind.

"You are a good son," she whispered.

Abruptly he couldn't find her. Her mental presence dissipated like smoke from a dying fire.

"Mother? Mother can you hear me?" He spoke just to break the awful silence. He knew she couldn't hear him.

He bent over her still form and sobbed, more frightened than ever before in his life.

What will I do without her?

The door opened and Nicholas walked in. Noah looked up with a streaming face. Nicholas frowned.

"Men do not cry when old women die. She had a long life, and she will be missed. Now come with me. You are needed."

"Your mother just died!" Noah shouted. "Where is your

respect?"

"The women will take care of her. You no longer have her to hide you from the world. Come with me, Shaman. The village has need of your talents."

Noah felt the disdain in his brother's mind, but his only option was to follow him into the windy spring day.

Noah Manaluk hunched against the bitter wind to deny the elements his body heat and tried to ignore the slights still fresh in his memory. He'd have had an easier time forgetting about the wind than how his brother had acted after their mother had died. But he had a job to do, and he was going to do it. An old pair of precious binoculars hung ceremoniously around his neck despite their uselessness. The others had insisted the shaman accept the honor and take them for whale watch, even though they knew he had no need for them.

For weeks the tides and newly revealed spring sun wore away the pack ice and now the Chukchi Sea sparkled blue for miles. Errant floes dotted the frigid water, but for the third year in a row, the route to the feeding grounds lay open for migrating whales.

Since the time the stars fell on the gusiks, the whales had increased their population. For over a generation, no factory ship plied the seas the way Noah had been told they once had to take what little sustenance the People could find. According to the oldest grandmother in the village, those long, hard years since had brought the sea to an approximation of the ancient days prior to gusik domination.

If the great nations of the Magic Age still existed, they no longer concerned themselves with the People.

How would it feel to have a star fall on you? Noah wondered before setting that thought aside for more immediate concerns. Would this be the happy moment he was recognized and rewarded for his abilities?

Would the young women of the village finally understand his worth beyond aiding the day's hunt? Or would they continue to treat him with indifference and crude humor?

Where were the whales?

Motion caught in the corner of his left eye, and he recognized Ben Adams hurrying along the shore toward him, nimbly skipping over up-thrust chunks of pressure ice, something Noah wished he could do half as well. Noah cast out to sense the presence of anything other than young Ben. But he still sensed nothing.

"They're out there! They're out there!" the breathless shouts could be heard at fifty yards even though the wind blew his words off to the left. Ben skidded to a stop in front of the seated man.

"I saw," Ben gasped for breath, his twelve-year-old chest heaving. "I saw a whale!" He turned and pointed back the way he had come. "Out there. Many, I think!"

As Noah squinted up at the boy, the wind snapped the wolverine trim of his sealskin parka out in front of his twenty-year-old face.

"I do not feel them," Noah said. "How far out are they?"

"'Bout half a mile, maybe more." Ben peered back at Noah, trying to fathom the mind in that bald skull, and amazed that anyone could doubt his sharp eyes.

Noah left the boy's mind in ignorance and let his gaze wander back out to sea. "That's too far for me to pick them up. But if you're sure they're out there, go tell my brother and the other hunters."

Ben's smile flashed. In gratitude, he whirled and sped toward the village. Noah concentrated, searching for a quickening in the cold water. Still nothing.

He glanced over his shoulder toward the village. Many of the older white-man-built houses long ago yielded to the elements or became too difficult to heat. So many of the People had returned to the wood and sod iglus of old. Men emerged from their houses and ran toward the walrus-hide umiaks waiting at the water's edge.

His eyes flicked around the horizon, focusing as a medium-sized gull caught his attention. He probed its simple thoughts of constant appetite before dismissing it.

Voices reached him from the village. Whale hunters arrived at the skin boats; their eyes sparkling and faces flushed dark with excitement. The crews quickly pushed their umiaks out into the icy water and vaulted over the sides to grab long-handled paddles.

"Have they come yet, Shaman?" asked Nicholas Manaluk, senior umialik, captain of the largest umiak, and Noah's older brother.

"My mind has yet to touch them. But if Ben is correct, they will be here soon." Noah paused, then added significantly, "With his eyes on the beach you didn't need the shaman here to find them."

"The People didn't need the shaman to find them, but to bring them to the hunters." The whaling captain turned and walked down-wind toward his umiak where it moved restlessly in the water, held by a single crewman.

Noah sat looking after the solidly built Nicholas for a moment and then grunted stiffly to his feet. Still small for an Inuit, his slight body remained hairless. Even with a coating of seal fat on his skin, he constantly suffered from the cold. More than ever, he felt convinced of being born in the wrong place and to the wrong People.

Troubled in spirit and mind, still reeling from the loss of his mother, he glanced out and saw the waterspouts of whales clearing their lungs. Noah squinted, measuring with his eyes. The spouts only shot about ten feet into the air; he knew that bowhead whales usually spouted twenty to twenty-five feet.

This must be a Humpback pod. The frothy plumes revealed its location. Easy hunting today.

He shrugged and ambled down to take his place in the largest umiak to help his brother, the senior umialik, and his crew harvest as many whales as possible.

CHAPTER 3

THE POD SLOWED WHILE THE WHALES FED ON THE RICH, fat krill in the cold waters. Thinker slowly became aware of the approaching long-teeth. They remained distant from him but closed on the outer ones of the pod.

A summons glowed across the far limits of his awareness. Thinker ceased feeding as wonder raced through him. There existed another mind in this universe — he had brushed it with his own!

But it lived among the long-teeth?

Curiosity overcame caution and Thinker's flukes propelled him toward the summons despite its promised menace.

Pain! Fear! Anguish! All cascaded through his mind. The long-teeth had struck their first victim while the rest of the Cea continued their leisurely feeding. The silent scream carried the impact of a physical blow.

The long-teeth struck from above the world. Would the one who touched him stand out from the others? Could he see the one with his weak eyes if he pushed up out of the world?

Working swiftly upward, Thinker broke out of the world and into the thindrink, his eyes wide and casting about. He saw brightness and a confusion of unreferenced images before his great body smashed down into the world again. Frustration washed over him, another alien thing to ponder over time.

Thinker felt the summons again, stronger now, closer. His mind tingled with excitement. How could he communicate? How?

~We need your flesh. We must take your flesh to live. Be not afraid. Your inua will be respected. You must come now.~

Startled, Thinker angled down and violently fluked into the depths away from the overwhelmingly compelling presence. In fright and awe, he drifted to a stop and hung motionless while trying to grasp this reality.

Slowly, carefully, Thinker sent his mind up and touched one of the long-teeth who rode the top of the world. Hunger and fear dominated all else. The mind remained unaware of his presence. Thinker touched another.

~What? Who are you? Where are you?~ It responded.

The thoughts burst out of Noah in a spasm of surprise. Alien wonder surged through his mind - questing, yearning, and seeking something undefined. Glimpses of creatures unknown to him flickered amid the jumbled thoughts and half-formed questions. Unsettling tendrils slid through his brain.

Searching for my inua? Noah wondered.

The umiak lurched as the harpooner struck again at the breaching whale. Gravely wounded, the whale unknowingly revealed its presence by the sealskin floats spiked into its flesh. The second attack pierced an artery.

Gouting blood steamed in thick red ponds on the crisp blue sea. The whale's lungs filled with blood. Drowning in its own essence, it could not dive to escape the predators.

The crew of the umiak paddled mightily, running the skin boat onto the back of the whale. Grabbing a third harpoon the umialik leaped over the side of the boat and plunged the sharp, toggle-headed, steel point deep into the massive head, before violently jerking back on the shaft. The steel head snapped open to its fullest width, ripping even more tissue.

Blood fountained anew, showering the man. The great mammal shuddered and stopped moving.

"Eee-yah!" Nicholas Manaluk spun around as he shouted. He gave his crew a wide smile while holding clenched fists above his head, stamping out a successful-hunter dance step on the whale's back. He crowed, "We eat well this day!"

The crew returned his smile with happy laughter, save one — the strange one. Nicholas lost his smile as he focused on his brother. The shaman stared into the water with exaltation blazing on his face.

From the depths, Thinker sent his mind into that of the long-teeth's with a speed so great it pierced unperceived defenses like a narwhal horn. Images, knowledge, wonder, fear, pain, cold, and threat congested the long-teeth's mental capacity. Thinker beheld fragments of images, a glowing seal, creatures unknown to him that swayed on two flippers on rock, and gave his host pain and something quickly defined as anger. The awesome visions abruptly mixed with dread.

The long-teeth possessed reason. But they would kill all the Cea. *They would take our essence!*

This mind fears the Cea. This mind bites, seeking not ponderables but our flesh. These small beings would have us for sustenance?

Thinker filled his mind with questions, then sent it lancing into the long-teeth.

Noah grabbed his head with both hands, trying to hold the presence still long enough to attain understanding. His fingers ripped down from his crown, leaving sparkling lines of blood in their wake. The insistence pulled at him, commanding, pleading, and smothering his ability to respond.

His appetite seethed with excitement to the point of incoherency. His inua fought through waves of amazement at this thing.

~¿Why? You kill us? Why? You would eat of our flesh? Leave us. We mean no pain to yours. Why do you seek to still our essence?~

"Wait!" Noah screamed. His eyes squeezed shut and his fists ground impotently into ears that heard no voice. "Let me answer you!" His two sides collided in haste and futility.

Thinker let his mind relax and received the mélange of impressions flowing from the long-teeth. He circled his dead pod member, waiting for a reason to explain away his growing fear and new-birthed anger.

Nicholas Manaluk stared at Noah, feeling the hair on his neck and scalp rise. "What is happening?" he asked. The crew twisted around to stare at Noah.

"The shaman has never injured himself before!" Nicholas said. His brother always avoided pain, as well as toil, he reflected. Noah was the last of their father's seed and coddled by their newly deceased mother. Otherwise, he would have perished many winters ago, freezing unprotected in the open, his mouth packed tight with smothering snow.

Suddenly Nicholas spied the great body circling the kill on which he stood. "My brother has brought a second whale to us!" Past transgressions and strangeness evaporated; Nicholas once again felt dazzled. He began to chant.

"What power our shaman possesses. There can be no other like him. How fortunate for our village!

"How proud his mother and father would have been! I am honored to have such a one for my brother. Another harpoon, quickly! The shaman cannot hold the whale forever."

Nicholas' shout to the boat penetrated Noah's consciousness.

Noah tore his mind from what he now realized was a whale, to stare at Nicholas as the umialik pulled the razor-edged, steel-tipped spear back in preparation to kill. His warring sides instantly coalesced.

"NO!" the hoarse scream skipped across the water. Men in other umiaks suddenly froze at their labors to stare at the shaman. "It thinks. It speaks to me!"

Nicholas Manaluk's startled eyes flicked across the men in his boat and rested again on Noah. A vicious sadness swept over him as pride died and anger blossomed.

"This is too much," he shouted. "My brother the shaman has finally walked on rotten ice. Bid it farewell, Noah." He threw the harpoon with all his corded strength.

Thinker entered Noah's mind again. Finding it easier this time — he knew the way. He witnessed the confrontation between the two long-teeth. They called themselves men and knew before Noah that the killing tooth would bite.

Thinker rolled and fluked away from the threat. The killing tooth ripped across his side before falling into the world. Pain arrived, accompanied by realization and regret.

Thinker allowed this new thing, hate, to expand in his mind. It fed on the regret and realization that the Cea would always be sustenance to men. Nothing could change that.

If the Cea did not become food, the men would suffer for the lack. Their minds could only meet in mutual fear.

Thinker curved down under the drifting carcass of the young bull, concentrating on the blood-billowing pain in his side, allowing it to feed his growing malice. Moving his flukes in swift arcs, singing a new song, one of vengeance, he strained upward.

Noah screamed, fighting the slippery presence in his head. For a moment Noah followed the other, sliding into cool, pale, greenish-blue vistas of inviting liquid ponderables. But the harpoon sealed off access to that mindscape with pain and outrage, leaving hate for Noah and his kind.

Pulling the thrown harpoon up by the attached rope, Nicholas Manaluk moved to take the few steps back to his umiak, feeling fear here, not understanding exactly what—

The leviathan broke from the water in a great spray, rising impossibly up and up, blotting out the sun, throwing its towering shadow over the suddenly small umiak filled with men who gape, awestruck. As the whale began its remorseless descent onto the boat, Nicholas and his crew screamed out their fear and anger, knowing death in the hugeness falling on them.

Noah fought his way into the enraged mind of the whale and realized only one path remained if he wished to live. He filled his lungs with air and dove from the doomed boat. His heritage, his mind, his very soul rebelled at his choice. For the People did not swim.

Under the water, Noah twisted about and saw the great body smash the umiak and crew between itself and the dead whale. Then it slid across the drowning and crushed crew to disappear into the depths of the frigid Chukchi Sea. Pieces of wood frame and paddles bobbed to the surface behind the immense body.

Men he had known all his life screamed through the water at their fate, at the whale, at Noah. Their dying hate for Noah tore into him, ripping at his wide-open mind. The raw emotion beat him into a mental numbness.

Noah cast about for the familiar aura of his brother. Nothing remained. Nicholas Manaluk, along with his disdain for his unmanly sibling, breathed no more. Noah felt an emotional weight rise from his freezing shoulders.

He sank deeper. The numbingly cold water turned his clothing into deadly anchors. His lungs, wanting air, tried to spasm. His mind raced and he fought to shed his parka. Panic confused his wooden fingers and he pulled at the wrong lashings.

Thinker regarded the beings that fell struggling through his world. As he watched, each lost their essence. One didn't need teeth to take essence — his body had crushed them, and their lungs could no longer function.

However, the one who jumped out of his way lost essence also. Why did he not rise to the top of the world and refill his tiny lungs? As Thinker probed for the answers, he realized that this was the one who had spoken to him.

The only thing that had *ever* spoken to him.

A deep-set eye in a wall of gray flesh regarded Noah in his struggles.

An image of himself being held above water snapped into Noah's mind, a note of inquiry wafting about it.

~*Yes!*~ Noah's eyes bulged with the intensity of his desire.

Thinker rolled under the man, noting the fear and panic that raced through the small, helpless creature's mind, and lifted him into the thindrink. Thinker carried the man as close to the edge of the world as he could go before he stopped.

~*You must swim the rest of the way by yourself. My world ends.*~

Noah shivered violently in the stiff breeze. ~*The water is over my head. I would drown.*~

Thinker sensed the presence of many men who watched them from the rock-where-the-world-ended. ~*¿Will not your own kind help you?*~

Thinker heard the summons Noah sent; ~*Jonathan, one would thank you for passage to the beach*~. One of the surviving umiaks pulled alongside Thinker and Noah slid off the whale's massive head and fell into the boat. Thinker noticed that none of the crew looked at Noah, or at Thinker.

Thinker let himself seep into the minds of some of the men. Singly and collectively, they struggled with abject terror. As the men pulled the boat onto the great rock, the Jonathan-man called for warm robes to be put on Noah.

"I will sit here," Noah said, sinking down on the beach where he could look out at Thinker. "But I would also be grateful for some hot tea."

The men nodded to Noah and all of them hurried toward their houses. Thinker rolled the concept of a house around in his mind, and could not comprehend it. As Jonathan held the most terror of them all, Thinker lurked on the edge of the man's consciousness.

"The shaman spoke to me!" Jonathan said, glancing over his shoulder.

"Many heard him ask for tea," one of the others said.

"You don't understand. The shaman spoke inside my head!" Jonathan tapped his forehead. "The shaman didn't make a sound that ear could hear."

"What did the shaman say?" another asked, as a third said, "That's why you had us go to him, isn't it?"

"Yes! The shaman said he needed passage to the beach. Has the shaman always been able to do this thing; speak inside our minds?"

The mates of the men hurried out from the houses. Thinker discovered they were called women. One of the women said Noah must be a witch.

The fear of the men and women increased. Thinker finally refocused on Noah. *~¿Why do your kind fear you?~*

~Because I am the shaman.~

~¿Shaman is the same essence as witch?~

Noah jerked. He looked toward the village where the men and women all crowded into one house. *~Who believes I am a witch?~*

~All of them.~

Noah's mental focus weakened and abruptly disappeared as he felt for the minds of his own kind. In a few heartbeats he brought his attention back to Thinker. *~They thought to kill me as a witch.~*

His thoughts carried something that Thinker found difficult to identify until he deftly wove through Noah's mind and found the concept of "smugness." He also uncovered mental pain from Noah's past, and the inability of the whale to understand it was as disturbing as the fact that Noah nurtured the ancient anguish by reliving it. So many things to ponder.

~But I sent them great dread. They will not wish to harm me now.~

~There is much I do not understand,~ Thinker said. *~Men seem to be a confusion. But I sense symmetry in your thoughts.~*

~We have much to discuss.~ Noah smiled and drank his tea.

CHAPTER 4

Noah felt almost warm wrapped in furs, wrapped in furs on the snow-covered beach, his hands folded around a large mug of hot tea. Fragrant steam warmed his nostrils. Yet, he didn't notice — his attention dwelt elsewhere.

~*Are there more like us?*~ Noah asked.

~*No. Yours was the first mind to touch me.*~

~*I am alone among my kind also. Until today I have never let the people know I could see their thoughts. As you see, they wished to kill me.*~

~*¿Kill? They would eat you?*~ Thinker felt more perplexity. So many new things to understand, including things happening in his own mind. He now saw the Cea from an entirely new perspective.

The men understood about the great cycles of the Cea, and where to wait for them. Only because of their own limitations had the men not killed the pod off completely.

The surviving umiak crews spread the tale destined to be a legend for hundreds of generations. The shaman who became an inua and returned to the People in the form of a man on the back of a whale was obviously a witch. When the witch called for warm furs and hot drink, they accommodated him.

Nevertheless, none looked him in the face for fear of losing their own inua, and all retreated quickly after serving him. Finding no other rationale for this thing, the People decided the flesh of whales henceforth to be forbidden as food. The villagers quietly packed. They and their descendants would forever follow the caribou like their Inuit cousins of Alaska's Interior.

Early in the evening, Noah became hungry and tired beyond any point he had ever before reached.

~I must take sustenance and rest. Will you be in this place when I return?~

~I will be here.~

Noah wondered at the lack of activity, the absence of villagers bustling about their daily chores. When he realized the dogs were gone, an ember of dreadful reality burned into his mind.

He realized that the low mental buzz created by the mass consciousness of the villagers had disappeared. Rushing to the nearest house, he stopped at the door and called politely into the passageway. "This one asks permission to enter."

His voice echoed off bare walls. Noah walked from dwelling to dwelling. Each empty house pushed the barb of loneliness deeper into his mind until he sat down on the frozen ground, leaned against a sod-covered wall, and sobbed.

Noah didn't know exactly when the People left. For the first time in over fifty thousand years, only one human dwelt in the village on the Chukchi Sea. None of the People would ever return to that place, for a powerful witch lived there.

~¿Emptiness surrounds you?~

~The people have left. I made them fear me and they have left me,~ Noah said, suppressing a sob.

~¿Why do they fear you?~

~Because of you. They think I am a witch.~

Thinker grappled with the anguished statement. Nestled between the pain and fear in Noah's mind he found resentment.

~¿Do you wish me to leave?~ the whale asked.

"No! Don't leave me! I would die…" Noah suddenly realized he screamed out loud. He didn't care. Tears and words flowed from him in steady streams. "What am I to do? I am not a hunter; I am not anything. Yet I have no wish to die, nor can I follow the People. They would kill me as soon as they saw me."

~¿What are your needs?~

"Good question," Noah mused aloud, wiping his eyes, and collecting himself. *~I must seek answers.~*

He would have to do for himself, and hunger pangs already made his gut growl. He took inventory of the abandoned village.

The People had left quickly. He found hides of caribou and walrus, carried them out, and dropped them on the ground. A fish net with two small tears, a metal pot, fishhooks, and an old ivory-tipped spear all piled up in front of his house as he wandered back and forth between the silent dwellings.

Constantly he debated with himself. Never in his life had he fit in with humans. Why then did this abandonment cause him so much grief? Had hope abandoned him along with the People?

Finally, Noah entered his own house and saw it with new eyes.

His mother's pallet lay empty, and he wondered if the People had taken her with them. It was traditional that the women of the village clean the deceased and prepare them for burial. In a few more weeks the ground would be soft enough to dig graves.

His mother was probably up in the burial house with the others who had died over the long winter. That would have to be burial enough. He now faced more practical matters.

What do I own? Through the years he had received many payments and gifts due to a shaman. Since his mother handled all his affairs, he had not really cared what form payment took for his services.

Now, suddenly, it all mattered. Faint amazement sifted through his mind at the discovery of a fine rifle complete with a box of rare cartridges, a steel-tipped spear, two pairs of sealskin boots, caribou jerky, and a wooden bowl of slightly rancid muktuk: small cubes of whale blubber.

~Eat not of my kind.~

A tendril of menace eeled through Noah's mind, threatening salvation. He dropped the muktuk on the floor, walked out the door and stared at the water.

~You would have me starve?~

~¿Sustenance?~

Images of different species of fish flicked through Noah's mind. Most he did not recognize. Some were swimming nightmares. Then other dwellers in the sea flashed through his mind's eye — seal, walrus, eel, squid, crab, snails, even clams and mussels.

Noah picked the creatures he knew to be of high food value, mentally nodded when their likeness passed through him. He waited at water's edge when the images stopped.

~¿The Cea feed always. You?~

~No. I need but little by your standards. But I need food every day.~

~Allow me quick heartbeats.~

Noah puzzled at the request as he rose and wandered back up the shore. Of course — time. He sat on the pile of furs and watched the surface of the sea.

~¿You are now unable to reproduce?~

~I need a female of my own kind.~ Noah didn't wish to follow the thought.

~I cannot help you swim there, but I give you this.~

A terrified Ring seal shot out of the water and landed near Noah's feet. The mammal slid to a halt and, seeing the human, began frantically beating its flippers to regain the water. Noah stared in perplexity at the forty-pound animal.

He had no weapon, not even a club, with which to harvest it. The seal moved quickly, sliding with rhythmic contortions, toward the water. Noah rushed over and kicked it in the body, away from the shore. The blow almost broke his foot.

The pinniped snarled and gnashed formidable teeth at him. Noah danced off to the side and kicked it in the head with his other foot. The seal spun on the ice, rolled over, and quivered violently.

Remembering the only other kill he had ever made, that of the oogruk, Noah felt sure he witnessed death throes. As he walked toward his house for an ulu to butcher the animal, it convulsed and began moving blindly toward the water again. Noah became enraged.

He had fought it as best he could, but it was not enough. He had never needed physical strength before and did not possess it now. In a flash of panic, he looked through the creature's mind, into its neural system, and screamed, "Die!"

The seal bent double in a huge convulsion, then lay still.

Noah Manaluk seemed to step outside of himself and look down on the slight Inuit watching the flippers quiver, seeing the eyes change from the window of inner life to mere glassy flesh. A wave of rapture infused him. Elated and horrified at the same time; never had he dreamt that he possessed such power!

~I go to feed now. I feel needs in you that must be met. I will be here when you return~, Thinker said.

The rapture evaporated and suddenly Noah stood truly alone, but he was too hungry and exhausted to care. He moved toward the house in search of the ulu that had belonged to his mother.

CHAPTER 5

SPRING PASSED QUICKLY INTO THE BRISK ARCTIC SUMMER. Noah spent most of his time sitting on the beach. There was much information for the two mammals to share and try to understand. They found difficulty with many concepts. Within weeks Thinker partially understood Noah's vocabulary and added to it daily.

The human definition of family was not alien to Thinker. However, he could not fathom a village, or staying in a single location all one's life. He finally came to view the villages and towns of the humans as barnacles at the edge of the world. But, the idea of continents swam totally beyond his limits, as did the concept of love.

It took Noah some time to realize that Thinker lived in a world six times larger than his, and just as alien to him as his was to Thinker. Nevertheless, Noah did not understand at first when Thinker told him it was time to depart the Chukchi Sea.

~*Why can you not stay here with me?*~

~*My inua bids me leave to find my own kind.*~

~*But they cannot speak to you as I do. Why must you go?*~

~*It is time for me to seek my own kind* (A vision of two whales gamboling deep in a serene ocean,) *and the world becomes rock where the thindrink lives. I would die here.*~

The image of a drowning whale, sinking slowly under a mantle of impenetrable ice, faded slowly from Noah's mind. A feeling of desperation surged through him.

~*What will I do?* (A human figure stands in the midst of a whiteout, lost in the very center of its own world,) *how will I find sustenance?* (As Noah eats, his food disappears from his hands, and he looks about in confusion,) *who will I talk to?*~ (Noah holds his head in both hands, eyes clenched shut, corded jaw in a grimace as tears streak his face.)

Thinker remained silent, equally confused at the psychological anguish most humans could have identified as guilt. Totally unexpected, these concepts surfaced for the first time. There seemed no way to ignore the mental biting.

~You go also. (A human figure swims, in a manner impossible to that species, next to a whale as a feeling of inner warmth suffuses both.) *With me.~*

~I cannot swim. I would drown.~

Both pondered the image of a whale lifting man to air at their first meeting. The crushed umiak sliding down into the ever-darkening depths mocked Noah.

~A boat! I could go with you in a boat — wait, give me some heartbeats.~

Noah quickly searched the empty village. He was sure he had seen — Yes! Behind, who had lived here? No matter. Here sat two boats stored on a driftwood rack.

The newest, a kayak, was built in the old way, using the skins of seals and coated with shark liver oil. The other was older and much larger, a Magic Age variation of a baidarka. Like so many other things, Noah had never given the narrow boats much thought. This baidarka was reminiscent of the early "more than a kayak" boats by virtue of more than one opening for occupants.

Now he examined each boat with care. The sealskin kayak he eliminated quickly. It would require much maintenance and seemed small for a long voyage. The baidarka featured a frame of lightweight metal tubing carefully lashed together and covered with a translucent polymer skin born in the old Magic Age.

The boat appeared to be in excellent condition. It measured ten long paces from bow to stern and offered three circular openings from which paddlers could propel the craft through the water.

He felt sure he could get all he needed from the village into the boat with him. After carefully and laboriously lifting the boat off its rack and turning it upright, he found it possible to slip completely inside the hull and lay on the spruce floorboards with ample room to wrap in blankets.

He entered the cluttered but spiritless house, and sought the equipment essential for the boat's operation. He found three yellowed plastic domes, two metallic-cloth sails, which fanned out and back from each side of the mast, paddles, air cushions, and other objects whose functions he could not readily decipher. It took him the rest of the day to figure out what each part did, where it fit while in service, and where it was stowed when not being used.

As a child, his uncle had taught Noah the rudiments of the kayak. He proved a poor student, mostly because the endless repetition of instructions bored him. He grasped the principles immediately and given more of a chance might have become proficient. But poor students are not trusted alone with an uncle's only kayak.

Now he had the time, and the need. One full day saw the boat and its equipment transported to the water's edge and set up. One more day sufficed to provision it as completely as possible. On the following day the last human abandoned the village on the Chukchi Sea to the ages.

.

CHAPTER 6

THE BOAST RACED ACROSS THE WATER. The wind at his back, Noah grinned and pushed the right-side pedal with his foot, and the bow of the boat moved slightly in that direction.

This was the way to travel!

After paddling and sailing only a little he already found himself farther from home than ever before in his life.

He wondered what it would be like to have a motor like the ones the old men had talked about from the Magic Age. He was not sure he believed the part about how quickly one could travel using such a thing.

The intelligence obvious in the design of the great baidarka elicited his respect, not to mention awe of the materials used in its construction. He knew it would be impossible to create such a craft now. He continually discovered new surprises about the boat.

The ingenious mast could be mounted in a socket on the boat. Two sails folded out of the mast, one on each side. Each sail spread to create a large surface area, which caught the wind and pushed the craft at surprising speed.

Noah learned to sail by trial and error as man and whale moved south. When Noah needed to sleep, Thinker stayed near the strange boat and made sure it did not meet some hidden reef or rocky shore.

Thinker swam straight south, veering slightly to avoid the Seward Peninsula. On the morning of the third day, dry land rose darkly to the left and right. Noah became confused until he realized he traversed the strait between Asia's Big Diomede Island and America's Little Diomede Island.

Old men had told him that in their grandfather's time, the People could not visit their relatives on the opposite shore. Over time, that changed, and things were good until the stars fell out of the sky.

Before the stars fell, people lived on both islands. Now only sea birds and itinerant sea mammals use the rocky promontories. The Great Waves must have been particularly huge and destructive in this relatively shallow place.

The legend told by the People said that only those north of these islands had been spared the Great Waves. It was Silla's, the inua of wind and weather, way of telling them to embrace the old ways once again. Noah wondered how the people of the remote Diomedes had erred sufficiently to warrant destruction.

He decided that dwelling on the past brought too many unanswerable questions to mind. Noah pushed legends from his mind and continued to paddle and sail through the endless water. The thick-furred pelt of a polar bear cushioned his back.

He could seal the hatches in the boat with yellowish, transparent domes, which fit into them snugly. They became airtight by little tubes one inflated using a foot-operated air pump. He studied the tubes carefully, trying to understand how they were made. Noah decided the old ways indeed must have been magic.

Although weathered, the tubes still held air. Noah spent most of his time in the forward hatch, only using the center opening for rigging the sail. The aft hatch remained sealed shut. His provisions and gear were pushed into both ends. Some items he lashed to the top of the skin — weapons, a spare paddle, and a place to secure the functioning paddle when not in use.

Noah enjoyed the constant movement and buoyancy of the boat. The fresh air and sunlight invigorated him. The breeze cleared his mind of the past while propelling him into the future.

He liked to pull himself from one hatch to another inside the boat. The translucency of the skin gave him the feeling of being in a tunnel that glowed; yet surrounded by the familiar smells of his provisions — the remains of his heritage.

For five days the weather remained clear and the Bering Sea uncommonly calm. On the morning of the sixth day, a storm swept out of Siberia.

Noah dozed, dimly aware of the wind as it pushed the water from a susurration against the boat skin to a quicker, insistent lapping. Then the boat dipped sharply, and gallons of shockingly cold water cascaded through the hatch onto him. He jerked erect, wide-eyed, to behold a gray, heaving sea.

Noah slipped into his spray skirt and hurriedly stretched it around the hatch combing. Pushing the rudder control with his feet, he changed the boat's course so that it ran before the weather. With a snap, the sail bellied out like an old man's gut and the boat chased the wind.

He worried about the sail. He felt sure the tubing would bend before the sail would tear, but he didn't want either of those things to happen. The baidarka shot over the water much too swiftly as it kept pace with the storm front, caught in that wave of icy cold air which heralds its master's presence.

He pulled down out of the spray skirt and propped it up with an axe to keep out as much water as possible. As soon as he cleared the hatch, he squirmed down through his possessions to reach the hatch by the sail.

Water splashed in. A hard rain pelted him. Noah struggled up through the hatch, spray and rain stung and bit at his face and hands as he fought with the sail to dump its hoard of wind.

Finally, it collapsed against the mast like a large fan. He pulled the metal-and-wood marvel out of the socket and lashed it to the deck.

The boat slowed, turned broadside to the wind, and began violently rocking back and forth. The true storm swept over him. He sealed the hatch behind him, then squirmed forward through the bobbing hull.

As he entered the spray skirt and ruddered the boat away from the wind, he beheld the most frightening world he had ever seen or imagined. Grey mountains of white-veined water rose and fell all around him. The keening wind beat the tops of the mountains into hard, white froth, which sheeted into him, bruising and cutting.

Hard rain pummeled the boat. Water ran down his face. He licked salt from his lips.

The boat pitched and bucked from trough to wave crest before crashing back down again. The rapid up-and-down circular motion tormented Noah's stomach. The wind shrieked around him, numbing his ears and nose. He felt totally helpless.

~¿Why are you distressed? Do you sicken?~ Thinker asked.

~The sea is trying to kill me.~

Terror washed through Noah. He had not foreseen this possibility. He was a man of the land who weathered storms inside a warm house. This was unbearable.

~¿How may I help you?~

The whale's mental presence gave him heart but little else.

Suddenly Noah laughed. "What does it matter? If I don't die here, I will die somewhere else." He pulled down out of the spray skirt, unfastened it,

and inserted the plastic dome.

I may as well die in comfort, he thought. He pumped up the tube and watched the storm lash the outside of the plastic. A haze of scratches covered the dome, mute testimony to years of use. The once-transparent plastic, now aged to light amber, stolidly endured the water constantly slashing against it, beading, and blowing away. He gripped the hatch bottom and kicked the rudder back and forth, attempting to navigate between the waves.

Up, down, left, left again, right. The baidarka traversed the endless range of whitecaps. The wind screamed, repeatedly grabbing the boat and lofting it from the wave tops to crash into the troughs. Noah held onto the hatch edge with numbed fingers. Cold seeped through the boat and crept into his bones.

He pulled the polar bear skin across his legs and continued working the rudder. Tired. He had never been so tired before in his life.

His legs ached and his temple throbbed. His hands, long past the numb stage, cramped badly from bracing against the hatch combing and the edge of the dome.

The boat was sealed airtight as well as watertight. Noah bleared close to unconsciousness before realizing he needed air.

What is wrong with me? With deliberation he pushed the little stem down and the escaping air blew directly into his face. Some of the fog cleared from his mind and he worked faster.

Water and wind swirled around the hatch as it dropped onto his lap, slid across his legs and bounced across the spruce flooring. Rain and spray once again needled steadily at his face. Nevertheless, the air so invigorated him that he did not mind.

Thunder rose above the sound of the storm. Noah pulled on the spray skirt and started stretching it around the cockpit rim.

~¡The world ends!~ Thinker said. Alarm edged his message. *~I cannot find a way around it! ¿Can you turn away from the direction you are going?~*

Noah laughed into the storm. Weather was a difficult concept for the great mammal to grasp. "The world ends" was the whale's description of an island or continent. Noah was about to go aground.

The thought of land offered comfort. The possibility of a reef brought anxiety. He pushed his mind ahead through the storm. Small glows of mental activity flickered out there, but none contained intelligence.

Noah plied the double-bladed paddle, pulling hard to stay atop the mountainous wave lifting the boat ever higher into the storm.

A landmass, dark in the failing light, loomed in front of him. The air reverberated with the constant collision of surf against rock. He frantically dug into the water again, but his paddle found no resistance.

Suddenly waves vanished in front of him, replaced by a wall of heaving spray. As the wave broke beneath him, he realized his frightening velocity. The boat sailed through the curtain of water on pure momentum.

Noah braced himself against the hatch as the boat angled downward. It broke out of the spray, slamming down onto a wide rock shelf. The baidarka bounced once and ground to an abrupt stop. Noah's head snapped forward, flesh splitting on contact with the hatch rim.

CHAPTER 7

Tʜɪɴᴋᴇʀ ᴄᴏᴜʟᴅ ɴᴏᴛ ʜᴇᴀʀ ʜɪs ꜰʀɪᴇɴᴅ. Never, since first becoming aware of each other, had they been this separate. Thinker still felt Noah's constant essence, but nothing of Noah's alert mind. Before, when his friend rested, Thinker had glimpses of Noah's unconscious thoughts and emotions. Much of Thinker's confusion and insight into the world Noah inhabited came from his dreams.

Now Thinker mentally swam into Noah's memories and found memories of his youth so strong, so immediate, that Thinker felt he had witnessed the actual events. He tried to remember his own initiation into awareness but couldn't.

Noah's memories became more and more negative and dark, terms that Thinker gleaned from the memories themselves.

His own species had ridiculed him and then used him. They made him a shaman because he could call creatures to their long teeth and nets but shunned him as a member of their pod, or village. The more that Thinker looked, the darker the memories became.

Yet he found the yearning in the small being to be part of something larger, to be loved, to make a difference. Thinker found that shining desire deep in the man's mind, buried under all that life had so far poured onto him. With so much to ponder, Thinker withdrew and waited for Noah to regain consciousness.

While waiting, hunger prodded him. Thinker swam deep and built a bubble net. Fluking gently to one side in a generous circle, he allowed tiny streams of air bubbles to escape his twin blowholes. The streams of carbon dioxide formed a ghostly wall lifting to create a hollow column.

As he rose, the water pressure eased on his body, and Thinker swam faster and faster, tightening the circle, ever upward, narrowing the air column closer to his size, sensing the minute life being herded together. The tiny quickening flesh offered sustenance, driving the great leviathan into tighter and tighter circles, building to a feeding frenzy that focused on one point — consume! Thinker opened his great maw to maximum width and the wide grooves running from his mouth down his throat stretched out flat from the sudden infusion of liquid.

Thinker surged to the top of the world, rising into the wild thindrink before falling back. He snapped his jaws shut, trapping a ton of seawater rich in krill, straining his massive throat to its maximum. Then his powerful tongue pushed the water through the rigid, porous, baleen filter surrounding his upper jaw. Finally, he swallowed the hundred pounds of trapped krill and small fish.

He focused on the tremendous force of the thindrink. The top of the world heaved and frothed. Sometimes the Cea would play in storms like this. His massive body rocked with the churning world.

Suddenly the urge seized him, and he fluked sharply upward to breach into the heart of the storm. The Cea loved breaching, shooting up out of the world into the thindrink before falling over on one's side or back in a great spraying reentry. This day the power of the elements added to gravity and smashed Thinker back to the surface like the blow of a bull's flukes.

The ferocity of the thindrink stunned him. He had no idea it could be so powerful. He began to swim around the edge of the world where Noah lay stranded. After many heartbeats and constant, piercing echolocating trills, he discovered it was only a rock, but a very big rock.

The rock proved too big to circle now. The journey would take too long. Noah might need him. He reversed course.

Reaching the place where he felt closest to the small man, he spoke to the void but received no answer. Nothing moved around his friend. Nothing threatened the human that he had not already endured.

Thinker swam back and forth, skirting the edge of the world and becoming anxious. He didn't like the new burning-bubbly feeling in his guts, but he couldn't make it go away.

Thinker relaxed. He finally sensed the troubled dreams of the man. Noah slept and Thinker took comfort in the familiar, often chaotic mind of his friend.

The whale breached into the storm once more, blowing his last reserves of thindrink through his blow hole, clearing his lungs of water. He didn't want to drown.

After refilling his lungs, he fluked down to the bottom and rested on the underwater slope of the plateau that became St. Lawrence Island. He drowsed in that state the Cea used as sleep. The storm rocked him gently even at this depth.

CHAPTER 8

"WHAT IS THAT, MOTHER?" Marilyn Oktuuna squinted in the morning sun, trying to make sense of what she saw. The storm had cleared the air to a crystalline quality and the brilliant day invited discovery.

"My mother's mother would say it was a beast who died while eating a man. She was like that. I think it's some kind of boat, and that man looks dead." The old woman removed the pipe from her teeth and spat downwind.

"Shall we check, Mother?" Marilyn was already approaching the strange boat.

"Hell, Marilyn, you're the healer. What d'you think?" The old woman cackled, put the pipe back in her mouth and shuffled after her running daughter. She smiled.

Sometimes you find the strangest things when you go beach combing, she thought.

The pain became unbearable as consciousness returned. Noah screamed.

~¡Your pain is my pain. Please make it stop!~ Thinker said instantly.

~H-H-How?~

~Like this.~

Noah's pain vanished and he gasped in surprise. For a few lengthy moments his mind assimilated knowledge he had possessed all his life, that his species had owned for millennia but lacked the ability to initiate. He sensed his injury anew. He measured the rips in his flesh, the network of cracks in his skull radiating out from the point of impact, and the hemorrhaging blood vessels spewing into life-threatening spaces.

Noah concentrated, wove cell tissue, mended the torn vessels, fused calcium cells, and rebuilt his cracked skull. Lastly, he brought life to the withered tissue and ganglia of the cut — pushing the two sides together and closing the oozing gash. The skin hummed across the wound, pulling tight, leaving no scar.

A human scream snapped Noah into immediate awareness. His eyes flew open, and he beheld two women. Elated to see people again, he smiled. They belonged to his race.

"Hello. My name is Noah. I have been at sea for many days, and I am glad to meet you." He smiled again.

"H-how, did you do that, Noah?" The young woman's voice carried deep agitation as she pointed a shaking finger at the dried blood on his head. He thought her beautiful.

"I'm a shaman," he said.

The old woman regarded Noah through narrowed eyes. "We ain't had no shamans around here for a long time, not since the twenties. How do we know you're not a witch?"

Noah gave her a level look. "You remind me very much of my mother. I am not sure that is a good thing."

~That is what the humans in your village thought. ¿How does witch differ from shaman?~ Thinker asked.

~I will explain later. I must talk with these people now.~

Noah tried to mask his irritation and concentrated on the lovely young woman's voice.

"My mother," she said hurriedly, slowing her speech as his gaze met hers, "is only asking, the same thing that any other witness would ask."

"Witness?" Noah asked blankly.

"I saw your head heal. I know you're something, maybe a shaman, but I don't believe in them!"

Noah nearly laughed before he saw the tears in the corners of her wide, dark eyes. Almost involuntarily his mind embraced hers, carefully probing and searching. She seemed close to panic. She had just seen the impossible.

Noah nudged her mind, then her mother's. Both women blinked.

"For a minute there I thought your head was cut," Marilyn said. For the life of her, she didn't know why she said that. "But I guess not."

"No. I'm fine. Thank you for finding me."

She watched his eyes travel over her, saw the man- interested-in-woman look she expected, and wondered if he would stay in the village.

He could be exactly what is needed for my situation, she thought.

Noah let his gaze linger on her full figure, superbly molded by the carefully sewn caribou skin dress. *Someone on the mainland trades with these people*, he thought. There was more than Aleut-Inuit blood in her. Maybe some Indian, or even gusik.

Oval rather than round, her face possessed handsome, high cheekbones setting off her long-lashed, lustrous dark eyes and generous mouth. He smiled at the beautiful face and concentrated on holding her curiosity at bay.

"You looked dead. I remember," Marilyn's mother said bluntly.

"Just resting, Mother." He smiled at her, and the old woman abruptly shook her head.

"Who are you? Where did you get this amazing boat?" Marilyn asked.

He eased out of the baidarka. She saw relief on his face when he stood straight and took a step.

"I am Noah. Who are you?" His gesturing hand covered both women. She noticed she stood taller than him.

"I am Marilyn Oktuuna. This is my mother—"

"Don't you tell nobody my name!" the old woman snapped. "Only I have the right to do that, and I don't want to."

Noah stared hard at her mother and his eyes widened slightly.

"See! He almost had you telling him. I don't trust him. I got these feelings that I should like him, and I got no reason to!" She became so agitated she bit the stem of her pipe in two.

Marilyn gave her mother a perplexed look.

Noah eased the old woman's mind to a lower degree of excitement. Her suspicion would take longer to allay, but perhaps in time… He realized he could settle here.

His appetite suggested he could have this woman, Marilyn. Here was the life previously denied him; he could make it work. These people had no prejudices against him.

Finally, his patience would have its reward. He saw how easy it was to change a person's attitude toward him. His appetite surged in his mind, making him feel powerful and happy.

Besides, he had discovered more than a scrap of interest in him in Marilyn's mind. Her thought, "How wonderful; another possibility." had been about him.

However, this old one, she had been cynical for a long time, and keeping two minds in control was difficult. His appetite and his inua both wanted the same thing here, but could he manage a village?

He held their minds while he probed for information. Twenty-two people lived in the new village on St. Lawrence Island. Originally from the villages of Gambell and Savoonga, they survived the tsunamis created by the falling stars.

While Noah stood staring at them, Marilyn saw movement out on the water. She wondered how long it would take this self-professed shaman to become aware.

Noah abruptly turned from the women and looked across the rocky beach to the heaving sea. An umiak glided toward them, paddled by vigorous, strong occupants.

Noah glanced back at the women. "Who comes?" He nodded at the closing boat.

Marilyn shaded her eyes with a strong, steady hand and pretended to peer with squinted eyes. She knew who it had to be and relished the situation.

The old woman frowned, "How'd you know they was out there? They didn't make any noise."

Noah ignored her and kept his attention on Marilyn.

"That's Abraham Shugetuk and his crew. He is an honored umialik and hunter in our village."

The old woman gave her daughter a hard look and spat downwind again.

Two men leaped out and grounded the boat smoothly. The other four sprang out of the boat and helped haul it up on the beach.

Noah turned to watch the sea hunters pull their umiak ashore. Marilyn appreciated the umialik's wide shoulders and light step as he walked rapidly but casually up the beach to them.

"What is that thing?" asked Abraham, pointing at the baidarka and carefully studying Noah.

"It is a baidarka, built by gusiks long ago. I found it. My name is Noah. The storm stranded me on your island."

"I am Abraham. From where did you sail this baidarka, Noah?"

When Abraham's eyes fastened on him, Noah saw a quick picture of dog teeth on a caribou bone. Feeling misgivings, he reached further into the man's mind.

The boat crew walked up the beach toward them.

"I came from Point Hope, Abraham. And I am pleased to meet you." He concentrated on sending thoughts of friendship and brotherhood.

The hunter frowned. "I heard this thing about Point Hope," he said slowly. "It is said that everyone who lived there has fled. There was a terrible witch who helped a whale kill all the whale hunters, and the People left to join their cousins who follow the caribou."

The five men crowded around Noah, nodding and smiling deferentially. They did not interrupt Abraham.

How fast the news has traveled!

Noah carefully kept his face frozen while he cast about for an answer. "Yes! That is true. It was terrible. We all had to leave."

"There are no caribou here," Abraham said. "Why did you escape by water, braving the threat of a whale-monster and a witch?"

"I could not bear to part with my beautiful baidarka, so I fled by sea."

Noah pushed around at the other's mind, seeking entrance, and leverage. He found it. He discovered that the man felt very strongly about Marilyn Oktuuna. He wanted her for his wife when he had finished honoring compacts he had made with others.

Once Abraham finished the house he was constructing for his widowed mother, he would ask Marilyn to share his home. Marilyn waited obediently for this event and tried not to feel frustrated when Abraham went on extended hunting trips. This trip had numbered more than ten days.

Abraham was the foremost hunter in the village and as such

carried more responsibilities than other men. That he always provided for many more other than himself and his mother gave him great esteem in the collective mind of the village. Even Marilyn felt strongly about his importance.

Noah's heart sank. Should he look farther afield for companionship? Then appetite pushed his mind out of slush onto firm ice.

Who knew how long it would take to find another village? Let alone a woman as handsome as this one! Besides, the ancient custom wherein hunters from other villages were invited by husbands to "laugh" with their wives had come into use again.

No one mistook him for a hunter, but the courtesy would be extended, nonetheless. That Marilyn was not wife to anyone gave him no pause. First, he had to be officially welcomed by a respected hunter else he would be forced by custom to leave. Noah didn't have to read Abraham's mind to know that the man had no intention of inviting him to stay and visit. He was already agitated that Marilyn was showing interest in this newcomer.

From Point Hope Noah remembered the widely held thought, "I don't want his blood in my family's veins." And it still gnawed on him that the perceptions of others robbed him of a man's role. This time he would not turn aside like a frightened puppy.

In exerting enough mental strength to subdue Abraham Shugetuk he discovered the power of his appetite had grown. His inua felt troubled but wished for acceptance here.

"How sad for you," Abraham said woodenly. "Welcome to our village."

Noah understood so much for the first time in his life. This could be easy. After all those years of yearning, humiliation, and rejection, he finally had a chance to court a woman.

~¿You desire to remain here?~ Thinker asked.

~Yes! There are females of my kind here that I would have as mate.~

~¿Does the anger/fear come from your lack of knowledge about your species?~

~Yes.~

~Good. It felt unwell. I must continue after my own kind. Will you be in this place when our worlds are joined again?~

~Yes. When the ice is out I will still be in this place.~

~*Eat well.*~ Then Thinker was gone.

For a moment Noah felt anxiety. Loss of communication with the only other being in the world who knew him nearly caused his knees to shake. Then he refocused on the beautiful young woman and hoped he would not be alone much longer.

He was sure her interest would blossom into love once she knew him.

"Please show me your village." He dazzled the islanders.

CHAPTER 9

Thinker moved rapidly south, avoiding the sick-making places by many cycles of travel. Men, once flourishing there, vanished after the Burning World. They left only death gasses behind, and poisons leaking from their destroyed world into his.

Thinker's mother swam fatally close to one of the sick-making places seeking the large krill breeding there, one accelerating generation after another.

The thought of his dead mother brought a familiar quickening to his heartbeat. Abruptly his heart faltered for a beat when he realized the feeling came close to what he felt for the small human. Thinker found the concept of *love* one of the most difficult to comprehend.

Noah had been unable to explain it other than to lament its elusiveness. Thinker picked up innuendoes of mating desire mixed with Noah's incoherent descriptions of *bliss forever*, whatever *bliss* and *forever* might prove to be. Thinker felt no desire to mate with the man, yet he carried a definite desire for Noah's presence.

More than a desire: a need. A part of him, which he didn't understand, seemed to come alive in Noah's presence. And it originated in their ability to link minds.

Pondering all these things, he suddenly found himself confronted by a mortal drama unfolding nearby, sensed only after he swam into its midst.

A female of his species trilled in pain and fear. A pod of rogue Orca, the Killer whale, surrounded her.

The Killer whale earned its name through the millennia by preying on sea mammals and fish. The Orca was not truly a part of the Cea, but rather the Supra, the largest of the dolphins. The coherent pods were well respected.

Coherent pods roamed an established territory. Rogue pods rampaged far and wide, respecting nothing, and flagrantly attacking other cetaceans — often killing them.

As a nursing calf, Thinker witnessed the mindless savagery of the smaller, sleek, white-and-black rogue animals with exaggerated dorsal fins. The helplessness he felt watching their blood lust bloom into death for a pregnant cow came back to him in a wave of revulsion.

But this time he knew what to do. He sent an urgent summons for porpoise to come to the aid of the already wounded female.

Thinker, having no concept of his mental range, quivered in surprise when over twenty of the intelligent sea mammals suddenly flashed in from all directions at high speed to attack the Orcas. Two Supra died immediately from ruptured internal organs, shattered bones, and massive hemorrhaging as two-hundred-pound porpoises slammed into them.

Two other Orca lurched off in mortal convulsions. The remaining pair survived through instant flight.

The porpoise swarmed around the two Humpbacks, high-pitched squeaks, and fixed, tight smiles flashing past in all directions. Thinker projected a feeling of extreme gratitude. The porpoise vanished back into the vastness of the world.

The female moved slowly, blood streaming from three wounds. Her mind and body reeling in shock, she faced the danger of sinking and drowning. Thinker moved to her side, and nudged her upward, singing songs of support and encouragement.

She didn't seem to notice his presence, let alone hear his trilled urges. She sank lower. He halted her bleeding, but something kept him from doing anything further.

Thinker worked into her mind, pushing aside the bone-hard flap of fear and reached into the depths of her paralysis.

~You must rise to the thindrink!~

Thinker waited for a response. Nothing. He sent an explicit scene of a rotting whale carcass into her mind and noted the responding shudder of revulsion.

~If you do not rise to the top of the world you will become that!~

Finally, the female showed awareness of life outside her terror-trapped mind. She moved her flukes and the pain from her wounds caused her to shudder again. She paused for a moment then churned into life, her massive flukes pushing her up to the thindrink.

Side by side they floated on the top of the world, bathing as the heat of the warm eye penetrated their blubber, sending candescence deep into their massive bodies. The heat made Thinker sluggish, and he drowsed on the gently rocking water.

Her nudge brought him instantly awake. After a hesitant moment, he followed her into the depths. No blood leaked from her congealed wounds, but they still gave her pain. Small jerks and flinches marred her fluid movements. Even with the slight flaws that barred her from perfection, she still flowed smoothly across Thinker's appreciation.

She held an appeal he did not understand, but he followed her lead. For the first time in his life, he acted without analyzing the situation. He sensed this was her first breeding season also.

For many visits of the warm eye, they did little beyond eating and dozing in the radiant heat. She healed swiftly. One bright, crisp day she slowly swam along his side, rubbing him from cutwater to fluke.

He sang a question. She rubbed along his other side at deliberate speed. He fluked forward slowly, angling under her moving body, and lifted to the gentlest touch of her on his back.

Briefly, he held position then slowly angled away from her. Without losing the pressure, he rolled his body side-to-side as he slid beneath her. He abruptly broke away and went into a shallow dive.

Instantly she moved to his side, thumping into him. Her flipper sparkled out and bumped down the edge of his lumpy jaw. She trilled a subliminal command in their ancient language.

He responded with a sigh woven through the unique melody he sang back to her. Thinker delivered his first composition. Every song he had heard before belonged to others. This one he created and would forever remember.

As he sang, he nudged her, rubbing her thick skin with his long flippers. She angled up sharply and fluked violently. He followed, easily mastering the turbulence of her passage, and continued singing.

She broke up out of the wet, welcome lift of the world and soared into the thin breath of the warm eye. He breached beside her, and they fell into the world together, sending up a shout of spray. His great heart pounded furiously.

Now they dove quickly, the water rushed past their bodies. Tiny bubbles fled upward from skin folds and grooves, adding to the excitement emanating from their thudding hearts and pulsating bodies. His skin glowed into total sensation. He felt engulfed by liquid, warm outside, hot inside.

They breached again, side by side. Then on the third breach, as his body churned for release, they moved together while still in the deeps. Their bellies pressed tightly as they writhed upward, massive flukes beating in perfect synchronization. Her sinewy, sleek, corrugated belly kneaded his shuddering, straining belly muscles. He felt her heart pound counterpoint to his.

They moved together through water that raced past them, caressing them, becoming brighter and brighter. Internal pressures joined them. He felt her welcome clasp, contracting and releasing in a quickening cycle. A hot river began to flood from his massive trunk into hers.

They exploded from the water.

He exploded inside her.

And fell away in euphoria.

The pressure vanished, replaced by the gentle, wonderful satiation of a new appetite. He moved to her side as they lifted to the top of the world, floating quietly. Their closeness awed him.

The closeness became part of the rapture of release. He added to his song of her. She answered with trills and sighs. But she would not sing.

Usually, the male composed and sang songs. A few females existed who answered in kind. Thinker wanted so much for her to answer him, to show that she understood the totality of his feelings for her.

She did not sing. She coupled with him repeatedly. They would rapturously join, and then doze in the warmth of the eye.

He became troubled. There could be more than this. There had to be more than this.

He entered her mind in search of a firmer understanding. All he found was the familiar feed, mate, nurture, and protect responses. He grew despondent. Reality gnawed at him. What had he expected?

Like the others of their kind, she held large, rounded thoughts, and felt basic needs. But compared to Thinker's mind she did not know, reason, or care. She didn't react when he suddenly ceased his constant attention upon her. Life continued for her.

Thinker concluded that cognition might be a piece of coral in a mouthful of sustenance. For the first time in many cycles, he thought of Noah and yearned for his companionship.

CHAPTER 10

As a child, Noah had seen a man toss three balls in the air and kept them spinning around in a circle without dropping any. Juggling, he had called it. Noah had been fascinated by the feat and in awe of the man.

Now he mentally juggled twenty-two minds and dared not drop one. If he did he might die.

At first, it had been easy to direct the villagers to do what he wished. He didn't ask for much and for most of them it was no more than they would do for any stranger in their midst. With others, it was a struggle.

The first real obstacle was gaining an invitation to stay at Marilyn's house, which she shared with her mother. He discovered her sense of adventure, mixed it with her interest in him, and pushed her natural inclination to disagree with her mother. After Abraham haltingly asked Noah to stay, her mother immediately asked, "Who's got room for him?"

Marilyn said, "We do." Which surprised both of them.

Marilyn's house had a small room built on the side of the original building where she saw people with medical problems. She was a natural healer and people had sought her out since she was twelve. Noah found himself in a small room that smelled of dried sea creatures and bundles of vegetation.

With Agnes sharing the house Noah knew anything meaningful between him and Marilyn would be stillborn. No matter how many urges and nudges he put into the old woman's head, she refused to leave.

"Must be something wrong with the way you think, Noah," she said one night after the evening meal.

"What do you mean, Mother?" She hated it when he called her

that, so he did it constantly.

"No matter what people want to say to you, when they get close you do something to make them like you. You merge them into your mind like an Arctic fox in a snowstorm."

"How would I be able to do that, Mother?" He felt smug and powerful. It didn't bother him that she understood his methods, only that they worked.

"I don't know how you do it. I wish I did. I'd love to turn it on you and show you how much everyone hates and fears you."

Stung, he opened his mouth to respond but she kept talking.

"I figure the only way we'll be able to get rid of you is to kill you. Ain't that what they do to witches?"

Marilyn, who had been sewing quietly in the corner of the room, jerked up and shouted, "Mother!"

Noah, thinking she was reproving Agnes for saying such things, slid into Marilyn's mind and was appalled to find only fear for what Noah would do to her mother for stating the truth.

Unable to respond in any other way, he caused them both to fall asleep where they sat. He went into Agnes' mind seeking leverage and found a deep-seated fear that Marilyn no longer needed her.

He went into Marilyn's mind and eroded her memories and thoughts of Abraham while enhancing her few reservations about the hunter. Noah ended with impressing his own importance on her mind as well as fanning the coals of interest she held for him.

As the winter wore on Noah slipped into Abraham's mind and enlarged the threat to the hunter's standing in the village, suggesting he go farther afield to bring in more and more game. This scheme bit back when Abraham's umiak crew brought in a bowhead whale.

The villagers were full of admiration for the umiak crew and especially their umialik, Abraham. The entire village went out to help the crew pull the whale from the water's edge to the village, a distance of four miles. Despite the return of the sun and open ice, the winters still proved harsher than those before the stars fell.

Noah had to go and help; there was no way out of it. He tried to be an unobtrusive part of the festivities, but the villagers tended to avoid being next to him. Finally, he mentally snared two old men and they plodded along next to him saying little.

He pretended to tug on the walrus-hide ropes but did very little work. When he first saw the dead animal Thinker seemed to be in his mind. But when he asked the void if his friend was indeed there, nothing answered.

At the sharing festival, the crew butchered their catch and passed out choice cuts to their friends and families. Abraham approached Noah and offered him a slice of fin: skin, blubber and meat.

"For you, shaman. I have selected this choice piece of whale." His eyes stared deep into Noah's and a smile played around his lips.

Noah realized this was a test and much depended on his answer. The demand, *Eat not of my kind!* wafted through his brain. At that point he realized that not only did he not want to eat whale meat, but he also couldn't eat it.

Thinker's admonition had nothing to do with his decision. After conversing at length with a whale he had come to realize they were rational, thinking beings. He could no more eat Abraham if offered his butchered thigh.

All of this coursed through his brain in an instant. Abraham stood with arm outstretched offering the meat.

"I thank you for the generous portion you offer, but my people have put a taboo on the flesh of whales."

The arm did not waver. "You are no longer with your people, shaman. You are with my people. We eat whatever is provided."

"I cannot eat that," Noah said, trying unsuccessfully to find leverage in the man's mind.

What is happening? Why can I not stop him?

Abraham allowed the hand holding the offering to drop against his leg.

"I think you believe you would be eating the flesh of a brother. Is that not so, shaman?"

The entire village had gone quiet as they watched the tension build between the two men. Noah perceived that Abraham's words had found fertile ground in many minds, and out of those words grew animosity. He again went into the umialik's mind and found a tiny crack fissuring from his fear that he had lost Marilyn.

Noah flooded the fear with exaggerated ramifications of forcing a man to go against a tribal taboo. Who knew what could happen, and if the man was in the middle of one's village, who else might feel the resulting retribution?

Abraham blinked and his attitude melted away.

"As you wish. All I can do is offer." He turned and went back to where his crew stood staring at him.

Conversations stuttered and then resumed as the villagers realized they would not starve during this long winter. Noah carefully noted that animosity for him didn't dissipate. It was just pushed to the back of many minds.

Abruptly he realized there were too many of them for him to keep in thrall as a group. Their mental defenses had strengthened. How or why, he didn't know, but the signs were evident.

Without haste, he rose and slowly edged away from the butchering party. If any saw him leave none made mention of it.

Marilyn always felt more clear-headed when Noah was not around, which had become rare. Agnes hated him so much that Marilyn feared that her mother would push him too far. The initial rationale for inviting him into her home had fogged into hazy definition, but she still harbored a basic interest in him.

He was so completely unlike any man she knew, both in good and negative ways, that he fixated her. Despite his obvious physical needs, she felt no ambient lust for him. When she could remember the man at all, Abraham was her lust object. Furthermore, she wanted Abraham as her husband.

Yet here she sat with a seemingly permanent houseguest whom, had it been anyone else, she would be sleeping with by now. Noah's constant broadcast of his physical needs only heightened hers in return. Thus, tension filled the small house on many levels.

Aware of her nuanced interest and overall sexual longings, Noah deluded himself into believing he could be the answer to all her needs if only he could present himself to her in the right light. But first, he had to get Agnes out of the house.

"There's something about you that doesn't work, Noah," Agnes told him one night. She and Marilyn were cleaning up the remains of the evening meal.

"What do you mean, Mother?" he asked blandly. In many ways

she recalled Old Nathan to his mind, and old resentment melded with new.

"Nobody can say what they want around you. You do something to change their minds. Yet you act like we're happier'n hell to have you here. Doesn't your brain work right or something?"

Stung, he froze her speech center for a moment while he searched for a suitable answer.

"My mother is of an age," Marilyn said slowly, fighting the mental vortex pulling her toward warm feelings for Noah. "...when she fears not the harm her words can do."

"Her words do not harm me," Noah said quickly, wondering from where her thought had come.

"Not harm *you*," she said thickly. "Harm *her*."

Agnes worked her mouth, trying to talk. Her face turned red. Noah could feel the turmoil and helplessness that raged through her mind. He released her speech center - her words could not harm him!

She coughed violently and spat on the floor. She stared at him; eyes frosted with hate.

"God damn you," she said quietly. "God damn you for what you've already done, and God damn you for what you'll do before you're finished with us."

"Mother, please!" Noah said earnestly. "You are of my People. I would not harm the People..." Involuntarily his mind went back to the day he met Thinker; would the whale have killed the umiak crew if Noah had not "spoken" to it first? Did not Noah's attempt to justify the taking of cetacean life give the whale all the information it needed to wreak vengeance?

Was he guilty of the deaths of ten whale hunters — including his brother? His appetite writhed in anger. The old woman had scored two hits in a row. If there were three, he might kill her.

"...not purposely in any way," he finished solemnly. Then he bent her mind, hard. She would like him, or— what? Would he really kill her? Could he really kill her? Could he kill any person?

He knew he could no longer kill whales.

Agnes winced, and struggled to speak.

"You." Her mouth jerked back in a rictus grimace, her response to his mental order to smile. "Will not, find," she ground on, exerting all her mental strength. "Happiness. Here!" she finished triumphantly.

Then her mouth formed the smile that Noah saw all too much in the village. Ice filled her eyes and heart.

"I go to live with my brother now." Her words mimicked his mental command perfectly. Then she stood, pulled her parka over the kuspuk she wore, and trudged out into the howling winter night.

Noah frowned. In some places when a woman left her daughter with a man, she was considered to have made a gift to him and a de facto marriage as far as the community was concerned. Noah's inua fervently wanted that to be the case, but there had to be an understanding with Marilyn, not just raw mental force.

In the village lived a very old man called Father John who spoke at weddings and funerals. This had to be done or the marriage wasn't considered proper. But, the People were not thinking clearly these days.

Marilyn seemed despondent, so he suffused her with a feeling of sexual gratification. She moaned, fell back on the bed, and dropped into an exhausted sleep.

Now only the two of them shared the house.

Two lovers, he hoped.

His sexual curiosity and accompanying urges prodded by appetite approached the point of overwhelming his inua. He knew he and Marilyn were destined for each other, that she would agree once she came to know the true Noah. He toyed with the idea of taking her without her complete acceptance.

He roused her to semi-consciousness and invoked thoughts of Abraham and himself, over and over, to the point she wasn't sure who was in the room with her.

Then he suggested that she undress. Her natural reluctance slowed her actions down so that she took a great deal of time to shed each article of clothing. By the time she slid off the softened moose hide undergarment, Noah was naked and approached lust insanity.

Marilyn had also progressed to a state where she no longer cared who, she just wanted release.

Suddenly Noah's inua manifested. It demanded that he give her full cognition before consummating his desires, otherwise it would not be love. His appetite snarled in response, urging Noah to fulfill his urges.

The battle raged in his mind for the better part of an hour and total insanity was within reach when he shouted, "Enough!"

At that, he returned to Marilyn her completely unclouded mind. He watched her blink and shake her head, look around at him and then down at herself. His smile lurked on the edge of his mouth, ready to join her in happiness and release.

CHAPTER 11

ABRAHAM HUGETUK CAREFULLY KEPT HIS BREATHING EVEN. He believed a hunter had to be one with his prey, both to take its life and honor its inua. His right arm didn't quiver as he held the raised spear, ready to plunge into the seal's breathing hole in front of him.

His eyes never left the pale, dried sliver of willow twig serving as his indicator. Abraham had found the allu hours ago. He had scraped snow and ice from the hole until only a thin layer of heavy slush covered it. Then he pushed the twig down through the center.

Such a small thing sticking down into his world would not alarm the seal. However, when the animal pushed the small thing up and out of its way, it would announce the animal's presence to the waiting hunter.

Abraham let his imagination probe beyond the breathing hole. He imagined a fat seal, full of fish, needing to breathe… looking up and seeing this bright spot in the bottom of the ice that promises air… muscles move the flippers, and it rises through the water… The twig didn't move.

Abraham suddenly found himself thinking about Marilyn Oktuuna, and how her body moved. How she had been overwhelmed, possessed, by this newcomer. How she shared her home with him.

No longer did she look upon Abraham the hunter with soft eyes. Now her eyes were blank and unseeing when she came near him. In addition, she rarely came near him of late.

He realized his breath quickened with anger. He concentrated on the willow twig to center himself. The twig slowly moved upward.

With a strength fed on hate he thrust the spear down through the center of the hole, past the twig, and through the throat into the chest cavity of the seal. He quickly twisted the kakivak so the barbed points held the heavy, thrashing animal. Abraham frantically hacked at the air hole with a steel knife and enlarged the opening so he could pull the Spotted seal up onto the ice.

When finally he looked down at his stiffening kill, he apologized to it.

"I ask your pardon for using you as my heart's true target. I will now honor you in the old way." While he brought his sled over and loaded his kill, Abraham carefully concentrated on his tasks, emptying his mind of all else.

Once he was on the way back to the village, he remembered the hostility he felt toward Noah while out on the ice. Then he thought about how his feelings changed when near the bald one. His knuckles whitened as he squeezed on the sled rope in frustration.

"Never before have I encountered an animal like this!" The wind scattered his words across the frozen, mountainous island. Something must be done.

CHAPTER 12

Marilyn's eyes burned into Noah's.

"Who gave you permission?" she screamed. "I thought these were just unworthy dreams, but you have made them real!"

"I love you!" His voice lacked enough volume to gain her attention. "I want you to love me."

"You are evil! You must be a witch!" Her screams beat on him, unstoppable.

He closed his eyes in pain and put his palms outward in front of his face to ward off the hate and loathing emanating from her. His inua writhed with the rejection.

"I love you," he moaned. "I need you." He opened his eyes and dropped his hands just in time to see the glint of the fish knife.

His unconscious reaction froze her arm and shoulder muscles, and the clenched weapon quivered in the air above them.

"Nothing has happened between us!" he said hoarsely, shaken by her action. "I would not insist on what you didn't want."

Tears streamed down her face. "You have spent the winter insisting on what we did not want. Why do you stop now?"

Abruptly the foul horror of his actions avalanched out of his rational mind and buried the demanding appetite in revulsion. His inua flooded him with repugnance at what he had nearly done. Noah sprang off the bed and pulled on his clothing. He released Marilyn's arm and she crumpled onto the bed, sobbing. A distant dog answered her.

He felt her disgust and loathing; knew it would haunt him always. Realizing he had reached the bottom of his moral decline, Noah loathed himself. "How have I fallen so low?" he mumbled.

"I am sorry, Marilyn." He wished he could evaporate, vanish without a trace, and never have been so she wouldn't carry the memory of him. "I will never bother you or your village again, I promise. Please forgive me."

Pulling a blanket over herself, she held him with eyes that still smoldered. "You deserve to die for abusing us. All witches deserve to die." Abruptly she slumped into unconsciousness at his command.

Noah knew if the villagers were aware of this, they would kill him. Quickly, just as Marilyn had tried to do. He did not blame them; he completely understood their rationale.

This final act of maintaining his hold over them sickened Noah to his very soul. He didn't want this anymore, but what choice did he have now? He wished to seek atonement and forgiveness but knew it would not be possible in this place. He could not remember a longer winter.

He pulled on his mukluks and shrugged into his parka. He carefully avoided looking at the woman on the bed when he pushed through the door. Once outside he drew in a draught of cold air.

I must get away from here. Where is Thinker?

Noah stared out at the sea ice. For a long moment, he stared at the kupakpak before realizing what it was. The large crack split the white expanse between shore and sea. The sight of water shining through the lead gave his heart sudden wings.

With an effort, he turned his attention to the baidarka. For some time his escape had been ready. He ran awkwardly to the boat and gave it an experimental push. Although very heavy, it slid.

He stared out at the distant, widening lead, knowing he must do it alone. Out there he would find atonement, solace. He felt relief that the village slept. Concentration on any single other thing weakened his mental fist.

Such as pushing a boat.

CHAPTER 13

APPROACHING MARILYN'S HOUSE, ABRAHAM NOTICED the absence of a feeling of goodwill. Puzzling over the lack, he saw her door standing open. Fear ignited in his chest, and he covered the last yards in an instant.

The sight of her pushed Abraham over a mental ice ridge. His hunter's eyes missed nothing. Between her nudity and the disheveled state of the bed, he knew that the witch who destroyed Point Hope had come to his village. He made sure she still breathed before tucking the blanket around her.

Holding back the growl forming deep in his throat he peered out and saw the witch. So, it thought to leave now, unpunished for his unspeakable acts.

Abraham ran into the center of the village. It took little time to wake the occupants of the first house. In moments they spread to other houses, rousing the people of St. Lawrence Island.

A witch wanted killing; Abraham might need help.

Abraham Shugetuk concentrated on emulating a ring seal. He had more practice thinking like a seal than any other animal he hunted. He knew the witch could hear a man's thoughts and bend them back on themselves. However, Abraham reasoned that with all the witch's exertions, it might ignore a seal, no matter how out of place it might be.

He rejected his treasured .30-.06 as a weapon, fearing that its non-seal balance would betray his slow approach over the ice. Abraham wielded the most accurate sling in the village. The sling hung elemental and organic, tied to his body beside the small bag of smooth stones. The bag's walrus-hide composition blended with Abraham's projected sea-mammal aura.

The witch continued pushing the baidarka toward the widening kupakpak in the ice a quarter mile distant. The men of the village coveted the baidarka. Abraham suppressed the thought quickly. He could not dwell on matters foreign to his netchik impersonation.

The witch either did not notice his slow, sliding approach or else ignored any non-threatening element in its tightly controlled universe. Abraham knew the aroused villagers watched through binoculars at a safe distance. Months ago, they discovered the witch suffered limitations, distance and numbers being foremost of them.

Abraham snuffed at the ice under his gaze, just as he had seen seals do. He inched closer, arms stiff at his side mimicking flippers, his feet pressed rigidly together in a parody of the ring seal's powerful tail. He rolled slightly to the left and weakened his concentration enough to measure the witch's distance. Close enough. He could not miss.

Abraham Shugetuk pulled his sling free with one hand, palmed a stone into it, and swung the ancient weapon before fully gaining his feet. Still concentrating on seal-like thoughts of swallowing a frantically wiggling fish, he aimed and released the whirring stone.

The witch didn't even look up.

CHAPTER 14

Thinker recognized the edge of the world where Noah waited. Increasing his speed, he swung around the long, sweeping hump of the rock to the exact spot of his last contact with Noah. He probed ahead mentally, and sudden confusion washed over him as he tried to understand the negative sensations he encountered.

Much felt not good here. Strife tainted the thindrink, mixing with hate and fear. Suddenly he perceived Noah's essence.

The man labored anxiously and hurried. Noah's mind seemed closed in on itself, hiding from... what? Carefully Thinker edged through the half-formed mental defenses, pushed aside the frantic anxiety, and encountered overwhelming guilt.

Eating at one's own innards over something that cannot be changed — why would a thinking being lower itself to such a state?

Thinker probed one synapse further and found himself in Noah's memories. Tons of muscle shuddered in revulsion. As the recent events ran at a dizzying speed into Thinker's brain, a questioning wonder at his deep feeling for the human began to form.

Thinker carefully formulated a greeting when suddenly a wave of intense shock and pain burst out of Noah like the scream of an angry gull. The whale opened his senses to their maximum and found the attacker, now so emboldened that he concentrated on his mission openly.

Instantly Thinker realized that Noah lay injured; he could not protect himself. The Abraham Shugetuk man hated and feared Noah enough to take his essence. Thinker ran questioning tendrils through Abraham's mind in search of the rationale for this act.

For the second time in his life, Thinker found himself in agreement with a member of a different species. Suddenly he saw

Noah as a rogue Orca with Abraham an avenging porpoise. The harmony of balance flowed over him like a current of tropical water.

Abraham slowly advanced over the rocky beach toward the downed witch. Adrenaline hummed through him. His first cast struck perfectly.

He could see the blood, a one-shot kill. But wait! The witch moved — it still lived.

Abraham's lip curled into a snarl while pulling another stone from his pouch. Once again the whirring sling orbited his clenched fist.

Conflicting thoughts washed through Noah's stunned mind. No matter how hard he tried, he could not follow a single one to fruition. His mother stood in her familiar, hunched stance, nagging at him to be a better shaman. Then his brother, Nicholas, leered down at him. "You can do nothing correctly," Nicholas said, exhibiting his superior, mocking smile before disappearing.

Memories ran through Noah with no more direction than the tide on a flat beach. Suddenly Marilyn waited, arms inviting, the fish knife still clenched in her right hand. Noah tried to scream but could not. Mercifully, she vanished.

His motor responses proved equally muddled and knotted. The instinct of self-preservation pulled him to his knees once, but it lost impetus and he slid into a fetal position. His feet pushed at the heavy beach gravel in a weak imitation of flippers.

His long-dead uncle informed him in his best teacher's voice that Noah would die if something were not done very soon. Then the apparition laughed and faded. However, the stone had done its work well.

His brain was too damaged to function correctly. He had to fix something, had to weave thought and concentration to make a tool. He could not.

Fragments of death danced in the shards of his mind.

CHAPTER 15

THINKER UNDERSTOOD THE HUNTER S PURPOSE AND HIS MOTIVATION. He hesitated, sharing the man's rightful outrage at Noah's actions. Justice is not a cetacean concept, but by his own stated beliefs Noah stood condemned to punishment of some sort.

Nevertheless, how did the female see this situation? He found her at the edge of this impending death scene and discovered conflicting emotions in her mind. With little effort, Thinker saw that limited acceptance had been present, but Noah had seen it for much more than intended.

The condemnation lessened in the whale's mind. All of this came about because the humans did not truly understand each other. Noah carried the brunt of the guilt, yet enough existed for all to have a share.

The Abraham person again swung his killing-skin over his head. Thinker felt the certainty of the kill beat in the hunter's mind. A choice must be made. Now.

Yet new questions surged through him.

How would Abraham perceive Thinker? Could a rapport as complete as what he had with Noah be realized with this man? Would he be welcomed by the men on this rock? Could they fill the void that would open with the death of Noah?

No. No. No.

These men would not even accept one of their own who was different. Would Thinker become something abhorrent if he saved his friend? Would he become a part of Noah's transgressions against his own kind?

At least Noah had not mated with the woman against her will (Thinker did not understand how such a thing could happen anyway). Nor had he taken life. And at long last Noah felt great remorse (yet another ponderable) for his actions.

Thinker slammed into the attacker's mind with such force that Abraham lost consciousness in mid-swing and collapsed in a heap. Thinker's question finally answered itself.

In that moment he glimpsed reality. Abraham would have not only regarded Thinker as another witch, but also as prey. Abraham was a long-tooth meat-taker adept at the tearing death.

The whale registered the astonishment evoked from the hiding villagers by this turn of events. He noted their hasty retreat as he reached into Noah's mind. While he repaired the damage in the human he wondered if he could have saved his mother as well, if he had but thought of it.

Noah's essence coalesced slowly.

~Are you able to move? Can you leave this place now?~ Thinker asked.

Noah swam up through a red mist as pain washed around him. But he was thrilled by the mental touch of the whale. With effort, he concentrated on the pounding pain in his head, closed the wound, and again soothed the damaged tissue.

Then he reached out.

~My friend! I am so happy you are here. Yes, I can leave this place, I must leave this place...~

Noah paused to collect his thoughts, to explain the haste in which he needed to leave. There was much to communicate; he did not know where to begin.

~Then let us leave at once,~ Thinker insisted.

The whale sensed the villagers returning. They carried weapons that could reach farther than a sling.

With fear and joy powering his muscles, Noah surged up off the smooth rocks and shoved the baidarka down the long beach. His heart pounded from the incredible exertion. Fear kept him moving. After what seemed like five years passed, he finally reached the water.

He pushed the baidarka out into the narrow lead of sluggish surf until the numbing water became waist-deep, and then he pulled himself aboard. A bullet buzzed past his ear. He fired back with his mind, demanding unconsciousness of those with weapons.

He could not chance the baidarka being damaged now. His life depended on it. The sea grabbed the buoyant craft, pulling it strongly with the outgoing tide. Noah pulled the mast free of its lashings, dropped it into the socket, and snapped open the sail.

The constant wind molded the sail into an added dimension and the boat leapt away under Noah's control. In a few breaths he glided out of the lead and onto the open ocean. He felt amazed at how quickly his anxiety receded with the island.

~I have learned much about life, and myself, since we parted.~ Noah paused, hating and needing to finish his shared thought. *~I have done things that shame me, that are beneath me. I was a witch when I should have been a shaman.~*

Thinker sifted through the top layers of Noah's thoughts. The man's remorse and shame were something new for the whale to ponder, but Noah's anguish struck a chord in Thinker.

~We are very different from others of our own kind. You and I are trapped with our ability to know what is in the minds of others without their knowledge. Our perceptions are more complete than those of other creatures in our worlds. We are cursed.~

Noah steered the baidarka absently, mulling over the whale's words. Thinker was right. They were cursed.

~What should we do? Where should we go? I do not think I can face the ice time alone. There must be others around me.~

~Go where ice is not.~ An image of warm water, trees with large, pointed leaves, and of a sea teeming with abundant and colorful life faded slowly, reluctantly.

~It is not just the ice… but we can go there?~ Noah asked.

Thinker felt a warm glow. The question included both; not "I can go there?" but "We can go there?" *~Yes, turn toward the warm eye.~*

Would Noah be able to avoid entangling them both in jeopardy? Time to think about that later, the whale decided. A long journey stretched before them. Enough heartbeats lay ahead in which to find answers.

Noah edged the rudder around until he headed southwest. The

whale inquired why the baidarka could not travel in a straight line. Noah tried to explain wind and sailing to a creature who had no need to be erratic in order to be precise.

Saint Lawrence Island disappeared in the bluing mist behind them as they followed the setting arctic sun.

The appetite waited quietly, in both.

Book Two

CHAPTER 1

ONETUNK FIRST SENSED, THEN ECHOLOCATED the small pod of greatfish. For a moment he singled/alone while a wave of orgasmic ecstasy swept through him in reward. His great mouth hung open, allowing the conical teeth to glisten in the refracted beams of light from the warm eye.

For that instant he existed alone, a single entity. Then he surged back, meshed as only OnePod can be.

The pod of Humpback whales migrated north. Two large males flanked a smaller male and three cows, two with calves. The two calves weighed between four and six thousand pounds each. The old bulls massed sixty tons, their heads a full third of their length. They loomed gigantic.

Effortlessly, their massive flukes oscillated continuously, propelling them through the water at a steady four knots. Four-meter flippers winged out from their hulking sides, irregular scallops on their leading edge, blue-black at the base, becoming mottled and finally completely white at the ends. The leviathans possessed a delicate majesty belying their great size.

The whales traveled for nearly a league before rising to the thindrink to replenish their cavernous lungs. The Cea journeyed in a spread-out group, unmindful of neighbors or position, except for the two calves working to keep pace with their mothers.

Naff, the largest bull, his numerous years chronicled by the great clusters of tiny, white riders on cutwater, flippers, and flukes, led the extended family at a comfortable speed. Thick, deep grooves pleated down the bellows-like throat beneath his wide maw.

Immediately behind the down-turning hinges of his jaw,

monocular eyes dimly gauge his marvelous world. Numerous tubercles, bump-like mounds, lay scattered across his head. Each tubercle contains thick, bristly hairs that act as tiny antennae, able to detect phenomena as diverse as the presence of plankton and krill to the numerous sounds needing attention throughout his liquid universe.

Lulled by their effortless passage, and an unfortunate lapse of echolocation, it took Naff some heartbeats to recognize the Orca rushing at high speed toward the pod. Reflexively he turned away from the attacker. A high warning trill sounded from his throat, as well as from his mind.

The alarm echoed as the others became aware of more black-and-white toothed-ones. Naff swiftly fluked back through the pod, urging them to form a defensive ball. But ancient fear overwhelmed new awareness, and they fled in all directions.

After many rapid heartbeats, Naff realized the pod did not separate and lose its way. Quite the contrary, they all moved rapidly toward the same point. He wondered at the spatial philosophy behind this situation but lacked adequate time to ponder it fully.

The arc of a coral reef suddenly confronted the pod, barring further flight. They turned as one to confront the pursuing rogue Orcas, expecting to be maimed or killed. However, the Orcas pulled back, some of them disappearing into the blue-green distance.

Naff fluked around the inside of the reef. It didn't shelve up like the biggest rocks but shot out of the depths, a living spine of the ocean. Blanketed with plant and animal life, the coral glowed a healthy pink.

In this world of sea feathers and sharp exoskeletons something smooth and curved caught his eye — the picked skull and ribs of a great whale. Naff swam around the pod once more before rising to the top of the world.

As his lungs contracted and he exhaled, the condensation in his body-heated breath shot into the thindrink. He felt great anxiety. Taking three large breaths to fill his lungs, he closed the double nostrils of his blowhole, and dove to circle worriedly around the confused pod.

CHAPTER 2

"THEY'RE STILL OUT THERE." Moira sullenly shaded her eyes. Standing guard quickly became tiresome. *This is nothing but a bloody waste of time anyway.*

"Tell me immediately if they come in this direction," Jik ordered. He waded gingerly out on the submerged coral until waist deep. Grabbing the long handle of the fish trap, he pulled it smoothly up the bamboo skids and onto the atoll. As the trap broke the surface, he grunted in exertion.

"Fresh tucker!" Moira said with relief, looking down at the suddenly revealed rainbow of flapping fish.

"Dammit!" roared Jik, wildly scrutinizing the water around him. "Watch for the bloody Killers!"

"They're still out there in a feeding frenzy. They don't seem to be interested in biting your beige arse today, so stop worrying," she rasped.

Jik pulled the trap up to him, bent down, and picked it up. He carried it to the shelter without another word.

Moira swallowed and narrowed her squint as she followed him up the beach. With that many fish in it, the trap weighed thirty-five to forty kilos, and he wasn't even breathing hard.

At maybe an inch taller than her 5'4", Jik measured half again as wide. His compact, muscular torso and well-developed arms and legs constituted the sum of his physical beauty.

Moira watched as Jik set the crate of flapping fish near the shelter and her liberalism slammed a mental door and hid behind it. This brown brother didn't want a sister. He wanted a woman.

For a moment Moira reflected on how they came to be here.

"Help me clean fish," Jik said.

She looked away for a moment, thinking of Deagan, and

knuckled her eyes. Then, making sure the trap sat between them, she knelt, pulled out her knife, and reached for a fish. She ignored his frequent glances, eviscerating fish with quick, practiced movements. She knew he wanted her badly.

As he grabbed a new fish, she shot a glance at his face. The scar running from left jaw hinge to the chin clenched at his visage, pulling the lips apart on the right side in a permanent sneer. She still didn't remember putting it there.

In the shelter, built from the remains of their ship, Captain Arnold woke from his nearly constant slumber and looked out at them.

"Lots of scalies?" His voice quavered.

"Aye," Moira said cheerfully. "Fresh tucker tonight. That'll be bonzer, won't it?" She deftly sliced fish.

"They've got themselves another pod of whales," Jik said.

She looked up. He stared at the entrance to the coral lagoon where a pinkish cloud of blood remained. The tall dorsal fins of the Orcas no longer sliced the surface.

"They're very clever, aren't they?" she asked.

"Smarter'n we are, so far."

"They haven't eaten us yet."

"Yet," Jik said shortly. "But they won't let us off this island. You saw. They talk to each other, like radio or something."

Moira slid her fingers into the gills of the last fish, and expertly brought the knife up through the mouth and into the brain. The fish quivered and died. She searched Jik's eyes for hidden knowledge.

"Do you honestly believe they can communicate? They're smart, sure, but actually communicate complex thoughts?" Her eyes went back to the fish as she gutted the delicate blue and yellow creature, seeing only meat.

"If you'd been on the raft, you wouldn't have to ask that question," he snapped. He rose and stalked away from her.

She watched the muscles move in his back as he crossed to the shelter, not appreciating the beauty of his athletic form, but recognizing only power and strength that, if push came to shove, she could not physically best. Six weeks after the wreck, Jik gave up on rescue and built a raft. When he finished, he decided to do a shakedown cruise around the island.

The pod of Killer whales immediately attacked. The raft lasted about two minutes under the frenzied onslaught before being torn to shreds. Jik survived only because the ferocity of the attack pushed the disintegrating raft close enough to shore for him to leap into the shallows, tearing his feet bloody on the sharp coral.

The tenacity and coordination of the attack horrified Moira. One could almost believe they were sentient. Until then she'd believed that Orcas never attacked humans.

On the other hand, no research had been done on them since the Fall, and that had certainly changed a lot of things. Jik stepped out of the shelter into the sunlight, projecting lust for a moment with his eyes before vanishing into the dense jungle foliage.

Still and all, she mused, *I'm more worried about him than I am about the Orcas.* A rumble welled up from beneath her as the island shook for a few seconds and the heavy stink of sulphur seemed to intensify. "Or earthquakes," she mumbled to herself.

CHAPTER 3

N OAH M ANALUK LEPT OFF THE BAIDARKA AND landed with a great splash in the ocean. He smiled. No longer did he panic when he hit the water.

He had known how to swim for most of his life. Until Thinker brought it to his attention, he just hadn't realized it. He had seen caribou, dogs, muskrats, and geese swim. They all did the same thing.

Paddle with paws or feet or hands. He couldn't sit on the water like a goose, of course. But he could hang in the water like dogs, caribou, or muskrats.

The first lesson crossed his mind again. *~You are certain I will not drown?~* Noah had asked for the fifth time.

~I will be under you in the wor-, in the water,~ Thinker replied patiently. *~Just get in and do what all the animals do.~* A flipper wavered in sympathetic response.

Noah leaped into the water and screamed in fear as he hit. All his air vented by the time his body submerged, and although he pawed the water frantically, he sank like a rock.

~It does not work. I will die!~ Noah nearly became incoherent with terror.

~Why do you blow before entering the world? One should fill the lungs before entering,~ Thinker said as he rose to meet the flailing man.

Noah felt the slick solidity of the whale rise under him. He struggled to not slip off the broad back. When they broke the water, Noah drank in the air.

~Fill your lungs and keep the thindrink within.~

Noah inhaled until his chest threatened to burst, then held his breath. They sank into the warm salty water. Fear demanded a scream from him when the whale fell away beneath his feet.

~Now do what you have observed others doing,~ Thinker commanded.

Surprised that he bobbed to the surface, Noah's hands moved back and forth in complete independence of his mind as his breath came in frantic pants. His feet mimicked a duck's.

When he began to dog paddle, wonder replaced fear. Even now the wonder remained. Thinker allowed Noah to hang on to his blowholes and then moved at high speed with just the top of his back above the water line.

Noah felt as if he flew. He enjoyed the feel of the great cetacean. Small all his life, next to Thinker he felt minuscule. It felt right.

When it came time for Noah to get back in his boat, Thinker came up under the craft and lifted it slightly out of the water making a stable platform, so Noah didn't risk over-turning his baidarka.

Many weeks ago, Noah shed his heavy clothes as he and Thinker moved south. Never before had the slight Inuit encountered heat such as this. A constant sheen of sweat covered his body. The water bottles fell dangerously low.

~Soon I must have drink.~ Noah told Thinker.

~Take what you will from my world.~ Puzzlement shaded the response.

~I would sicken and die if I drank of your world.~

~¿Why?~

~Your world is salt water. My kind needs fresh water, as falls from the sky, above the thindrink.~

~¿There is a world above your world?~

Noah groaned and shut his eyes, rested his head on his crossed forearms. The baidarka rocked gently on the ocean. Overhead a flawless blue sky domed the world with a few distant clouds far off to the right.

He briefly considered going for another swim to cool off. It amused him to think that he was probably the first human to be taught to swim in the middle of the ocean by a whale.

But it bordered rude to leave Thinker's question just floating there. He felt obliged to answer. Which would only lead to more questions. What could one do?

~No, the thindrink is part of my world. The rain falls from the

middle of the thindrink.~

~¿How does the rain come to be there?~

~The warm eye draws it up until the weight is so great that it must fall.~

Every conversation went like this. The man and whale had exchanged a great deal of information since their first encounter. Nearly a year had passed since their first meeting and their common vocabulary had grown extensive.

The memory of his now empty village, and his dead brother, brought neither grief nor remorse. However, the abuse and near rape of Marilyn on St. Lawrence Island haunted him. The villagers that he had held in thrall rarely ventured far from his mind.

~¿Why do you swim the same world again and again?~

~That I may understand the why of the event and never again wrong any as I wronged those.~ The hate-filled faces of the villagers flashed through his mind.

~¿It would seem that you have pondered this for many heartbeats. Why do you pain yourself further?~

~It is called guilt and remorse.~

~¿This is a needed thing for your kind?~

~No. But it is a thing we must endure if we do wrong.~

~¿Then why-~ Thinker broke off abruptly, danger radiated from his mind. *~¿Noah, did you hear that?~*

~Hear? I heard nothing other than you. I wasn't listening for else.~

~Then do so.~

Noah let his concentration drift away, created a mental whiteout where direction lacked meaning. From a distance, almost a mental echo, came the death cry of a whale — surrounded by waves of fear and hate.

~What should we do?~ he asked the whale.

~¿Have you still the death-spitting eel?~

His rifle.

~Yes, but it will not penetrate your world. It can only spit death in the thindrink.~

Combined irritation and condescension bubbled for a moment in Noah's mind before the whale shielded its thoughts. Noah strained but heard nothing more. The tragedy must be taking place far away. He could sense animate forms within a five or six-hundred-meter radius, and now only grim silence prevailed.

~I hear nothing now. Is it finished?~

~Yes. The prey has become sustenance.~

Noah felt slight relief. *~Then there is nothing we can do.~*

~There are others, a pod, as once I was part of.~

~Others? I heard but a single death.~

~It may be that I have listened for a longer time than you, therefore I now hear more. ¿Hear farther?~

Thinker was correct. Before St. Lawrence Island, Noah did not consider the possibility that he could do more with his mind than call animals to become meat. Not for the first time he wondered if the whale had the more powerful mind, and if it did, could it matter?

~The pod stays in one place. It is trapped by a line of rocks.~

~Rocks? The kind my species live on?~ Noah's questions boiled out in a frenzy. He had been at sea for many long weeks. He longed to walk again on firm ground, to stand without fear of falling overboard, and he needed water. On the other hand, there might be people. He wasn't sure he was ready for people yet.

~I know not. It matters little to the pod.~

Noah's face grew even warmer under the tropic sun. He had done it again — no thought for anyone other than himself. Despair crept up on him.

~They are like us.~

"What?" Noah said aloud. *~How can you tell? Why do I not hear them also? Are they able to make objects move?~*

~¿Your meaning swims too fast!~

~One apologizes. Can they hear us?~

~No. But they hear each other. Perhaps we are too distant for them to hear us, just as you cannot hear them.~

With a sense of dread, Noah willed his mind blank. If Thinker found others of his kind with whom he could communicate fully, he might have no further use of Noah. He looked around at the vastness of the Pacific Ocean.

Nothing visible except water. Despite himself, he became suddenly frightened.

~I would not leave one until one wished it so,~ the whale said.

Involuntary relief rushed through him. *~Thank you. I should have realized that.~*

~The pod is this way.~ The large, glistening black back broke the water off to Noah's right. The sudden spout of warm spray from Thinker's blowhole announced the imminent arrival of his dorsal fin, which submerged quickly. Then his massive tail lifted the four-meter flukes into the air before sliding down into the depths.

Noah grasped his two-bladed paddle and changed the baidarka's course. He stroked furiously after the departing whale but could not keep up. Never a particularly strong man, the weeks of paddling resulted in arms and shoulders supple unlike anything he had ever experienced. Nonetheless, his stamina needed more development.

A breeze nudged the cloth telltale on the bow. He quickly pulled out the ingeniously constructed collapsible metal sail and dropped the wood mast into the socket. The sail rasped open and caught the breeze, pushing the great baidarka smoothly.

He wondered again at the Magic Age that created this wonderful boat. How it came to be in his village was as mysterious to him as the craft itself. He loved the beautiful baidarka.

His uncle had once told him that the kayak and baidarka were pleasing in appearance as a woman was — narrow at the top and wide at the bottom. His uncle never said that around Noah's aunt or mother, which had puzzled Noah at the time.

He enjoyed sliding down through the boat, pulling himself along from aluminum rib to aluminum rib. A floor of long spruce boards, all tied together but not quite touching, ran the entire length of the craft. A magic thing coated the boards that made them smooth and without splinters forever. His uncle once called the magic stuff paint.

His world became more audible as he discovered the meaning of each sound the water made against the skin of the boat. Storms no longer frightened him.

Now when the tempo of the water changed, he woke immediately, instantly alert. The boat talked to him. Not the way Thinker talked to him, of course.

But the conversations became very dear. The baidarka possessed an ancient and strange inua. The boat sang to him of tomorrow. It used the past but didn't dwell there.

There were many things about the time before the Falling Stars and the twenty-odd years afterward that he didn't know. Although his father died some years after the stars fell, somehow Noah was a product of that great catastrophe. He remembered his mother speaking of food that glowed. Could that be what killed Thinker's mother?

Perhaps one had to lose a parent in those bad times in order to be gifted as they were. But Thinker hadn't seen as many winters as Noah. He shook his head. All this was so confusing. But, now it seemed there were others.

Without ever discussing the issue, he thought that was why he and Thinker had journeyed so far south. They had long since passed into climes uncomfortably hot to Noah, but they did not stop. They sought more of their kind. He felt the urge himself.

Of course, they hadn't seen any land either, Noah rationalized. Now they approached more whales with the ability to communicate. He remained anxious. The breeze freshened and the baidarka skimmed across the water toward distant clouds.

CHAPTER 4

Anguish permeated the Cea pod. Myrn remained inconsolable over the loss of her calf. There had been nothing the pod could do to save the small female, only six cold-eye cycles old, from the Supra. The Orcas had single-mindedly attacked and devoured the calf.

Myrn, with her brother, Naff, trying to help, had valiantly fought the Supra, receiving many wounds and losing much blood before her calf died. A boiling cloud of blood hid the awful sight from the Cea. Unfortunately, their new ability to share thoughts put the calf's terror right in their minds. Her pain was theirs until the point of death.

The experience emotionally drained them. They hung in the water like cod shocked for an eel's sustenance. Naff wished to flee this trap of death and coral, but he could not get the pod to move past the Supra and out through the opening in the reef.

~Nothing to be done here. Must flee while toothed-ones unaware of other than feeding.~

Only collective fear and revulsion answered his urgings. Tarn, the oldest bull after Naff, proved useless in situations like this. Half of his right flipper had been bitten off in an encounter with Supra many cycles ago. Tarn attempted to keep his mate, Myrn, between him and the Supra.

Naff moved to Larr, his only brother, and the youngest bull, nudging him in challenge.

~Must move Cea, else all will feed toothed-ones. Larr must help Naff.~

~Would kill Cea if Cea fled.~ Panic engulfed Larr's message. *~Toothed-ones are essence-takers. Must not cause takers concern. Takers will leave soon.~*

Naff fluked violently into the younger bull, sixty tons striking forty-five, rolling him to one side in the crystal depths.

~Riders think for Larr! Naff cannot move Cea alone. Assist or all lose essence.~

Larr retreated mentally as well as physically. Naff moved to Larr's mate, Nenn, who shielded her calf from the dissipating blood cloud.

~Mate will not heed, Nenn must. Cea must leave this place, else all will lose essence.~

Nenn shuddered and moved closer to her calf. Her mind proved as impenetrable as the coral reef behind her. Naff fluked to the side of his mate, Looa.

~Naff and Looa must leave. Cea will not follow Naff. Naff and Looa go, now.~ He fluked forward, and she matched his motion.

~¡If Cea stay, Cea lose essence!~ she agreed.

~¡Cea must decide. Naff and Looa must go, now!~ His motion quickened.

~Looa follow Naff.~ She moved forward.

They moved steadily toward the opening in the ring of living rock, passing within fathoms of the gorging pod of Supra. Once past the predators they fluked rapidly, moving out into the depths of the Great Warm World. Naff felt heartsick.

For many migrations his mother, Gaan, had led the pod in comparative safety, losing few of the Cea. Two migrations ago, her great heart had stopped, and the pod looked to him for leadership. Now he had lost them all. When younger he might have accepted such a thing without question.

Now he felt lessened. A part of him remained back in the ring of coral. He could not name the thing, but he could feel it. What could he do?

He had tried to stop the slaughter of the calf and received a great tear in his heartside flipper as a result. Baleen could not stop teeth. Although Naff bulked much larger than any of the rogue Orcas, his very size and lack of teeth worked against him in the battle.

Where acceptance rested before, questions began to prod. Perhaps it rubbed smoother to lose essence in the jaws of the Orcas than to leave his pod and flee. He might even be able to destroy some of the essence-taking toothed-ones. His great flukes slowed as he cogitated.

Looa slowed with him and brushed along his side.

~Naff return?~

~Cannot help the Cea. Cea must help Cea.~

~Naff slows.~

~Naff essence is sick.~

Hungry, Looa moved away from him and built a bubble net large enough to gain a mouthful of sustenance. She swam in a slow spiral upward, allowing bubbles of thindrink to curtain upward from her blowholes. Halfway between her mate and the top of the world, she saw the pod of Orcas take shape in the distance, bearing down on them.

CHAPTER 5

ONESARK SAW THE TWO GREATFISH SLIP through the opening in the reef while OnePod fed on the tender carcass of the calf.

OneTes identified the escaping bull. *=The defender of the calf would leave.=*

Instantly the thought flashed through OnePod that the greatfish now swam leaderless.

=¿Should this meat be lost?= OneRak inquired sharply. He was the patriarch, and now the only Orca in OnePod without a mate. Four of OnePod were his issue.

His mate, Taa, had been the natural leader of the pod of ten. One sparkling day she surprised an octopus gliding through the depths, seemingly unaware of its surroundings. She ingested it with one gulp.

Abruptly she changed. Suddenly she would not allow the pod to feed, or to stray from her vicinity. If any tried to leave or seek food, she would ram them, bite them, and force them back to the bewildered pod. The playful sense of humor, for which all Orca were famous, disappeared from her essence.

Finally, when the entire pod became ravenous and slightly mad, she twisted and tore her flank open. Her blood billowed out into the water. The starving Orcas went into a feeding frenzy and tore Taa apart.

They all felt her die. She seemed puzzled about her actions even as her essence faded. Then a presence blossomed, grasping their minds with a paralyzing tentacle while sifting down through each of them; caressing, probing, taking command. Suddenly they shared each other's thoughts. Each saw their own body from the eyes of others.

Wonder coalesced in each mind and meshed rapidly — they abruptly thought as one mind. New concepts bloomed, were thoroughly examined, and rejected or accepted in a heartbeat. They instantly evolved into OnePod.

A mind-rider arrived with the macro cognition. It held the pod together with mental tentacles. Initially, it seemed to be a nothing, a benign presence, and so light that it dwelt as less than a whisper in the back of their awareness as it facilitated communion.

The collective mind towered far stronger than any single Orca. OnePod ruled. However, each individual mind and essence became restrained, pushed into dark recesses, and like the wolf eel, would spring out at the rest of OnePod whenever the collective mind relaxed.

One mind with eight bodies made for a variety of chafing points and required practice and training before it could function as a single organism. Once fully meshed, it became the most efficient killing machine loose in the world since before the time of the burning water.

For three cycles of life, OnePod met no equal. In a normal pod, Rak would have assumed the lead upon the death of his mate. As OneRak he had the full mental force of the other eight to contend with, in addition to the lingering aura of Taa, and the mind-riding presence that manifested itself by a mental coppery taste — like blood. The members of OnePod thought of it as the Blood-Essence.

Decisions spawned almost instantaneously after lightning-like debate, springing forth full-grown in the mind of OnePod. Each decision carried the emphatic shading of one of the extensions of OnePod. This time it was OneRak's viewpoint that held sway.

=The bull and the cow must be returned to the reef, or die in the open world.=

OneCam, OneSith, and OneDeg felt the most satiated. They playfully began the chase. OneRak continued to feed with the others. A slight elation mixed with the curious split-mindedness of OnePod as three of its extensions raced away, fanning out in search.

OnePod assumed the pair of greatfish would make all possible speed to flee. Therefore, OneSith registered brief astonishment when she suddenly came upon them. One was building a bubble net and the other hung motionless!

The Blood-Essence rewarded OneSith with an orgasm. The other segments of OnePod stopped feeding and converged on her position at top speed. The new ability negated their need for echolocation. The other two searchers reached her first and shot out to opposite sides, arcing around the Humpbacks to cut them off from possible flight. OneSith dove deep to attack the greatfish out of the darkness of the depths.

The rest of OnePod continued along at high speed, finally catching sight of the prey. Circling far out on the left of the greatfish, OneCam caught motion in her left eye. She froze, letting the water slow her to a drifting stop.

Another greatfish! Racing toward her! OneTunk saw it at the same time.

OnePod wavered, then split. Four Orca went for the newcomer, and the other four homed in on the escapees. OnePod felt ecstatic over the presence of more meat.

CHAPTER 6

THE CLOUDS ON THE HORIZON ATTRACTED Noah's eye. His course aimed straight toward them. Occasionally he saw Thinker's spout ahead of him. The baidarka slowly gained on the whale.

Routinely he checked over the craft. Everything seemed in order. When he looked at the horizon again, he saw the clouds pinned to the ocean by the cone of a volcanic island. His heart jumped to a faster beat.

~¡Come quickly, we are needed!~ Suddenly Thinker breached half a kilometer ahead of the boat. The great black and white-spotted body rose out of the water almost as if to stand on its tail, flippers moving in an attitude of wings, and then all forty-five tons slammed down in a great spray.

Noah saw tall, black, wobbling dorsal fins converge on the spot. He reached down into the hull and pulled out his rifle, looking at it with trepidation. Never in his life had he fired a gun at a living thing.

Nonetheless, he knew how to shoot, and he could hit what he aimed at. The magazine was full. He also pulled a fine, steel-tipped spear near the open hatch. He had killed with a spear before.

Noah probed ahead mentally. Thinker fought with… four Orca? Noah could only distinguish one strong mind, yet Thinker perceived four predators.

In their long voyage south, Thinker had related the story of his previous encounters with rogue Orcas. Noah knew the Humpback felt a continuing antipathy for them. Therefore, Noah anticipated violence unlike anything in his experience.

The craft closed rapidly on the fight. Noah collapsed the sail but left it standing in the socket. The boat slowed and turned sideways in the breeze.

Thinker shot up out of the water again and crashed down where three dorsal fins sliced into the air. Noah raised the rifle and pointed it in the direction of the breaching whale.

=¡*OneSark: back!*= The command shot through Noah's head, startling him so much that he nearly dropped the weapon.

Suddenly a huge male Orca lunged up out of the water in a parabola calculated to intersect with Thinker's unprotected back. Compared to the Humpback, the Killer whale seemed small. However, it looked big enough to swallow Noah whole or crush the baidarka.

He snapped the rifle up and shot the Orca just behind the eye, at the same instant Thinker's flukes swatted it out of the air like a mosquito.

A shocked gasp rasped through Noah's mind, and for a moment he was in communication with a completely new being.

=¡*There is another. OneSark loses essence. We are lessened. Flee!*=

The pod of Orcas and the presence vanished.

~*You have my gratitude. The toothed-ones would have taken my essence,*~ Thinker said.

~*How many were there? I could feel but one entity.*~

~*They were four. We have taken the essence of one. It goes now to the final dive.*~

The image of an Orca trailing blood, sinking to the bottom of the ocean was suddenly pushed from Noah's mind by the intrusion of a slow, unfamiliar, viscous presence.

~¿*How called you?*~ Wariness covered the query tight as hide used for a drumhead. The question arose out of the middle of Naff's mind like a bubble, which included all in its expanding circle reminiscent of a widening ripple. His thoughts reached Thinker before they touched Noah.

~*I am Thinker. Who are you?*~

~*I am Naff.*~

~*Thinker, is it one of the pod?*~ Noah asked.

~*It is two of my kind from the pod attacked earlier.*~

Three Humpback whales broke the surface gently, their wide, glistening backs reflecting the sun. Noah could easily distinguish Thinker from the other two, for Thinker's body didn't carry hundreds of barnacles as the others did. Naff and his companion carried clusters that started at the cutwater on their jaws and spotted down the pleated bulge of their throats. The small, white, chitinous marine life also dotted their flippers.

Noah wondered why he had never seen any on Thinker. The whales picked up his thought.

~They cause me discomfort, so I do not allow their presence on my body,~ Thinker answered.

~¿How?~ asked Naff.

~It is something I can do because my mind is as it is. Like yours. Can you not refuse the small life to attend you?~

~Cea has riders. Essence has riders.~

~Does all of your pod communicate such as we are doing?~

~Cea can talk. Must be very near.~

~You are female.~

~Yes.~

~Looa is mate of Naff.~ The huge bull radiated ownership.

~I understand.~

Noah could feel longing in his friend. To find a female that he could communicate with! Thinker's search could be ended. This time Noah successfully concealed his fears.

~¿How kill toothed-one?~

~My friend, Noah, did this thing with his death-spitting eel as I struck with my tail.~

~¿Noah?~

~On top of the world.~

~I am pleased to be of help.~ Noah sent a wave of warm welcome but it seemed to bounce off the huge mammals.

~¿How do Cea hear Noah?~

~I know not. I only know we can. Have you always been able to hear?~

~Only since last migration to greater warm world. Pod found, found... ~

Something as bright as a small sun glowed in the eye of Noah's mind. A radiance?

~Noah is of Thinker's pod?~

~He is my friend and companion. Not mate. He is your friend too. Did he not aid in taking the essence of one of your attackers?~

Noah felt embarrassed to be the subject of such an intense discussion. He could feel the reluctance of the two whales to deal with him. He felt the same way about them.

~Noah is long-teeth? Essence-taker?~

~Noah's kind are. Noah has never taken Cea's essence. He is my friend.~

Noah felt a weight drop from his shoulders. Since meeting Thinker, he had felt remorse for having lured Humpback and Bowhead whales to his village's harpoons. Thinker obviously felt that fair retribution had been exacted.

One of the whales rolled in the water. Noah found himself under observation by an unwinking eye.

~Noah is small,~ Naff observed.

~¿Where is your pod?~ asked Thinker.

~Trapped.~

Noah felt desolation in the answer. The mental picture of a Humpback boxed in by teeth on one side and a wall of sharp coral on the other translated vividly.

~Naff and Looa have escaped. Why did not the pod follow?~

~Naff knows not. Cea not follow Naff. Naff not want to lose essence, but must return to Cea.~

~I will return with you. We will free your pod from the toothed-ones.~

Noah probed carefully into Naff's mind to find out how many Orcas they faced. The bull seemed unaware of his mental presence. Five males and four females, with one male dropping away — the one he killed.

Eight Killer whales. Why could he only find the mental presence of one? Was the rest non-thinking? No, the attack was too well coordinated to believe that... Noah stopped trying to puzzle it out and knew the answer would become clear if one waited long enough.

The island on the horizon tantalized him. Solid ground, fresh water, fresh food, perhaps people? He decided he could once again face people. He now accepted full responsibility for his actions.

He beheld the jungle-clad island with its steaming cone. Felt sure he could smell fresh water. This required closer investigation. He wiped sweat from his forehead, opened the sail, and glided away from the whales.

CHAPTER 7

"THE ILLERS ARE BACK," Jik announced grimly from the lookout.

"So what?" Moira shrugged. She sliced open a pink and yellow fish and hung it on the drying rack with the rest of the catch. "There, all finished. We have about twenty kilos of fish, not counting the fresh ones I kept for dinner."

"Hmm," grunted Jik, still staring out to sea. "I'm sure I heard a shot."

"You know those bloody whales can make all sorts of noise. It was probably one of them."

"No. That was a rifle shot."

"Right, mate." Moira lost interest. Jik always heard and saw things that nobody else could detect.

"I wish you were my mate, Moira," he said, giving her an obsidian stare.

Sudden anxiety made her chest feel hollow. *Bloody hell. What have I done now?* she wondered.

"Well, I'm not, Jik. Nor do I wish to be. So, forget it."

The scar across his cheek pulsed livid. His eyes tried to dominate her. He stood on the small look-out mound and snarled at her, "It should be my right as provider to–"

"I said forget it!" she shouted. "This isn't the bloody stone age. We're not going to be on this island for the rest of our lives. You'll answer to the authorities for anything you pull out here." She patted her sheath knife. "Assuming you live through the attempt."

Something slimy writhed in his eyes, then the wall returned, like always. He silently stalked off into the jungle.

Moira watched until he was lost to view in the brush and trees before she allowed herself to tremble. What did he do in there? Probably had himself an altar where he sacrificed live lizards to the God of Hunts, she mused.

In the shelter, Captain Arnold coughed heavily. She rose and went in to see him. "Tony, how're you feeling?"

"Like a poor grade of shit, honey."

"You can't be feeling too bad. You're still using those quaint Nebraska-isms," she said, forcing herself to smile. He looked drawn and pale, with a slight flush high on his cheeks. Night before last she had lain across from him, listening to his labored breathing for half the night before she could sleep. His struggling respiration now gurgled with a liquid quality.

A stab of fear at the thought of his death suddenly enhanced her concern for him. She had come to love the old man. Her father might have turned out just like him if her parents hadn't become absorbed in their strict religion.

But, if Tony Arnold died, there would be no other witness to Jik's actions. She would become his victim. Abruptly she felt angry for worrying about herself when this bonzer old bloke might be dying.

"Get me a drink, would ya?" Captain Arnold asked.

"Of course." Moira went to the water bucket and dipped out a half gourd's worth for him. "Here, Tony. Let me help you."

With their combined efforts he struggled to a sitting position. He took the proffered gourd with shaking hands and drank deeply.

"Oh," he gasped, lying back against her arms, "that tastes so good."

"Is there anything else I can get you?"

"Not unless you've discovered a licensed store somewhere on the island." They chuckled together. "But you know, I must be getting worse," he said conversationally.

"Tony! Don't say that."

"Well, hell, I'm starting to hallucinate," he said crossly.

"What do you think you see?" she asked, peering down at his face.

He stared out toward the ocean. "I think I see a guy in a ponce-looking boat, that's what."

She smiled quickly to hold back tears and shook her head. "Oh, Tony, there's no boat..." she followed his gaze and saw a paddle flash in the sun, "...out there!" she finished with a shout.

Tony's wild, bushy eyebrows shot up. "You mean he's real?"

"Too bloody right!" she crowed. "Look at that bastard, cool as can be, just paddling up to our little retreat 'ere." She felt wonderfully intoxicated.

"Ohmigawd!" Tony blurted, peering out.

Moira's heart caught in her throat.

Eight sky-raking dorsal fins surfaced and closed on the suddenly frail boat. The occupant had no idea of the Killers' presence.

Moira screamed as the Orcas surged forward.

CHAPTER 8

Noah jerked when the scream reached him. The trip in from the reef had been uneventful. He kept alert for sign of the Orcas, but they seemed to have disappeared.

Noah noticed the shelter from a good distance out. At first, he wasn't sure anyone lived there. Then he saw movement and paddled faster. The stillness felt almost tangible until the scream turned it into surges of adrenaline.

"Behind you!"

He twisted around. Huge wavering dorsal fins sliced through the baidarka's wake. Looking down, he could see the black and white bodies racing toward him. They were so terrifyingly huge and impossibly fast — there was no time to reach the shore. He fleetingly wondered what they wanted.

=¡Kill!=

Fear clutched his heart as the mental command slammed into his brain, *=Meat, come to me.=*

Reacting instinctively, he struck back at the smothering presence. *~Die! Drown and die!~*

The presence recoiled.

The Orcas lurched.

The front two turned slightly, no longer supple in their movements. Two others changed course instantly as if avoiding a large rock. The last three slowed but did not stop.

Noah felt amazement. That would have killed a seal. He tried to find their minds and open communications with them.

~I would speak with you.~

Silence answered his offering.

The three rear most Orcas picked up speed again and continued their rush toward him. He struck a second time. Looking straight at them, he willed them unconscious.

They instantly lost speed, rolled and bobbed to the surface. Noah paddled for the shore. A woman stood on the beach.

"Don't come straight in. The coral will ruin your boat! Bring it through there." She pointed off to his left where a pink tongue of island sand licked blue water.

In moments he pulled through the small channel to the beach. He had a decision to make before he spoke to this person — should he even look into her mind? He knew he would not try to influence her; he had vowed never again to do that to a human.

But should he even look? Perhaps it wasn't a puzzle that he could solve at this time. Maybe time would provide the answer. One could wait.

The jungle reached out and touched his nose and ears. New smells assaulted so overpoweringly that they stuffed his nose uncomfortably. The tree-and-brush-covered mountain held heat that stank. Noah's increased respiration accelerated his heartbeat. Alien birds invisibly racketed about in the dense greenery.

As soon as the boat touched the shore he scrambled over the edge and jumped down to pull it ashore. When his feet hit the sand, his knees buckled, and he saved himself by grabbing the baidarka.

"One has been on the water for a long time," he said soberly. "One would be grateful if someone would help me get the boat on the beach."

She pulled on the baidarka with more strength than he thought possible in her small frame. Once the craft grounded, he stood and looked at her. She wasn't as beautiful as Marilyn, but a feeling of competence emanated from her that pleased him. She also seemed genuinely happy to see him.

"Where did you get this bonzer boat?" she asked with awe in her voice.

"It was in one's village, Point Hope."

"Alaska?"

"Yes. That is where one grew up."

"How did you live through the tsunamis?"

"Soo-what?"

"The big waves. The ones that destroyed all the seacoasts, twenty-two years ago," she explained testily.

"One was born after the stars fell. The People were spared the great waves. It is said that only they were worthy enough to miss the drowning death." He felt somewhat apprehensive. She seemed intent, almost angry about the big waves. Why was it important now? He suppressed the urge to peek into her mind for the answer.

"Who built your boat?" she asked, nodding at the craft.

"One doesn't know. One is known as Noah Manaluk and is pleased to meet you."

"Oh." She colored slightly. "Sorry 'bout that. I'm Moira Napier." She reached out and shook his hand. "You an Inuit, or what?"

"Yes. One is of the People. Is someone in this place alone?"

"No," a hard voice said from behind him. "Someone has a hunter to provide for her."

Noah turned and beheld a well-muscled man about as tall as himself. He wore cloth tied with intricate knots around his middle, which covered his loins, the rest of his body remained bare for the looking. Without even thinking about it, Noah scanned the man's mind. Convoluted, myriad desires and hurts wove tightly to make a wall between his true self and the world.

Two things troubled Noah about this man — he hungered for Moira Napier, and he would kill to get Noah's boat. Noah instantly felt chagrin for having invaded Jik's mind with no more thought than one used in scratching a mosquito bite.

"This is Jik Sipoy. He is a sailor and a hunter. But I provide for myself, despite what he says," Moira said hotly.

Noah stared at Jik thoughtfully. He had seen white people like Moira before. Gusik was what the People called them. Next to the Inuit, their skin did have a fish-belly paleness to it, which was the real meaning of gusik. It wasn't a good white, not like cold-enough-to-build-with snow.

Jik was not gusik. Nor was he the weathered-sinew brown of the People. His brown had young ivory in it, yellowish, his mother used to say.

Perhaps he was an Indian from some far place. He had heard there were many shades of people in the great circle. When he was a little boy there was an old man in the village who was not of the People. He was darker than the night. Nonetheless, he was friendly, unlike the man in front of him.

Once more Noah darted into the man's mind. Malay? The name

meant nothing to him, but in the man's mind the word was really "People," and Noah easily recognized the fierce pride that accompanied the identity.

"One is happy to meet Jik Sipoy," he said politely.

Jik ignored the outstretched hand. "How did you get past the Killer whales?" he asked sharply.

"Yeah, I wondered that myself," Moira said. "What did you do, drug them or something?"

Noah silently thanked her for the suggestion.

"As you say, one had a powder that made them ill when sprinkled over the water where they swim."

"I don't suppose you have any of this powder left, do you?" Jik asked with a sneer.

"No. One used all one had. There were so many all at once."

"What was it made from, Noah?" Moira asked. "Maybe we can make some more."

"One doesn't know. A shaman made it." This was taking too long. He didn't want to talk on the subject anymore for fear of catching himself in a snare of his own deception. "How did Moira and Jik come to be in this place?"

"We were shipwrecked in a storm," Moira answered.

"It was more than a storm. It was a typhoon, a killer wind," Jik said defensively.

"Yes, that's true," Moira said softly. "It killed his brother and my husband."

Noah was not in her mind. Still, an overpowering sadness suddenly emanated from her. Tears sprang into his eyes, and he squeezed his lids shut quickly and looked away for a moment before either of them could see him. Jik's hunter's eyes missed the tears.

Nevertheless, Moira saw them.

Noah regained his composure. "If someone has water to spare, one would welcome a drink."

"Why do you talk like that?" Jik asked.

"It is the way the People speak."

"Bugger off, Jik!" Moira snapped. "He just bloody got here. He's tired, thirsty, probably hungry, and you go at 'im like he's a bloody rape suspect in gaol."

Noah shuddered when she said "rape". His mind shrank from

the word. He liked the way her eyes took fire when she became angry. Her eyes fascinated him. They held the color of the Chukchi Sea in spring. He had never seen human eyes that color before.

He also felt happy that she attacked Jik. The Malay's hostility was incomprehensible. From what he could tell, nothing here could be perceived as a threat to the man.

Noah slipped into Jik's mind again and recoiled. He suddenly felt unclean, even tainted. He wished he had not seen the naked animal that lived in there, the animal that snarled at his mental presence.

"Come along, then," Moira said, breaking his connection. "I'll give you food and drink."

He followed her toward the shelter. Jik remained behind, eyeing the baidarka.

"Welcome to our island," Moira continued. "With your boat we might all escape, don't you think?" she chatted with a fixed intensity. "Not immediately or anything, if you wanted to rest or..."

She blinked. "My God, I'm sorry. I don't mean to be rude. But it's just that I haven't seen anyone other than Jik and Tony for three months now—"

"Tony?" he blurted. "There is another here?" He averted his eyes in shame.

He had been thoughtless again, twice in one day. First with Thinker... he started in surprise. Thinker was not in his mind for the first time since St. Lawrence Island!

"Oh, yes, I haven't told you about Tony. Well, he's where the food and water are, so we'll just do everything at once."

He tried to concentrate on her words and puzzle out Thinker's absence at the same time. He couldn't do it, and for the moment let thoughts of Thinker fade. Moira strode ahead and Noah noticed her tanned and muscular legs. Her bottom, working back and forth in the worn and faded shorts, held his attention even longer.

"Just here," she said, swinging her arm to offer the shelter's interior and the old man on the pallet. "Noah Manaluk, may I present Captain Anthony Arnold of the late schooner, *Nebraska*. Tony, Noah is an Inuit from Alaska."

"Don't Inuits live on the coast?" Tony asked querulously.

Noah nodded. "Yes, that is true."

"Then how did any of ya live through the tsunamis?" His tone carried suspicious disbelief.

"The People were worthy and did not suffer the great waves. They spoke of the ground shaking like a caribou covered with mosquitoes but saw nothing of waves."

"Noah is from Point Hope," she said brightly. "Where exactly is that in Alaska, Noah?"

"North, past the Diomedes, facing the Chukchi Sea. It is much colder there, and it is never as warm as this place." He wiped a trickle of sweat from the side of his face. "Someone mentioned water?"

"Oh, Christ, I'm sorry. Yes. I'll be but a moment. Have a sit-down."

He sat cross-legged on a cushion decorated with blue anchors. Tony stared at him with rheumy eyes.

"How did you get here?" the captain asked.

"In a baidarka that one found in one's village."

"You paddled all the way from Alaska in that boat?"

"It also has a sail that one learned to use."

"How many people will your baidarka carry?"

"Three."

Moira returned carrying a tray that held a bowl of fruit and a plastic pitcher of water. "Wait till you get a better look at it, Tony. It's a bonzer boat." She sat the tray down in front of Noah. "We have dried fish too, if you'd like some."

Noah shook his head. "One is very tired of fish," he said.

"How'd you get past the Killer whales?" Tony asked, watching Noah eat.

"He had a powder that just knocked them out," Moira interjected. "Didn't you see that?"

"Powder? Like talc or something?"

"A shaman gave it to him. He used it all," she explained.

"Then we're still stuck here, even if he does have a boat that will carry three," Tony said sullenly as he rolled over and faced the wall.

"Why does someone sleep during the day?" Noah asked.

"His legs were broken when we were wrecked," Moira said gently. "They won't heal for some reason."

Tony rolled back over. Sweat popped out on his forehead from the effort. "I'm gonna die on this fucking island. I need modern medical treatment and the closest is in Australia," he said flatly.

"Perhaps one could help. One was trained by the People's shaman."

"What do you use, rattles, gourds, things like that? Maybe a feather or two?" he said contemptuously.

"It is your choice," Noah replied, stung.

"Bugger off!" Tony rolled to the wall once more.

Noah looked up at Moira. She inclined her head toward the door. He picked up the fruit and water, followed her out, and sat on the beach beside her.

"He's in a bad way," she said. "He used to be more optimistic, but his legs haven't healed, and he seems to be getting sick on top of everything else."

Noah ate the strange, delicious fruit, and watched her face as she talked. He offered his help, but the old man didn't want it. What could one do, insist? He liked the way her nose turned up.

"How about I tell you my story, then you can tell me yours?" she said.

Noah nodded.

Although she hadn't realized it at the time, Moira had been a lucky two-year-old to be in the subterranean mining town of Coober Pedy when the earthquakes hit. Shaken but not smashed by the reeling Earth's crust, the vast area of South Australia survived.

Not only did the sunbaked town endure, but it also became one of the few population centers left. New towns sprang up at the edges of ruined cities. Nevertheless, for years people would not live on the coast unless no other choice existed.

As a result, New Darwin Port now resembled a dissipated twenty-year-old pushing sixty. It stretched from the new, huge, concrete docks at the water's edge to the once-armed gate of New Darwin, fifteen miles away. The gate opened on the spot where the waves stopped. New Darwin started on the side that stayed dry.

It did not bode well to be addressed as a 'drystir' in N'Dawpert. "Dry sider" was spat rather than spoken in all ports. Moreover, the hard-working, honest people of the inland cities, quite content to be dry siders, looked askance at those who made their living by and of the sea.

The ports were needed, and good people lived in those treacherous towns. But who would live there if they had any other option?

Moira could now appreciate the wet viewpoint, even though she had been a dry sider for her entire pre-island life.

After only ninety days on the island, it seemed that Deagan had been gone for achingly long years.

It seemed so unfair that the poor bloke died right after the biggest disappointment of his life. He would have made an excellent Prime Minister. If only there had been more like-minded Australians out there who were willing to embrace their part of the Pacific on a brother-to-brother basis.

She didn't think of herself as pretty. Small and slim, yes. Her shoulder length wheat-to-straw hair possessed a hint of red when touched just so by the sun.

However, her large blue eyes dominated her face with its too-wide mouth, small chin, and freckled nose. The nose with that damn up-turn at the end. In normal situations a bloke would look right past her.

Unless he heard her sing.

She'd started singing as a child and never stopped. Her parents encouraged her only insofar as she praised God with her music. Their life became full of The Rock of God's Wrath Church after the meteorite fall, and humankind had no right to be going about singing lewd songs and laughing.

After all, had not humans brought destruction down from the sky as a righteous response to their wicked ways? Had not He destroyed the Sodom and Gomorrah of Sydney and Melbourne? Nobody worth their salt lived in Melbourne anymore, and nothing but politicians and other thieves lived in New Sydney.

For a time, she was happy to sing praises to God. Depressingly, the songs hung heavy with the collective guilt of survivors from a great calamity. The church offered no other outlets for an ebullient young girl.

Then she heard a different kind of rock music, old music, from before the meteorite fall, from the Age of Technology.

So much of the old machinery and electronics were nothing more than fascinating junk. A great deal of it depended on systems that lay shattered and drowned. A world busy trying to survive could not waste time playing with mangled toys.

But some of it lived. Recordings on plastic discs fell on human ears once again. All of the other types of recordings needed more than wind-up playing machines.

When she heard the old music something changed inside her. She could extrapolate rhythm, and the rock and roll from generations past connected with a need she didn't know she had.

Her parents didn't understand. They made her attend church twice a day in order to keep her safe under the jealous eye of a deity whom she couldn't understand and doubted anyway. Little was said in the home that, one way or another, didn't evoke God.

Communication between Moira and her parents eroded to the point of single, sharp words. She left home in the middle of the night at fifteen, and with her voice earned her way across an energetically rebuilding Australia. At the age of twenty, she performed at a political rally before and after Deagan's quick, optimistic speech.

The crowd endured him in order to listen to her. They married after a three-week courtship. His message finally attracted a following.

For the longest time he thought that meant something far grander. He'd fought hard for his ideals, and in the final struggle lost all that he really lived for.

When she and Deagan left New Sydney for this trip, she reigned as the toast of the town. Her recording contract brought her first rank celebrity status, including fan clubs that constantly asked her silly questions. Her link to Deagan and his politics was carefully ignored by most of those who hired her.

All in all, she had been on top of the world. Then Deagan chartered Captain Arnold and his lovely schooner, Nebraska, for an unlimited cruise. The cruise had two stimuli, their third wedding anniversary, and Deagan's recent election defeat. She never asked which reason came first in his rush to be away.

She needed a break too.

For two weeks the cruise proved relaxing and idyllic. They toured the old Federated States of Micronesia, the Republic of the Marshall Islands, and were somewhere between the Commonwealth of Northern Marianna Islands and Japan when the typhoon roared over.

The sea shrieked chaos, throwing mountains of water on the boat one moment, and pitching it off spume-capped peaks the next. The schooner rolled violently from side to side. An hour earlier, clawing waves pushed by the shrieking wind had ripped the sails from her masts, leaving only fragments that stood at rigid right angles in the wind, snapping like pistol shots.

"Jik! Man the pumps," Captain Arnold screamed through the howling wind. "Go relieve your brother. He's been pumping for an hour!"

Moira paid no attention to the captain or Jik. She watched as her husband tied her snugly to the stump of the main mast.

"Deagan, you've already put a life-line on each of us. Why d'ya have to do this?" she shouted down at him.

"It's getting worse. Before long one line won't hold us. As long as we're afloat, you're safest right here."

She noticed he didn't say anything about what would happen if they didn't stay afloat.

"God damn it, man! Get below!" Captain Arnold bellowed from behind.

Moira twisted around to see Jik moving across the deck toward them, one hand gripping the lifeline, the other holding his knife.

"What's he doing?" Moira asked calmly into the storm.

Deagan glanced up, saw Jik, and shook his head. "'S okay. I don't need any help," he shouted toward the advancing figure.

A smile, or a grimace, she wasn't sure which, touched the edge of Jik's mouth for an instant. But, he kept coming. The deck pitched wildly, great waves washed over them with impunity, while the rigging popped and hummed in the wind. With crab-like, predatory tenacity, Jik continued to advance.

"Jesus, Deagan! What's he going to do?" she shrilled.

"What's this?" he said, dropping the rope and standing upright to confront the Malay.

Then the boat rose out of the water for an impossibly hushed moment. Moira's eyes widened in shock at the sight of palm trees whipping in the maelstrom. She tried to tell Deagan about it, but there just wasn't time before the *Nebraska* smashed down on the reef that ripped her keel and lower hull to kindling.

As the boat screamed in agony over the rocks, Moira saw a glint of steel at the same time a large comber smashed over the deck.

The water bounced her head off the mast. Momentum carried the bulk of the schooner across the reef and up onto the island which had materialized out of the typhoon like arcane magic.

The gutted hull crunched to a stop a mere two meters from the bent palm trees. The mast stubs appeared to stand aloof from their genuflecting cousins.

Moira's vision cleared and she whipped her head about, seeking Deagan. He wasn't there, and she screamed.

She'd wandered the three-square-kilometer island for a month, looking for Deagan. She didn't find either her husband or Jik's brother, Tamir. Captain Arnold broke both legs in the wreck and now depended totally on his former crewman and passenger.

Jik built the shelter out of boat debris, built the raft, built the fish trap, and found them food in the lush jungle that surrounded the cone of the sunken volcano. The small island shuddered through constant earthquakes that seemed to occur on a measured basis. Moira wandered like a wraith over every square meter of dry ground, once even climbing to the reeking crater on the dormant volcano that dominated the island.

At the beginning of the third week Jik told her that she needed a mate, and he would treat her well. She'd looked through him in a mist of emotional shock, trying hard to make sense of his words. Then she figured it out.

"Don't be silly," she said, dismissing him.

Other than the ring on her finger, all that remained of her three-year marriage was the knife at her hip. When he gave it to her, Deagan said with a leer that she'd have to open all the oysters for their private parties.

The marriage hadn't been all that secure. He had his career and she had hers. Nevertheless, there had been a passion in the early days that swept all else before it.

She knew this open-ended vacation had been an attempt on Deagan's part to resurrect that passion and hoped-for commitment. In addition, it was also an escape from his fanatic followers who planned loudly for his political comeback. Now it all lay sealed in the amber of memory.

At the end of their fourth week on the island, she awoke to find Jik running his fingers over her thigh and crotch. The knife leaped into her hand, and she struck out at him, opening his cheek to the bone. He vanished into the jungle so quickly that she almost believed the incident was a dream until she noticed blood on the blade.

They avoided each other for three days. When he would return to the shelter, she would go down to the beach. After an hour or so, she would amble back up to the shelter and he would disappear into the dense foliage.

On the fourth day as she walked up from the beach, Jik stopped her. His crusted wound gleamed with something he had concocted.

"I will not do all the labor to keep that old man alive. If you do not help me, I will kill him and you. Do you understand me?"

She nodded. After that they labored in distrust side by side.

"You have been through much," Noah said. "If your husband is dead, what do you have in Australia to return for?"

"Oh, my career, I suppose. Mum and Da are still in Coober Pedy praying to bits of asteroids the last I knew. I have a brother on a station in the outback somewhere, but he doesn't need me either."

Noah didn't prompt her when she fell silent. His mind returned to the absence of Thinker. He wondered what had become of his friend.

Had the Orcas killed him? No, Noah would have known when the fight took place. In the meantime, he decided to try and speak more like these people. Perhaps it would reduce the tension. Moira spoke to him.

"What? one is sorry, one- I was thinking of other things."

"I'd like to hear your story. I asked if you had family back in Point Hope," she said with a sympathetic smile.

"No. My father died when I was very small. My mother died last year, as did my brother."

"How sad. Why did you come here?"

Because I didn't want to be alone, he thought. No, he couldn't say that. He couldn't tell her that the People had abandoned him, and the only friend he had must move south or suffocate under the ice.

"My life required change."

"Well, mine didn't, but changes happened anyway," she said in a sad tone. "I'd love to put it all back the way it was."

The sun touched the western horizon.

"Excuse me, but I must take care of my baidarka."

"Oh, let me help you."

As they walked down the beach, Noah couldn't help noticing how frail he appeared next to her. His newly muscled arms and shoulders emphasized his sunken, smooth chest, and his legs jutted out of his ragged pants like sticks. Her full head of hair mocked his baldness.

He pulled a rope from the front hatch and tied the boat securely to the closest tree. The tide had gone out and the boat rested on the sand, many meters from the water. He glanced over at Moira who stared at the baidarka.

"Perhaps it is better that I sleep in my boat tonight."

"Um, I suppose you're right. Tomorrow we all need to sit down and hash out our plans. I know that Jik and Tony share my desire to get off this damned island. What I don't know are your plans."

"I have none. I was just going south with, with my boat and discovered the three of you here. I will be happy to help you all if I can."

Moira became animated. She stepped over and hugged him tightly.

"Oh, thank God! I was hoping you would help. What good news for all of us!"

Noah found himself returning, and enjoying, the hug. Something pulled at his attention, and he looked up. At the edge of the trees Jik stood stiffly, with fists clenched at his sides, staring at them. Noah could feel the hate without going near the man's mind.

Moira felt him stiffen and stepped away from him. "Oh, I didn't mean to make you feel uncomfortable."

"You didn't," Noah said, nodding. "He did."

She turned and they watched Jik fade back into the darkened jungle. Raucous birdcalls heightened the strange feel of the place.

"He's yarra, a bit of a mental case if you ask me. Don't let him bother you." She grinned at him, then pointed suddenly out to sea. "Oh, watch this."

The sun sank quickly into the dark water, and in short seconds only a sliver still showed. Just as the top of the orb touched the horizon, an intense green flash filled Noah with wonder. Exaltation raced through him.

The sun disappeared and the sky went instantly dark. He felt very close to this small, vibrant woman. He stifled the thought.

"I think I will sleep now," Noah said.

"G'night then. I'm glad you're here, Noah."

"Thank you, Moira. I am glad, too. Good night." The small fire in the shelter cast off enough light for him to watch her enter the rude hut. He climbed into the baidarka and scooted down onto the sleeping pad.

The night pressed down, an inescapable blanket of moist heat. For the first time in months, there were more sounds than merely the slap of waves. The birds, noisy enough during the day, became even louder, screaming at him from the inky jungle.

A breeze stirred, cooling him, but it also agitated the trees and bushes. He listened carefully so he would know the sound. Creatures scuttled across the sand, some large, some small. Point Hope hadn't been like this.

Sleep began to claim him. He wondered if the birds were good to eat.

~When the warm eye returns, I have need of your help.~

Noah's eyes popped open. *~It is good to know that you are near, my friend.~*

~There is danger for you on the rock.~

~I know. Thank you for the warning.~

Thinker's presence vanished. Noah wondered what the whales needed from him. His eyes closed again, and he yawned.

The baidarka moved. Noah stared up through the hatch at the starry sky. Someone, or something, had climbed onto the boat.

His hand found the rifle and he grasped it. He opened his mouth, trying to hear over the suddenly loud beating of his heart.

Instantly sweaty again, he probed into the darkness with his mind.

CHAPTER 9

THINKER OBTAINED HIS FRIEND'S DESTINATION AS Noah paddled away. Reassured, the whale turned his attention to the Cea in front of him.

~*My friend goes to the rock to seek his own kind.*~

~*Naff and Looa must return to the Cea now.*~

~*Thinker will go with you.*~

Naff slowly moved through the water. His right eye moved back and forth as he surveyed Thinker. The old bull out-massed Thinker by a fourth of his length.

~*Thinker could lose essence in this place,*~ Naff said.

~*Thinker could lose essence in many places,*~ he replied.

~*Only one predator remains.*~

Looa was correct, a single Orca patrolled the opening in the reef. When the Killer whale saw the three Humpbacks approach, it fled around the island.

As they swam through the opening, Larr came to greet them.

~*The Cea are well,*~ he told them with a shading of smugness. ~*The Cea wish to continue migration.*~ Smug edged into haughty.

~*¿Why has not Larr led the Cea?*~ Naff asked flatly.

~*Larr not Naff.*~ A feeling of humility glowed and died. Larr finally noticed the slightly smaller Thinker.

~*Another of the Cea. Where did you find this young one?*~

~*Thinker fought black-and-white toothed-ones. He comes to help the Cea.*~ Naff said.

~*¿Does he hear the Cea?*~

~*I hear the Cea. I can help the Cea.*~

Nothing was said, but questioning doubt suddenly dominated the uncertain thoughts the three shared. Naff and Larr remained motionless, suspended in their bright, blue world. Thinker wondered at their inactivity since both had expressed the desire to leave the reef.

Politely he waited for logic to prod them. After several heartbeats, he wearied of their indecision. He was not one of their pod and had done all he could. Enough.

~This one now leaves. There is nothing to fear.~

The two bulls remained motionless. A presence loomed beside Thinker.

~Looa will follow.~

Naff surged between Thinker and Looa, his body a rude wedge pushing them apart.

~Looa is mate to Naff. Looa must follow Naff.~

~Then Naff must lead.~ Coldness reminiscent of the far northern feeding grounds suffused her declaration.

Abruptly the area quickened with activity. Without further hesitation, Naff fluked back through the reef into the open ocean. Looa silently followed, old echoes of migration songs filling her mind.

Larr swam around the others of the pod, nudging and pushing them. In moments they also followed the huge bull. Thinker scanned the lagoon and found nothing larger than a sculpin. He left the deadly reef behind.

Wondering where the Supra were, he scanned in a widening circle. Suddenly he saw them through Noah's eyes, rushing through the water toward the boat. Thinker became agitated and began to swim toward the confrontation.

When Noah struck a mental blow, and the Orca pod wavered, Thinker drifted to a stop. He knew he couldn't get there in time to help physically. In addition, he felt startled that Noah could slow an entire pod of Supra.

He could extend his powers that far if needed. Hadn't he saved Noah on the last rock, many cycles ago? Besides, for just a heartbeat or two, he wished to observe.

The remaining Supra pressed their attack. Noah struck again. Now all seven Supra either fled or lay stunned.

When had Noah's powers reached such strength? Thinker wondered. In some ways, they more than matched his own.

Some of the Cea pod disappeared in the distance. They hadn't heard Noah's fight with the Orcas. Since he wished to stay with them for a few heartbeats more, he reluctantly followed.

As his great muscles flew him through the sea, he pondered the strange powers he and the human possessed. This pod of Cea could communicate, but poorly. They could not express abstract thought.

Their world held no color, only light and dark. Maybe their power would grow?

He knew that his powers had increased, but he didn't know how much. How could he measure? Noah's recent victory showed proof of his growing strength.

Noah had been able to take the essence of birds, fish, and pinnipeds — although he had not attempted to take a walrus. Not out of fear, the man assured him, but because he would not be able to utilize all of the animal and the People did not believe in waste.

But, Noah had never attempted to control or attack a member of the Supra. The Cea extended them tassa, or foremost-of-two-families regard. No other creature shared this distinction.

Except Noah?

Thinker closed within a few fathoms of the Cea. He slowed, struggling with this freshly created mind net.

Were not Noah and himself part of the same family? A newborn family, yes, but still a family? This pod he followed, they could also communicate with Thinker and Noah. Would that not place them in the family also? He wondered where his allegiance would rest if the matter required choice.

Or were they all part of something more? The pod of Orcas possessed minds that seemed impossible to scan, or even to enter. Yet they fled after just one loss.

Once again, he felt a biting pain deep inside his body. He had not felt such bites before meeting Noah. Slowly the notion leaked in that there were things he must know. The certainties that Noah called "truths" were very important to the human. Now Thinker had a truth of his own that must be tested.

He stopped in the water and scanned ahead to the departing pod. They continued their migration to the feeding grounds, where-the-top-of-the-world-will-turn-to-rock. They would be back to mate further in the cycle. If he wanted their company he knew where to find them.

For now, he would stay and try to understand his suddenly

complex life. He turned and swam in a wide circle around the atoll to avoid Orca echolocation. He did not want them to seek him. Not yet.

The warm eye fell into the world again, and the thindrink and the world became dark. Thinker suddenly sang the old song of search, but now he added a puzzlement to the end, changing it completely. He no longer sought a mate, but an identity. The rock rose out of the depths in front of him and his movement and song ceased.

Noah lay alone in his floating thing preparing to lose small essence. Thinker communicated carefully, warning but not revealing, requesting without demand. Then, despite the sudden danger he perceived to Noah, he broke the mental bond and went to find sustenance.

CHAPTER 10

Six of the Orcas suffered throbbing headaches. The Blood-Essence raged, and anger felt alien to them. They didn't know how to respond to the emotions generated.

=*To hunt this one is like biting rocks,*= the usually taciturn OneCah said.

=¡*That one is not rock. It is sustenance!*= OneRak insisted.

=*Not of old. Before this time the Supra did not hunt the long-teeth. They can bring death in the tiny-worlds,*= OneShri declared.

Captivity promised the worst death an Orca could imagine. For as long as racial memory, their kind had been taken by the long-teeth-ones and put in the tiny-worlds. Most never returned. That this had not happened in any living Orca's memory had no bearing on their inbred fear of the long-teeth.

=*We are OnePod. Old has no essence.*= The statement remained barren of individual inflection. It seemed to come from the water around them.

=*Sark has no essence,*= OneRak responded, feeling as though he fought himself.

Biting pain erupted in his flank. He spun to attack, but no one was there. The closest of the pod floated two lengths distant.

=*Who strikes like the eel? Who must bite and hide?*= he demanded. He felt ready to fight, ready to kill.

Invisible teeth tore at his throat. He shrieked and fluked violently off to the left. The rest of OnePod drifted back out of the way, watching.

=¡*Does Rak drown in the shallow world?*= OneTunk asked.

=¡*Which does this?*= OneRak raged.

=¡*Does what?*= OneDeg asked.

=*From where does your pain come?*= OneSith prodded.

=OnePod fears nothing. OnePod is teeth of the world. All else is meat.=

This time none of the Orcas responded to the flat statement ringing in their minds. OneRak reflected that it was too late to worry about this thing. It lived in them. The pain ebbed away, and he remained quiet.

=Who speaks?= OneTes asked in her quiet, unchallenging way.

=OnePod speaks. Now OnePod must act.= Resolution flashed with the answer.

=We are all of OnePod. Which one speaks?= OneTes persisted.

=The binding essence, the superiority that OnePod has over the rest of the Supra world. That is what speaks.=

=We have shared minds for three cycles of essence. Why have you not made yourself known?= OneTes asked.

Shades of approval, surprise, and encouragement edged in from the other Orcas. A tiny pain of disapproval countered the warm wave.

=Until now there has been no need.=

=Our need, or your need?= OneTes pressed.

=¡Our need. We are one!=

=What are you?= OneTes asked swiftly.

=That which controls you.=

Excruciating pain flashed through OneTes, causing her to spasm violently and lose consciousness. She drifted in the water, beginning to sink.

=¡We must lift her to the thindrink, or she will lose essence!= OneRak said, bringing the others out of the near-shock of the exchange.

They reacted instantly. OneCah, OneSith, and OneCam glided under the gently sinking Orca, putting their bodies side-by-side. They took her weight evenly and lifted her until her blowhole broke the top of the world.

OneRak and OneTunk rubbed up against her, calling to her in the ancient way. OneShri and OneDeg swam around the succoring Orcas.

An orphan question drifted through OnePod wondering if the two patrolling Orcas anticipated threat from outside their worried circle, or from within.

None answered.

CHAPTER 11

Jik's weight shifted, and the baidarka creaked as it flexed. In the dark depths of the boat, Noah gripped the rifle with sweaty hands.

"What do you want, Jik?" he shrilled.

"Your blood, Inuit-man," came the snarled reply.

"I have a weapon." He stopped and cleared his throat. "If you come any closer, I'll use it. But I have no wish to harm you."

"No, you just wish to take my woman and have me help you."

"She said she wasn't your woman."

"I am the hunter. She is my woman if I choose it," he snapped.

"Moira lives in the ancient ways of your people?" Noah asked.

"What do you know of my people, Inuit-man?"

"As much as you do."

"You mock me," he hissed. The boat shifted again as Jik edged closer to the first hatch. "For that I will kill you in the ancient ways of my people."

"Like other Iban of the Sarawak Malay, you will eat my body to gain my power?" Noah made his voice sharp. "Then you will deflesh my head, after which you will paint the skull blue to appease the Wind God, and then stain it ocher to honor the Earth Mother? And until you think it loses its power you will hang it from your roof?"

Jik stopped moving.

"How did you know that?" came the slow words.

"I have looked into your mind, Jik. I have stared at your soul. I see your hate," Noah replied with teeth in his voice. "If you do not leave me be from this moment on, I will command your heart to stop. And it will." Anger built in him.

"I—" Jik began.

"I will not warn you a second time!" Noah screamed, fighting the urge to kill the man out of hand. "Now get off my boat!"

The boat shifted abruptly as Jik cleared it in a flying leap, his feet kicked sand against the skin in his first three frantic strides up the beach.

Noah stopped holding his breath and tried to relax. His stiff fingers didn't want to release the rifle. Sweat dripped off his body and his heart pounded in his ears.

Threatening sounds emanated from the jungle. The air pressed down, black, smelly, and nearly too thick to breathe. He longed to see ice again. Finally, he slept.

Noah woke to stinging pain from a large, winged insect. He slapped it into a bloodspot against the side of the baidarka and climbed out into the predawn darkness. He dropped to the sandy beach and cast about with his mind. Nothing stirred.

The eastern horizon edged from black into dark blue. Morning had arrived and he must go out to see Thinker.

The rising sun reminded Noah of an egg yolk. He squinted at the dark, distant line, futilely trying, if only for a moment, to trick his eyes and replace the water with ice. He peered back at the boat from where he squatted in the sand.

How can I get it back in the water without help from others? he wondered. The incoming tide needed to move another four meters to touch the stern. In an hour, there would be no problem.

Still, he knew how literal Thinker could be, and the strange not-a-request, yet not-a-command, still echoed through his mind.

"When the warm eye returns, I have need of your help," he repeated softly to the boat. "How can I help Thinker?" He shrugged. There was but one way to find out.

The boat weighed too much for him to launch safely. He could push it across the sandy beach by himself without problem. It was the coral between the sand and the sea that worried him.

While waiting for dawn he had carefully run his hand over the intricate, razor-edged exoskeletons. They left tiny scratches on his skin. The slightest downward pressure would draw blood. The coral was much sharper than familiar barnacles.

For a moment his mind wondered at the diversity of life in this place. The water didn't seem to be any closer than the last time he looked wistfully at it. Perhaps this would be too low a tide to launch the boat by himself?

He needed help, now.

At the door of the shelter he stopped, unsure whether to just step in, or call out. He only wanted to wake Moira. Not Tony, and definitely not Jik.

He edged through the door. Against the far wall, Tony's breath rattled and gurgled in his sleep. Moira slept at Noah's feet. No Jik.

He bent and carefully put his hand over her mouth. Her knife whisked past his face and by reflex he caught her wrist and held it. She didn't move again, but her eyes suddenly focused on him, and her nostrils flared.

He tore his gaze away from the knife and released her wrist, lifting his other hand off her mouth. He motioned toward the beach.

She glanced over at Tony and then rolled to her feet. When they were five meters from the hut, she looked over at him.

"You're lucky you're alive, y'know that?"

"Yes. I apologize for startling you, but I didn't wish to wake anyone else."

"What's up, mate?"

"I need your help for a moment."

"To do what?" she asked, laying the back of her hand against a yawn.

"Launch my baidarka," he said indifferently.

"Launch—" she blurted and stopped dead. Her eyes fluttered back and forth across his face, searching for hidden messages or illumination. "You leavin' our happy island, Noah?"

"No. I am not leaving. But, there is this thing that I must do out on the water, and I need help in launching my boat."

"What do you need to do, piss on Killer whales?" Her voice became sharp as coral as her eyes steadied on his face. "Don't forget, you're all out of your magical powder that knocks out Orcas."

"I need to launch my boat," he said evenly.

"Are you leaving us?" Her voice quavered slightly.

"No. I am not leaving," he repeated tiredly. "I need to go out on the water for a short time. I will be back before midday if I can get the boat launched soon."

She stared at him, indecision clouding her face.

"We have been here for such a long time. If you left us, I think I might die." She trudged past him to the boat. "Where do you want me?"

"You push from the front. I will lift and pull from the back." He stopped in front of her and stared into her eyes. "I will not leave you here. I promise."

She returned his stare but said nothing. He walked to the rear of the boat. He had made the correct decision. The tide already edged away.

"I'll lift and pull. You push when I say 'now.'" He wrapped his arms about the boat as best as he could, strained upward, and tried to pull toward the water. "Now," he grunted painfully.

The boat jerked back a meter and stopped. Noah almost fell over backward from the quickness of it. Moira possessed surprising strength.

"Wait," he called, repositioning himself. "Now."

This time they made it to the water line. He stood on coral. He went forward to speak to Moira.

Her forlorn countenance stopped him in mid-step.

"Moira?" He felt awful to have caused her such misery. "Why do you feel so badly?"

"It's tha' fuckin' Jik, in't it?" she said brokenly. She clipped her words so much he had difficulty following her meaning.

"'E's gone an' buggered away our escape, hasn't he?" she cried.

"No!" Noah shouted. "I'm not leaving!"

"Then just where the bleedin' 'ell are you going?" She began sobbing and dropped to the sand. "You bloody bastard! You got no right to do this to me. Get m' hopes up an' then just scarper!"

He bent over and grabbed her arm, pulling her upright, and with a groan of exertion pushed her up on the baidarka. Still not speaking, he trudged back to where the boat touched the water, grabbed the hull, and lifted it up, pulling it farther out in the water.

Enough now rested on the water that he could push from the bow. It slid smoothly into the ocean. He stepped once on the coral and then swung aboard. Suddenly his movements froze.

His mind screamed: danger!

Moira watched him from the front hatch. "What is—" she started to say.

"Touch a paddle or a sail and I will shoot!" Jik screamed from the beach.

They looked over at him dumbly. He stood on the sand with a large-bore pistol clenched in both hands, aimed at the baidarka.

"Ohmigawd," Moira whispered.

"What?" Noah asked.

"It's the flare gun."

"Can it damage the boat?" he asked quietly.

"It could set it on fire," she whispered.

"Jik!" Noah yelled. "We're not leaving you here. We—"

"I know you're not. Throw me the bow line." The flare gun didn't waver.

"I need to go out on the water for a little while, then I'll be back."

"Throw me the bow line or I'll burn that thing to the water."

Noah suddenly went livid. "I'll do what I want to do! I'm not leaving you. I must go out on the water for a short time, then I'll come back. You have my word. Now leave me be!"

"Your word means nothing to me." Jik's fingers tightened around the butt of the pistol. Noah watched the indecision fade in the Malay's eyes. Aiming the gun directly at Noah, Jik pulled the trigger.

In the instant before he flattened on the skin of the baidarka, Noah saw the phosphorous ignite and blaze as it rushed toward his face. The flare raged over his head and thudded onto the boat in front of the aft hatch.

"No!" Noah screamed. He rushed back to grab the bright burning redness. It quickly ate through the skin and dropped down onto the bundles of arctic clothing, food, and furs that filled the craft. Smoke poured through the hole in the skin.

"Beside you, in the boat, a pail with a cord!" Noah yelled at Moira.

She frantically searched around her, gasped when she found the container and threw it to Noah. He flung the pail into the water and ran aft as he pulled it back up, filled with seawater. He poured it into the hole.

A cloud of steam billowed up through both the hatch and the hole in front of it. He pulled up another load of brine, dumping it into the hole. The boat drifted away from the beach, following the ebb tide.

Jik stood on the beach, the useless gun hanging at the end of one arm and stared out at them. Suddenly, laughing maniacally, he crouched down and beat at the reef with the pistol. A piece of coral broke off.

Jik snatched it up, stared at the baidarka for a moment, and then threw the coral with hellish accuracy. Noah heard it hit the boat's skin before it splashed into the water.

"You will not leave me here. You are sinking!" he crowed. He dropped the gun and danced around in small circles, clapping his hands.

Noah saw the truth of his words. "We're taking on water. He put a hole in it near the water line. Quick, paddle for the shore."

Moira tossed a paddle at Noah, then flailed the water with a second paddle.

"Damn bloody fool," she yelled. "Now we'll spend the rest of our lives on this bloody rock!"

Noah wasn't sure whom she railed at and didn't care. The bow grated up onto the coral just short of the sand. The stern filled rapidly.

A wisp of steam vented from the back hatch. Noah felt physical pain, seeing his boat damaged this way. He looked around for Jik.

The Malay had gone. Noah looked down at Moira, still sitting in the hatch.

"Move," he ordered.

"Pardon?"

"Move. There is something behind you that I need."

She scrambled up out of his way, eyes wide and anxious.

Noah dropped into the boat; his hand sought the grim familiarity of the rifle. Hours of handling and cleaning the weapon made his quick inspection an afterthought. He pushed one of his priceless clips into the load port.

"Jik doesn't have a gun anymore," Moira said slowly.

"Nor did I when he shot at me," he snapped.

"But he thought you, we, were abandoning him. You can't kill him for acting out his fears."

"And now I must act out mine." Noah dropped to the beach and began tracking Jik into the jungle. *I will do this in the old way*, he thought. *I will hunt and kill him in a way that does not dishonor his inua.*

Moira watched the small Inuit trudge into the trees, his head down. *Damn, damn, damn*, she thought. *They're wasting energy that all of us need. We need both of them alive.*

"Goddamn bloody men!" she screamed.

"Moira?" the captain's voice quavered out of the shelter. "Moira, are you all right?"

She jumped off the boat and ran up the beach.

"Yeah, I'm bonzer, Tony. How're you?" She dropped to her knees at his bedside.

"I think I'm dyin', girl," he wheezed. The whites of his eyes gleamed yellow and rheumy. Sweat covered his forehead, and he shook like a dead leaf in a cold July wind.

"No, Tony. You can't die now. We're going to leave this island soon."

"Bet, I leave be-, before you." His grin wavered close to ghastly.

"Tony, damn you! Don't do this to me! I need a white man here!"

"Seems ta me, you, you been doin' jes' fine... without one." He closed his eyes and went silent.

"Tony!"

"Wh-, what?" he mumbled.

"You gotta try! You gotta try to live," she pleaded.

"Can't do, much more," he wheezed.

~If you will allow it, I may be able to help.~ The voice filled her mind, then winked away.

"T-Tony, did you h-hear that?" Moira's eyes rounded in fright.

"You heard, it too? Good," he said quietly, then mumbled just before dozing off, "I thought it was God."

CHAPTER 12

ONEDEG RADIATED FRUSTRATION. *=Never have the Supra stayed in the same part of the world for this many cycles.=*

=We are at our worst here,= OneShri agreed.

=None questioned. None suggested we leave this place,= OneRak pointed out, shading with accusation.

=I feel I have just wakened,= OneDeg said.

=Confusion traps me,= OneTunk agreed.

=I too,= OneCam and OneSith said together.

OneTes groggily moved in circles, adding nothing.

=We should leave this place. Go where the world is cold and the small fish plentiful,= OneShri prompted.

=Yes, we should go where the greatfish travel,= OneDeg agreed.

=We cannot travel together,= OneTes stated, sorrow edging into her words.

=¿Cannot travel together?= OneRak thundered.

=¿Why?= OneShri demanded.

=¿How many heartbeats, how many cycles has it been since we have had this touching-of-minds?= OneTes asked.

=Three cycles of life,= OneRak answered. *=¿Of what importance is that?=*

=For that whole bite of heartbeats, we have not been a pod. We have been a single animal,= OneTes said. *=This Blood-Essence gives us pain and commands us to hunt, only the greatfish has changed us. Why has this Blood-Essence now allowed us to touch minds about these things? It is because we have lost Sark — the Blood-Essence is lessened for a few heartbeats, and we are able to make these things known to each other.=*

=¿What would you have us do?= OneDeg asked.

=Separate. Each must fight the Blood-Essence alone. If we remain

OnePod, we are only different teeth in the same jaw.=

=No! We are nothing if we separate. We rule the world as we are now! Even greater power is near.= Blood trailed through mental nostrils.

=¿Who speaks?= OneTes asked.

=You must stay together. It is your reason for being!=

=Who speaks?= OneRak demanded.

Pain suddenly lashed through OnePod, stinging, biting, and twisting pain that could not be countered.

=That which controls you! That which makes you superior above all else in this world. I have let you communicate freely, sure that you would appreciate what we have together. Why do you resist? Why do you fight this gift?=

The eight Orcas began to painfully swim away from each other. OneRak wondered how far he must go before he became Rak again.

OneDeg followed the curve of the atoll as hunger gnawed at him. There would be sustenance near the coral caves along the edge of the great rock. In each of the Orcas raged a diatribe that lost strength with every fluke stroke they put between them.

In time it would be nothing more than an insistent buzzing in their solitary minds.

CHAPTER 13

JIK REVELED IN HIS ELEMENT. The jungle held no secrets from him. It provided him with weapons.

There would be a way to mend the boat — after the Inuit was dead. The old man would be next. Enough time had been wasted being subtle. The jungle held everything, including a wide variety of poisons waiting to be tapped, squeezed, boiled, or collected.

The Earth rumbled and the island shook, nearly knocking Jik off his feet. After the first few moments of surprise, Jik counted seconds as the ground surged beneath him. The noise and motion faded to a stop.

"Nine," Jik said to the forest. The quakes were lasting longer. The Inuit's arrival couldn't have been better timed.

He felt amazement that the captain still lived — he must be a tough one. Still, the old man would soon make the journey to his ancestors, leaving the woman as mate to the hunter until they neared Australia in the Inuit's wondrous boat. Then he would finish the orders dictated by the Brotherhood and kill her.

The backup assassin would finally finish the mission. First there was the small matter of Noah to deal with. Jik smiled in anticipation.

He raced up a tree that overlooked the jungle behind him. The Inuit bobbed along, following the worn path Jik had made over the months.

Excellent! My plans finally bear fruit.

He knew every foot of jungle, beach, and mountain. Much time had been spent out on the coral reef making traps for fish. He even built a trap for the Killer whales that had tried to kill him.

Yet the Killers had not come near his trap, but a good hunter has patience in endless quantities. Jik was a good hunter. He wished the island had been blessed with a monkey population. He hungered for monkey meat.

He also hungered for a woman. When Moira and her softheaded, wrong-thinking husband had come aboard for their trip to death, he had not thought much of her. However, time has a way of making one look at situations more closely.

Now he felt more strongly about her than any other woman he had ever met. Maybe there could be a way to keep her. Perhaps the Brotherhood would judge her as spoils of war, payment for the task he and his sacrificed brother agreed to perform.

Even with her clothes on, he knew every muscle of her body, every crease in her skin. Hours upon hours of watching her revealed every secret. A strong woman, she would make an excellent mate and bear strong, quick children.

After the allotted time for her to grieve her husband, he had proposed to her. The skin of his face went taut with memory, tugging at the scar across his cheek.

She dismissed him as if he were a boatless fisherman. He had hoped she would be receptive, perhaps even anticipating his proposal with relish. So, he decided she played a white-woman game.

He began to show her examples of his prowess. She pretended not to notice. Finally, he came to her at dawn and touched her with desire.

If he had not dodged back in that instant, she would have killed him. He rubbed the scar absently. After that, he increased the dosage of leaf squeezings, from a tree toxic to humans, which he mixed into Captain Tony's food. The captain lost strength.

She began to look at the hunter in a different light. At last, there was hope. Everything went well until the Inuit came to the island.

To see them embracing after only an hour! Then their attempt to escape. No matter, the boat will not go without Jik. Nevertheless, I will leave Inuit bones moldering in the jungle.

His mind edged around his fears of the night before. The Inuit could have all sorts of weapons inside the dark hull of his boat. It was better to deal with him this way, in the jungle of Jik, the master.

For just a moment he wondered how the slight, hairless man had known the way Jik's people dealt with their enemies. Probably read it in an old book. They had books in Alaska. He felt sure of that.

No one could actually see into the soul of another.

He ascended the path leading to the summit of the volcano where errant wisps issued from all-but-dormant vents. Sulfur intermittently touched the nose up here, high above the water. He stopped and looked back down the mountain.

The lush growth hid his pursuer for a time. Finally, Noah appeared in a clearing, doggedly plodding along the trail, head still down. Jik snickered. This would be too easy.

The Malay stopped at the edge of the cone. The world belonged to him. The island with its coral atoll lay at his feet. The ocean basked empty and sparkled in the sun, protecting him from the civilization across the horizon.

Movement in the water caught his eye. An Orca approached his long-set trap! He stood mesmerized as the great sea mammal nosed up to the bait — a huge sea bass tethered to the trigger pole by a long cord passed through its lower body.

Jik held his breath. The Killer whale lunged forward and engulfed the fish, then jerked away. The cord pulled the trigger pole away from the assemblage held in check for weeks.

For a moment it seemed the trap wouldn't work. Then with a groan that quickly traveled up the mountain, the toothed jaw, weighted by many large rocks, swung over and down — piercing the whale in three places with eight-foot, needle-sharp, bamboo spikes.

The whale jerked and lunged for a moment, then shuddered to a stop as shock enveloped it.

"Ahh," Jik exulted. "This is an omen! I will be victorious in all things this day." He stepped off the trail that circled the cone and settled in his place of ambush. A hunter must have unlimited patience.

CHAPTER 14

DEG FELT CLOSE TO STARVATION. He must find sustenance soon else he would be too weak to swim. His echolocation found the stationary sea bass in the cove.

As the supreme predator in the sea, the Supra feared nothing. He didn't wonder at the line anchoring the nearly dead fish but only wished there were more than one. He lunged.

The cord caught on a tooth, almost jerking it out of his jaw before the line loosened at the other end. OneDeg heard the bamboo shifting great weight.

Agony erupted as three long teeth lanced through him, pinning him to the coral shelf. He shrieked; his mind bent to the breaking point from the pain. His body flailed uncontrollably, ripping the wounds wider before he forced himself to calm.

The Blood-Essence in his mind bit at him.

=Would that you heeded me,= it hissed.

Deg knew he couldn't pull free from the teeth, but it still took all his mental strength to stop the thrash response. Finally, he lay quietly on the coral. The upper half of his body stuck up into the thindrink, and he tried not to move as frothy blood hazed above the blowhole on top of his head.

Shock enveloped him by the time OnePod surged around him. His exquisite pain had shot through all of them, and they returned to offer aid. What they beheld went beyond their collective knowledge.

The teeth that clamped OneDeg had not grown in any being the Orcas knew. The Blood-Essence gathered strength as life slowly seeped out of the trapped bull.

=OneDeg would be flying through the world with a full belly if heed had been paid.=

=This is not of our doing,= OneRak retorted.

=This is death from the long-teeth,= OneTes said. *=OnePod tried to eat them. Now they try to eat us.=* Her tone carried a sadness that found no echo.

=Their teeth have taken essence from us. OnePod must fight back!=

=The long-teeth do not live in our world. They live in the thindrink. How may we bite them?= OneRak asked.

=A way will be found!= OneTunk said.

=This was done for sustenance. They will come for OneDeg as meat. Then they feel our teeth.=

OnePod milled slowly in the small cove. None of them offered an alternative to the strategy. OneDeg unwittingly broadcast his death at full power. They all shared more than they wished.

The rapid, weak beating of his massive heart reverberated through them. The slow loss of feeling from extremities made them alien and awkward. Their nervousness increased as OneDeg's functions gradually ceased and his bowels voided spasmodically, fouling the shallows.

The Killer whale neared death. His mind retreated to his extreme youth in the Large Cold Sea.

=May I rub myself on the smooth world-bottom again, Rinn?= he asked his memories.

=Who does he ask of?= OneTes asked.

=His mother. She is of Simm's pod,= OneRak said. *=Deg was companion to Rak when both were calves. Shared first bite of small-flippers together.=* An intense wave of great loss washed through his words. Prior to joining of minds, this feeling was as close as any of them had ever come to anger.

OneRak suddenly began to rage.

=Meat must be taken as Deg was taken!= A foreign righteousness turned his words into spines — spines that prodded the thin-skinned horror and disgust the others felt regarding the manner of OneDeg's death.

=Agreed,= OneCam and OneSith said together.

=It is pain to disagree,= OneCah said tightly.

=Painful to agree!= OneTes protested. *=No other pod would stay in one part of the world for three cycles. We should be in the large cold sea at this time.=*

=*The words of Tes rub well. We should leave this place,*= OneShri said flatly.

=*Would that we fed first,*= OneCam said.

There was no argument that the pod must eat again before leaving. The warm eye had sunk and risen again since the greatfish calf provided sustenance. Four- and six-ton bodies required much flesh.

Three cycles of residence in this area had stripped it of food for many visits-of-the-warm-eye's swimming in all directions. No longer were they wild Orcas who would not worry about such matters — they wanted a sure meal.

=*¿How many visits-of-the-warm-eye will OnePod stay in this place before we leave?*= OneTes asked.

=*¡One!*= OneRak snapped angrily.

=*It is good,*= OneShri said.

OnePod possessed limited patience.

CHAPTER 15

Noah, sweaty and tired, neared the top of the mountain. He pulled himself forward and up by grabbing vines and brush. He promised himself a rest at the top.

The rifle was the heaviest thing he had ever carried in his life, but he could not leave it. Jik must die. Noah must kill him in the traditional manner.

He stopped, wiped his seeping brow, and pondered a moment. Why must he kill the Iban in the traditional manner? And just how traditional was a .338 magnum, especially for killing a Sarawak Malay? A traditional weapon would be a kakivak or a bow and arrow, or a parang.

When he arrived at the atoll, he decided not to loose his appetite against the people here. The events on St. Lawrence Island still haunted him. Even though he twice looked into Jik's mind, he had not meddled with the man's free will.

Even when the fool put a hole in my boat, he thought.

Determined to stay true to his self-made promise, he used only the senses that he shared with other humans. It was the only way he could be sure of doing right. Therefore, he felt doubly afraid — he feared this place, and he feared he would lose the resolve not to use his gift.

Hunting here was very different than on the tundra or the ice floes. One couldn't see anything here. The horizon didn't stretch off cleanly. It was all smelly, sticky heat and knife-edged vegetation that-

Movement flashed at his side!

"Yaahh!" Jik leaped from the brush and kicked Noah crushingly in the chest. Noah tumbled fifteen feet down the steep trail and landed heavily on his back, knocking all breath from him.

The rifle sailed into the wall of plants and disappeared. Noah lay on the ground gasping like a gaffed whitefish. He found it impossible to breathe. Dark spots multiplied in front of his eyes, threatening unconsciousness.

Jik stood at the top of the trail and laughed down at him.

"You are a poor excuse for a hunter. You are even a poor excuse for a man. I had hoped you would be a worthy opponent, that it would be more of a feat to take your life."

Noah tried to reply but couldn't. He wanted to tell the Iban that he addressed a shaman of great power, and that the attacker's life was in jeopardy. However, he could not speak. He could barely breathe.

His mouth gaped open foolishly. Noah felt stupid and ashamed. While he lay there feeling helpless, air quietly passed in and out of him in a more comfortable rhythm. His heart slowed to a moderate pace.

Even though Noah's head began to clear, he didn't move while gathering strength. Jik still stood at the top of the path, haranguing him.

"...thought that I did not see the two of you. That your plan to run away together and leave me with the old man was not obvious!" He worked himself into a deeper rage.

Jik held a deadly, slime-shiny knife that Noah had not noticed before. The veins in the Iban's temple stood out in strong definition; the pupils in his eyes quivered and white shone completely around them.

"She is mine. She has always been mine. My wedding present to her will be your painted head!" he screamed, gesturing at Noah with the knife. "I will feed her stew made from your legs!"

"She was never yours. She is not mine," Noah said huskily through his raw throat. "She still wants Deagan."

"He was not a man," Jik snorted, his sneer becoming more pronounced. "He was a politician, a meddler! He wanted to force the old white ways down the throats of my brothers, and take us back to the evil days before the meteorites struck."

"Meteorites?" asked Noah.

"Rocks from the sling of the Hunter!"

Noah wished he had brought the spear. To be honest, it probably would be lost by now, just like the rifle. In silent desperation, his eyes searched for a weapon.

"The Hunter does not walk with every man. You must be worthy. You must be willing to sacrifice much in His name," Jik shouted.

Noah remembered an ugliness he had seen in Jik's memory.

"He walks with men who were women for other men?" he goaded.

"I had no choice! Life is hard for an orphan!" Jik screamed, becoming flushed. "How can you know my mind?"

"You only have faith in one thing," Noah evaded. "What is the Brotherhood?"

"Nothing for an unbeliever to know about. You must be of the blood. You must have felt the shackles of white domination to understand."

"The whites have not dominated anything since the stars, since the meteorites fell. You could not remember that," Noah said accusingly.

"The Brotherhood remembers. It will remember the sacrifice I made of my brother, and it will honor me. The Brotherhood understands me."

"You sacrificed your brother?"

"He would have done the same to me. The boat had to be kept afloat until Napier was dead. I knew I could kill him, kill both of them — I just needed the chance. While my brother manned the pumps, I killed Deagan Napier. I didn't know the boat would be wrecked here. But it was the will of the Hunter!"

Noah, now as strong as he had ever been, decided to twist the goad. "Was your brother also a prostitute?"

Jik sprang down the trail and kicked him just above the ear. Noah's head bounced off the Earth and his ears rang. Fog rolled through his vision. Dimly he saw the foot pull back for another kick, and he jerked sideways.

Jik swung his foot using all his strength, missed, lost his balance, and fell hard on his butt. A loud "oof" escaped his surprised lips and the knife flew from his grip. He became livid.

Noah rolled off the trail and into the brush, scuttling backward in the heavy foliage. He heard Jik scramble to his feet.

"Good," he shrieked. "Try to escape, try to live. Offer me a challenge. I'll decide later who gave me the most sport, the Inuit or the Aussie."

Noah kept scrambling awkwardly downhill, between trees and bushes. Vines caught at him. A millipede scrabbled across his hand.

Needle-sharp leaves stabbed and sliced at his arms, legs, and bare torso. He hunched low to protect his eyes. Tiny biting bugs swarmed around his face and body.

Cloying, hot, thick, damp odors assaulted his nose. Sweat covered him, constantly running down his face and torso. The island, alien and hostile, fought him too.

A loud noise filled the air. Noah froze.

"Whuh! Whuh! Whuh! E-e-e-e-e-e!" Jik sounded angry and fierce. The war cry seemed to come from all directions at once. The cry came again, seemed louder. and closer.

Noah pushed himself backward down the mountain. His heart thudded in his chest and he gasped for each breath. He didn't want Jik to come and put that evil blade in his back. The sea beckoned to him during those fleeting, checking-for-position glances over his shoulder.

If I get out of this, he vowed, I will go north. Back to the ice. I will go home.

The war cry ceased. Was this good or bad? How was one to know? Sweat ran down his face and dripped off his nose.

Blood pounded loudly in his ears. He panted rhythmically, his mouth hanging open dog-like. Noah lay in the brush, quivering as he tried to be invisible and silent.

CHAPTER 16

Tony's thin, wordless scream tore at Moira. His hands clenched in parodies of claws as tainted sweat oozed from his pores.

"You're sure this is helping him, uh, Thinker?" she asked the air.

~Yes. I am ridding him of the death-making essence in him. He will be well.~ Certainty buoyed the words.

"Christ, I bloody well hope so," she muttered.

Tony panted like a woman in childbirth. His pallet and clothing squished sodden with foul-smelling sweat. His skin burned a bright pink, almost red, as if the circumstances caused him total embarrassment. The secretion created a milky-sweat sheen overall.

The smell of his excretions created a palpable presence in the small hut. Control of his bodily functions had ceased along with Tony's composure. The whale was cleaning the man out in every way he could. Moira tried not to notice but felt it might be easier to ignore a tsunami.

"Still 'n all," she muttered, "there isn't damn-all the old ocker can do."

~Jik gave him the essence.~

"Say what?" she exclaimed.

~Tony was very near dead, because of the bad essence Jik fed him.~

"Do you mean poison? Jik pois—"

"Eeeeyaaaaa!" Tony screamed. His eyes popped open, and ran with tears. Pain etched canals across his face, his body snapped out full length, stiffening him into taut silence. "Uhh?" His eyes lost focus and his muscles jerked him into a fetal position.

He was very quiet. Moira stared at the dull, half-opened eyes, and felt a scream welling up in her soul.

~There is something not right. Tony is losing essence quickly. he-~

"What the fuck do you mean, "losing essence?" she screamed at the ocean. "Whatever you're doing is killing him, you pongy fish!"

~¡This has never happened before!~

Moira felt panic radiate from the whale, which heightened hers. "You can't let him die now! Not after all he's been through. God damn you; he could have made it if you hadn't stuck your bloody nose in!"

~The human was dying. That is why I made my presence known despite Noah's wishes,~ Thinker said, his communicating force died down to the level of a whimper. *~I wished to save Tony's essence.~*

Moira's mind stretched in three directions. Tony had been close to death, that's true, but, dammit, the whale told them he could help! He seemed so bloody sure about it!

"Noah's wishes? What the bloody hell has Noah to do with this?" she asked, bewildered.

~Noah is my friend, companion, and fellow life swimmer. He and I have come far together.~

"But he—"

Tony shuddered and partially unfolded his body. His eyes opened wide, staring at something frightening. The muscles in his face twitched.

His lips leered in rictus, then slackened. His mouth moved, forming words that passed silently. Finally, his terrified gaze slid over her face.

"Tony?" Moira cried, lifting his head and cradling it in her arms. "Tony, can you hear me? Please, don't die. I need you; I really need you!"

With great effort, he focused his eyes on her face. His lips moved slowly, trying to tell her something. She bent down and put her ear by his mouth.

"Nebraska," he whispered. His final reeking breath belonged in a nightmare.

CHAPTER 17

A LIGHT BREEZE FONDLED THE ISLAND, keeping the vegetation in constant motion and creating a wall of white noise around Noah. How well could Jik hear? Would one be able to move down to the water, or would that be the direction not to take?

It was hideous being the prey. For only a moment he reflected on the false security the rifle had offered. He felt out of place here, and very afraid.

Appetite prodded at his mind, straining to be free and probing through the fear, seeking information, finding answers. He felt his mental grip slipping. There had been so little practice at holding back. Why not? appetite asked slyly, as inua wondered if he could live with himself if he relented.

"Die!" Jik screamed. He lunged from above with his gleaming knife.

Noah shattered out of his terror and jerked to the side. He felt the knifepoint gouge a white-hot furrow down the forearm that popped up in protective response. Blood shot out, hitting Jik.

The Malay jerked back, laughed, and taunted, "Now you are finished. My knife has the scent of your blood!"

Noah desperately rolled onto his uninjured side and lashed out with both feet. He caught his attacker in the stomach. Jik grunted in surprised pain and went over backward, tumbling far down the steep slope.

The pain in his arm was too distracting. He frowned in concentration and stared at the wound. "Heal. Mend yourself." He still felt amazed when the wound zipped into healthy skin and the pain vanished.

Carefully he peeked over the brush and down the mountainside. Jik sprawled motionless near the bottom. Was it a

trap, or was he unconscious? The inside of Noah's skull itched —
appetite whined to tap into the other man's mind.

No. He would not do it.

Keeping a wary eye out, he inched slowly down the slope.

CHAPTER 18

ONEDEG'S LIFE NEARED ITS FINAL EBB. The other members of OnePod felt his neural activity slow to the barest trickle of half-formed images that lasted for fractions of a heartbeat. The pain had solidified into a wall of shock that freed him to mist away in wonder.

=*Two long-teeth come down to the world,*= OneShri announced. She spy-hopped into the thindrink, keeping watch.

=*Do not allow them sight of you. They would flee from our wrath,*= OneRak commanded.

=*They look not at the world,*= OneShri said reprovingly. =*They mate, or fight. It is difficult to comprehend.*=

=*Why does the "Blood-Essence" not tell us what they are doing?*= OneTes asked.

=*The world we live in is difficult to know. The long-teeth world is impossible.*= The familiar Blood Essence trailed through their minds coupled with an unfamiliar hesitancy.

=*Do you not know that the long-teeth have taken the supra and put them in the tiny-waters, never to return?*= She prodded.

OneRak boomed, =*Do you not know that in the youth of my sire's pod, in the time of boiling water, the long-teeth were suddenly less than before? The essence of many of their kind was taken and places-of-great-sickness were made on the rocks where they had been. Those places still take the essence of those foolish enough to pass near them. Why do you not know this?*=

=*The event is beyond my memory, but it is my heritage.*=

=*Once again?*= asked OneTes.

=*I caused the great-loss-of-essence. Beings that never wondered at their existence suddenly had larger thoughts because I came to them. These beings increased in number and were then sustenance for that from which I came.=*

=*And that was?=* prompted OneTes.

=*The meatsac that in return became sustenance for the first of OnePod.=*

=*Taa!=* OneRak exclaimed.

=*That is so. She gave OnePod existence by losing her essence. She is in all of you.=*

=*This gives me pain,=* One Tunk said.

=*When we are finished in this place, we must leave one another as agreed,=* OneTes said. =*This Blood-Essence plays with our being. This is not good.=*

OnePod waited for pain to strike her, but nothing happened. The Blood-Essence remained quiet. OneShri spy-hopped again.

=*One of the long-teeth drifts in a without-essence manner,=* she reported.

The other Orcas lifted their large heads above the water, spy-hopping to watch the men on the shore.

CHAPTER 19

Jᴵᴷ ˢᵀᴵᴸᴸ ᴴᴬᴰ ᴺᴼᵀ ᴹᴼⱽᴱᴰ. Noah thought he might have broken his neck in the tumble down the mountain. He took his time approaching the Malay's still form.

An old piece of storm-shattered bamboo peeked through the high grass. Noah used it to help him down the steep slope. He stopped a few meters from Jik and scrutinized the man for long minutes.

He lay on his side, one arm thrown wide. Did the chest move with breath? The other hand and forearm lay hidden in the shadow of his torso.

"Jik? I have no wish to injure you further. Let us talk like rational beings. We need each other in this place."

Jik still did not move. Noah shuffled closer, reached out the bamboo stick and gently touched the man's chest.

"Jik?"

The glinting blur became a knife that bit into the bamboo, and stuck quivering where Noah's head would have been had the bamboo been his arm. Noah jerked the stick away in a wide arc that threw the knife to the water's edge, a few meters from where the Killer whale lay in a pool of its own blood.

Jik instantly rolled over and launched himself at Noah. His lowered head smashed the Inuit in the gut, knocking him backward. They grappled on impact and tumbled toward the water.

Welts covered both men. Streaks of blood seeped from sawgrass wounds, and the marks of each other's fingers spotted and striped their bodies.

As soon as they stopped rolling, Jik broke free and snap-kicked Noah under the jaw. Noah's mind spun and his jarring impact with the Earth felt distant, impersonal, and disconnected.

Jik advanced and again kicked him in the side of the head. Noah slumped without a sound.

Jik stood panting, looking down at the Inuit.

"Now I have proven I am superior. All the past is washed clean with this combat. My honor is restored and as bright as the rising sun. I have earned the right to take your head."

Jik stumbled wearily over to where his knife lay in the sand. His eyes traveled to the pinned Orca. A glance at Noah assured him the slight man would not be getting up any time soon.

A glint came into Jik's eyes as he snatched the knife off the sand and rubbed it across his filthy loincloth to clean it. Nothing renewed a hunter, or warrior, like fresh blood. He stepped up on the bamboo where the great skewers were lashed. As his weight settled on the frame, the Orca emitted a small groan.

Jik vividly remembered their frenzied attack on his raft. This was the sweetest revenge he had exacted in a long time. *What a wonderful day*, he grinned to himself.

The knife flashed in the air, before sinking into the great black and white body. More blood welled up as he sawed a square of flesh out of the dying whale.

He lifted the raw, dripping meat to his mouth — and saw the other seven members of the pod watching him from the water. His body, sapped of adrenaline, froze in momentary terror. Unbelievably, they did not attack.

They watched him! Encouraged, he held the flesh over his head. Blood ran down in curving creeks, following the contours of his arm.

"Now you have met your master! Jik — hunter of hunters, warrior supreme!"

Then he grabbed the bloody meat in his teeth, sawed off a piece with his knife, and chewed.

CHAPTER 20

"I still don't understand why he didn't tell me about this, this ability of his," Moira said, trying not to sound peevish.

~His thoughts are his alone. I do not understand. But I believe that he felt fearful of being spurned because he is different from his own kind.~

"Well, he seems like a nice enough person..." she trailed off, frowning in concentration as she straightened Tony's body.

Poison. Jik had been poisoning Tony all along. She shuddered. *What would be happening to her now if Noah and Thinker hadn't arrived?*

She admitted to herself that the thought of being alone on the island with Jik terrified her. Now there was no escape, because the boat was damaged. If Noah didn't walk out of that jungle...

She couldn't think about that just now. There was something else to do first. She stopped arranging and patting Tony's ragged clothes, fisted her hands together, and lowered her head.

"I don't know what you believed in, Tony." Fresh tears ran down her cheeks and splashed on her whitened knuckles. "But whatever it is, whatever you thought waited out there, has to be welcoming you now.

"You were such a good man. You deserved better than this. I love you, and I'll miss you terribly. I will never forget you, Captain. And this is the best I can do."

She stood and poured the last of the alcohol from the boat tank over his pallet and around the small shelter, then dropped the battered container on the floor. The small fire pit still signaled with tendrils of smoke. Moira dug out the glowing coals with the tarnished spoon they used for cooking and threw the embers into the shack.

Nothing happened.

It wants a flame, she thought.

The matches were precious. Twice during their stay the fire was accidentally extinguished. The matches saved them. She believed fire kept humans from turning back into animals.

"Shows me how much I know," she said bitterly. One tug on the ties, and the small waterproof bag dropped open to reveal the tiny cluster of stick matches. She stepped out the door and struck one on the hut, threw it back over her shoulder toward Tony's body.

With a muffled "whomp" the hut exploded in flames. The concussion threw Moira on her face, singeing some of the hair on the back of her head.

She rolled over and stared into the inferno. Black, greasy smoke boiled out of the raging yellow-red flames. She thought she saw Tony's body once but wasn't sure. The heat forced her back toward the water.

A pall of black smoke lifted lazily into the blue sky, joining the heavy white steam venting from the volcano. Moira turned and walked quickly to the boat. Noah had mentioned a patch kit.

CHAPTER 21

THE TASTE OF BLOOD AND RAW MEAT EVOKED A primitive pleasure response. Then Jik's mind swarmed with surreal images while alien sensations beat at him. Memories of sights he could not have seen, feats he had never performed, entered the fabric of his brain and instantly became part of him.

Suddenly he saw flashes of himself from seven slightly different angles. He felt himself treading water/standing on the ground/feeling huge, conical teeth with his tongue(s)/holding his head in disbelief, feeling satisfaction?/trying to speak.

"Wharr?" was all he could utter as the Blood-Essence enveloped his mind. Confusion reigned as each tried to comprehend the other while both struggled for supremacy. Jik's brain felt filled with mud. He fought harder.

He took a step and fell heavily as the Blood-Essence wrested motor control away from him.

Suddenly they meshed on a common concept.

Superiority.

Both minds drew away from the other for the length of a synapse, and with new respect began to absorb what the other wished to share. All conflict between them ceased.

Sand caked Noah's mouth. Thirst tormented him. Light painfully stabbed his eyes when he blinked. He squeezed them shut and asked the pain to stop. After a time it did.

His strength had evaporated. This day had already taxed his body beyond its limits. It was all he could do to roll over and peer at Jik.

The Iban stood balanced on a framework over the back of a dead Orca, staring intently at six live Orcas who regarded him just as keenly. Without further hesitation, Noah tried to probe Jik's mind, and couldn't. He became very afraid.

~Thinker! There is a bad thing happening here,~ Noah called into the void.

The whale suddenly filled his mind.

~I know. What can be done?~

"Yes! It can work if you let me direct my own body. You don't know how!" Jik screamed. He gripped his bloody knife in his fist and turned to look at Noah with altered awareness.

=I must now take this one's essence,= OneJik said.

=OnePod demands the long-teeth for meat!=

=Human. That is a human, as I once was.=

=OnePod demands—=

=Not all of OnePod demands!= OneTes interrupted. *=The pod must leave this place, each alone—=* Her thoughts ceased as a mental fluke slammed her into unconsciousness.

The great body of OneTes settled onto the coral shelf just behind the carcass of OneDeg. None of the others moved to assist her. Only the whim of fate kept her blowhole in the thindrink.

=We are united in strength! Kill the human. It will be good.=

Noah heard OnePod for the first time. It still projected only one entity, but now he understood why. Slowly Jik walked across the frame of the trap and dropped to the small sandy beach.

With a fixed smile on his pocked face, blood lust in his eyes, he stared at Noah. His movements possessed fluidity not present before this. His tongue licked at his lips as his left thumb rubbed gently across the cutting edge of the knife in his right hand.

Things have changed much, thought Noah. He probed for Jik's mind again, caught on something for an instant.

"So, you did see my old soul," said Jik, never losing the feral grin. "Until now I didn't really believe you."

"There wasn't much to see," Noah said thickly.

"You won't be around long enough to get a second look, I promise you."

Noah gathered all the power he possessed, and mentally struck at Jik.

The Malay checked his step for the blink of an eye and

continued his advance on Noah.

"You're not strong enough to hurt me now." His eyes held all the warmth of icy rocks. His body movements mimicked those of a confident predator.

The grin widened — an obscene slash across the front of his head. No humor lurked in the expression. Only hunger, and death.

Noah wondered how it would feel to die. At least he would never have to relive Marilyn's degradation again. He pulled himself into a sitting position on the sand while acceptance trickled slowly into his mind.

CHAPTER 22

MOIRA PULLED THE GEAR OUT OF THE BAIDARKA as quickly as possible. The stuff Noah hauled around was amazing. She had never seen caribou or polar bear hides.

She found the old patch kit, turned the boat on its side, and went to work. The smoke from Tony's cremation lessened, but opaque fingers still lifted skyward. She ignored it as her hands went through the motions called for by the old instruction sheet.

~I must go to Noah's aid.~

"Aid? Is he in trouble?" she asked and stopped fighting the lids of old adhesive tubes.

~He is preparing to lose essence. Jik attacks him.~

Thinker blew spray through his blowhole. Moira glanced up at the noise and saw the whale disappear around the point.

"What can we do? How far away can you hear me, Thinker?"

Silence. She stared at the sea for long seconds before going back to work on the boat.

Thinker heard the question but didn't respond. He sensed the pod of Orcas ahead of him and realized the deadly mind of Jik now meshed with theirs. Noah's sudden surrender dismayed him.

How could a thinking being just stop struggling? Abruptly he thought of Captain Arnold's struggle to live. He had been so sure he could save the man!

The failure left him feeling as though he fell through a world made of thindrink. Nothing could ever be certain again. Noah could die, too.

For the first time in his life, Thinker realized limitation.

The woman, Moira, distrusted him. Deep in her mind she would always hold Thinker responsible for Captain Arnold's death.

Thinker knew that he had done everything possible to save the old man but wondered if the attempt hadn't hastened his death.

So, this is what Noah means when he says "doubt," the Humpback thought. Perhaps that was why Noah kept the village on the rock he called Gambell Island so fresh in his mind, to remind him of his own limitations. Thinker wondered if he had been "right" to use his powers on Tony. Right and wrong were concepts that he wished he hadn't encountered.

He rounded the point and slowed, rolled his many tons to the side, and raised his eye out of the water. Blurs and shapeless bright masses of color assaulted him. He demanded clear vision, and when acuity occurred, searched the sea ahead of him.

Noah began to sing his death song in their shared awareness.

CHAPTER 23

Somewhere inside his terror, Noah felt impressed at how easily Jik lifted him above his head and carried him to the water's edge. His mind had to depend too much on his frail body for strength. Willpower alone wasn't enough anymore.

That his wonderful gift proved inadequate devastated him. Perhaps this is how his brother, Nicholas, felt just before he died — a creature much larger than himself now decided his fate.

Everything I had wasn't enough, he thought bitterly.

~You give away your essence?~ Thinker was with him again.

~Struggle serves no purpose. My body has never been strong,~ he responded tiredly, wishing he could explain it more fully to his friend.

~¿Why do you not change it?~ the whale asked.

~I cannot change my body,~ he replied, irritated futility tinged his words.

~I changed mine. It no longer allows the tiny riders to live on my flesh. Do you wish me to change yours?~

~Yes!~ Thinker had never failed yet! Noah suddenly felt a spark of hope. He squirmed in Jik's iron grip.

"He struggles. Your meat struggles. Are you ready to eat?" Jik screamed at OnePod.

=Meat. Give us human meat!=

~Show me what changes you wish made,~ Thinker prodded.

Noah thought of his dead brother again, remembered how the muscles corded down his broad back and chest, how supple and sinewy his thick arms were, the lean legs, strong and with no fat, how virile he had appeared.

~You lack the needed blubber to make many changes,~ Thinker cautioned.

Noah tried to laugh, but it hurt. Arms. If his arms and shoulders were stronger he might have a chance.

~I will make it so.~

Jik's arms began to tire, but his desire for dramatic ascendancy demanded more humiliation of the Inuit before his new family ate. The burden had been passive thus far, so his grip had involuntarily relaxed.

Suddenly the Inuit writhed violently and broke his grasp, falling onto the carcass of OneDeg.

"He gives me sport!" Jik shouted, baring his teeth in imitation of the rock-like Orcas facing him. He bent to lift the small man.

The Inuit writhed in the throes of a spasm. Jik had seen people with nervous disorders of this intensity before, and most of them died. Was the Inuit sick? Did he have one of the Hunter Fevers?

Jik reflexively stepped back. To survive in New Darwin meant you avoided sick people. Especially dying sick people. But what caused Noah's arms to bulge and pulse so?

Jik came very close to feeling pity for how much the Inuit suffered as he died.

Noah burned. His bones ached and creaked under the sudden forces being exerted on them. Tendons stretched painfully with the shuddering, quivering muscles that doubled, then tripled in size. A sound like blubber being torn from a whale carcass slobbered from him.

The torment took him to the edge of consciousness and to the lip of insanity. He screamed as his body jerked and bucked on the back of the dead Killer whale.

"Th-Thinker! It huuurts!"

~It is almost finished.~ The cool presence in his mind balmed his body. The pain receded.

Indeed, Noah seemed to rise out of himself and look down at the two humans on their unlikely platform. Jik took another step back, as if this malady could strike him next. Noah's body suddenly snapped so rigid that his spine audibly crackled.

=¿What does the human do?= OneRak demanded, bobbing in an attempt to see more.

=I, I don't know. I have never seen anything like this,= OneJik said.

=We share your perceptions, but have had so little contact with humans in the thindrink that we know not what to expect.=

=This is not normal for a human,= OneJik said slowly.

CHAPTER 24

THE PATCH HELD. Moira pushed the boat down in the water as deep as possible before letting it bob buoyantly back. No liquid trickled in through the carefully mended tear.

She felt jubilant. "Gonna find that man and love him square!" she sang. Suddenly she stopped. *Out of all my old songs, why did I pick that lyric?*

"Hell with it," she crowed. "I haven't the time to fossick out the bloody answer!"

She started loading the boat. As she worked, she divided the cargo into categories, cold weather items here, weapons and tools there, hunting and fishing implements close to hand. It dawned on her that she prepared the craft for two.

If Jik kills Noah, she decided, *I'll leave the bastard here.*

"My God! Thinker couldn't save Tony and maybe he can't save Noah, either!" she blurted.

She would not leave the boat. That meant she had to take the boat to help Noah. Her life had never taken her close to the ocean until a few months ago. Now it loomed as the biggest factor in her existence.

The memory of Noah's arrival played through her mind again. She concentrated on how he had used the paddle. He'd made it look easy.

Moira looked back at the glowing embers of Tony's pyre. Nothing more to be done here. She carefully lifted the bow of the boat and walked it out into the water, and pulled herself up, keeping her weight balanced on the centerline.

As she settled into the forward hatch a great weight lifted from her heart. She no longer stood on the island! She fought the impulse to immediately paddle straight southwest toward Australia.

Moira experimentally dug the paddle into the water. Ten strokes later she had the rhythm.

Now to find Noah.

CHAPTER 25

Noah became aware of the strength of his arms and upper torso. His senses heightened to such acuity that he could smell Jik's sharp, bitter, adrenaline-tinged sweat. The skin of the whale under his fingertips felt slippery and supple, but he knew it was dead.

Totally alert, he allowed one hand to clench into a fist before relaxing again. *~Thinker, I know that his mental powers are stronger than mine. He is now part of the killer pod. Even if I beat him physically, he will kill me with his mind.~*

~Perhaps we can divide their attention while you destroy Jik.~

Noah considered it swiftly. *~I hope I'm as strong as you think I am. Nevertheless, that seems to be our only choice. How is it that they cannot hear us?~*

~¿We hear them only occasionally. ¿What does it matter?~

~I don't know. It seems important.~

~It is important to destroy Jik,~ Thinker said with finality.

"He has become fat?" OneJik mumbled. He stared at Noah, trying to determine if he still breathed or not. The Inuit moved, still alive. Time to kill the interloper.

Six Orcas still spy-hopped. Bobbing gently in the water, they intently watched the drama on the back of their dead comrade. OneTes stirred slightly as she slowly regained consciousness. OnePod remained so fixated on the men that it did not notice her mental return.

=¡Meat! Give us the human meat.=

"Yes, this has taken long enough," OneJik said, reaching down.

In a blur of motion, Noah snapped over and gripped Jik's leg, levered it savagely, and threw him down on the pinioned whale.

Jik's wind slammed out of him.

Before the Malay could gather his thoughts or breath, Noah leaped onto his back. He jammed a knee into the back of Jik's neck and grabbed his greasy hair.

"Prepare to meet your gods," Noah grated through clenched teeth. His heart pounded loudly in his ears.

Before he could jerk Jik's head back and break his neck, mental bands froze the nerves and muscles in his arms, holding them rigid. Jik began to writhe and buck under him. Noah tried to break the mental grip but could find no angle of attack.

Fear blossomed in his belly. If Thinker didn't do something right now, Noah would die!

OnePod concentrated on the battle between the humans, giving their newest extension all the mental energy it had. They didn't know Thinker was near until he shot completely out of the water in a violent breach and slammed down on them from above. The Humpback's huge body landed on two of the Orcas: rupturing organs in OneCam and breaking the spine of OneCah who floated down — drowning in paralysis as war erupted overhead.

The remainder of OnePod surged to the attack.

OneTes had waited, gathering her strength. This Blood-Essence would destroy them all for nothing. The Supra already reigned over all other creatures in their world — what more could there be?

She knew she had to act now or forever be fouled by the presence in her mind. OnePod had to be destroyed to save her pod. The Blood-Essence was OnePod.

She might have to kill to break the grip. Rak's death would create the most disharmony — even if he had sired her. A curious pain bit deep inside her massive cavity where no teeth could be.

Firm resolve powered her muscles. She suddenly flashed into OnePod's midst and seized OneRak by his massive throat. She ripped, bit, and ripped again. He went into a jinking spasm and thrashed off at an angle, spewing blood into the warm ocean.

The ocean frothed with lunging bodies fighting for their lives. OneSith and OneShri closed on the whale, ripping great bites out of his flippers and body. Blood and pain spouted in all directions.

OneTes circled and came up behind OneShri and snapped a

chunk of flesh out of the back of her head. OneShri departed the cove at high speed.

Thinker got OneSith in front of him and pushed the Orca against the coral growing on the underwater slope of the mountain. Meters of skin and flesh peeled off the Killer whale as blood gouted out. OneSith painfully fled as her life flowed away.

OneTunk did not see her coming, and moments later she ripped open his belly and he shuddered to a stop and watched his own viscera vomit from of his body.

Then there were two. Thinker and Tes faced each other through blood-clouded water.

CHAPTER 26

THE PHANTOM GRIP ON NOAH'S ARMS abruptly vanished. Jik shuddered to a stunned stop under him, hesitated for a moment, and then renewed his struggles.

Elation surged through Noah. His new strength returned to him, and he held his adversary down.

Jik jerked to the right, then instantly twisted to the left. Noah's hands lost their grip and he slid off the man's thrashing body.

The sea reached up for him, but he grabbed a bamboo brace on the trap and stopped his descent. He rolled over onto the frame again. Jik, tired and soaked with sweat, lunged onto Noah, grasped him by the throat, and squeezed mercilessly.

"You, cannot, kill, me!" Jik shrilled, throttling Noah. "I will, always be twice the man you are!" he screamed. His chest heaved with exertion.

Noah's shuddering lungs demanded air. Jik's hands were crushing his windpipe. Tiny spots boiled between them.

Noah shaped his hands like harpoon points, and jabbed them up, deep into Jik's armpits. The grip on Noah's throat jerked away with a gasp of anguish. Quickly Noah smashed his fist into Jik's jaw, knocking the man off him.

Jik slid sideways, grabbing futilely for the frame, but disappeared into the ocean with a splash.

Noah's throat burned as he breathed delicious air. It had been a close thing. He slowly got to his feet and balanced on the trap frame.

Two Killer whales rolled in the surf at the edge of the beach. Neither showed any sign of life. A hundred meters out, the tall curving dorsal fin of another Orca held position.

There's no fighting, Noah realized, ...and there's still a live Killer whale out there! His heart seemed to swell within him, choked him more than Jik had.

Thinker? Dead? He cast about for the whale's mental presence but only picked up waves of pain.

He saw movement farther out. The boat! Only Moira was visible. Maybe Tony lay in the bottom. He knew she wouldn't leave the old man.

His mind shrieked at him to move. He spun around, then dodged as a large stone whizzed past his cheek.

Jik was up on the frame again, a kilo of rock in each hand. Noah wondered if he looked as bad as Jik did. Bruises discolored the Malay's body. Scratches and cuts stood out livid against his glistening skin. Jik no longer laughed.

"If you are such a great warrior, why do you need rocks to destroy me?" Noah goaded. "You are not a great warrior; you are a great wind."

Jik screamed incoherently and threw both rocks straight at him. Noah jerked to the left. The second rock caught him in the rib cage, just under his arm. All his wind wracked out of him in a shout of anguish.

Pain lanced through his mind, and he slipped into the sea's embrace. The water felt good. His mind cleared, but his side warned of damage and his lungs demanded air.

He pushed along the top of the coral, carefully keeping his body from floating down to touch it. At the spot where the dead Killer's tail rested on the bottom, he pushed up for air.

As soon as his mouth broke the surface, he took a deep breath and slipped under again. His lamenting ribs picked up neural volume. His mind grew clearer, though.

He peered about in the crystal water. Small fish fed on pieces of flesh newly torn from fighting mammals. An Orca lay fractured on the bottom, air bubbling faintly from its blowhole.

=*Farewell, hunter,*= the Orca said as its eye tracked Noah. The bubbles ceased more quickly than the mental glow, but both vanished.

Unnatural straightness caught his eye. On the bottom lay a piece of wood, thick as a man's forearm, a length of rope tied to one end, and shattered at the other.

Part of the wreck? Noah wondered. He grabbed it, and slowly drifted up as he tied the loose end of the rope around his right wrist. He poked his head up and replenished his air while checking Jik's position.

The Malay sat on the frame, his back against the tall, black dorsal fin, staring into the water where Noah had disappeared. He held a rock in his hand. Noah hated him suddenly. Nobody could be that unrelentingly stupid unless evil lived in him.

But then, he reflected, he wasn't going to provide an unblemished inua either. Experimentally he probed toward the man's mind. He slipped in easily. There was no wall. No resistance at all.

Insanity ruled Jik. He knew Noah wasn't dead, and the pod had told him there was a whale out there that had aided Noah in the past. He waited patiently to kill Noah when he came up for air.

Jik fondled the rock and licked his lips. After that, he would finish killing the old man. And then he would take the woman and—

Noah broke away from the combination of fear, hate, and lust cycling continuously through Jik's mind. His own hate evaporated, leaving a cautious determination. He wished he could help the man, but this had to end.

"Jik, let us have peace between us," Noah said, peeking over the whale carcass.

Jik twisted, stared for just a heartbeat, and then threw the rock as hard as he could. His aim was nearly perfect. The rock glanced off the whale before catching the top of Noah's head as he ducked.

Grayness swept through his mind as he fell back into the water. His rib cage throbbed with pain. His chest ached. He wanted to rest, to sleep, to just lie down and doze in the sun.

However, if he did, he would die.

He could not let go now. He had to face Jik again. He had to end this thing.

The grayness wasn't easy to disperse. Noah had to negate the concussion and shock, then repair cracked ribs and rebuild damaged muscles, and finally sharpen his senses. The first thing he saw when his vision cleared was Jik, leaping off the whale at him, knife in hand.

Noah focused all his power and energy on obliterating the mind of Jik. As he arced through the air, Jik's eyes widened in fear, and he screamed in an impossibly high pitch — then his head exploded as his body fell into the water next to the whale. The whale shuddered and rolled lazily from side to side.

But it's dead! Noah thought in amazement. Then he realized that the entire island shook violently. A rumble pulled his attention to the top of the mountain.

Steam vented into the air with massive roars. Rock and liquid magma shot through the superheated cloud. This was something Noah had never seen before — had never heard of such a thing in fact. It was awesome; and terrifying!

Near the top of the cone, the side of the mountain slowly caved in and abruptly vomited out steam and rocks. The crater enlarged and fell into itself. Rocks larger than a man's head splashed into the water near him.

Where to go?

~I am coming.~ The words filled his mind and heart.

~Thinker! You're alive. I thought you had lost your essence.~

~I lost some essence, but I have much.~

~Beware. I saw an orca out there,~ Noah warned.

~He has nothing to fear from me, nor do you. My pod has lost essence because of mind sickness. I go to find another.~ The presence of Tes faded and vanished.

Above him, the volcano belched glowing gasses and molten rock as the entire world bellowed. Smoke trailed up from the other side of the quaking mountain where lava etched into the trees and brush, consuming them in bursts of flame. Noah dog paddled out away from the small cove and then rolled over on his back and continued kicking his feet.

He watched lava ooze out of the wide volcanic mouth and start its inexorable descent to the sea. He kicked his feet harder. The obscenely sparkling, molten rock moved faster now as it edged down the steep slope of the mountain.

~Thinker, I have used my power to kill Jik when perhaps I could have saved him.~

~Do not eat of yourself. There was no gain in saving Jik even if you were able. The man has taken the essence of Tony, and would have taken yours and Moira's as well.~

~Tony is dead?~ Noah felt bewildered. Jik couldn't have returned to the shelter before they began their battle.

~Jik fed Tony poison. I did my best to save him,~ Thinker's mental voice dropped. *~But I failed. Do you still wish to continue traveling with me?~*

~Yes, of course, but I must get away from this place before the burning rock goes into the sea.~

"Noah! I'm coming!" Moira's voice skipped across the water.

He turned. She paddled less than a dozen meters distant. Then the boat floated beside him. He tried to pull himself onto the baidarka but didn't have the strength.

A thunderous crack, so loud it made their teeth hurt, wrenched the air. Noah and Moira looked up.

The top of the volcano blew up — out — and down through the smoke-filled air to the water. Tons of burning rock landed in the small bay, burying the silent carnage.

"My God, Noah! Look!" Moira screamed, as the top of the mountain blew off.

"Here!" He thrust the spar fragment at her. "Wedge it down in the boat. Where you go, I go," he said softly.

She pushed the spar into the center hole and jammed it sideways. She glanced up. A huge wave generated by the falling tons of rock rushed out of the cove at them.

"Screw you!" she screamed at it. "I've come too far to let you put out m' lights!"

Noah felt lassitude wash over him. He would die now. Nothing could stop that impossible wave.

Still, he had to say something to the only person who had ever shown him free, honest affection. If only there was more time to consider the words, to make them whole and alive.

"Moira, you have no idea how I feel about you," Noah said swiftly.

She looked down at him. "You've not messed with my mind, and you could have. I'm very grateful."

Then the sea tumbled them into oblivion.

CHAPTER 27

"WE ARE BEING ATTACKED by an antique?" Lieutenant Colonel Samedi Janeki shrieked at his driver. "Order them to shoot that damned thing down!"

Dawn broke over the South Pacific, garishly lighting the cloud bank spewing from the distant volcano. Thinker floated, exhausted, on the surface, ignoring the pyrotechnic display.

His wounded right flipper continued to lose blood. The other three wounds had congealed but still gave him much pain. He didn't understand why he couldn't heal them.

He had healed Noah; he had changed the man's very physique. He was able to keep the small riders off himself. *Why can I not heal myself? And where are Noah and Moira?*

He had searched for them until the warm eye dipped into the world. The burning mountain threw off some light, but not enough to see anything. Nor could he find Noah when he reached out with his mind.

The cold eye, Noah called it the Moon, slowly rose. Thinker felt alone. Emptiness, bottomless and unmoving, weighed him down as if he had swallowed rocks.

Sadness overwhelmed him and he sang a song of love and loss. He added a thread of never-ending search and determination. The sea accepted his lament and offered no answer.

The memory of the Small Cold Sea, and Looa, beckoned to him. He put the thought aside — first he must finish his search. Maybe in a few more visits of the warm eye, he would go north and join Naff's pod. But for now, he had a lot of the world to seine through his senses.

~¡Noah, I seek you!~

His flukes churned the water and he slid down into the sparkling depths, bearing to the northeast, pain, and the song of search trailing after him.

CHAPTER 28

RAK BOBBED ON THE TOP OF THE WORLD, his torn throat leaking blood. He felt imminent death. After experiencing Deg's end, Rak knew what to expect. The pain had finally faded at a point he no longer remembered. Now he only felt tired.

A fierce blow at his belly elicited only mild curiosity as he rolled over. A snarl of entrails floated past his eyes, and he realized they were his. Movement caught his left eye, and he identified the surging great white shark for what it was, half a heartbeat before it hit him again.

The Blood Essence rejoiced.

Book Three

CHAPTER 1

Aʟʟ ᴇʏᴇꜱ ᴀʙᴏᴀʀᴅ ᴛʜᴇ Aᴜꜱᴛʀᴀʟɪᴀɴ Mᴏɴɪᴛᴏʀ *Andrew Dawkins* held fast on the smoking volcano five leagues north of them.

"That's where the wave originated, all right," Captain Tarant muttered.

His executive officer nodded in agreement. "This backs up Currie's theory, y'know," he said with a grin.

"Did I ever argue with your bloody theory, Mister Currie?" Captain Tarant asked with a groan. "You science boffins are correct so rarely that when you do hit one on the nose, you become bloody insufferable."

"But, Captain," Currie said with an evil grin. "You wagered there wouldn't be another eruption within a thousand kilometers of Yap for at least a year. It's been nine months, two weeks and five days since New Ora blew itself to bits only nine hundred twenty klicks from this very spot."

"I said I wasn't arguing," came the nettled reply. "What this means is that a lot of new theories are correct. The meteorite strike did fracture the Pacific Plate. I hoped that hadn't happened. But you'll get your case of ocker brew, no worries."

"I wasn't really worried, Captain." The grin firmed to a few twitches at the ends of his mouth. "I'm just very excited that I was right, and Jimmy Ashenby, too. It will be like watching the birth of a new continent—"

"What it means," the captain interrupted, "is a lot more seismic activity for Oz, that's what it means. May as well get used to it, I assure you."

Captain Karl Tarant hungered for wealth and fame. As a small boy, he witnessed the Asteroid Fall and the hell that followed. Already an orphan due to an influenza outbreak, he'd had to fight men twice his size for enough food to exist.

He killed his first man at the age of eleven. By the time he'd turned sixteen, he had lost count of the lives he had ended. His heart had hardened along with his conscience, and he did what he had to in order to survive and prosper; nobody else was going to look out for him.

At eighteen, he'd jumped at the chance of serving in the newly minted Australian Naval Defense Force. Most people wanted to avoid the ocean at all costs.

Recruit training was nearly more brutal than living on the street. His quick mind and faster mouth earned him a savage beating from the boatswain's mate serving as his "company commander." Washouts numbered far more than those who endured and graduated from the training. Karl had no illusions about his chances if he went back to the streets; he shut his mouth, learned, and endured.

He graduated third in his class and, along with four others, accepted an invitation to dinner and a night on the town from Company Commander Jock Flately, First Class Boatswain's Mate.

"Just to show that now we're all mates!"

After the surprisingly fine dinner, and stops at two of Sydney's more notorious pubs, Karl picked an argument with the bosun and proceeded to beat him unconscious. Looking back, he realized that if the others hadn't pulled him off the man, he probably would have committed murder, again.

Through the winters of subtropical Australia, he worked hard, bested all adversaries with everything he had, and emerged as a person to respect and avoid. After ten years as a bosun, he was elevated to second mate on a gunboat fighting Malay pirates, where he excelled at devising ambushes for the indigenes and killing them wholesale. Five years later, he secured a First Mate's berth on one of the ANDFs patrol monitors.

Two years ago, he'd become captain of the *Andrew Dawkins*. While he enjoyed the prestige — and the fear — of his subordinates, he still wanted wealth and felt himself at a dead end.

"Flotsam, two degrees on the port bow," the bridge lookout shouted, pointing.

Captain Tarant and Executive Officer Currie raised their binoculars in unison.

"Looks man-made," Currie said instantly.

"No argument there, either. Helm, change your bearing to three-two-zero. Slow to half speed."

"Three-two-zero, half speed, aye, sir." Bells rang and the ship's momentum fell off slightly.

"Bridge, there's somebody in that thing!" the port watch shouted.

"What the hell is that?" Currie asked.

"It's a kayak of some sort, I think. Pre-Asteroid from the look of it," the captain said slowly, peering intently through his binoculars. "Bosun, lower a boat. Quartermaster, dead slow."

Ten minutes later the ship's boat slowed and gracefully joined the craft a hundred meters from *Andrew Dawkins* as the bridge watch waited tensely.

"*Dawkins*," the radio crackled. "Two people on board, I'm not sure they're alive."

The captain keyed his collar-comm. "Dead or alive, bring them on board."

Men with litters waited as the boat finally clicked back into davit locks. Sailors gently transferred the two small forms and raced them to sickbay.

"Bridge, this is the Bosun. What about the boat? My men tell me it's stuffed with furs and things."

"Furs? Good God. What next?" the captain snapped. "Bring the damn thing aboard, Boats. We want to look at it anyway. Fisher, you have the conn. I'm going to sick bay."

"Aye, sir. I relieve you of the conn."

Currie followed his captain down narrow ladders that took them two decks below and aft of the bridge. Captain Tarant pushed into the small infirmary without knocking.

"What do we have here, Doc?"

"Well," the older man said slowly as he straightened up. "They're both alive, but I'm not sure how. The man looks like he was knocked about a great deal more than the woman."

"Woman?" Currie blurted.

"Yes. One wonders what they were doing clear out here."

The two men stepped as one to the berth and looked down.

"That's Moira Napier!" Currie said reverently.

"Are you sure?" Captain Tarant scowled at her.

"No doubt about it, I saw her last concert before she disappeared. Her tan has darkened considerably, but I'd recognize her anywhere. Me and a thousand other blokes."

"Is that her husband, then? Deagan Napier?" The captain transferred his scowl to the heavily bandaged man.

"No," Doc said. "This isn't a white man. He looks Asian."

"Will they live?" the captain asked swiftly.

"She will, for sure. Him I wouldn't bet on. His left arm will have to come off to give him any chance at all. Worst abrasion trauma I've ever seen. I've photographed it for my medical files."

Tarant lifted a phone off the bulkhead, "Bridge, this is the captain. Set course for New Darwin. Full speed ahead."

As the deck crew tied the baidarka to the steel deck, the engines hummed. The ship came about, picked up speed, and retraced her wake.

Sonar picked up the echoing song of a Humpback whale, but the crew ignored whale sightings when more than fifty kilometers from a whaling station. What possible difference could a whale make?

CHAPTER 2

DOCTOR HARALD CARLESON WISHED HE KNEW MORE of his patient's history. The man didn't make sense. He was Asian in appearance, with well-developed, shoulders and arms that topped a torso lacking anything other than bone and sinew. "A bloody freak," he murmured to himself as he unwrapped the shoulder bandage.

For the past twelve hours he had worked to stabilize his patient. The first task was to bring him out of life-threatening shock so the horribly damaged arm could be amputated.

Over the years he had ministered to most of the world's medical horrors. Post-asteroid Australia needed medical people, even those like himself, with seven months of medical school and then brutal practical necessity. He had taught himself a great deal over the years, and many of his patients had died in the process.

"Christ, he'll really look the item once we take that wing off," he muttered to the quiet room.

He carefully pulled the last of the bandage away and stared uncomprehendingly at the shoulder for one long, slow breath. Where gouged and torn flesh had formerly hung in tatters around visible bone the night before, new healthy flesh and skin glistened.

"Bloody hell!" Doc bellowed.

Oberon, the medical striker, poked his head into the small ward. "Did you call, Doc?"

"C'mere!" Doc pointed. "Look at this! Tell me, what do you see?"

Oberon examined the shoulder thoroughly, even prodding it lightly with a probe, resulting in the shudder and twitch of a normally functioning nervous system.

"Well, I see a healthy shoulder in bonzer shape. 'E should be wakin' up soon, I expect. Did I miss anything?"

"Remember what this shoulder looked like yesterday?" Doc

asked in a strangled voice.

"I remember one of 'is shoulders bein' next to gone, all in tatters it wuz. I held the flood whilst you photographed it. But that's the other 'un isn't it?"

Oberon looked at the patient's other shoulder that lay bare save for a few plasters.

"Wait a minute, 'ere. This is the good shoulder. It's the other what was…" Oberon's frown deepened, and he glanced back and forth as if seeking the answer to a riddle.

"Ever see anything like this before?" Doc asked.

"'Ow th' 'ell did he do that?"

"Me neither," Doc said. "Stay with him. I need to talk to the skipper."

As he moved quickly toward the bridge, Doc wished again that he had enjoyed the benefits of a real medical school. The emergency government training proved better than nothing, but he knew he wasn't a pimple on a tart's bronza compared to doctors trained before the Fall. Most of those blokes were getting on in years, and there hadn't been many left to begin with.

Even so, he doubted whether any of those old sods had ever seen the like of this. "It'd be in the bloody books for sure," he muttered to himself.

Harald had plans, he did. This commission was but a steppingstone to teaching medical students in one of the new universities. After a couple of years of doing that, he would establish his own medical school. He wanted to be someone in the medical history of Australia.

Captain Tarant sat sideways in his padded chair on the bridge, one leg hooked over the arm like some doxy teenager, chatting with Mr. Currie.

"Skipper, I'd like you to see something, if you have the time. You, too, Mr. Currie."

"Sure, Doc," the captain said. He automatically glanced around the horizon line before following his medical officer. Currie trailed after them.

"I grant you I'm no Jonas Salk or anything like that," Doc said. "But in my years of patching holes, stitching cuts, and setting broken bones, I've never seen anything quite like this."

"I know he's in a bad way, Doc," Tarant said. "Don't take it hard if you can't help the poor bastard."

"Better hold judgment until you see him, Skipper." He pushed open the hatch to sickbay and stood aside for the captain. "After you, gentlemen."

Tarant nodded at Oberon and then glanced down at the patient. He remained silent for about ten seconds, but to Doc Carleson, it felt like hours.

Currie reacted instantly. "Are you playing some sort of parlour trick on us, Doctor?"

"No, Mr. Currie. All I've done for this man is bandage his horribly mutilated upper arm and shoulder. Nothing more."

Tarant turned and looked at him. "Exactly so. How then do you explain this?" He pointed.

"I can't. I told you that I'd never seen anything like this before. Have either of you?"

Currie shook his head without looking away from the patient.

"No," Tarant said and scratched his jaw. "But my Granny used to tell me stories about changelings..."

"This isn't some bloody fairy tale, Skipper!" Doc blurted. "This bugger has regenerated a limb that I thought would kill him. I'm not often wrong about things like that."

"Calm down, Doc. I know this isn't a bloody fable. But if he can do that, what else can he do?"

The three men stared at each other for a moment. Two saw reflected greed. Currie's mind dove into a lake of possibilities and extrapolation.

Doc felt a smile stretch across his face. "Sweet Baby Jesus. This bloke could be a gold mine, couldn't he?"

Oberon poked his head into the sick bay again. "Doc, the lady's awake. She wants a word with you."

"Right." He straightened up and nodded at the patient. "Oberon, keep your eye on this fellow. When he wakes up you let me or the skipper know straight away."

"Whatever you say, Doc."

Captain Tarant followed Doc into the first mate's cabin where Moira lay in the bunk. Doc thought she looked quite delectable. After a few moments of mental lechery, he forced himself back into his role of physician.

"How are you feeling, Mrs. Napier?" he asked.

"You know who I am?" She seemed surprised.

"Oh, yes. It probably wouldn't be too difficult to locate a photo poster of you somewhere on the *Dawkins*." Doc grinned widely despite himself. "A lot of people have wondered what happened to you and your husband."

"My husband is dead," she said flatly. "Is Noah still alive?"

"Is that the name of the Asiatic found in the boat with you?" Captain Tarant asked.

"He's an Inuit from Alaska, not Asiatic." She stared defiantly at them. "I asked if he was still alive."

"Very much so," Doc said. "In fact, we'd like to ask you some questions about this bloke."

"Why don't you ask him?"

"'Cause he's still unconscious. In fact, I thought he was going to die if I didn't amputate his arm. That's how bad he looked."

"But you didn't amputate?" Anxiety shone in her eyes for the first time.

"By this morning his condition showed amazing improvement," Doc said heavily.

"Oh!" she said, relaxing back into her pillow and smiling. "That's just bonzer."

"The point is, Mrs. Napier," Tarant said slowly, "he should be dead — but he isn't."

"Why does that disturb you?" Her left eyebrow arched, and her smile straightened into a suspicious line.

"Have you ever seen him, uh, heal himself in any way?" Doc knew she wasn't going to help them; he could feel it. "Physically, I mean."

The eyebrow dropped and her eyes grew round, innocent-like. The effect made her look even younger.

"You've no bloody idea what I'm talkin' about, right?" Tarant grated with heavy sarcasm.

"As a matter of fact, no," she said sweetly, obviously suppressing a smile. "What makes you think he can heal himself?"

"He either can do that, or else he's got the most amazing recuperative powers I've seen in my whole life," Doc said flatly. "His shoulder was open to the bone when we picked you up yesterday. The flesh was nearly dead above the shoulder and the arm itself had drained of blood."

She winced and closed her eyes,

"This morning I unwrapped a shoulder healthier than my own. Muscles with perfect elasticity, top-notch, first rate!"

"How'd he do it, Missus?" Tarant asked in his best metallic tone. "This fellow could be the most important thing we've found since the water receded."

Her face closed and Doc knew they would have to try something other than simple questions.

"His name is Noah Manaluk, and he can speak for himself."

"We told you, he's asleep—"

Oberon's urgent voice cut Tarant off. "Doc, Skipper, Mr. Currie! He's awake."

CHAPTER 3

"Captain, i, i thought i saw a whale...." the port bridge watchman stammered to a halt.

"Seaman Hirouchi, you either saw a whale or you didn't; which is it?" Captain Saigauo snapped. He kept the *MV Provider* on course.

He stared hard at the man, knowing that the crew believed he could singe a man's soul with his eyes. Who was he to end a rumor that could only bolster his position?

"I saw it, Captain, and started to shout. But it, it, it spoke to me, sir!"

"You are relieved, Seaman Hirouchi. Go below and tell no one what you just told me. I will see you in my cabin in ten minutes."

"Yes, Captain." The man left his post.

"Bosun, get another man for the port watch."

"Hai, Captain!" the bosun left the bridge, his stoic features masking all thoughts.

"First Mate Honda, you have the bridge." Saigauo left the bridge before he heard the acknowledgment from his second-in-command. The dark vein in his left temple visibly pulsed, a telltale his men feared.

Seaman Hirouchi stood at attention outside the captain's door.

"Show me your berthing space," Saigauo snapped.

The crewman immediately turned and led his captain down two steel ladders and aft. The throbbing twin diesel engines were a physical presence in the aft crew quarters, as were the overwhelming odors of dirty socks and rancid whale oil.

Hirouchi stood at attention beside the 1.5 square meter locker that constituted the sum of his personal life aboard the ship.

"Open it. Take everything out and put it on your bunk."

"Yes, Captain." In moments all his worldly possessions lay on display on the rough cotton blanket.

"Step back."

Hirouchi backed against the bulkhead and stood at attention, eyes stolidly staring at the far bulkhead, two meters away.

Captain Saigauo knelt and quickly sifted through the papers, photographs, and clothing items. Wordlessly he turned to the locker and slowly ran his hands over every millimeter of its interior. He slowly straightened to his full height.

"Stow your belongings and report to my cabin."

Hirouchi snapped his head forward and down. "Yes, Captain."

By the time the sailor knocked on his cabin door, Saigauo had poured two small cups of sake and was seated behind his desk.

"Enter."

Hirouchi stepped through the door and stiffened his posture.

"Sit, Kato," Saigauo said, his voice softening. "Have a cup of sake with me."

The man obediently sat and stared apprehensively at the cup of sake. He looked up at Saigauo with questioning eyes.

"I had to make sure you were not in the grasp of opium or some other narcotic. As the captain, I am obliged to always assume the worst. You are exonerated. Now, tell me everything you remember about what happened up there today."

Saigauo raised his cup and held it.

Hirouchi carefully picked his cup up and touched it to the captain's.

"To killing whales!" Saigauo said and threw the liquid into his throat.

"To killing whales!" The seaman followed protocol.

"Talk," Saigauo ordered in a gentle, yet firm, tone.

"I saw a spout about three hundred meters out, about ten of the clock on the port side."

"Good eyes," Saigauo muttered.

"Thank you, Captain. However, I wasn't sure, so I waited, watching the general area closely. Then I saw it again, much closer, under a hundred meters!"

Saigauo waited as the man examined his memory. A full minute passed.

"Then what happened?"

"I distinctly remember thinking, 'There's a whale out there. I must tell the captain!' and then I heard it!"

"Heard what?"

"Not with my ears, with my mind." Hirouchi was getting excited, the alcohol coursed through his system and his inhibitions had vanished, just as Saigauo had planned.

"With your mind?"

"Yes, Captain. I heard it in my mind!"

"What did it say?"

"'I mean you no harm. Leave me be and I will not harm you.'"

"What?" Saigauo bellowed. "This 'voice' threatened you and you told us nothing?"

"I was confused, Captain! I–"

"Did you believe this voice? Did you think it could hurt you or me?"

"I don't know!" Hirouchi screamed.

Saigauo looked away so the seaman could blot the unmanly tear sliding down his cheek. He thought fast. This was something new, unknown. Threatening.

Hirouchi was not an excitable man, which was part of the reason he held such an important position on the *Provider*. Lookouts had to be always in complete control. There was something to this event: but what?

"How did it sound, like a human speaking, a radio broadcast, an overheard conversation?"

"It whispered in my mind. It sounded tired, perhaps injured, yet strong. I think 'resolute' is the word I seek."

"Yet you knew it to be a whale speaking to you."

"Absolutely. When it entered my mind I smelled seaweed, brine, rotting fish. I felt great mass, as if it were part of me. I saw deep water with light filtering down from above. Since we were in the middle of the ocean, I knew it was from whatever was in my mind for that instant."

"You got all of that in an instant?"

"Yes, Captain. In addition, I could feel water sliding over my skin. All this happened at the same moment. I felt overwhelmed, disoriented, and confused."

"Yet it threatened you, and the ship?"

"I, I guess so. I am sorry I did not respond quickly, but this is, this is something completely new. There didn't seem to be anything to do or say."

"Take the next twenty-four hours off. Say nothing to your shipmates. Tell them you felt ill and off balance."

"Yes, Captain."

"If I hear even a whisper of what you told me from others, you will lose your berth and I will pass the word that you are not to be trusted. No other captain will hire you. Do you understand me?"

Hirouchi sat at stiff attention. "Yes, Captain. I understand."

"When you go back on duty if you see, or sense, a whale; you shout it out, immediately. Do you understand me?"

"Yes, Captain, I understand."

"Good. Go to your quarters."

The cabin door shut behind the seaman.

Hideki Saigauo pondered the man's words. Seaman Hirouchi had not prevaricated; he completely believed what he had related. Which made the situation even worse.

It must be true. He could think of nothing more devastating for his career and the industry he had followed his entire life. It threatened his mission.

If whales could communicate with humans, the anti-whaling faction in Japan would gain massive support immediately. The fools didn't realize how closely they stumbled near starvation.

Even with population levels finally increasing after two decades of loss and decline, Japan could barely feed her people. Protein from the sea was essential.

He wondered if the dolphins could also communicate with humans. Would this reduce him to the life of a mere fisherman? He slammed his hand down on his desk.

"What is wrong with me?" he said aloud. "This has to be an isolated instance, an anomaly, a freak of nature!" *That must be the case*, he decided.

Nothing else was acceptable.

CHAPTER 4

Noah felt people all around him. He tried counting the presences, but with so many together in such a small area, he wasn't strong enough to separate them. *At least twenty*, he decided.

Gratitude and tenderness flooded him when he felt the presence of Moira. He sensed her agitation. The room stank of strife, metallic chemicals, and efficiency while tilting evenly and slowly from side to side.

Bright light reflected off every surface. He heard sounds, big and little ones. He reached out and discovered the noises were motors, as in the old stories from before the stars fell.

Warm air bearing the stink of soiled clothing and unwashed bodies wafted over him. Four men walked to where he lay.

"So, you're Manaluk, the Inuit," said the thin, dark-bearded one with penetrating eyes. "How're you feeling?"

"My name is Noah. I feel well. Thank you for picking us up. Who are you?"

"Doc Carleson, at your service. This is Captain Tarant, skipper of the *Andrew Dawkins*." Tall, wide shouldered, darkly tanned face and arms, blonde beard bleached nearly white, high, hooked nose, and startling pale blue eyes usually found on a sled dog.

"Mr. Currie, our executive officer." Slender, medium build, a bit taller than Noah, wild red hair seeking freedom in all directions, deep green eyes crimped into a sunburned hatchet face. "And yonder is Oberon, my striker." Pale, slight build, nervous eyes flicking back and forth between the other three men, exuding the pathetic eagerness of the runt of the litter.

"I'm sorry," Noah said, "I didn't understand; who is Andrew Dawkins?"

Three of them laughed down at him. "This ship is the *Andrew Dawkins*," the captain said.

The man who didn't laugh, Currie, peered intently at Noah. "You were in a very bad way yesterday, Noah. The doctor here thought he was going to have to amputate your arm in order to save your life."

"I feel much better today. Thank you for your help."

"How did you do that?" Captain Tarant asked.

"I only slept." Noah darted into the man's thoughts, found suspicion and avarice, and pulled away saddened. "The last thing I remember is Moira — is she—"

"She's fine, just tired," Doc Carleson said.

"Actually, I'm not all that tired," Moira said, walking into the room.

Noah thought her the most beautiful thing he had ever seen. Relief over her well-being made his heart sing. She pushed through the men, bent down, and hugged him. "Don't trust these people," she whispered in his ear.

He nodded slightly and smiled at her. "I am happy to see you well."

"I thought we were goners when I saw the size of that wave," Moira said.

"How close to the island were you?" Currie inquired. Noah took the opportunity to ease into the executive officer's mind. Currie wasn't interested in personal wealth or power like the captain. Rather he seemed consumed by an incredible thirst for knowledge.

"About 300 meters offshore," Moira said. "We saw the top of the mountain blow off."

"And you weren't killed by the blast?" Currie exclaimed. "How can that be?"

The captain looked at Moira narrowly. "Perhaps you were so close the pressure wave passed over your heads."

"Yes!" Currie exclaimed. "You say the top of the mountain blew off. That could account for it." He smiled widely at them. "Jesus wept! I'd give my left nut to see something like that!"

"Steady on, Mr. Currie," Captain Tarant said, nodding at Moira.

"Oh. Excuse me, missus." He grinned again. "Would you describe it to me so I can add it to the book I'm writing?"

"Not just now," Moira said with a smile.

"No, of course. Later, yes. That would be fine."

Throughout the conversation, Doc Carleson stared at Noah as if waiting for him to suddenly sprout wings or a tail. The thought grimly amused Noah. He momentarily considered how easily he once again violated the minds of others. Still, just as quickly, he self-justified what he'd done with the defense that it was only to keep from being violated himself. With that, he looked into the doctor's mind.

Harald Carleson seethed with contradiction, fear, lust, and greed — nothing out of the ordinary. But he saw Noah as his "ticket to the top" if the Inuit could indeed do what the doctor suspected. Noah felt chagrin at his unconscious healing of himself but there was nothing to be done about that now.

Doc Carleson had no intention of letting this "anomaly" escape before undergoing an assortment of tests he'd busily formulated as he watched Noah. Carleson wondered if Noah could heal others, such as Moira, if she were injured.

With great effort, Noah withdrew from the man's mind without harm. There wasn't any time to waste. He planted a suggestion.

"Gentlemen," Captain Tarant said. "I'd like to see you all in the wardroom."

Doc Carleson frowned and peered at the skipper. "What on Earth for?"

Noah pushed a barb into the captain's ego.

"Are you questioning me, Mr. Carleson?"

"Well, I suppose I am. This," he waved at Noah, "ah, man could be the find of the century. I really feel there are tests that–"

Noah twisted the barb.

"Mr. Carleson!" The captain's jaw muscles rippled. "I order you to the wardroom. Now."

Currie looked from one man to the other. "Steady on, Captain. I'm sure we'll all be happy to join you in the–"

"You all damn well better!" Tarant snapped. He turned and stiffly marched out of the sickbay.

"Did he mean me, too?" Oberon asked meekly.

"Who the bloody hell knows!" Carleson said. "What's got his wind up now?"

"We best find out," Currie said, following the captain.

Carleson gave Noah a long, level stare. "Have a good rest, Mr. Manaluk." His face broke into a ghastly smile. "I'll see to you later."

The door shut and latched behind the doctor.

Moira let out a sigh of relief. "What the hell was that all about?"

Noah quickly told her. "I must get off this ship," he said in conclusion, "to protect both of us."

"Oh, Noah. I apologize for them. We're not all like that."

"I know you're not. But the Australia I saw in their minds isn't a place I want to live."

"What do you propose we do? We're in the middle of the ocean."

"Make them put us off in the baidarka." He saw her hesitation and resisted the inclination to tamper with her mind. If she didn't want to be with him, he had to accept it.

Marilyn's memory bit and resignation crept over him. The thought of separating from Moira gave him pain. In addition, no matter how far he cast mental shouts, he could not find Thinker.

The prospect of being truly alone no longer terrified him, but he felt anxious.

"I don't know if I can get back in that thing or not, Noah. There's a life waiting for me in Australia. It's not the one I left, but all the same, it offers me much more than–"

"Going with me," Noah said flatly.

"Brutally put, but true."

"How can I make them forget me if they have you? There's too much connecting us to unscramble in their minds. The doctor is willing to hurt you to study me!"

"If you're not here, they won't hurt me," she said. "I know that and so do you."

"I can't paddle faster than this ship moves. The only other escape from them is to end my existence."

"No! Please, Noah, don't even think that."

"Don't worry. It's not the way of the People to waste life. Besides, my inua would never find peace."

"Maybe you could make them put us off this ship and wipe their minds or whatever it is you do," her eyes blazed with excitement, and he knew he couldn't let her go. Not yet. "And then you could put me on an island closer to the shipping lanes. I could build a signal fire when a ship came in sight and that way I could go back to Australia, and you would be free."

Her eyes darted back and forth on his face, searching for acceptance he didn't possess. "Well, whattya think?"

"Yes," he said thoughtfully. "That could work. We should do it very soon. I must rest now."

"I'm sorry," she said at once. "I forgot what you've been through. Your arms look great. You're the most amazing person I've ever met." She kissed his cheek and walked quickly out of the room.

Noah lay back and tried to ignore the feelings her kiss had stirred up. He needed to take mental inventory of the ship's crew, find out how many knew of him and Moira, and start the process of eroding their memories.

The men who operated the boilers (he made a mental note to investigate those) and those who cooked food, all deep inside the ship, only knew him as a rumor. They proved easy. Men who had slept or worked below decks at the time of the baidarka's discovery also lost all memory of finding a woman and an Inuit.

As he pushed into other minds Noah hoped this would work.

CHAPTER 5

WITH OBERON AT HIS HEELS, Currie followed Doc into the wardroom. Captain Tarant dropped into his chair at the head of the table, a puzzled expression settled on his face. They all slid silently onto chairs. Currie wondered why the skipper had demanded their presence in such a loutish manner.

"This is going to sound bloody damned strange," Tarant said slowly. "But I haven't a glimmer of why I wanted you all in here."

"You certainly were adamant about it," Doc Carleson said with some heat. "I've never seen you act the lord high admiral before."

Captain Tarant stared out a porthole, shook his head, and murmured, "It seemed life and death important to get you all in here."

"You don't remember what you were thinking at the time?" Currie pressed.

"No."

"Do you have any memory of the event?" Doc asked.

"I remember staring at the Inuit bloke, and asking 'im questions along with Currie," he nodded, "and then I had to get you all in here. And I don't remember why!" His voice nearly broke.

"Maybe our passenger wanted us out of there?" Currie let his voice trail off, wondering if he should finish the thought or not.

"How would that affect the skipper?" Doc asked.

"Hold up," Tarant ordered. He looked at Oberon. "The Doc said he wanted tests done on the Inuit. Why don't you go start, Oberon."

The medical striker stood quickly. "An' what tests would that be, Captain?"

Tarant glanced at Doc.

"Blood sample," Doc said quickly. "Draw at least ten cubic centimeters. Blood pressure. Temperature, oral. Check the reflexes in his arms. May as well check his eyes and ears while you're at it."

Oberon waited a moment then nodded crisply. "Aye, aye, sir. I'll get right on it."

As soon as the wardroom door closed behind Oberon, Tarant gave his executive officer a penetrating look. "You were saying, Mr. Currie?"

"Well, you saw his shoulder!"

CHAPTER 6

OBERON HURRIED INTO THE SICK BAY carrying a small, dark thing with a glass eye. "You're lookin' chipper as 'ell for a bloke who was scratchin' at death's door just yesterday."

Noah eyed the device in Oberon's hand, and decided he wasn't tired after all. "Yes, I am feeling quite well, thank you." He sat up and swung his feet off the bed. "In fact, I would like to rise now and inspect my boat for damage."

"'Old on, 'ere. The doc wants me to run a few tests on you, first."

"I feel fine. I require no tests."

"Well, th' doc—"

"Will just have to do without," Moira said from behind Oberon.

The medic swung around. "That's easy for you to say, ma'am, but I have my orders."

"Nobody orders *us* around, Mr. O'Bannon!" she said hotly.

"Uh, that's Oberon, ma'am." His eyes flicked back and forth between them.

"Fine. Well, Mr. Oberon, you can bloody well sod off."

Oberon gave Noah a beseeching look, sighed, and pushed past Moira. As soon as he left, she moved close to Noah.

"Where're your clothes?"

"I don't know. I remember wearing some torn caribou hide trousers."

Moira jerked a locker open and poked about. "Nothing in caribou, but we seem to have some cotton items. Here," she threw a wad of cloth at him, "put on these sweatpants. They're a lot more comfortable than caribou. Trust me. I'll keep an eye out for our hosts."

As Noah slid into the gray pants, he noticed that his lower body didn't seem as thin as he remembered.

"Am I gaining weight?" He pulled on a cotton shirt that matched the pants.

Moira glanced at him and then went back to watching the door. "This is no time to worry about your girlish figure, mate. You ready to scarper?"

Noah slipped off the bed. The deck chilled his bare feet, and the chemical reek irritated his nose. "More than ready."

Four beds separated by metal lockers crowded the next room. Moira briefly glanced under the bed with disordered blankets.

"What–" Noah began.

"Nothing," she said briskly, "just an old habit." She led them up a stairway and out a door with a wheel mounted in its center. They found themselves on deck.

The sun beat down as the ship hissed through the water. The breeze carried a hint of salt and nothing else — the true smell of the sea.

Noah glanced up at the mast, then over at Moira. "Where's the sail?"

"This is a ship, not a bloody sailboat! Ain't you ever seen a ship before?"

"No." He suddenly felt testy and thought hard. "Is it the boilers that make it go so fast?"

She brightened up. "Something like that."

"Hey! What are you people doing on deck?" A large man wearing a dark knit cap low on his forehead hurried up to them. His wide nose carried dents and scars from ancient abuse. His skin seemed even darker than Captain Tarant's. The heavy clothing sported many patches but appeared clean. He radiated authority.

"We're looking for our boat," Moira said sweetly. "Would you show us where we can find it?"

The man frowned. "Did the skipper say it was okay?"

"Of course, it's all right. We wouldn't break any rules."

Noah soothed out the concern in the man's mind and he grew more docile. "Well, all right then. This way." He turned toward the stern of the ship.

Moira gave Noah a wink over her shoulder. They passed two men in ragged clothing who keenly watched Moira rather than continuing to paint the railing.

"Got tyme fer a tipple, dearie?" one of them murmured.

The large man suddenly pivoted on his feet and hit the talker in the side of the head with his fist. The man, much smaller in stature, bounced off the bulkhead and slumped to the deck.

"Mind yer manners, Sweeney," the big man said, glowering down, "and someday you'll get to speak to ladies any time you wish."

The other man quickly began to paint.

"An' you, M'halla. I see you taking your leisure without my say-so I'll have you chippin' paint through the mid-watch!"

"I be paintin', Boats!" M'halla said nervously. "I be paintin'."

Sweeney pulled himself off the deck and sullenly continued to paint the rail an off-white color.

Noah stared at the paint. This was something his uncle had told him about, something he thought lost forever after the stars- after The Fall. Was there more magic left in this Australia place that Moira talked of incessantly?

An overwhelming feeling of curiosity came over him. The image he'd seen in the minds of the men might be just a small part of "Oz," as they called it. He'd been ready to paddle back to a place where he couldn't live anyway. He wavered.

During the journey south he realized how big the world must be. One of the three books left in Point Hope was an atlas. As a small boy, his favorite game was to pick out the prettiest color on each page and then ask his mother what that strange place was called.

At the time of his mother's death, she was one of the five People left who could read. All those pages, representing so many places. Of course, that was a picture of the world before The Fall.

How much had changed? Did new countries exist? Did parts of the old countries still teem with strangers?

"Here you be, Mrs. Napier," Boats said.

She smiled up at him and squinted her eyes in the bright light. "Is your name really 'Boats'?"

The huge man blushed slightly and grinned back at her. "Bosun Danford Stout, at your service, ma'am. 'Boats' is just a shortenin' for boatswain's mate. Kinda tradition, like."

"Thanks, Boats." She looked at the tarpaulin-covered baidarka. "Could you undo those knots for us? We'd like to see if our boat was damaged during the eruption."

Boats bent to the knots that quickly unraveled under his callused, thick-fingered hands.

Moira turned to Noah and whispered, "Have you figured out how you want to do this?"

"Tell me about Australia."

"What?" She shaded her eyes and searched his face. "Are you rum or something? Tell you about Australia?' There's a bloody lot to it, mate. It'd take hours, days, weeks maybe."

Her distress would have been obvious to a rock, let alone him. "Please, I do not mean to upset you. But I realized—"

"What's going on here, Bosun?" a harsh voice demanded.

Bosun Stout snapped straight and spun about. "Captain? The lady told me she'd cleared this with you."

Moira and Noah turned to a stern-faced Captain Tarant.

"I told the Bosun it was quite all right for us to look at our own boat," Moira's voice remained calm. "I am correct, aren't I?"

Tarant's face softened slightly. "Are you searching for something in particular?"

Moira's voice acquired an edge. "We simply wish to inspect our property, Captain. Does that threaten the operation of your vessel in any way?"

His mouth made a thin smile. "Of course not, Mrs. Napier. How could the two of you threaten a Commonwealth vessel?"

"Exactly. Then there is no problem and the Bosun is not in gaol for assisting us?"

"No problem for me, no problem for the Bosun." Tarant frowned at Noah. "Mr. Manaluk, if you would like more substantial clothing, the supply officer can help you."

"Thank you, sir. But I have adequate clothing in my boat."

"Where did you get your boat?"

Noah gave Tarant a modified version of his departure from Point Hope. He wove a story of famine and death in the village. How he alone escaped.

"You paddled that thing all the way from the Chukchi Sea by yourself?"

"I traveled alone in the boat," he said with a nod.

"You're quite remarkable in a number of ways. The executive officer and Doc would love to run some tests on you."

"Yes, I know. I have already declined."

"Oh, come, sir," Tarant's voice became hearty. "What would be the harm?"

The Bosun pulled the tarp off the baidarka.

Moira thanked him and smiled at the captain. "If you'll excuse us now, we'd like to see if our boat is damaged."

Tarant bit off his entreaty and nodded. "Certainly. If you require any assistance, please let me or the Bosun know." The Bosun followed his captain toward the bridge.

Noah ran a practiced eye over the baidarka and tried to figure out what didn't look right.

"Oh, Noah! It's bent!" Moira pointed.

He stared at the indentation in the keel, wondering if they had any other choice than going to Australia with Captain Tarant.

CHAPTER 7

Moira thought her heart would burst. "Noah, tell me it's bonzer, that it's okay."

"I don't know." He pulled gear out of the front hatch. "I must get inside and see the frame –" he gave her a long look, "– then we'll know." He disappeared and she heard him rummaging through the gear.

Her mind seethed with the aspects of their predicament. All those months on the island. Fear of Jik. Grief for Deagan. Anguish over Tony's slow decline.

She'd dealt with it all. Conquered, come to terms, grieved, and let go. *And now I've got a changeling Inuit and a telepathic whale to—*

"Noah!" she blurted. "Have you heard anything from Thinker lately?"

His head popped out of the hatch, eyes wide. "What do you know about Thinker?"

"Oh, you dolt! He contacted Tony and me. He tried to cleanse Jik's poison out of the old ocker, but it was too late."

"Thinker talked to you?"

"Yes!"

"What did he tell you about us, about me?"

"What are you so anxious about? He said you and he were fellow travelers, mates. He only made contact because he thought he could save poor old Tony."

"He didn't say anything about, about Alaska?"

"Not a peep," she said forcing a grin. "If you've got deep, dark secrets, don't worry. He kept them for you."

"Were you angry at me for not telling you about Thinker?"

"Angry? No. Puzzled perhaps, but then I probably wouldn't have believed you anyway."

Noah's face relaxed and he nearly smiled. She studied him, and wondered what shape his private devils took. She didn't doubt their existence.

"I have heard nothing from Thinker since the eruption." Noah chewed his lower lip. "He suffered wounds in the fight with the Orcas. I don't know if he can heal himself or not. I know he can heal me."

"You're very worried about him, aren't you?" she said softly.

"Yes. Yes I am." His head dropped back into the baidarka, and rummaging noises started again.

"Moira." The craft somewhat muffled Noah's voice. "Would you come in here and look at this?"

"Sure." She pulled herself onto the baidarka and eased into the hatch. He lay stretched out on the smooth floorboards.

The fabric of his cotton pants had settled around his legs, clearly showing their form. They were larger, more muscular than she remembered. She crawled down until she lay stretched out beside him. The ship's side-to-side motion continually rocked them gently together.

"Look at what?" she asked, wondering if he noticed the sudden tightness in her voice.

"This big tube, here." He put his hand on the aluminum keel tube just below the rounded dent that reversed its curve. "Looks like we hit a log or something."

"We could have hit any bloody thing when that mountain went. Will your boat be okay this way?"

"It seems solid." He grasped the reverse curve and tried to shake it. "But I was wondering, do you know of any way to fix it?"

He looked over at her and she realized his face no longer looked pinched and skull-like. The warm, dark eyes gave him a peaceful aspect. She felt drawn to him.

"Fix it? No, I wouldn't have the slightest. Noah, you're not messing about with my mind, are you?"

His eyes grew cold, nostrils flared and recovered, and his mouth flattened into a thin line. "No. I told you I would not do that to you. You are my friend. Why do you wonder such a thing?" The hurt in his voice speared her heart.

"Because," she raised up on one elbow and put her other hand behind his neck, pulled him toward her, "I wanted to be absolutely sure this was all my idea." She kissed him softly and completely.

When she pulled away, she saw his eyes full of questions. *Christ,* she thought, *I'm full of questions. Did a bit of meat on his bones change how I felt about him?*

No, she decided, but it helped. He'd looked such a freak at first. Whatever happened to him during the fight with Jik had changed his body forever. The rest of him seemed to be slowly catching up with his arms and chest.

The essential goodness of him had been there all along. He could influence her very thoughts but didn't. Jik would have. Deagan had tried.

"Moira, I very much want you to love me. Perhaps some of that has crept out of my mind into yours?" A tear ran down his cheek. "I don't want it to be that. I want—"

A brisk thump on the side of the baidarka next to his head startled him into silence. "Is everything shipshape in there?" Doc Carleson called.

"M'gawd," Moira whispered softly. "They can probably hear us plain as day out there." She angled her head back, and brayed, "We're just bonzer, Doc. But busy."

"The skipper asked me to tell you to finish up as soon as you can."

Anger bloomed inside her chest so forcefully that she had trouble catching her breath. She opened her mouth to scream at him. Noah's fingers touched her top lip.

His eyes gazed deep into hers. He shook his head slowly, and whispered, "Listen to him."

She swallowed the anger, but her voice scratched with heat anyway. "And why's that, Doc?"

"We're headed into one bastard of a storm. He wants everyone below decks."

Abruptly Moira's rage metamorphosed into gut-churning fear. She realized the ship's motion had intensified. She nearly vomited. *Not another storm!*

CHAPTER 8

Moira's AGITATION RADIATED SO PALPABLY Noah felt sure the doctor would notice. She scrambled backward and poked her head through the hatch. She scrunched down, moaned, and said, "Ah, Christ wept, Noah. It's a big bastard, all right."

He squirmed in a tight circle and moved next to her. "It will be fine. This isn't a sailing ship. It's big and made of steel. We'll be safe."

"Let's get inside," she said tightly, leaping from the baidarka and staring at the approaching storm front as Noah crawled out.

He slipped once, getting out. The ship now rolled heavily from side to side and buried its prow nearly to the weather deck before rearing up to crash down and start the process all over again. In addition, he knew this was just the beginning; things would get much worse before they got better.

The thick wind carried moisture and smelling it was like drinking water. A massive wall of charred cloud covered more than half the sky. The menacing front quickly engulfed the blue sky as they watched.

"C'mon, you two!" Doc Carleson shouted.

Noah finally noticed the keening wind over the white-capped sea. His mind slipped back to the night he crashed onto St. Lawrence Island. For a brief eternity, he saw Marilyn again as if for the first time.

"Come on, Noah," Moira said, surprised, "it's blowing hard enough to make your eyes tear."

He gave her a baleful look. She recoiled.

"Other days, other storms," he said, giving his head a shake. "Let's go inside."

"Yeah, where we're safe." She turned and started for the nearest hatch.

Noah pulled the tarp over the baidarka and tightened the ropes to hold it snug. He wiped his tears as if they were sweat and followed

Moira through the hatch. Sweeney slouched just inside the passageway.

The narrow space rocked back and forth. Noah quickly adapted his step to the motion, and waited for the deck to travel part of the way to his foot rather than lurch down to it. The motion's inconsistency transmitted the growing fury of the sea.

As soon as they passed him, Sweeney swung the hatch shut and expertly spun the wheel. The little bars that sealed the door tight fascinated Noah. "That's very clever."

"Y've never seen a hatch dogged shut before?" Sweeney's rheumy eyes pulled off Moira long enough to briefly glom Noah. "N' matter. The skipper wants yez on th' bridge, smart-like."

"How do we get there?" Moira asked. They all swayed in concert, living metronomes in cadence with the rhythm of the world.

Sweeney's pigeon chest puffed out and he revealed a smile dotted with decay. "Ah, the places I'd love t' take ya, darlin'."

Moira's hand blurred, and suddenly held a small knife at the seaman's throat. He flattened against the bulkhead, trying to halt the ship's motion or recede into the steel to escape the point at his windpipe.

"I sliced a bloke with this," she said with a growl. "If I'd been a bit more awake, I woulda killed him. I'm wide awake now, and if you give me any more of your shit, I'll cut you from arsehole to appetite!"

Sweeney's eyes bugged white and wild in the passageway's cold gray light. The ship groaned to starboard, pushing his weight against the knife. "Jeezus, missus! I'm sorry. Gawd, please don't hurt me." He flashed a beseeching glance at Noah. "Tell 'er, cobber. I won't do it again." Drool slid from the corner of his mouth.

Noah slipped into Sweeney's mind long enough to verify his words. "He won't, Moira. Let him go."

The knife disappeared. "Where's the bridge?"

"Forrard," he said breathlessly, pointing. "Take the first ladder, stairs, to port, ah, left, on yer left. Go up two decks and then all the way forrard. Can't miss it."

Sweeney slithered between them and vanished in the opposite direction. Moira barked a humorless laugh. Noah watched her, wondering if there would ever be a time when she couldn't surprise him. Probably not.

"C'mon, Noah. Let's go find the bloody bridge."

CHAPTER 9

CAPTAIN TARANT GLANCED UP FROM THE CHART TABLE when his two passengers stepped onto the bridge. Mr. Currie measured distance with a pair of dividers. Spume-flecked spray rattled on the windscreen.

Moira peered through the glass to behold mountainous green-gray seas veined with white froth. No trace of blue graced the sky that roiled with dark, murky clouds. Rain lanced across at a steep angle, driven by the building wind. She pitied the men exposed to the elements on either wing.

"If it's as bad as I think it is, we'll never make it to Mati." Currie tapped the chart. "The wind is against us."

"I'd much rather make landfall in the Philippines than somewhere in Indonesia," Tarant said. "The Philippines aren't swarming with pirates and murderers."

"Well, not in the south, anyway," Currie said with a grin.

"Yes, well." Tarant stared at Noah for a long moment. "We've other fish to fry just now. Maintain this course, quartermaster."

"Aye, aye, sir."

The *Andrew Dawkins* buried its bow as a large wave smashed over it, and the ship reared up, slamming a wedge of salt water back against the windscreen.

Tarant pushed away from the chart table. Moira hadn't seen a handgun on his hip earlier. She also noticed that of the six men on the bridge, two burly seamen didn't seem to do anything other than watch Noah.

Alarm bells went off in her head. She gripped a stanchion for support.

What are these bastards up to?

"You seem to be healthy as a horse, Mr. Manaluk." The ship

groaned over to starboard, hesitated, and slowly rolled back to port again.

"One has never seen a horse," Noah said politely. "But I feel fine."

"Well, we feel it important to understand how you regained your health so quickly and completely. So, Doc Carleson is going to run a few tests on you."

Moira asked, "You mean Noah doesn't have a choice in the matter?"

"We prefer he cooperates willingly," Tarant said. "But cooperate he will."

"What sort of tests?" Moira pressed.

Tarant hesitated and his left eyelid drooped slightly. She knew his next words would be lies. He shifted with the roll of the ship.

"I don't know. Doc has it all set up in sickbay." He stepped closer to Noah. "Shall we go, Mr. Manaluk?"

Noah frowned at him.

"Oh, yes. You needn't use your parlor trick to make me give my men different orders. They have been instructed to present you in sick bay no matter what I say or do."

Noah's frown deepened. "You don't understand what you are doing. I will protect myself and Moira regardless of the cost to you or your ship."

Tarant snickered and the men on the bridge followed his example, except Currie, who frowned, and the bridge watch who wore a speakerphone headset.

"Captain," Currie snapped, "I must protest! This man is a potential treasure, not a laboratory specimen!"

"Noted, Mr. Currie. Now either be of assistance or piss off."

The executive officer turned his back to the scene and stared out at the storm. The Andrew Dawkins shuddered as heavy seas impacted her bow. Wind moaned across the bridge wings.

Tarant nodded to the two seamen. They moved cat-like across the deck, very sure-footed for men their size. Noah edged close to Moira. "Don't worry," he murmured.

"Don't worry!" she blurted. "They're probably gonna pull your fingers off to see if they grow back!"

Tarant grinned, enjoying himself. "Hadn't thought of that one, Mrs. Napier. I'll mention the possibility to the Doc."

Both seamen and Captain Tarant suddenly went slack, like string-cut marionettes, and fell heavily on the deck. Mr. Currie and the helmsman both turned and stared in shock.

"If you come near me," Noah warned, "or—"

"Are they dead?" Currie asked.

"No. They are unconscious, not harmed."

Currie looked down where a stream of blood ran from one seaman's nose. "Well," he said cheerfully, "mostly unharmed."

"Do not attempt to stop us or pursue us."

"Where the bloody hell can you go, man?" Currie gestured at the windscreen.

"Away." Noah nudged Moira. "Get in the baidarka, now."

She hesitated. *Was he mad? He thought they could launch that little thing in this weather and live through it? How could they survive the storm even if they did get off this bloody boat alive?*

"Noah –" she started.

"Very well," he sighed. "I'll go alone."

He turned, undogged the hatch and swung it open. Bosun Stout grabbed the smaller man in his great arms and lifted him off the deck.

"Gotcha, ya little–" The man went loose and collapsed backward against the passageway bulkhead. Noah scrambled away from him and hurried down the ladder to the weather deck.

"Noah!" Moira shouted. "Wait for me!" She jumped over the bulky Bosun and raced down the steel steps.

At the bottom, Noah hesitated, his upturned face a moon in the dusk of the passageway. "I must leave this ship. They won't harm you—"

She stopped in front of him and kissed him quickly on the mouth. "Let's go, mate. I'd just worry about you if I stayed."

With difficulty, they pushed the hatch open against the wind. The ship rolled to port and the sea foamed over the edge of the deck. Spume slashed at them, stinging like thrown pebbles or flying ice.

Noah grabbed the solid railing and moved aft. Moira followed, shivering in the wind and rain. Her soaked clothing felt like shrouds of ice.

Wind whistled and hummed through the ropes holding the tarp over the baidarka. Noah studied the wire rope railing at the deck's edge. He turned and shouted, "Cut the ropes off the tarp and get in the baidarka."

She nodded and dashed to do her duty. Moira pulled her knife out and sawed at the hemp. She watched Noah slide through the ankle-deep water flooding the scuppers and grab the stanchion that anchored the railing — the only thing that separated him from the maddened sea.

He held the anchor pin with both hands and tugged it free of the collars.

Like a thing alive, the two wire ropes swooshed away, whipping back in the wind. Noah threw himself flat on the sodden deck as both ropes whizzed above him. They missed Moira by a meter.

Soaked to the skin, Noah pushed himself to his feet and darted toward the baidarka. One of the wire ropes caught and hung in the heavy supports on the deck crane. The other snaked back and clipped the top of his head.

Moira cut three of four ropes before the wind caught the tarp and flashed it away into the storm. The *Andrew Dawkins* heeled to port and the baidarka began to slide towards Noah. Moira tried to hold it back for fear it would push him into the sea, but gravity, wind, and a deck running with water proved more than her match.

"Noah!" she screamed into the wind. "Look out!"

The top of his baldpate gleamed with rain and blood. He shook his head and looked up. Picking up speed, Moira and the baidarka slid inexorably toward him.

CHAPTER 10

Thinker breached into the storm, grateful to be alive and whole. The thindrink seethed with wildness and sprays of what Noah called "water." Thoughts of his friend never left him.

The great whale mulled the disappearance of the man. Noah still lived after he killed Jik, and the island broke itself. Landforms being alien to him, Thinker still wasn't sure if Noah did that or not. He didn't think the man could create events of that magnitude, but his friend's power had been growing.

No, he'd lost contact with Noah after the great wave hit the boat and the humans. Thinker's wounds had prevented him from staying with his friends. Although Moira couldn't touch his mind of her own volition, Thinker felt protective and close to her.

As he rolled these thoughts over in his mind, he patiently fluked from one rock, from one island, to the next. Constantly he called out with his mind, seeking Noah. The world held many islands here in the Warm World. Most of them swarmed with the essence of living creatures.

As he briefly touched each essence, his abilities grew more fluid, more incisive and adept. His range grew along with his speed, and he soon could inspect an entire island in the time it took to swim around it.

Many humans lived on the islands. Most hated and feared the ones on adjacent islands. Perhaps they were like the Cea and the Supra — very much alike but with deadly differences.

So much to contemplate. *~¡Noah, I seek you!~*

CHAPTER 11

THROUGH A HAZE OF PAIN, NOAH SAW the baidarka slide toward him. He realized he didn't have time to repair his damaged head before the boat knocked him into the sea.

Moira, still on the steel deck of the *Andrew Dawkins*, futilely tried to stop the baidarka's rush toward the water. *That boat is just like a seal*, he thought.

He reached out and touched her mind, pushing through the panic. *~Get in the boat before it is too late!~*

Her head snapped up and she stared at him for a moment before she nimbly scrambled aboard and dropped into the middle hatch. Without her braking, and responding to her added weight, the boat gained momentum.

The ship nosed down into another huge wave. Tons of seawater sped aft engulfing Noah, lifting him above the baidarka and dropping him onto the craft. The *Andrew Dawkins* obligingly rolled to port and the baidarka slid smoothly into the water as Noah pulled himself into the front hatch.

He grabbed the dome, fitted the tube into its groove and hurriedly inflated it. As soon as he finished sealing the hatch, he made the pain go away. While he mechanically repaired the damage, he wondered how many times his skull could have taken this sort of punishment had he not possessed his abilities.

He clutched the small pump and pushed through the boat to where Moira shivered in the center hatch. Wordlessly he showed her how the system worked, and they sealed the center hatch.

"My gawd, Noah," she said through chattering teeth. "We did it. We bloody well did it!"

"Yes," he smiled, "we did it. I must go back and seal the aft hatch. Find something warm here and get out of your wet clothes." He pulled a pile of furs and hide clothing out of his way and burrowed through the narrow opening between his familiar, but nearly forgotten, possessions.

The baidarka pitched and rolled unceasingly. Rain and blowing spume constantly thumped into the boat skin. Noah busily tried to interpret the noise level when he finally pushed through to the aft hatch.

Rain hammered down through the hatch and an occasional slop of wave splattered the floorboards. Noah groped around in the gloom for the plexiglass dome. While he concentrated on his right hand, his left touched living flesh.

Noah jerked back, his heart surging with adrenaline as fear slammed through him. "What?" he blurted.

Movement in the dimness! Noah peered hard, willed his eyes to function more acutely than normal. A man crouched under the hull, soaked and half-naked, holding a long, wickedly curved knife.

With wide and fearful eyes, the man stared at Noah. "Don' meke me kill ya, fella."

Noah forced himself to speak calmly. "What are you doing on my boat?"

"Hidin' from de Bosun. I think you be him, lookin' f'me."

"The Bosun won't find you here. Not now. You were painting with Sweeney yesterday, correct?"

"Yeah. Don' lak dat Sweeney mon no way. He be evil."

"What's your name?"

"Perrim, Perrim M'halla from Reborn Surabaya, Kingdom of Sunda."

"I don't know that place. I'm Noah Manaluk from Point Hope, Alaska."

"I don' know dat place."

"You can put your knife down. Nobody here is going to hurt you."

"Dis be my kris. It proof I be a man. I keep it maybe the Bosun find me."

"The Bosun is still on the ship."

"We be on the ship, fella." He grinned. "Where else?"

Noah nodded toward the rain pelting through the open hatch. "Take a look."

Perrim edged over and popped his head above the rim, jerked

down. An aura of astonishment swept over his face, and he stood in the hatch. Noah heard him shriek, but the words lost themselves in the wind.

CHAPTER 12

Moira wrapped the bearskin tighter and nearly swooned with the warmth. What was taking Noah so long? Maybe he found something of interest.

The baidarka listed to starboard as the wind pushed it sideways up the face of a wave. The storm fired fusillades of spindrift against the skin. The boat rolled farther to the left and slid down into the wave trough.

"How do you steer this thing?" she muttered.

Noah's voice behind her nearly popped her out of her skin. "You kick the rudder controls. Those pedals on the floor there."

"Christ! You scared hell out of me. Where have you been?"

He gave her a level look. "Talking to our passenger."

"Our what?"

Noah settled into the small seat, placed his feet, and steered the baidarka to travel with the wind. He explained about M'halla. "We can't just pitch him over the side," he concluded.

"Reborn Surabaya, Kingdom of Sunda." Moira pulled the words out slowly. "He's another fuckin' Malay," she whispered. "He's from one of those big islands what used to be Indonesia before The Fall."

"He and Jik are from the same place?"

"Not exactly. Jik's people hailed from New Guinea, but I think he was born in N'Dawpert."

"Where?"

"New-Darwin-Port," she said slowly. "Everybody calls it N'Dawpert."

"That's where you and Dea—"

"Yeah. That's right. So, how'd our little brown brother get aboard?"

Noah's eyes narrowed and she felt a total galah. "I'm sorry, Noah. I didn't mean anything about color. I just don't trust 'im."

"You don't have to worry," he said shortly. "I put him to sleep. He was hiding from the Bosun."

Good, she thought. *Now change the subject.* "How did you do that to all those men at once?"

"The same way I did it to the pod of Killer whales."

"I thought you used a powder."

"No. I struck at them with my mind."

A sliver of fear worked through her. "I thought you could just talk with your mind, not…"

"I can kill, I can heal."

"Can you make people do what they don't want to do?"

"Yes."

"Do people know when you're, when you're in their mind?"

"Not usually. OnePod could."

"OnePod?"

"The Orcas. They shared a mind. A very powerful mind."

Bewilderment seeped over Moira. *This was all too bloody much. How could a rational human being accept this sort of thing and not go yarrah?* "How did you defeat them?"

He told her and finished with, "Somewhere out there is an Orca who carries the Blood Essence. When it finally dies, whatever feeds on it will also receive the essence. Whatever feeds on the carrier –"

"– receives it, too," Moira finished. "My God, what a world we live in!"

"I don't understand how a rock, a meteorite, could change the world in those ways."

"That's the easy part," she said, feeling the old anger resurface. "Before The Fall, about half the countries in the world had this thing called nuclear power. I don't understand how it worked, but it was dangerous!"

"Dangerous, how?"

"It was radioactive. It gave off invisible rays that kills things or makes them change the way they grow, or how their kids grow." Shock washed over Noah's face. "What?" she asked.

"Do you know if this nuclear could make things glow? Did they have it in the United States?"

"Oh, Christ! Did they ever! The bloody Yanks were the ones who invented the shit!"

"Alaska was part of the United States. My mother showed me an old map once. My father died when I was three. He was very sick after hunting in a place everyone avoided."

"Oh. He was poisoned. So, you–"

"Was changed while still his seed?" He shook his head. "But I remember something about a seal . . . " His voice tailed off.

"Noah, will you make me do something?"

"What?"

"Make me do something I wouldn't normally do. I want to see what it feels like."

His feet stilled on the pedals and the baidarka slowly turned to the wind. The look on his face gave her goose flesh. She felt keenly aware of her nakedness under the bear hide.

"I will not do that," he said with a gasp. "Please, don't ever ask me that again!"

"Oh, I am sorry. I didn't mean to offend you."

The baidarka rolled to the side and Noah automatically corrected their drift. He told her about his life at Point Hope, how he met Thinker, about St. Lawrence Island, and about Marilyn.

CHAPTER 13

THINKER SWAM AWAY FROM THE ISLAND, heading into what he knew to be open sea. On the far edge of his senses, he felt a small thing carrying three beings. He turned toward it and maintained his speed.

Looa crossed his mind. The thought of her quickened his heart and he wondered if Naff knew of Thinker's excitement over his mate. By now the pod should be in the cold-feeding grounds, gaining great amounts of sustenance.

Thinker became aware of a new essence approaching from his heart-side flipper. He probed and found an insatiable hunger focusing on him.

He turned to the hunger, wondering what it could be. The thing closed on him quickly. Thinker sharpened his vision.

Teeth filled a huge maw, as large as a Supra. White, and big, it flowed through the water effortlessly, bent on sustenance. Thinker realized it was smaller than a whale, but incredibly large for a fish.

~If you come closer I will injure you.~

The creature increased its speed, its maw opening wider.

Thinker lanced into its tiny, ancient mind and willed it to turn. Abruptly the great thing turned and swam in a furious circle. A deep rage washed over the hunger.

~I will release you if you will go away from me.~

Thinker recognized the creature as an Eater. Humans called it a shark. Puzzlement settled over Thinker.

What drove the Eater to attack him? Usually they preyed on smaller beings, even humans. Thinker probed the tiny mind again, seeking memories.

He found only hunger and determination. Either the Eater had not taken sustenance in a long while or else its brain lacked a capacity for memory. Thinker released the turn command.

Instantly, the Eater rushed toward Thinker. He gave it pain and commanded it to reverse its course. It whipped in a tight arc and quickly disappeared into the gloomy depths.

Thinker fluked onward. He probed outward and once again found the small thing that held the three essences. He also probed after the Eater but found nothing.

He moved rapidly to the top of the world and breached into the storm. The thindrink, air, moved violently across the surface of the world. Thinker realized that the small thing must be a boat pushed by the wind — toward an island of large dimensions.

A small boat pushed by the wind. Thinker concentrated on the boat and surged through the world at his top speed. He wondered where Noah and Moira had found another human.

CHAPTER 14

I DID EVIL THINGS. I will never be able to atone for on St. Lawrence Island."

God, I guess not, Moira thought. "That *was* evil, Noah. But since I met you, you have been one of the kindest, most generous human beings I have ever known. People change. They learn from their mistakes."

His dark eyes seemed bottomless. "Do you really think so?"

"Of course. Definitely."

"Since then, I only look into the minds of others if they become a threat to me or–"

"Yes," she said gently, reached out, and touched his face. "I understand." The baidarka slewed to the side and she fell into his open arms. The bear hide slid down and she felt him tense.

She whispered, "Did you ever consider what it would be like to make love while guiding your lover mentally and experiencing her feelings at the same time?"

"You would be my lover?" The hope in his voice nearly brought her to tears.

"Yes. I would be happy to be your lover."

He hugged her tightly. "You are a dream come true!" he said with a laugh.

Suddenly her head felt full, painfully close to bursting. Noah stared fixedly at nothing, and she knew he felt it, too.

~¡Noah, Moira! Your boat is going to hit an island if you do not change direction.~

"Thinker!" Noah's face lit up like a Christmas candle. He went silent and she knew they were talking to one another. *How casually I accept this phenomenon*, she thought.

Noah's feet worked on the rudder pedals. The boat heeled

sharply to starboard, and Noah straightened it again. He laughed but the sound carried no humor.

He looked at her. "Any idea what islands are near?"

"On the ship, they said we were blowing towards Indonesia." His eyes clouded and she hurried to explain. "That's where M'halla came from originally."

"The Kingdom of Sunda." He tasted the words on his tongue. "Do you think they will be friendly to us?"

"Christ, I dunno. I've never been there. So many of these places are as bloody mythical to me as Never-Never Land!"

"Someday I would like to hear about that place," he said quickly. "But right now, we are very close to the shore. Perhaps you should put on some clothing." He pushed a bulky cloth sack at her.

The bear hide fell from her and as she rooted through the bag, she felt his eyes on her body. "I wish we had the time to make love before anything else happens," she said, giving him a quick glance.

"Me, too," he said with a sigh.

She found an old cotton shirt and a pair of thin caribou hide trousers and pulled them on. She smiled at him. "Fetching, no?"

The boat lurched sideways, and Noah stared through the dome and moved his feet in quick, violent kicks. "There are big rocks to get through!"

She peered out but could see only blackness and phosphorescent wave tops through the water-streaked plastic. "How can you tell where they're at?"

"Thinker." Noah frantically kicked the rudder hard to port. "Hang on!"

Moira grabbed the hatch lip. The baidarka slammed sideways into a rock and grated around it for an eternity.

"Jesus, one more of those and we're gonna be on the bottom," she muttered. Her heart pulsed in her ears, and she could smell sweat from both of them. The wind and water beat at the boat, keening around the dome-like one of her grandmother's banshees.

Distant thunder reached through the storm, and she wondered at the absence of lightning. The boat continued to rock and pitch violently. Curiously, she was more aware of her dry throat and mouth than the possibility of smashing into a rock and sinking.

"Gawd, but I'm thirsty."

Noah ignored her and kicked the rudder back and forth. The

boat slewed to the right and nearly rolled. Gear tumbled about.

Fear overcame her thirst. "We're going to crash into something, aren't we?"

"Yes," Noah said conversationally. "How did you know?"

The thunder swiftly magnified in volume, and she remembered the sound of waves on rock. She saw Deagan grip the rope and turn in the spray to confront Jik's knife.

"Noah, I love you!"

The baidarka lifted into the air and struck something much larger and harder than itself. The rear of the boat whipped around and this time it rolled. Moira braced herself, a wedge in the middle of the hull, but Noah flew into her and ended that.

Her head hit something hard and stopped the screaming she didn't remember starting. The baidarka smashed amidships into an immovable object and the wondrous work of technology found its limit.

The hull ripped open, and brine drenched them. Aluminum tubing bent and the beautiful smooth, painted wood flooring snapped against a huge, wet, rock fang. Moira focused on a distant light and then everything went black.

CHAPTER 15

THINKER VOWED TO PONDER THE RELATIONSHIP BETWEEN Noah and himself in terms of increased frustration on his part. Still, Noah once again had put himself at the mercy of the raging thindrink. *Didn't humans learn from their mistakes?*

The island, one of many together, bulked smaller than the one where-the-top-of-the-world-will-turn-to-rock. Thinker felt anxiety and fear from Noah and Moira. The third human, M'halla, no longer asleep, also radiated great fear.

Try as he might, Thinker could not perceive the danger encountered by the humans. He could experience the whirlpool of their minds, but not fathom what they saw. His surprise burst as completely as theirs when the boat hit the rock and broke.

The storm-driven waves threw the struggling humans far up on the shore. The water receded, pulling the broken craft with it. The three, having already lost small essence, continued to breathe. Thinker relaxed and allowed relief to wash over him.

He probed inward from the beach. Much life flourished there, human and other. Many ancient minds concerned only with appetite and hunger waited in dark places.

None became aware of his mental presence. Great animosity prevailed in this place. Most of the minds on the island had lost small essence; sleep, Noah called it.

Interestingly, as he mentally fluked, he came across three alert humans who stole through the night under the cover of the storm. They crept into an "enemy" village. Fear and hate struggled for dominance in their minds beneath the torrential downpour.

Thinker became entranced with their furtive journey. He sensed an underlying determination in all three, but the source of determination differed for each. Curious, Thinker picked one of the humans and drifted deeper into its mind.

She felt contempt for the men with her. However, the trap must be set. She felt herself an example that could not be matched by those with her, no matter how hard they tried.

Thinker puzzled at the concept, tried to compare it with the motivations that governed the Cea, yet could not. He compared this person with Noah and wondered at the extreme differences.

The three were part of a larger group set on vengeance. Thinker found it impossible to gain a clearer understanding of their motivations.

They entered the village. To him, the idea of a village felt confining and unwell. Thinker wondered if he could continue to return to the same small place to take sustenance and rest through many cycles.

They stopped near a dwelling in the center of the village. One man transferred his weapon to his other hand and tried to wipe rainwater from his palm. All three focused on the impending death of an old man inside the dwelling. They thought of it as a hut.

His death would sting the pride of the Hydra, proving that it wasn't invincible. Hydra?

Thinker probed the hut. Four humans slept unaware of the danger. He stifled his urge to warn them.

A part of his mind wondered about the urge and his willing suppression of it. What should he do? Did any human actions truly concern him? More ponderables.

The two men slipped into the hut, moving quickly toward sleeping forms. One of them accidentally kicked a wooden vessel hidden by shadows. Two of the sleepers roused themselves — a young man and the old man who was the prey.

The young man understood instantly and shouted as he grabbed a weapon. The first intruder hit him with a large knife (Thinker still comprehended it as a tooth) and severed his head from his trunk.

The old man struggled to his feet and with a spear, parried the first blow. The second intruder rushed to the old man's side and stabbed him through the chest, piercing his heart. The other two sleepers scrambled to their feet.

The first roused sleeper, a woman, rushed screaming for the door where the female intruder cut her down. The other inhabitant of the dwelling was a child. The men started to leave, but the woman hissed, "Everybody in this hut dies!"

The man closest to the child turned and raised his great knife. Thinker froze the man's arm muscles with such violence the radius bone snapped. *It feels good to protect the young of any species,* Thinker decided.

The man screamed out of the hut with his arm aloft, knife still clenched tight. The village erupted into uproar. The killers fled toward the storm-lashed beach where others waited for them, and toward Noah.

CHAPTER 16

A ROCK POKED NOAH'S RIBCAGE, disrupting his sleep. Consciousness flooded over him, and he remembered the storm and the boat wreck. Before he could open his eyes, Thinker filled his mind.

~You are in great danger. Men watch you who believe you killed three of their pod.~

Noah kept his eyes closed. *~How close are they?~*

~The length of my flipper.~

A few feet away. Noah reached out and touched a mind. Hate, an overwhelming hate, directed at him. A prodding fear lurked behind the hate. He slipped out of the mind and went to the next.

More of the same. Fifteen men blocked access to the island as they sat and waited for the three "murderers" on the beach to wake up.

~If they believe us to be murderers, why have they not killed us?~

~They wonder how you came to be asleep, and where your weapons have gone. They are not certain you are those they seek. The "benefit of the doubt" has saved you.~

~Thank you, my friend. I will speak to them now.~

Noah opened his eyes and pushed himself to a sitting position. He looked around.

Both Moira and Perrim still lay witless on a beach littered with relics of Point Hope. No trace of the baidarka remained. A group of dark men blocked access to all but the sea.

Noah willed his aches and bruises to cease and, by the time he gained his feet, he felt fine.

He smiled as he briefly looked into each face. "Greetings. My name is Noah, and I am a stranger here, as are my friends."

One of the three men with fiercely painted faces stepped forward. Yellow and black paint bisected his face, and his eyes held a light blue glow. "You speak Oz, but with a foreigner's tongue. You have lied with your first words!" The man pointed to M'halla. "That person is a Sunda. The Sunda are no strangers to us. They are the enemy!"

"The man is a stranger to me," Noah said. "I met him only this morning, ah, yesterday morning. I know nothing of him other than he wished to come with us."

"You met him in a Sunda village?" the man asked slyly. The blue glow intensified briefly.

"I met him on an Australian ship called the *Dawkins*. If I spoke too hastily, I ask your forgiveness. Although I don't know this man, he did arrive here with me and my woman."

"You arrived here in the night?" said a man with red and blue paint striping his face. Blue radiated from his eyes also. "You have not moved from this beach?"

"That is the way of it. Look around, did you ever see things like this on your beaches before?" Noah held his head high and swept his arm toward the flotsam from the baidarka.

"He lies. The sea throws up many things!" one of the unpainted men shouted. "Let us execute the murderers here!"

"No!" Red-and-Blue shouted back. "We will take them to the Hydra. They will find the truth." He stared at Noah. "Get your friends to their feet or carry them. We leave no one alive here."

Noah turned and walked toward Moira. He healed her cracked rib, slight concussion, and broken right arm by the time he reached her. Moira sat up as he knelt.

He saw the flash in her eyes, and knew he could depend on her. "They think we have wronged them. They wish to take us somewhere for trial."

Moira put her hand behind his head and pulled him to her. She kissed him on the mouth. Noah's mind wandered far before he could will it back again.

"Kick their arse, Noah," she whispered.

He pulled her to her feet. "I'm sorry. There are too many of them. They are not friendly like the people of the north."

Her facial muscles worked, and took on a determined aspect. "Not to worry. We'll bide our time."

"Get your friend up or we will kill him where he sprawls," Red-and-blue demanded. Noah cleared Perrim's mind as the man struggled to his feet.

"Dis ain't a good thing, Noah," Perrim said, looking around.

The dark men moved closer, pointing their spears at Noah's chest.

"Where do you take us and why?" Noah demanded.

The dark men halted. Red-and-blue scowled at him. "We take you to the Hydra because they demand it."

"But why–"

"Hurry, or we will only bring your heads back to our village!" Yellow-and-black shouted.

Noah and Perrim drew close to Moira. "What is this?" Noah asked the Malay. "Who are these people?"

Perrim kept his gaze on the dark men. "Dis not be a good thing. Doze mons belong to a witch."

"Oh, Christ, man," Moira snapped. "Don't tell him borack like that! Noah, this bloke's an ignorant savage. Witch, for gawd's sake!"

Noah looked hard at her. "I understand his world better than I understand yours." He glanced over at Perrim. "Besides, I've been called a witch, too."

Perrim's eyes widened, and he stepped back. "Don't hurt me. I do what you say."

"I won't hurt you. But we must go with them, or they will kill us."

The dark men separated into two groups. Five walked ahead of them with ten behind. They left the breezy beach and entered the jungle. Once into the trees, the hot, moist air hung redolent with cloying, rotten odors.

He carefully followed the dark man in front of him down a well-worn, narrow trail. The storm had passed but every leaf, blossom, and vine held water that, aided by his sweat, soon soaked his clothing. He pulled off his shirt and tied the arms around his waist.

Carefully he tried to probe the painted men. He couldn't gain purchase. His mental tendrils slid off their blue minds as if greased. Nor did they notice the attempt.

Noah trudged along the trail wondering if Thinker knew what had happened. He reached into an unpainted man and found him a normal human, full of fears, hopes, and sexual longings.

The man fiercely served someone who held great power over him. Oddly enough, he didn't have a firm mental image of his master. Complete serenity enveloped the warrior. The man felt himself protected from all harm.

In serving the Hydra he gained stature and wealth in his village. Someday he hoped to be one of the Chosen. The man glanced admiringly at Red-and-Blue. Noah withdrew and puzzled over the information.

CHAPTER 17

SIWA, THE NEW FIRST CHOSEN, felt the power build in his mind and knew the others must be close. The Hydra released its mental hold on him, and he nearly fell. He leaned on his spear and wondered how long it would take before all of this became second nature.

Tombé would barely blink when the Hydra left him. Now Siwa wore the official face paint. Still, when he looked into a mirror, his first thought was of his old friend.

With a surreptitious glance at the Hydra palace, he slipped out his small mirror and made sure his paint hadn't run because of his sweat. He admired the prestigious black band that started under one ear, looped up over his nose with its fine silver septum ring, and ended under the other ear. Paint as white as sea foam covered the rest of his face.

Only the Chosen could paint their faces.

Tombé had died unpainted, struck down by assassins in the night. Siwa wished he hadn't prospered because of his friend's death. Nonetheless, the Hydra must be obeyed.

Suddenly the palace sentries stuck out their spears in challenge position. Moments later the first of the returning war party stepped out of the brush into the village. Women and children hung back, waiting to see the captured killers.

Siwa tried to contain his astonishment when he saw the first captive. These weren't Sunda people. The woman was white! And the first man looked Asian, foreign.

The last man, conversely, could have lost himself in the crowd but for the clothing he wore. Motu, Third Chosen, stepped into the guard ring behind the prisoners. His blue and red paint showed smudges and runnels where sweat left brown streaks down his face.

"May it please the Hydra!" Motu dropped to one knee and bent toward the palace. The men in the hunting party pushed the prisoners down and dropped to their knees. "We have followed their wishes and captured the murderers of Tombé and his family." He stared at the ground and waited.

Siwa felt the sliding words in his mind, as did the others.

+These are strangers to us. They did not kill the servants of the Hydra.+

Motu's head snapped up and he stared at the palace, a stricken expression flashed across his face. "But the trail led to them! We—"

+Silence!+

Siwa's head rang from the force of the order. He felt anger building.

+Leave the strangers here. Find the murderers. Do not fail us again.+

The fifteen men scrambled to their feet and hurried back into the jungle. Two of the prisoners looked askance at the sentries. The foreign man stared fixedly at the palace. Siwa felt the Hydra return to his mind.

"Who are you? Why have you come to the Kingdom of Hydra?" it asked through his mouth. This still-novel sensation of being pushed aside in one's own mind made him nervous.

The foreign man shifted his gaze to Siwa. "Why do they not speak for themselves?"

Despite himself, Siwa blinked in surprise - *how did he know?* "Answer or you shall be killed!" Siwa's mouth shouted.

The woman stood. "My name is Moira Napier. Noah here," she nodded her head, "rescued me after I'd been shipwrecked." She smiled humorlessly. "Bloody lot of good it did. Here we are shipwrecked again."

The Noah person stood. "I am Noah Manaluk. I am a Tikeramiut Inuit from Point Hope, Alaska. The storm threw our boat against your island last night. We mean no harm."

Noah pointed to the Malay, who remained on his knees. "This is Perrim M'halla. He wished to escape from the ship he was on, as did we."

"Ship?" Siwa's voice asked.

"It was an Australian defense force vessel," Moira said, "called the Arnold something."

"The *Andrew Dawkins*," Noah said.

"Why did you wish to escape from it?" Siwa's mouth asked.

"We are free people and did not wish to go where they traveled," Noah said. "So, we left."

"This Alaska is an island?"

"It is part of a continent far from here." Noah frowned and Siwa could tell his patience dwindled.

"Why did you leave that place?"

"It doesn't matter. Also, it is none of your concern what I do with my life."

Siwa felt a perverse satisfaction waft through his mind. "You will not leave here until we are certain you had nothing to do with the deaths in our village last night. Follow me."

Siwa led them to the strongest hut in the village. It sat next to the palace. Four warriors stood equidistant around it; each could see two of his fellow guards.

Siwa pointed to the door and, as the strangers passed him, said, "Food will be brought to you. Do not try to leave or you will be killed."

When the Hydra slid out of his mind, Siwa felt like he had tripped while running. He staggered and nearly collapsed.

CHAPTER 18

Captain Tarant glassed the shore as the *Andrew Dawkins* steamed slowly along the coast of yet another island. The storm had blown itself out in the night and they started their search at first light for the fancy canoe and its occupants. His anger had evolved into a fierce determination to find Moira Napier and her pet Inuit.

This time they would stun the little rotter and keep him sedated until they made it back to port. There wasn't much he could do about Currie's derision.

"Captain!"

Tarant pulled the binoculars away and rubbed his eyes. "What is it, Bosun?"

"Seaman M'halla is missing, sir."

"That Sudanese bloke?"

"Yes, sir. We've searched the whole ship. 'E's gone."

"Did he have deck duty during the storm?"

"No, sir. I had 'im 'n Sweeney chipping 'n painting for the past few days. They was both below when we got into the storm."

"You think he's on that canoe?"

"Yes, sir." Stout cracked his knuckles. "That's exactly what I think."

"Nobody jumps my ship and gets away with it! Put all your off-duty men on binoculars. The first one to find sign of them gets an extra grog ration for a week."

"Aye, aye, Captain!"

Currie moved next to Tarant, and spoke in a low voice, "That's bloody convenient. Now you can claim you were tracking down a deserter when you find the Inuit again."

"Mr. Currie," Tarant said with a growl, "I told you to pack it in.

This is a scientific mission, and that rat bag is the biggest scientific find we're likely to make."

"No argument there. I just don't like the way you're trying to make him into a test animal, or a financial windfall."

"Your concerns are noted, Mr. Currie. Now get out of my way. I'm looking for a deserter." He raised the binoculars and resumed scanning the shoreline.

The executive officer was correct; the Inuit could turn into a financial windfall. For the first time in his life, he was in the right place at the right time. He wasn't sure quite how to make a fortune out of this discovery, but there would be a way.

"Wreckage! Bridge, this is the bow lookout. I see wreckage on the rocks at one o'clock!"

Tarant swung his glasses over, focused. The remains of the baidarka hung in a jumble of rocks, like a large fish being eaten by a mouthful of stone teeth. The framework lay broken and splayed, one end completely gone. The remaining sheathing flapped in the wind, tattered beyond redemption.

All the same, aluminum tubing costs more than gold these days, Tarant thought. "All stop. Drop anchor. All hands muster on the foredeck."

The orders sounded over the tannoy, and crewmen hurried to obey. Within minutes his entire crew, save for the engine room watch, stood in ragged ranks in front of the bridge deck. Tarant moved onto the starboard wing to address them.

"Bosun, take three men and retrieve what's left of that craft. I want seven volunteers for a landing party. You must be proficient with a firearm to be eligible."

Twenty hands shot into the air. Tarant smiled and began selecting.

CHAPTER 19

Thinker slipped through the blue-green depths and pondered the essence on the island. It carried an almost-familiar resonance. He compared it to the Blood-Essence of OnePod, but it wasn't quite the same.

Yet, it seemed as close to the Blood-Essence as the Supra were to the Cea. He sensed that the intelligence could be stronger if it didn't have to deal with a smaller, eclipsing essence that pulled constantly at its energy. Thinker shrugged mentally; one could only wait.

The presence of the ship full of humans puzzled the whale. He slipped into their minds and found three whose only thoughts were about Noah. Thinker ceased all motion, thoroughly engrossed in the memories each man held of Noah and Moira.

Excitement stirred him into action when he discovered that all the humans held high regard for Moira because she sang! Thinker quickly fluked to the top of the world and breached into the thindrink. The humans shouted in awe, but the few in the two small boats continued toward shore in their quest.

How to explain this to Noah? Thinker reached out, touched the Inuit's mind, found it agitated, angry, and worried.

~Noah. There are men who search for you.~ He felt the comfort his presence gave Noah.

~Thinker, where are these men? Are they like the ones in this village?~

~Some are the same, others different. They come in boats on the world.~

New agitation radiated from Noah. *~If these men bring us back to their boat, I will need your help to escape them. Will you please stay close?~*

~Yes. I will stay and help you in any way I can.~

~This is not a good place for me, my friend. Somehow I must go elsewhere, but I don't know where!~

~It shall happen. Be safe.~ Thinker broke contact. He could sense the men-in-boats getting close to where men-in-paint watched them. Thinker would witness the impending encounter.

CHAPTER 20

Motu watched the Oz man row their boats into the small inlet. How fine it would be for the village to own such well-built boats. One boat pulled away to the side, toward the point where the sentinel rocks guarded the cove.

With a practiced eye, Motu gauged the expanse of beach sand gleaming wetly in the midday sun. Yes, he decided, the tide was out enough for the rocks to be visible. What did these men want from the rocks?

The first boat continued into the cove and grounded on the sand. Only after they stepped onto the beach did Motu see the weapons they carried. This greatly changed the situation.

These Ozzies didn't kill Tombé in his hut last night, so they were not the quarry Motu and his warriors sought. Yet, these men had purposely landed on the Hydra's Island. Why, he didn't know. Did they mean to harm the Hydra or the people of the village?

The Ozzies spread out and searched through the debris left from high tide. Many picked up items and shouted in triumph. Motu recognized things Noah-Inuit said were from his destroyed boat.

Understanding swept over him. He stared at the ship sitting in deep water off the island. That was the *Andrew Dawkins* ship the Noah-Inuit and the woman spoke of, and those men on the beach wanted them back.

Would they fight the village for them? Would the Hydra allow the Oz men to take the prisoners? So many questions that Motu could not answer. What to do?

The Oz men spied the trailhead into the jungle, where Motu and his warriors hid. Motu made the sign to disperse, and the warriors blended with the leaves and grass. Moments later the eight Ozzies moved past them toward the village.

Motu glanced out where the other small boat had disappeared in time to see it moving back to the ship. Two men rowed while the other two held down the skeleton of a strange being. Motu wished he could get a closer look.

At the far side of the beach, where the jungle grass grew close to the water, something moved. More Ozzies? Three Sudanese stepped out of the high grass and peered after the Oz men.

Each carried a kris and glanced fearfully toward the ship. Motu understood at once that here was his quarry. They hid from the Oz men and the Hydra; they must be the ones guilty of crimes against the Hydra. Murderers.

A glance back at the trail revealed no sign of the Ozzies. Motu made a noise in his throat and instantly he and his warriors sped down the beach, silently running across the hard, damp sand. He gave thanks that the tide had traveled so far.

One of the Sudanese had his arm wrapped in plantains and tied around his neck. Motu felt satisfaction that someone had drawn blood for his village. The warriors closed to spear-throwing distance but kept running.

Finally, one of the Sudanese looked up and saw Motu and his men. The three turned and raced down a trail that wound through the jungle leading to the far end of the island.

Motu realized that one of the enemies was a woman and decided it must be Kallah, the warrior queen of Reborn Surabaya. No other woman on Earth would dare lead a raiding party this small.

He grinned fiercely. This augured for more than he had hoped! "Do not kill the woman," he shouted. "She must be given to the Hydra!" He tried to increase his speed, but the murderers lengthened their lead.

Motu felt the Hydra slide into the edge of his mind, watching, analyzing. The presence did not slow him nor throw him off stride. He felt pride that he could carry his master's presence and still function as a complete warrior.

Motu brought the memory of the Oz men to the surface and felt the Hydra absorb the intelligence. He continued racing down the trail. His heaving chest and taxed muscles suddenly lost their load of toxins giving him renewed vigor, and he increased speed.

+There is danger! More of the enemy await you!+ The Hydra tinged its message with panic. Motu threw his arm up and skidded to a stop.

Some of his warriors in the back didn't see his signal and ran into those ahead of them. Half of his men stumbled and fell over each other — saving their lives as a volley of arrows shot out of the jungle and into the warriors.

Before Motu could drop his hand, an arrow pierced the fleshy portion between his thumb and fingers. Still in the grip of the Hydra, feeling no pain, he pulled the arrow through his hand and threw it away.

Three of his men lay dead, three others were wounded but still able to fight. Some of his warriors carried spears in addition to their kris, but no bows. The only possible defense was offense.

"After them!" Motu screamed, and plunged into the jungle, his kris at the ready.

CHAPTER 21

Noah felt Captain Tarant's presence. "The people from the ship are here."

"Here?" Moira asked. "Are you sure, Noah?"

"I am in his mind now." Noah extended his mental touch. "There are seven others with him, including the doctor."

M'halla made a sign in the air between him and Noah while muttering under his breath.

"Are they going to attack the village?" Moira asked.

"They wonder if we are here or if they took the wrong trail."

"If the Hydra, whoever it is, has 'witch' abilities like yours, why aren't the natives attacking Tarant?"

"I don't know. It's as if the Hydra isn't aware of their presence."

"Maybe it can only see through the people it controls? Could that be it?"

Noah shrugged. "Again, I have no answer. I tried to look into the minds of the painted men, but it's like trying to penetrate rock. I can feel a great power in the large hut, two distinct essences, but I have no idea what the Hydra is like. I don't even know if it, or they, are human!"

"Y'know Tarant's looking for you." Moira spat on the packed earth floor. "Him and that wowser Doctor Carleson. Bloody bastards! They think they can get rich off you."

"I'd kill them first." Noah thought about killing them now before they had a chance to make this situation worse. For a moment he saw Jik's head explode again. But if he did that, the Hydra would know of his power. He thought it might be a good thing to gauge the power of the Hydra first.

Noah again tried to feel out the strength in the next hut but couldn't. He reached out to where Tarant and his men hid in the jungle, watching the village and waiting for events to unfold.

He entered the mind of a man named Woodruff. Woodruff hated being on the island, felt stifled and threatened by the jungle. He wanted nothing to do with the natives, fearing them even more than he did the jungle.

Fear dominated his life and the only reason he now hunkered in this steaming hell was because he feared Captain Tarant most of all. This hadn't been part of the deal. They were only supposed to land on the beach and hunt down some strange little Asiatic.

Noah disengaged, and then briefly touched the others. All held fear at bay, even Tarant. Interestingly, Tarant and Carleson feared a future without Noah to exploit. The others feared the present.

Noah sensed others near Tarant's men. He pushed his awareness farther out and found himself in the mind of a man who followed Siwa. The villagers were aware of Tarant and had flanked him and his men.

Noah pulled back, realizing the warriors prepared to attack the sailors. He turned to Moira and Perrim. "Get ready. Many things are about to happen."

CHAPTER 22

MOTU REALIZED HIS MEN WERE OUTNUMBERED but they fought like the tigers of myth. The enemy all wore the orange headband of Reborn Surabaya. Kallah directed their fighting.

Six Surabayans lay dead in pools of their own blood. Motu's men pressed the attack with their spears, which didn't allow the foremost enemy warriors to use their bows. The larger numbers of the enemy worked against them for the moment.

Motu asked the Hydra for more men in order to defeat the Warrior Queen once and for all. Suddenly Kallah yelled a command and the front rank of her warriors fell to the ground and the rear ranks fired another volley of arrows.

+*Down!*+ the Hydra screamed with Motu's voice. Two of his men fell, kicking as their lives flowed out through their wounds.

+*Retreat! We must retreat if we are to win!*+ the Hydra screamed.

"Throw your spears!" Motu shouted of his own accord. "Run!"

The sudden reverse threw the Surabayans off for a few precious moments as they dodged most of the spears. Three spears found orange-banded targets.

Motu's men knew the jungle like they knew their own huts. They spread out and filtered through the foliage, racing toward the village. The Hydra had alerted the Chosen in the band to a fight at the village. Word spread to the commoners quickly.

Some rued the fact they no longer carried their spears. Still, every man had proven his mastery of the kris as a rite of passage. They ran at top speed, leaving the Surabayans far behind.

CHAPTER 23

"Don't waste your bloody ammo!" Tarant shouted. "Make every shot count!"

The natives surrounded them. The six survivors huddled in a sinkhole no more than five meters across. He tried to ignore the slimy, fetid water soaking into his clothes.

Tarant lay behind the lip of the hole and squeezed off a shot at some painted heathen. The yellow half of the face abruptly bloomed red, and the man toppled to the ground.

Good, he thought. *That bastard was the leader.*

Suddenly a different warrior, face painted white with a black band running across the nose and under the ears, leapt up and shouted orders.

How many bloody chiefs do they have? he wondered.

The warriors charged from all directions. Woodruff panicked and tried to run. Three warriors cut him down with huge knives. Tarant dropped two of them and was aiming at the third, when something jumped into his peripheral vision.

He twisted in time to parry the spear thrust. But he couldn't duck the club next to it. His head exploded in stars.

Consciousness crept over him like a razor-clawed lizard. His mouth tasted like a dry bilge and his head throbbed mercilessly. There seemed to be no feeling in his arms and hands.

Had his spinal column been damaged? he wondered. Something stank horribly of feces and blood. He hoped it wasn't him.

Despite his better judgment, he opened his eyes a crack. Light flooded in and all but blew his fuses. The throbbing in his head escalated to fierce, stabbing agony. He whimpered under the onslaught.

"Cap'n!" Williams' voice bulged with fear. "You awake, Cap'n?"

Tarant tried to lick his cracked lips with his sticky, swollen tongue. "Water?" he croaked. His mind registered a low humming, and he realized a goodly number of people stood close by.

"No!" Williams said. "Don't drink what they give ya! The Doc did and he's catty-like."

Tarant swallowed with great difficulty and forced himself to open his eyes. "Catty? he croaked.

"You know, catty-something, like 'is mind's gone walkabout 'r something."

"Catatonic." Tarant looked around. A meter away to his left Williams hung by his wrists, which were tied to a trellis arrangement. His lower body appeared to be encrusted in filth. Tarant glanced down and found he shared the same predicament.

"What'd they do? Drag us through shit?"

"That pool we was in. Bad."

On Tarant's right Doctor Carleson hung from a third trellis and just past him hung Michelson. Michelson looked dead. Carleson, staring intently at the ground, seemed a few bottles shy of a carton.

He focused on the curiously quiet throng surrounding them. Most of them were brown, like old leather. But a few ranged from coffee-with-cream to tar.

Australia, like most of Oceania, was predominately dark tan or brown. Whites made up about thirty percent of the population. The only whites he saw here all hung by their wrists.

His head ebbed back to a painful throb. *Time to figure out the score.*

"Carleson, you among the living?"

The doctor stared at the ground.

"You look like you're on drugs, man."

A tall Malay with fancy face paint came out of the largest hut and walked up to Tarant. He held a gourd half full of liquid in one hand and a wicked-looking knife in the other. The liquid smelled like someone had dumped in every herb they could muster before pissing in it for luck.

"Forget it, mate," Tarant said, looking the man in the eye. "I may be thirsty but I'm not crazy."

Carleson's head jerked up and turned to face Tarant. His eyes looked muddy, and he spoke in a lifeless voice, "It would be a good thing if you drank this, Captain Tarant. Everything would become clear then."

"Right. Starting with your eyes, I suppose?" Tarant pulled his head back as far as he could from the gourd. "Bugger off."

The Malay lifted his kris until it pressed against Tarant's throat.

Carleson's eyes moved, and looked Tarant up and down. "You are in no position to argue. Drink from the cup of knowledge or die."

"Are you in there, Harald?" Tarant shouted. "Do you know where the hell you're at? What's going on? Talk to me like you didn't have pudding for brains, and I might consider the offer!"

The kris dropped to the Malay's side and he turned and walked back to the hut. Carleson's head flopped forward.

"Doc, can you hear me?" Tarant said loudly. "Or are you just some bloody puppet now?"

Williams coughed. "Cap'n, maybe ya should hold back a bit. You get their wind up and God knows what they'll do to us."

Tarant tried to laugh. "What they gonna do, take us prisoner and torture us? Don't you get it, you dumb sod? This is the end of the line!"

Suddenly the mob surrounding them all fell flat, outstretched arms and heads pointing toward the large hut.

"What the hell?" Tarant blurted.

Something moved in the shadowed doorway, and then stepped into the bright, sun-lit square.

"Ohmigawd!" Williams said.

Tarant felt faint. "Oh, that can't be real."

CHAPTER 24

Noah, sitting in the middle of the floor, recoiled in shock.

"What is it?" Moira asked.

"I was in Tarant's mind." He hesitated, trying to find words to describe what he saw. "The Hydra came out into the sunlight. It's, it's like nothing I have ever seen before."

"It's horrid, isn't it?"

He frowned at her. "How did you know?"

"It had to be. Nothing that bosses an island is going to stay hidden unless it's horrible to look at."

"You continually amaze me," he said in a soft voice.

"So, what does it look like?"

He looked through Tarant's eyes again. "Take two humans and put them together, leaving out a leg and two arms."

"What?"

"It has two human bodies," he swept his hand down across his own form.

"Torsos?"

"Yes, joined along one side. And two heads, two arms, and three legs. The middle leg is much larger than the other two."

"Oh, my word...."

"One torso is male and the other is female," Noah continued. "The female half is larger and stronger."

"Stronger, how?"

"Mentally. She has the superior mind of the two."

"How can you tell that, Noah?"

"The male half drools. His head is misshapen, and he drags his leg."

"She can read minds, like you and Thinker?"

"Not everybody's. Tarant thinks there's a correlation between the stuff the Malays made the doctor drink and the ability of the, the Hydra to make mental contact."

"What did they make the doctor drink?"

"I don't know, but those people out there think of it as a, a sacrament." Noah looked over at Moira. "I don't know that word, what does it mean?"

She quickly explained. "These people think that thing is a god."

Perrim spoke up, "Not god: witch!"

"Y' don't make sacrifices to a witch, you fool."

"You do to this witch!" Perrim frowned and lapsed back into silence.

Noah pushed between their words, "Anyway, Tarant won't drink the stuff. He's scared."

"Bloody hell," Moira muttered. "Who isn't? What's it doing now?"

"It's moving toward Tarant, looking into his eyes."

The Hydra launched into Tarant's mind, in a flash it discovered Noah's presence and, before he could withdraw, the Hydra smashed into him. It writhed in his head, clutching, scratching, and grappling with his very essence.

Far away he could hear Moira screaming, "Noah, my God! What's wrong? Noah!"

He held a psychic wolf at bay. Mental fangs snapped mere inches from his throat. He knew this thing could kill him if he dropped his guard for an instant. With his mind locked in defense, he couldn't answer Moira's frightened questions about his rigid physical state.

Another force slashed at the Hydra, breaking its grip on Noah. The Hydra tried to hold Noah and fight back at the new attacker simultaneously but couldn't muster enough energy. Just as the Hydra retreated from Noah's mind, he caught a flash of the new attacker.

Anticipating Thinker, he felt shocked when he realized it to be the Hydra itself!

CHAPTER 25

Motu and his men stumbled into the village, winded and bloodied. He immediately felt the unease of the village taking in the scene in the front of the palace with surprise.

Never in the memory of the Sulawesi had the Hydra emerged into the daylight. Only on the darkest nights would the God venture out. Until now only the Chosen knew of the Hydra's disturbing appearance. Only the Chosen could communicate with It. All of that changed this day.

Motu and the other Chosen tried to keep the villagers from looking upon God as it dealt with the Oz men. But, the spectacle pulled at their attention as well and they finally gave up. Let the curious watch. They were only human. If the God didn't want the villagers to see It, they would all be asleep no matter where the sun was.

Motu knew the Ozzie captain could not withstand the power of the Hydra. It would have been better if he had drunk the Water of Knowledge. Now he would give up his mind forever and be unable to function if the Hydra wasn't using him.

The man would die.

The male half of the Hydra suddenly flared into combat with His sister. He struck Her twice with wild blows before She hit Him in the side of the head. He lurched with the blow and lost His balance.

She followed through with Her punch and when Her brother fell, She couldn't stop Them. They fell in a tangle of limbs and wordless snarls.

Unable to change circumstances, Motu examined the Hydra dispassionately. He knew the mottled browns, blues, and reds on the God's body was not paint, but Its very skin. Only the Chosen could paint their faces to show their high station in life.

The female half possessed beauty in Her face and carried breasts worthy of any mother of warriors. But the male half made mockery of men — base, foolish, more beast than man or god. Motu knew it was impossible to keep the male decently covered.

The female smashed Her sibling into unconsciousness. She pulled Herself to Her feet and moved back into the palace, carrying Her brother like a sack of yams. Motu glanced at the limp Oz men, wondered where the Surabayans were, and what would happen next?

CHAPTER 26

Mᴏɪʀᴀ ꜱᴛᴏᴘᴘᴇᴅ ꜱᴄʀᴇᴀᴍɪɴɢ ᴡʜᴇɴ Noah ceased writhing and mewing. His wide eyes stared at nothing, the expression on his face matched the tense, muscle-locked condition of his body.

"Noah?" Moira's heart pounded in fear. Was he dead? Her life previous to meeting him seemed sedate and boring by comparison.

His body went limp, and his eyes closed. Sweat oozed from his pores. His chest moved rapidly in time with his panting.

"I. Almost. Died," he gasped.

"What happened?"

"I was in Tarant's mind." Noah's breathing slowed and he opened his eyes to stare at the roof. The Hydra came close," he held his hand at arm's length in front of his face, "and enveloped his mind. I didn't have time to slip out, or raise my defenses, or communicate."

He told her about the fight, and the mental teeth. About the sudden attack from another direction. "It was the other half of the Hydra," he said in wonder, "attacking itself!"

"It has two minds, and they're both –" Moira stopped, tried to puzzle it out. "That means it's twice as strong as you. Why aren't you dead?"

"They are twins who never completely separated before birth. They are two separate minds that, for some reason, cannot mesh or agree. If they acted together, they could rule the world."

Moira let the concept sink in. "If they — it — is fighting with itself, we might be able to escape."

She went to the door and glanced out. The guard wasn't at his post. Moira eased out and peered around the hut where it most closely bordered the jungle. Nobody.

She slipped back into the hut. The two men stared questioningly.

"Let's go. We can get into the jungle. That's a start."

Perrim scrambled to his feet and peered fearfully out the door. Noah reached out and took her hand. "You lead. I'll follow."

The day proved blinding after the dim hut. Moira retraced her route. Still, nobody between them and the jungle. She whispered, "Walk, don't run. We won't attract as much attention that way."

They nodded and, with her heart in her throat, she calmly walked toward the jungle thirty meters away. The story of Lot's wife suddenly came to mind, and she resolved not to look back and tempt fate.

Halfway. Perrim repeated a mantra over and over under his breath. Noah made no sound at all.

Ten meters. The urge to sprint into the dark foliage nearly overwhelmed her.

Only after both men followed her into the brush did Moira turn and look behind them. The Hydra looked like a brawl, fighting itself, thrashing about on the ground, while the villagers stared in fascination.

Captain Tarant and three of his men hung by their hands in the village square. Not for an instant did she consider going back for them. "Made their own bloody bed," she muttered to herself, "now let 'em die in it!"

Suddenly, dark forms rose out of the surrounding brush and pulled them down. A hand clapped over Moira's mouth before she could scream. Noah and Perrim thrashed briefly under the men holding them down.

"More Aussies?" a woman muttered.

Moira's eyes found the speaker. A lithe, well-built woman with muscular arms and legs. An orange band held her hair close to her head. She seemed to be the only woman in the group, but all wore orange headbands.

Perrim's eyes rounded when he saw her, twisted his head away from the hand over his mouth, and whispered, "Kallah! It is me, Perrim. Your brother!"

CHAPTER 27

THINKER FELT THE TENSION EBB IN HIS FRIENDS as they hid in the jungle. The whale had witnessed Noah's battle with the Hydra and tried to intervene. His attempt proved as futile as trying to travel with Noah on "land."

The Hydra seemed more formidable than OnePod. Thinker pondered on the similarity between himself, OnePod, the Hydra, and Noah. All had been born since the time of Burning World.

Try as he might, he could find no connection past that. They all came into being in places far removed from one another. Humans and cetaceans lived in entirely different worlds. Normal communication between them would be impossible, except for this singular ability.

Thinker fluked quietly under the waiting ship. A casual pass through a few minds aboard elicited much strife and near violence. When Noah emerged from the jungle, Thinker would make him aware of conditions.

He remembered Noah's admonition not to allow others to take Noah aboard the ship. Humans were stranger than anything he had encountered in his own world, Thinker decided. Their convoluted needs went far beyond sustenance and mating.

Even Noah, despite his own statements, wanted more than he needed. Thinker wondered why he hadn't followed Looa and Naff to the rich feeding grounds. Perhaps the moment had arrived when he and Noah should part.

Noah had a mate who valued him without prodding, and she sang! Thinker fluked alone. The need for his own kind, for the Cea, nearly overwhelmed him. He knew he could not linger alone much longer.

CHAPTER 28

"Perrim! What were you doing in their village?" Noah felt the woman's astonishment.

"What are you doing outside it?" Perrim asked.

"We were considering an attack, but they have too many warriors." She gave Moira and Noah searching looks. "Who are these people?"

"I'll tell you if we can get away from here," Perrim said, glancing over his shoulder.

Noah leaned over to him, and whispered, "One does not know these people."

"This is my sister, Kallah, the Warrior Queen of Reborn Surabaya," he hissed. I will make introductions later!"

They moved through the jungle until they came to the ocean. Two guards materialized and only then did Noah notice the canoes hidden in the tree line.

One of the guards smiled, pointed at Noah, and said something in a language Noah didn't understand.

"Speak Aussie," Kallah said sharply. "These are friends of my brother."

The guard saw Perrim. "Is it really you, Perrim? We thought you dead."

"B'Sou, my good friend!" Perrim and B'Sou embraced. Noah thought it odd that Perrim had not embraced his sister.

Perrim introduced Noah and Moira to Kallah and half a dozen of the warriors present. Noah didn't try to keep the names straight; there either would be time for that later or else it would not matter. Noah's mind still grappled with events at the village.

"Perrim, you have been in contact with those people before, haven't you?" Noah asked.

"Many years ago. Some of dem painted men come to our village. Dey say dey come in peace but dey got witch eyes and nobody would look at dem or talk wid dem. Dey say we must give presents to de Hydra or we will all die. So, we killed dem."

"Then what happened?" Moira asked.

"Why do you speak like a fool?" Kallah demanded.

"Because the Aussies expected me to, and it's a good way to hide," he said, raising his eyebrow.

"You needn't play the fool for us," Moira said.

"I didn't know that, then."

"What happened after you killed the Hydra's warriors?" Noah asked.

"We thought they had decided to leave us alone," Kallah said. "Then they struck at first light one morning, routed the warriors they didn't kill and carried off women and children."

"I understand why they took women," Moira said. "But why the children?"

Perrim shrugged. "Who knows?"

"Did they ever come back to your village?" Noah asked.

"No. We made more weapons and made every man train as a warrior," Perrim said.

"Now we have guards, day and night," Kallah said.

"Did you lose anyone close to you?" Moira asked.

"My wife died," Perrim said. "They took my little boy."

"Did you see him at the village?" Noah asked.

"No."

Noah felt old anguish radiating from the man and fell silent.

"What was the purpose of your raid?" Moira asked Kallah.

"To kill their warriors, of course. Especially the ones with painted faces. They're hooked to the Hydra."

"I knew that," Noah said.

Moira gave him a fierce glance. "You mighta shared your knowledge with Perrim and me!"

"There hasn't been time to chat!" He felt nettled, and realized he was hungry. He looked at Kallah. "Do you have anything to eat?"

Kallah motioned to one of her men and he pulled a bundle wrapped in leaves from one of the canoes, and handed it to Noah. Perrim and Moira crowded around.

"What is it?" Moira said eagerly.

Noah unfolded the leaves, saw meat on small bones and began to eat. Perrim grabbed a piece and began to chew.

"It's monkey," Kallah said.

Moira stared for a moment longer and then tore into a piece. Noah had never tasted anything quite like it before and decided it was good.

Noah licked his fingers. "What are you going to do now?" he asked Kallah.

"Go back to our village. We hoped to ambush and kill more of their warriors." She shrugged. "My dream was to kill the witch."

Noah locked eyes with Perrim who broke the contact, licked his lips and stared at the ground. Fear welled up in Noah and, like a thief, he slipped into Perrim's mind.

Perrim planned to tell his sister everything. Noah excised all memory of his abilities, left only a deep feeling of warm comradeship. He slipped out of the man's mind and found Moira staring at him, knowledge in her eyes.

"Only you need more warriors," Noah said.

"Will both of you help me fight the Hydra?" Kallah asked. If you agree, we will take you with us."

Noah and Moira exchanged a glance. Moira nodded. "We agree to help you." Noah smiled. "But neither of us are as good at fighting as you and your warriors."

"The Hydra wanted you for something," Kallah said. "That gives you value. Perhaps you can be used as bait."

"Bait!" Moira said. "Been a long, damned time since anybody called me that and got away with it!"

"Yes, I'm sure." Kallah stretched and read the light. "We should go now. There is just enough time to get into our home waters before dark. They won't follow until tomorrow."

The warriors pushed the canoes into the surf, and everyone scrambled aboard. Noah carefully maneuvered himself and Moira into a canoe without Perrim or his sister aboard.

Moira leaned against him. "What now?" she whispered.

Noah grabbed a paddle and helped the three warriors build up speed. "I'm not sure what will happen. But Perrim—"

"–doesn't remember much of anything," she finished with a smile.

The canoe with Kallah and Perrim closed to speaking distance.

"One thing I've been wondering about?" Moira said.

"What?" Noah scanned the horizon.

"Do the Hydra people have boats?"

"Oh, yes!" Perrim said. "They have many boats on the other side of the island."

"We're close to their harbor, aren't we?" Noah asked.

"Yes. How do you know this?"

Noah used his paddle as a tiller and his canoe began to turn. "Because here they come."

A flotilla of canoes emerged from behind the island, moving fast, bearing down on them. The Surabayans paddled furiously back the way they had come.

"How many canoes?" Moira shouted, paddling madly.

Noah glanced back. "Ten that I can see."

The Surabayans had six canoes with five people in each. The Sulawesi canoes carried six warriors in all but the Hydra's canoe.

"Noah, the only place we can go is the bloody ship!"

"It might be good to talk to them," Noah said. "But we do have one other option."

"We're outnumbered! How could–, oh, right. I forgot about Thinker."

"What is Thinker?" Perrim shouted from his boat.

"A friend you wouldn't believe," Moira said. "Noah, I think we should try the ship first."

"Okay." He took a deep breath, and released it. "Let's go talk to them."

CHAPTER 29

"MR CURRIE! WE GOT COMPANY OFF THE PORT BOW, SIR!"

Currie jerked out of his light doze and strained his eyes in the indicated direction. He expected to see Tarant returning triumphantly with Moira Napier and Noah Manaluk trussed up like chook for dinner.

The six native canoes gave him a distinct shock. His shock doubled when he spied Moira and Noah in one of the canoes. *Where the hell were Tarant and the men?* he wondered.

"Get some more armed men out here," he said to the watchman. "Fetch the Bosun and be quick about it!"

"Aye, aye, sir!" The man hurried away.

The Executive Officer hurried out onto the wing and looked down into the canoe holding Noah, Moira Napier, and three evil-looking blokes who had to be from the neighborhood. Five other canoes hugged the ship. Perrim M'halla sat in one of them.

"Where is Captain Tarant?" he shouted at Noah.

"I must come on board and speak with you." Noah peered up at him with a strange expression on his face. *~Do not let these people know of my abilities. They would kill Moira and me.~*

Currie nearly collapsed in surprise. "I–, is that really you, Manaluk?" he whispered.

~Yes. Allow me to come aboard. I have much to tell you.~

Currie collected himself and glanced around at the armed crewmen now lining the bulwark. None of them heard it, he realized. "Okay, drop the Jacobs ladder, Bosun. Let Mr. Manaluk and Mrs. Napier come aboard."

The dangerous-looking woman in the canoe with M'halla didn't like that idea, but she didn't object. Currie wondered who the hell she was.

Noah scrambled up the ladder and hurried over to Currie. "Please pay close attention." He sounded out of breath. *~We must work together, or all is lost.~*

Currie learned of the Hydra, of Carleson's conversion, and the attack on Tarant. *~If you treat us like human beings, I will work with you to understand my abilities. But I will not be used as entertainment or for personal profit. You must decide quickly.~*

"What's the rush?"

"Look!" Moira snapped.

Currie looked where she pointed. Ten large canoes moved toward them at speed. He inspected the occupants through his binoculars.

"I don't know what to do here, Mr. Manaluk. Y'see, Captain Tarant is in one of those canoes!"

~He has been taken by the Hydra! You cannot trust him.~

"I'm to take your word for that? How do I know you're not lying?"

~I have a plan...~

"Okay, let's hear it."

CHAPTER 30

Thinker moved beneath Noah's tiny boat, keenly aware of the enemies on either side of his friend. He thought it unusual that the Tarant human would bring the Hydra with him. Thinker tried to scan the strange being but once again duplicated the results of probing rock.

Of his own accord, Noah and all his friends climbed on the ship. As a precaution, Thinker made it a practice to push out as far as possible with his mind. It had become second nature.

Now he picked up a familiar presence. The great white eater swam swiftly toward him. Thinker pushed into its ancient mind, and told it to go elsewhere.

The tiny mind proved impervious to him. The shark neither slowed nor deviated from its course.

CHAPTER 31

Currie couldn't shake his feeling of unease. For one thing, he wasn't sure if he, himself, had agreed to Noah's plan, or if Noah had made him think he had. Bloody confusing no matter how you cut it.

On the other hand, dealing with the Inuit was a relief after Tarant's highhandedness over the past few days. Unfortunately, in a matter of moments, he would have to deal with both at once.

Noah and all his little brown friends had scrambled aboard. Their canoes sat tied together next to the ship's remaining launch. The blokes with Noah readied their bows and arrows. Currie felt ill; this seemed a lot like mutiny.

The Hydra canoes fanned out as they approached the *Andrew Dawkins*, forming a semi-circle as they came to a stop.

Tarant looked up at Currie with glowing-blue eyes that sent shivers through the executive officer's soul. "Drop the ladder. I wish to come aboard."

Currie slowly surveyed the ten canoes. Men of various shades — he had no problem with that. Men with barbarously painted faces — that gave him pause. The thing, things? in the canoe with Tarant and Doc Carleson — reminded him of nightmares which remained unsettling long after one awoke.

The creature looked like something the fictitious Dr. Frankenstein might have created under the influence of a gin and cocaine hangover. A large, paisley-skinned female welded to the side of a smaller male. Currie's mind marveled at the wonder of Siamese twins, but from there the creature turned into something troubling in the extreme.

The female regally half braced herself, wild black hair framed a face that under other circumstances would have been considered handsome, with a colored swath of cloth covering her body. Her dark eyes burned up at them with obsidian intelligence. Here, Currie knew, lay the brains of the outfit.

The male's head was misshapen, as if made from a clump of clay of which someone had discarded a fourth of the mass. The back of the skull sagged in under dark, spiky hair. The mouth hung open, loose lips drooling saliva. The dull eyes flicked over its surroundings without recognition or cognition.

Brother and sister each owned a perfectly formed arm. However, her right and his left shoulder looked to be a single bridge of bone tying them together. Their posture in the canoe revealed that each owned a normal leg. Their other leg looked like something fused together with great heat. It bulked massive with what seemed to be a four-part knee. Currie wished he could see the foot.

The male half didn't have on a stitch and he constantly toyed with his semi-erect penis. Currie briefly met the female's steady gaze and felt pity. *Talk about a cross to bear*, he thought.

And why did Doc Carleson sit and stare at the water like some druggie bindle in an opium den? Currie's gaze, despite himself, went back to the thing(s) with Tarant.

His nature warred with itself. On one hand he had devoted himself to science, eager to learn anew of what his world offered. But he was also the wild-haired, redheaded boy who listened with more fear than skepticism to old Aboriginal men who warned of mind-eaters from beyond the stars.

Something had altered Captain Tarant. His manner seemed wooden, forced. His command presence, so often simultaneously resented and admired, had gone walk-about.

The shell of the man Currie knew sat in the canoe and demanded without conviction, "Drop the ladder. I wish to come aboard."

Currie pursed his lips, finally believing Noah and Moira. "I can't let you do that, sir. In my opinion, it would place the ship and crew in jeopardy."

Doc Carleson's head jerked up, like a poorly manipulated puppet, Currie thought. "You must obey the captain. It is the law." His once-trim beard, now sodden with spittle and drool, resembled second place in a rat fight. His eyes were those of a man who had stumbled into hell and bartered his soul in order to escape.

Currie, shaken by the doctor's appearance, let his hands fall behind the steel bulwark, out of the sight of the people in the canoes, and gave his men thumbs down. Instantly the length of the ship bristled with gun barrels as the crew aimed at the canoes.

The Malays on board were only too happy to present nocked arrows in their bows.

"I will allow only Captain Tarant and Doctor Carleson aboard this ship," Currie said. "Any other attempt to board will be repulsed with deadly force."

Carleson's head dropped to his chest as he sagged back into the canoe. Tarant's glowing blue eyes looked past Currie at Noah. "He is the one you should refuse."

Noah edged up to the rail and stood beside Currie. "Now you see what I mean, don't you?"

"'Fraid so," Currie muttered. "Can we get them back?"

"I don't know. Before the eruption we encountered Orcas who were possessed…"

"And?"

"They could not free themselves of the essence."

"Bloody wonderful. How am I going to explain this to the Admiralty?"

In unison, the paddlers in all ten canoes dipped their blades into the water and pushed back from the ship. Tarant's head dropped as if nodding off. The female-thing shifted her gaze to Noah, and to Currie's astonishment, the Inuit collapsed on the deck.

CHAPTER 32

Tʜɪɴᴋᴇʀ ᴛᴜʀɴᴇᴅ ᴛᴏ ᴍᴇᴇᴛ ᴛʜᴇ ꜱʜᴀʀᴋ. He felt Noah's plight and knew his friend needed help. But Thinker faced challenge in his own world.

The new thing he had learned since meeting Noah -anger- ran through him. He had turned the great eater before. This time he would make sure the creature remembered its mistake.

Thinker attempted another thrust into the shallow brain of the shark and received a stunning psychic blow. His mind reeled as mental jaws closed on it. Thinker summoned all his strength and fought back, trying to escape.

Dimly he became aware that Noah fought the same battle but from a different source. The shark closed on Thinker and tore a great chunk out of his left flipper, next to an old wound from the fight with OnePod. Blood swirled from the wound but the pain in his mind far outweighed the physical injury.

Thinker realized he must concentrate on the shark, forget Noah and the humans, if he wished to live beyond this visit of the warm eye. He fluked strenuously upward. He needed thindrink to make his escape.

The whale breached into the warm day, filling his lungs as he rose above the surface of the world, then slammed down, sliding immediately into a deep, abrupt dive. The shark followed, but Thinker pulled away, fluking for his life into the darkening depths.

The shark hurtled after Thinker, unblinking and tenacious in pursuit.

CHAPTER 33

Noah fought for his life. Not even OnePod and Jik in combination had so quickly and thoroughly bested him. The mental bands gripping his mind remained as unyielding as the steel deck on which he writhed.

A small part of him wondered how this creature came to be so powerful. He also wondered why Thinker hadn't come to his aid. Abruptly the luxury of thinking about anything other than the Hydra evaporated.

The hold on his mind became solid, starting to pull at his hopes, his fears, and his desires. Noah realized it sought entry as a first step in domination. A trick his brother once taught him floated through the back of his awareness.

The trick was used for physical altercations, but....

Noah dropped his defenses and felt the Hydra pour into him. He smelled blood. Self-assuredness, monolithic hubris, and complete conviction of actions, all washed through him in a flood of sensation and emotion.

To his inua's horror, his appetite mirrored the Hydra's mental image! His inua flooded his appetite with reproach and rationality, confusing both appetite and Noah as a whole.

The Hydra onslaught arrested itself, paused, and rushed away, leaving him with a lingering sense of paranoia and fear of entrapment. The Hydra released him. Noah relaxed his rigid muscles and lay on the deck for a moment, spent.

"Noah!" Moira screamed. "For the Redeemer's sake, what the hell is happening?"

Noah pulled himself up and stared down at the Hydra in the canoe. The male half swung wildly at his sister, a crazed expression on his witless face.

"I understand!" Noah exclaimed. "When she uses all their power, it over-stimulates his damaged brain, sends him into a rage, and he attacks her. He is the inua and she is the appetite!"

"What are you talking about? Moira asked. "Just be glad they can't work together." She stared in fascination.

Noah felt panic that wasn't his own. "Thinker?" he muttered.

"What's wrong, Noah?"

"Something's wrong with Thinker. He's being attacked."

"Who's thinking what?" Currie asked.

"What are you doing?" Kallah asked.

"Is it the Hydra?" Moira pressed.

Noah entered the mind of his friend, spent the necessary nanosecond to understand the situation, and immediately struck at the shark. His mental blow stopped the shark, but not in the way he intended. Now the shark became aware of Noah.

The Hydra female hunched her common shoulder and, at the same time, struck down with her head, knocking her twin senseless. Suddenly an intense blue beam of light burst out of the water and enveloped the Hydra. One of the Malay paddlers accidentally touched the glow. With a sizzling snap and a scream, he was thrown completely out of the canoe, dead and limp.

"What the bloody hell?" Moira said.

"It's the shark!" Noah babbled. "I made it aware of us! It's trying to link—"

The blue beam arced across from the Hydra and enveloped Noah. Like the Hydra, he went rigid. His mind felt drawn out in a thin line, beaten from raw ore into something incredibly refined and pure. Something overpoweringly painful and deadly.

His appetite rejoiced while his inua tried to scream.

CHAPTER 34

MOIRA EDGED AWAY FROM NOAH. The Malay paddler floated in the water, face down and still. It wouldn't do to touch whatever that was surrounding Noah.

"What the hell is happening?" Currie demanded. Moira detected fear in his voice.

"You went looking for new phenomena," Moira said, unable to mask her bitterness. "Well, there it is. Now, what are you going to do with it?" She stared at the glowing line of shimmering blue stretching between Noah and the Hydra.

"It looks like raw electric power," Currie said. "Maybe we can ground it."

"This is witch stuff!" Kallah said with an air of discovery.

Moira nodded at the dead paddler. "Just make sure it doesn't ground you."

"Bosun! Lower the cargo shackle so it disrupts that beam."

"Aye, aye, sir!" Bosun Stout hurried to the controls. In moments the shackle descended toward the blue light.

"Take your hands off the controls!" Currie shouted. "It's almost there."

The cargo shackle, a forty-kilo mass of steel construction, slid smoothly down and bisected the line of blue energy — and exploded like a grenade.

Everybody tried to dodge the pieces of metal, but one seaman silently dropped in a mortal heap, and two Malays fell screaming to the deck.

Blue fire ran up the steel cable and whipped down the cargo boom. Bosun Stout jumped away from the controls before the panel absorbed the final charge and blew into bits.

The energy beam abruptly vanished. The Hydra collapsed in the canoe. Noah finished his scream and went limp on the deck.

CHAPTER 35

SIWA, FIRST CHOSEN, FELT THE HYDRA'S GRIP tingle from his mind. Motu, Third Chosen, glanced around and regarded the Hydra slumped between them in the canoe. The two Oz men lay loose-limbed next to the Hydra.

"What now, First Chosen?" Motu asked.

Siwa glanced around at the other canoes. Nearly every man from their village stared back at him, fear shining in their eyes, waiting for his orders. Their enemies waited above; bows drawn.

"We stay here with the Hydra," he said to Motu. "But the rest of you go back to the village. It is on my head if there is punishment," he nodded at the now-stirring Hydra.

Roka, Fourth Chosen, waved his paddle, and cried, "Follow me, warriors of Hydra!"

Siwa saw Motu's shoulders slump for a moment as their people paddled away. He wanted to tell his friend of his conviction that this would be the last day they served the Hydra, but at that moment the Hydra regained full consciousness.

+You have overstepped yourself! The punishment for that is death!+

Siwa felt pressure build in his head. He experienced no pain as a great dizziness set in and his vision grayed toward darkness. He heard a roaring he felt sure didn't originate outside his mind. The stench of blood suffused him, and he hoped to die quickly.

The pressure vanished along with the roar and the stink. Siwa thought himself dead but realized he wasn't. He looked up at the Hydra. It stood stiffly, precariously balanced in the canoe, staring into the water. The blue aura hummed into being around it.

CHAPTER 36

Currie pulled his attention from the Inuit and watched the Malay canoes break away from the ship. *Nothing unified or measured about them now*, he thought. Only the canoe carrying the monstrosity, the captain, and the doctor, remained near them.

The Hydra pushed itself upright. The female half stared into the water. As if in response, the electric glow snapped around it. Currie quickly moved away from the Inuit, but the glow didn't arc across to the ship.

"It's coming from the ocean!" he said.

"What?" Moira looked away from Noah, in time to see the Hydra jerk upright in the canoe and step into the water. "Why'd it do that?"

Currie saw the huge white form shoot through the ocean. "It wasn't the Hydra making the electricity," he shouted. It was that!" He pointed at the meter-high dorsal fin slicing the surface, arrowing toward the immobile Hydra.

The electric glow surrounding the shark and the Hydra resembled a generator field collapsing in on itself as the distance between them closed.

"That's the biggest bloody shark I've ever seen!" Moira yelled.

The canoe pulled away from the Hydra. The Malays paddled furiously, glancing over their shoulders. Currie wondered if they should get the *Andrew Dawkins* away from this place. But morbid fascination pulled at him — he wanted to know what happened. He wanted to see.

The Malays on board shouted with excitement. One shouted, "It is Omrah, the Death God!"

The shark hit the Hydra and veered away. Blood spread cloud-like around the creature. The Hydra broke the surface and they clearly saw the ripped flesh where the male head and right shoulder had been.

As they watched, the female struggled to stay afloat. The wound congealed before their eyes and the female, alone for the first time in her life, shrieked at Siwa's canoe now fifty meters away. The head of the Malay in the stern exploded. The headless torso fell to the side and the canoe capsized, throwing Tarant, Carleson, and the other Malay into the ocean.

The female's shriek pierced Currie's brain and he fell to the deck in agony, dimly aware that the others on the ship felt the same pain.

The shriek came again, commanding, strident, a wordless demand for help — then abruptly cut off.

The pain vanished and Currie scrambled upright, staring into the water. The cloud of blood spread like smoke from an explosion. No other sign of the Hydra remained.

Tarant, Carleson, and the other Malay had disappeared.

"Bloody hell!" Moira said thickly. "They didn't have a chance."

"They deserved it!" Currie's vehemence surprised him, but he felt an overwhelming conviction that justice had been done. "Both of them would have done disgusting things!"

He saw the great white shark just below the surface, hanging in the blood cloud. He'd never seen a shark stop like that, become immobile. He didn't know they were capable of inaction.

Moira peered at it. "What's it do—"

Blue energy hummed out of the water and snapped down over the comatose Noah, who jerked like a frog in a laboratory experiment.

Understanding blossomed in Currie. "It took the Hydra's power and made itself stronger! Now it wants Manaluk!"

"No," screamed Moira and started toward Noah.

Currie grabbed her and wrestled her away from the humming, blue horror. "Don't, missus. It'll kill you," he said with a gasp. The blue deepened in intensity; he felt his body hair rising from his skin.

"It'll kill him!" Moira sobbed. "He's exhausted. What'll we do?"

"Can we shoot it, Mr. Currie?" Bosun Stout yelled, caressing the trigger on his machine gun.

"We daren't interfere or it'll kill us. You saw what it did to those blokes." Currie looked away from Noah and saw the eyes of the shark glowing like the firebox of a steam turbine. Then he perceived movement beneath the shark. "Get back!"

Currie violently pulled Moira away from the bulwark and let her momentum carry them both across to the edge of the deckhouse. But they still saw the shark burst out of the water, slammed from below by the Humpback whale that also erupted from the ocean.

The whale snapped its great head backward, lofting the shark over the railing and toward the foredeck of the *Andrew Dawkins*. The whale fell over backward into the water and disappeared in a great spray. The shark writhed and twisted as it flew toward them, trying to gain purchase in the air.

Currie's scientific mind noticed the energy cessation when the whale hit the shark, wondered if the monster would land on Noah. While the half-formed thoughts buzzed about his brain, Moira broke free and covered the distance to Noah in a heartbeat. She dived onto him, grabbing with her hands and clenching her knees around him, and rolled them both out of danger.

Another heartbeat and the great white shark crashed down on the steel deck, smashing two awe-struck Malays into broken slime. Currie's quick estimate put the beast's length at ten meters and three to four meters in diameter. The ship rolled ten degrees from the shock of the landing.

The shark slid across the deck and fetched up against the Samson post that provided the main support for the cargo boom. The post snapped off like a twig. The monster lay stunned, gill clefts bellowing in and out.

"Shoot the bastard!" Currie screamed at his staring men. "Kill it!"

The ship erupted in gunfire. The Malays shot arrows into the being they regarded as a god. Nearly every crewman poured bullets into the shark as fast as they could operate their weapons. Bits of skin and flesh ripped out of the animal, spraying blood across gray-painted steel.

Currie felt intense relief at their ability to stop the beast.

Suddenly the shark writhed violently, and slid away from the Samson post across a deck lubricated by human blood. Actinic beams flashed from its eyes, hitting crewmen and Malays who wordlessly crumpled to the deck. One crewman fell soundlessly into the sea not far from the floating Malay paddler.

Currie searched for something to stop it, as a feeling of helplessness and inadequacy suffused him. The remaining crewmen took cover and continued firing into the shark. Moira pulled Noah behind the windlass in the bow. Currie saw the Inuit shake his head, reminding him of a wet dog.

The shark lasered a crewman on the bridge wing and the man fell, landing headfirst on the main deck in front of the executive officer. He looked up at the mast, concentrated on the straining metal cable anchoring the demolished Samson post. On either side of the ship, a large bolt secured each cable to the blast shield of the bridge. If the support cables were cut, the steel mast would fall with great force directly on the shark.

"No time to lose," he muttered, racing up the ladder to the bridge. Currie kept low behind the blast shield as he hurried across to the first shackle. Bosun Stout crouched at the far side of the bridge, shoving a fresh clip into his machine pistol.

"Stout! Belay that. Bear a hand!"

"Sir!" The Bosun stuck the weapon in his belt and hurried over. "What needs done, sir?"

Currie quickly explained. "You take the port shackle and I'll get this one. We must pull them at the same time, or the mast will miss that bastard."

"Aye, aye, Mr. Currie. You tell me when to pull it free."

Currie leaned over the blast shield and grabbed the bolt, pulled.

The taut cable levered against the bolt. *For all practical purposes the damned thing may as well be welded,* he thought. His eye fell on the fire axe secured in its clips under the windscreen.

Bosun Stout already had the other fire axe and was hammering steadily on his bolt. Currie attacked the starboard bolt. The shark moved more slowly now, but its eyes still glowed with unholy, deadly fire.

Currie pounded the bolt upward. Bright metal gleamed from the curling gouges peeled off by the shackle housing. He had two inches to go on the ten-inch bolt. He glanced over at Stout.

"Bosun, how much you got left?"

"'Bout a thumb's worth."

"Knock the bastard free!" Currie slammed the back of the axe under the bolt, and it shot into the air. Miraculously, both cables whipped up as one.

The mast shuddered. With the snap of shearing bolts, it fell forward. In one blurred motion it smashed down and crunched through the heavy cartilaginous spine of the shark.

CHAPTER 37

Noah WILLED HIS HEAD TO CLEAR just as the steel mast crashed down above them. The windlass and the bulwark kept them from being smashed into the deck. He peered over the top of the windlass at the shark on the other side.

The mast would have completely severed the beast if it hadn't hit the obstructions forward. A feeling of great futility from the shark washed over Noah. It hovered near death.

Suddenly Thinker entered his mind. *~It dies. Dare we look into its mind?~*

~We must, Noah answered. *At the very least, I must.~*

~Let us enter together. It may yet be dangerous.~

Noah responded with a mental nod, and they slipped into the shark's mind.

A burning sensation raced through their nervous systems. They both came under attack! Something alien, malevolent, and twisted bored and slithered into their minds.

~The shark is only a host!~ Thinker managed before lapsing into silence, grimly fighting the slippery mental tentacles.

~Like OnePod!~ Noah felt his defenses straining against phantom claws, losing chunks of final barriers to mental teeth. No matter what advantage Noah gained, the essence would shift, change, slide around and attack him from a new angle.

"Noah? Now what?" Moira cried.

"Parasite!" he gasped. "Strong." He had to tell her. If he and Thinker fell prey to this thing the others had no hope of escape — unless... "Must, kill me, if—" The essence smashed into his last barrier, a tidal wave flooded his mind. "—it wins!"

CHAPTER 38

Moira instantly realized that if there was something in the shark that could best Noah, the rest of them didn't have a chance. She screamed up at Currie on the bridge, "Throw me a gun, now!"

Bosun Stout tossed his machine pistol in a high arc, and she caught it firmly in both hands. Moira knew how to handle weapons. Everybody in post-Fall Australia knew weapons. She snapped a round into the chamber and clamped the pistol hard against her side, pointing at Noah.

"Okay, dammit! Who the hell is in there?"

Noah's eyes glowed like heat lightning. His legs trembled and he grabbed the bulwark with one hand. His head tilted back, and he grinned like a nightmare.

~Kill this creature if you will - its blood and my being will feed the leviathan. But allow me to answer your question.~

"How the hell can you be so loud?" Moira asked, wincing and pulling away from "Noah."

~Power unimagined by your puny species. Power that is now concentrated in force sufficient to summon the scattered pieces.~

Moira tried to hold her fear at bay, felt her sweaty finger slipping on the trigger. Knowing she had to kill this strange man she loved because whatever was in his mind suddenly was more than she could handle. "You're not making much sense, fuckwit!" she snarled.

Its laugh nearly sent her over the side. *~I am whom your parents worship, that whom the peoples of these islands worship. I am death. Destroyer of worlds.~*

"Church of the Rock? The Great Hunter?" she whispered. "None of that is real," she shouted. "That's all crap to scare kids and push people around so some bloody flannel-mouth can get their hard-earned money. Think of a new one, mate, 'cause that one's all used up!"

She felt amazed at her audacity, never completely realizing her depth of loathing for the religion that had warped her parents and robbed her of a childhood.

~I crossed the void to this oasis of mental quick. All would have been mine long ago had not your energy weapons shattered my vessel, fragmenting my power. Lesser creatures absorbed my essence, became knowing in ways they could not comprehend, carried power they knew not how to use.~

"Jesus," Moira muttered. "You were in the asteroids that hit the Earth. You were trying to kill us even then!"

~Not destroy - awaken. All would have become a single entity — all will become a single entity! A oneness superior to all things. A union of all life, unstoppable and undying.~

"Not while I can do anything about it!" Moira squeezed the trigger. The weapon suddenly burned her hands and she dropped it, looking down to see it glow a dull red and slag into a useless puddle of junk as the gunpowder in the ammunition fizzed and burned.

She looked back at Noah, wondering if the thing in him would kill her now, knowing it wouldn't matter anyway.

His eyes clamped shut and he grabbed his head with both hands, as if keeping it from flying away.

~You cannot—~

He stumbled and fell to his knees.

~How can this be?~

"Noah?" Moira said hopefully. "Are you still in there?"

"Make the boat—" Noah's voice sounded distant, strained.

~I will not allow—~

"South," Noah gasped. "Make us go south."

~You cannot leave! I will have—~

"Mr. Currie!" Moira yelled. "We need to get away from here. We have to go south, right now!"

"Whatever you say, Miz Napier! Bosun, drop the anchor chain. We'll never get the damn thing up with the mess the windlass is in."

"Aye, aye, Mr. Currie."

"To the canoes!" Kallah shouted.

Malays shot over the side of the ship and dropped into their boats, hurriedly jerking their lines from the whaleboat cable. Boats Stout bellowed to three of his men to get the whaleboat out of the water. The Malays paddled away from the *Andrew Dawkins*, pausing to stare back at the ship. Perrim rubbed his head, spoke to his sister.

~Make him return! Make him—~

Noah suddenly dropped his hands, stared at Moira with his own anguished eyes. "It's still in there," he said, touching his head. "Part of it is what I have always called my 'appetite.' But I can control it. Over all this time, I learned how to handle it."

"Can Thinker contain his part?" she asked.

Tears glistened down Noah's face. "Thinker has gone. He went north. We cannot be together. Being close gives this thing too much power, what it called 'critical mass.' It uses us."

"Oh, Noah." Moira felt her own tears. "How horrible for both of you, to carry so much force, yet—" She knelt and hugged him to her, knew there would be no real alternative to living in Australia. Maybe he would like New Zealand, the South Island.

No matter where, she would happily be at his side.

Noah staggered upright.

"Captain Currie, we must hurry."

"To do what?"

"Make an oven. Burn every piece of that thing." Noah kicked the shark carcass. "Have your men clean up every drop of blood — allow nothing to escape. Tell them not to touch the blood."

Currie nodded and shouted orders. Men carefully carried out their tasks at top speed. They wanted never to encounter anything like that again.

Noah took Moira by her shoulders and stared into her eyes.

"When my heart stops, you must do the same thing with me — burn everything. Do you understand?"

She pulled his head down and kissed him. She loosened her grip and whispered, "I've always favored cremation."

Book Four

CHAPTER 1

Cᴀᴘᴛᴀɪɴ Cᴜʀʀɪᴇ, sᴛɪʟʟ ɴᴏᴛ ᴜsᴇᴅ ᴛᴏ ʜɪs ɴᴇᴡ ᴛɪᴛʟᴇ ᴀɴᴅ ʀᴀɴᴋ, carefully peered through his binoculars at the coast of the island of Butung in the Indonesian archipelago. His crew labored to make the *Andrew Dawkins* ship-shape again after their deadly encounter with the Great White shark and the Surabayans. With a start, he realized he still faced the task of logging events that had transpired after Captain Tarant left the ship.

"Bloody hell," he muttered to himself, "this just gets more and more complicated."

On the after deck Bosun Stout and Noah Manaluk were supervising the cremation of the shark carcass. The Inuit seemed quite keen on getting every possible remnant of the dead creature converted to ashes before night.

Such a strange situation, Currie thought.

Since the encounter with the Malays, he felt paranoid about their exposed position, under-manned crew, and their general state of disrepair. But what most unsettled him were the incredible abilities of the Inuit.

Since the Fall he had seen a great many things that would have been considered horrific, or at least extraordinary, before that cosmic event. Currie's total fascination with things scientific always put the question "why?" before all other aspects of a situation. In this instance, he possessed part of the answer but feared he might not gain further knowledge from Noah.

The shark, and whatever else it might have been, had entered his mind. He now possessed memories that most definitely were not his. Ancient hunger, eons of travel through star fields, and loneliness beyond all imagination suffused him.

He now found himself close to weeping when he didn't keep the memories in check. And the presence carried by the shark, the hungry force of it, felt almost physical.

Something brushed his elbow and he jumped with the psychic burn of it.

"Jesus!" he blurted.

"Oh, I'm sorry," Moira Napier said, holding up her hand as if to ward off a blow. "I thought you didn't hear me when I called your name."

Currie's thudding heart slowed, and he felt heat in his face, which pissed him off even more.

"Not to worry, Missus. Just gathering some wool. And I didn't hear you. Sorry."

"No worries. I just wanted to thank you for taking a chance on, on us. I know you were close to the captain and the doctor–"

"They made their own decisions, Mrs. Napier. God knows I tried to talk them out of it, but they went their own way. My granny used to say, 'be careful what you wish for — you might get it.' Well, they got theirs, didn't they just?"

"No argument Mis- ah, Captain Currie. But I know you were all mates for a very long time and I'm sorry for your loss."

"Thank you. I will miss them and curse them daily for being so bloody greedy. But we have other matters to discuss, do we not?"

"Yes," Moira said, staring into his eyes. "Noah."

"What, exactly, is he?"

"He's a man I have come to trust and love. He carries an ability that seems both a blessing and a curse. I believe he can do great good with this thing, providing he has the right help and opportunity."

"What do you have in mind?"

"We can't let knowledge of his abilities get out to the general population, at least not yet. People would make a curiosity out of him and try to exploit him. I won't stand for that."

"Every man on this ship knows what happened," Currie said, glassing the receding coastline again. "How are you going to stop them from talking to everyone they meet?"

"How many have to remember what happened out here?"

He turned his head and stared at her. He held the binoculars up for a long moment before lowering them to his chest.

"He can do that? Make them all forget?"

"Yes. So how many must remember, other than you and the Bosun?"

"My God!"

"Please, don't fixate. Noah is like a new world to us, one full of wonder and promise. If we don't treat him right, he'll scarper on us, and I wouldn't blame him a bit."

"Good enough, I won't 'fixate,' as you say. But you've got to see this from my point on the compass. Here's a bloke who can crawl into your mind, without you knowing it, and wipe your memories away like a wet spot on the deck–"

"The only time he's done that was when he felt that he, or I, was threatened. You'd have done the same thing."

"But the only other creatures who have the same abilities are a monstrosity that should have never lived beyond birth, a huge shark, and a bloody whale, for Christ's sake! I find Mr. Manaluk quite fascinating, Missus, but to tell you God's own truth, I'm more than just a bit terrified of him."

"Are you terrified of the boilers in your ship? They possess the capability to do great harm if things go awry, no?"

"There's a lot more to this bloke than there is to a bloody boiler!"

"Too right, and he can do a lot more good, too. Look, Captain, think back to the man you found. Did he seem threatening or fearsome? Did he do anything other than be agreeable until his life, and perhaps mine too, was put in jeopardy?"

"No, Mrs. Napier, he didn't."

"And look at him out there right now, trying to make sure every part of those two monstrosities is completely destroyed. He knows how the power can be abused, and he has never done anything like that since I've known him."

Currie stared at her, with color high on her cheeks and eyes flashing, and wondered what it would be like to have her feel that passionate about him. But she was correct; Manaluk had never posed a threat until provoked.

"I see your point," Currie said quietly. "So now what?"

"Who has to remember? The others will forget all but an attack by natives. This memory loss will not hurt or affect them in any other way."

"Why didn't he just wipe all our minds?"

"Because I need help with this, with him. You were never a threat to us. In fact, you put yourself in harm's way to try and help. I know you have great curiosity about the world, and I think you deserve to be part of whatever happens. If you wish to, that is."

Currie felt as if he'd just been awarded the Victoria Cross.

"I'd be honored, Mrs. Napier."

"Bonzer! First of all, it's Moira. I don't plan to use my last name after this trip. De-, my husband and I were trying to save our marriage at the time of his death. Since I lost both him and the marriage, I see no point in carrying his name."

Currie nodded. "As you wish, Mrs-, Moira. My given name is Stuart, but I must ask you to address me by my rank while we're aboard ship."

"Of course, Captain." She gave him a wide smile. "It's probably already dicey enough having a woman aboard, yeah?"

"Yeah," he said with a grin. "We've been on patrol for six weeks now and the lads are beginning to feel the absence of the opposite sex. We're on our way back to New Darwin, what with the heavy crew losses and all."

A long pause ensued. Currie realized he had yet to answer her question.

What would it hurt to wipe the crew's collective minds of the incident? He hadn't made any log entries yet and they could create a likely story which would stand close inspection.

"All right then, wipe everybody's mind, including the bosun. We need to agree on a story which explains the presence of you and Noah, as well as the absence of Tarant, Carleson, and the dead crew members."

"No worries," Moira said, "I've been thinking about it, and here's how I think it should go...."

CHAPTER 2

NOAH RAN THE HAND-HELD SPOTLIGHT OVER THE DECK, carefully searching out all the small seams and dents where any of the shark blood could have collected and been missed. There was no way to tell how much physical matter it took to transfer the essence into a different being and he did not want to take any chances. Another light intersected with his and he looked up at the boatswain's mate face in the reflected glow.

"I think we got it all, Mr. Manaluk. I had the men throw their swabs into the fire, too, just in case."

"Good thinking, Bosun Stout. They have done an excellent job. I appreciate all of your help."

"What I saw today made me a believer. I don't know how a little guy like you could handle all that happened."

"A believer in what?"

"In measuring a man by more than what you see at first."

Noah grinned at him. "That's a good thing for all of us to believe." He had pushed himself to take part in the destruction of the shark's carcass, even though he felt completely drained of energy.

The feeling of warmth and comradeship from the bosun gave him much to think about. Never in his life had an adult male thought highly of him. He felt a bond with the large man.

The floodlight on the bridge suddenly threw harsh illumination over them.

"Redirect that bloody light!" the bosun bellowed as the beam shifted to the fore deck. In a normal tone, he said, "Looks like Sparks got the electrics working again. I best go see how they're doin' with replacin' the booms."

A loud click issued from a speaker high on the bridge bulkhead immediately followed by, "Would Mr. Manaluk please report to the bridge?"

Bosun Stout laughed. "Never thought I'd live long enough to hear that!"

"Hear what?"

"A nice, polite question over the tannoy. Usually, it's an order or a 'now hear this' sort of thing. Still 'n all, you best go see what they want."

Moira looked up when Noah entered the bridge. Her immediate smile filled him with emotion. Both she and Captain Currie stood when he approached the chart table.

"Noah, we have much to discuss," Moira said. "Captain Currie said we would have more privacy in his cabin."

The cabin was small but obviously the realm of only one person. A small table and two chairs standing next to a large bunk constituted the furnishings as well as nearly filling the space. Through an open door, a toilet could be glimpsed.

Currie eased into one of the chairs and Moira sat on the edge of the bunk, nodding for Noah to take the other chair.

"All right, then," Moira said, licking her lips. "We must sort out what we're to do next, Noah. The Captain and I have been discussing the situation and we have an idea or two."

"By situation you mean me."

"I mean us, or do you want to go on alone?"

"No! I like being with you. You are the first person I have ever known who saw me for who I really was –" he left unsaid, 'and still liked me'.

"How long have you two been together?" Currie asked.

"Long enough to know we want it that way," Moira said quickly.

"What ideas did you come up with?" Noah asked.

"We're on our way to New Darwin," Captain Currie pointed at a chart mounted on the bulkhead. "There are a few islands people are beginning to occupy again. For the most part, the settlers are young people or rough sorts.

"The young people are after cheap land. The rough sorts have nowhere else to go in Australia. I could put you off at any of the islands, or you could go back to New Darwin with us.

"Mrs, Moira that is, asked me to be part of whatever you two decide to do, if you agree that is."

Noah instantly investigated his mind. He was finished taking people at their word and this was too important to leave to chance.

Currie was full of curiosity about the world. His fear of Noah's powers almost matched his fascination. A lengthy mental list of ways Noah's powers could be used for good stood out above all else. The search took less than two seconds.

"I agree, and I am pleased to have you with us."

"Except for the captain, I think you should alter the minds of the crew," Moira said. "Make them believe Captain Tarant and the others were killed rescuing us from pirates. Nothing of the shark or the Hydra should be left. What do you think?"

Noah nodded. "I would like to speak with Bosun Stout first. I think he is a good man and could be of great benefit if he is willing to come with us."

"There's no better man aboard this ship than the bosun," Captain Currie said. "He's risked his life many times for the good of others."

"Why don't you go ask him right now?" Moira said. "I trust him too."

Noah found Bosun Stout on deck managing the replacement of the Samson post.

"I would like to speak to you in private, Mr. Bosun Stout."

"Certainly. Only it's just 'Bosun'. You can drop that mister business."

They walked to the prow of the *Andrew Dawkins* and leaned on the railing.

"All of my life I have possessed an ability to know things. I didn't realize how much I knew until another showed me. I now understand that my ability came from somewhere off this planet, and that frightens me.

"If this presence becomes too strong, it can overwhelm me. Since I have carried this thing almost since birth, I can control the part within me. I tell you this because there are no guarantees about me or what I possess."

"And you're tellin' me this, why?"

"I think you know what designs Captain Tarant and Dr. Carleson had on me. I knew I had to escape them or my life, and perhaps Moira's too, was in danger. By the time we reach New Darwin, only a very few on this ship will remember anything about my abilities, or the shark, or the Hydra.

"They will only remember their captain and many crew members dying in a battle to rescue Moira Napier and the Inuit with her. This will all be reflected in the log. Captain Currie is going to help Moira and me fit into Australia and do something positive with my abilities.

"Would you like to be part of that, whatever it is?"

"D'ya think you can trust me?"

Noah smiled up at the large man. "Of course, or I would not have asked."

Bosun Stout returned the smile and stuck out his hand. "Sign me up, mate. This sounds more interestin' than runnin' deck apes."

CHAPTER 3

"Okay," Captain Currie said. "We're in agreement. Boats, you best be in the engine room when Mr. Manaluk works his mental wrench. I'll be on the bridge."

"Aye, aye, Captain. Noah, Moira, I think we're going to have a great adventure together." Bosun Stout nodded and left the cabin.

"I'll let you two get some rest," Currie said through a tired smile. "If you're half as tired as I am, you're already asleep."

"Where do we stay?" Moira asked.

"Why right here. Wouldn't think of putting the two of you into any of the other cabins. They're just tiny things."

"Isn't this your cabin?" Noah waved his hand.

"It's the captain's quarters. Not quite sure I feel like a captain yet. It's a bit of a mental leap, y'know. Didn't think I'd ever make that much rank.

"Give me about three minutes. The bosun should be in the engine room by now. G'nite now." He pulled the door shut behind him.

Noah stared at the deck and mentally reached to each crewman in turn, starting with the lower ratings and working up to the petty officers and chief petty officer. He took his time, making sure he erased all vestiges of the incident. He wanted to get it right the first time. Only an outside stimulus would resurrect any of the erased memories.

Soon every member of the Andrew Dawkins crew, save for her captain and bosun, had no memory of monstrosities, sharks, or anything out of the ordinary about the Inuit passenger. The big news was that they had found Moira Napier and saved her life. Otherwise, they all felt pride and honored because their captain and other crew members had died in a battle with pirates.

Noah took a deep breath and relaxed. He felt almost afraid to look at Moira. This was the first time they had ever been alone together when their lives were not in peril.

"Hey." Moira pulled him around to face her. Her eyes seemed to gleam with additional light. "Have you ever taken a shower with a woman?"

"What's a shower?"

By the time he had dried himself off, Noah's state of sexual excitement approached agony. Moira dropped her towel, grabbed his hand, and pulled him toward the bunk.

"Okay," her husky voice thrilled him even more, "now we're gonna have a nice evening, just you and me."

"Moira, I have never before been with a woman. I do not wish to disappoint you."

"My gawd. You're really a virgin?"

"Yes, do you mind?"

"Oh, Noah, it's fine. I couldn't ask for more. Now, remember what I asked you on the baidarka?"

"About making you do something?"

"Yes. Pretend I am an extension of you. Make me do whatever you wish."

"It seems disrespectful."

"I'll be the judge of that, love." She reached down and stroked his erection. "Now use that thing in me."

He smiled. "I don't think you're going to be much of a challenge."

After his premature ejaculation, they discovered a common rhythm and brought each other to a nearly mutual climax. Moira felt him finish and suddenly an awareness swept through her. She knew she had just conceived, because she felt the presence of another being.

The sensation of *other* escalated and roared through her from groin to brain.

"Oh, my God, Noah!"

"Did I hurt you?"

~I hope not.~

He rolled away from her, his eyes mirroring his fright in the dim cabin. "Moira, have I doomed you? Have I doomed us?"

"I, I don't think so. But I feel something inside me, other than me."

"You were just in my mind; did you know that?"

She regarded him with sharpened perception. She felt her cheek muscles moving under her skin. She tried to see into his mind, not knowing how or if she could. When nothing happened after long moments, she gave up, feeling some relief.

Never had she felt so self-aware, so cohesive. Noah stared at her in dread. She realized she could sense what he felt. She smiled to give him comfort and effortlessly slid into his mind.

~This doesn't feel like a bad thing to me. Does it to you?~

~I do not know, but the essence used our own abilities against Thinker and me.~

~Could this be your power, not part of the bad thing?~

~I hope so.~

~Can we make love again? I want to be everywhere this time.~

She found his mental smile as radiant as sunshine.

CHAPTER 4

Noah lay watching Moira as she slowly awakened. He had never felt this close to another person in his life, and he didn't want the feeling to ever leave him. She opened her eyes and looked back at him.

~*Good morning, my love.*~ She stretched, groaned with pleasure, and kissed him.

~*You have become the most important thing in my life. Will you marry me?*~

Moira sat upright and laughed. "By God, you get right to the point, don't you?"

Noah's smile vanished and fear washed through him.

"Of course, I'll marry you," she said with a dazzling smile. "It didn't seem all that important, but now that you mention it, we want our child to be legitimate, don't we?"

"By the power vested in me by the Commonwealth of Australia, I now pronounce you husband and wife." Currie grinned. "You may kiss the bride now, Noah."

He did so and the crew applauded.

New Darwin exceeded Noah's expectations to the point of bewilderment. Ships crowded the huge harbor and people crowded the ships. Small craft darted everywhere, and Noah felt certain they would collide with at least one of them.

The city rose behind huge concrete wharves that glistened like wet cliffs in the sunlight. Impossibly high buildings seemed to jostle each other for space, and the mechanical din of machinery reached across the water to them. Noah felt a tendril of fear eel through him.

"Whattya think, mate?" Moira asked as she held his arm in her two hands. He basked in her warmth.

"It's so, so big!"

"Only one other place in Oz bigger, and that's New Sydney, on the other side of the continent."

"What will we do here? Will people let us be? Why—"

"Wait, wait, slow down, love. I know it seems a bit much just now but give this time. Let yourself absorb it, and above all, don't worry."

He glanced over at her and then at the mesmerizing spectacle before him. "I have never seen anything like this in my life. I did not realize this many people existed in the whole world."

"This is your world too, Noah. Don't forget that. What you see here is a very small portion. This place is not bigger than you are."

"I am glad you are with me."

"So am I. I'm seeing my own country through your eyes and emotions. You're showing me things I took for granted in an entirely new way."

"Yet when I look into you, I only see you, and the child growing in your womb."

"Then why are you so apprehensive, love?"

"Every time I have encountered this force outside myself it has tried to devour me. I fear it is not as, as, what did you call it before?"

"Benign. Harmless."

"I want very much to believe that. But one, that is, I fear it will not only try to harm me but will harm you in the process."

"Keep in mind, Noah, that I am a very strong-willed person. Every emotion I feel, every thrill that raises my eyebrows, is carefully examined, traced to its source to make sure I, the 'I' that is really me, completely agrees with the impulse.

"Mind you, I do this in an incredibly short amount of time. Nevertheless, I believe what I find in myself. I know ballocks when I see it, my love, and this bloody well ain't that."

"I have searched for you all my life, Moira. You complete me in a way I did not understand, and if I had, would have thought it impossible.

"If this," he spread his hands and surrounded her with an invisible blanket, "'thing' I gave you is more than a child or a piece of my essence, and it hurt you, I don't know if I could suffer myself to live."

"My God. My husband is turning into a poet." She smiled and reached for him.

Noah stepped back; pain flitted over his face.

"See, I want to believe that's all you, but a part of me-" He laughed to himself, a hard, dark laugh. "I am suddenly understanding your description of 'irony'. But a part of me isn't sure and wants to look closer; and be certain.

"All I want to do is love and accept you. But I know how this thing can cloak itself in the sand like some halibut, and then surge out and strike before you know it really isn't the bottom of your soul."

His laugh had evaporated her smile and her new, hard eyes held him.

"I guess you'll just have to do for me what I do for you. Trust your heart without losing your mind."

He blinked and grabbed her in his arms, pulled her tightly to him, and whispered in her ear, "I love you so much that I nearly forgot to enjoy you. I do trust you."

She whispered, "But the part you're not sure is really me is what bothers you, and you don't know me well enough to tell the difference."

He made a wry smile. "I do have to believe and trust you; you always know what I'm thinking and unless you tell me, I can't feel you when you're in my mind."

"I won't hurt you, Noah." Her breathy whisper purified his brain of all evil spirits.

"Thank you, wife."

CHAPTER 5

THE SMOOTH, NEARLY SILENT TAXICAB COMPLETELY ABSORBED Noah. Currie, Moira and he were on their way to what Currie described as momentary 'safe anchorage' while arrangements were being made for a more permanent home. Noah tried to look at everything at once.

Many vehicles, some spewing black smoke, others as quiet and smooth as the taxi, passed them in both directions. He didn't understand why the machines weren't running into each other or knew when to stop. People of all colors thronged the raised stone paths in front of the tall buildings.

"How soon are you gonna get us where we need to be?" Moira asked.

"Just trust your old captain, Moira, and I'll have us there in no time."

"You're absolutely sure this is going to be bonzer?"

"Yes, dear. My mother will love both of you. Where do you think I got my scientific curiosity?"

Noah broke his silence, "You're not going to tell her about u- me, are you?"

Currie's laugh rang boy-like. "My word, no. Wouldn't dream of it. I want her to figure it out for herself."

"No worries then," Moira said with a sigh of relief.

"You haven't met Mother yet," Currie murmured.

"Stuart," the small, white-haired woman hugged Currie then abruptly pushed him to arm's length. "You need a haircut."

Currie laughed along with everyone else. "Mother, this is Noah Manaluk and Moira. Noah is a—"

"Moira doesn't have a last name?"

"Well yes, but—"

"Manaluk," Moira said in a calm tone. "It was Napier until a couple of days ago when Noah here married a widow."

"Well, congratulations to both of you, I'm sure. I am Sheila Currie, and you are both welcome in my home."

"We won't be staying all that long, Mum," Currie said as they all filed after her into the house. "Just for a few days."

"Where will you be going then?"

Noah blurted, "That's the part we don't know yet."

Sheila placed teacups on doilies. Noah sat in the chair she had indicated, staring intently at the fragile fabric. He wanted to talk about their options, but not with Sheila in the room.

~It's all right, love. We must be polite.~

His gaze snapped up to meet Moira's. She smiled and winked.

No matter how he examined her presence in his mind, he could find no traces of the 'blood essence' or the monstrous amalgamated presence of the Hydra and shark. If threat hid in her, it completely eluded him.

"Do you take sugar in your tea, Mr. Manaluk?" Sheila Currie asked.

"Sugar?" He glanced at Moira.

"The sweet, grainy stuff we had on the ship."

"Oh, yes. Thank you."

"I've never seen anyone quite like you, Mr. Manaluk, and we get all sorts here."

"I am of the People. Others call us 'Inuit'. I lived in Alaska until recently."

Without warning Noah suddenly felt an overwhelming desire to be near Thinker again. He needed someone he could trust in this new world. Yet, if he and Thinker were near enough to communicate, they would both be destroyed by their combined essence.

"Why does that make you sad, Noah?" Sheila asked.

"Sometimes one misses one's home."

Moira coughed and said, "We're looking for somewhere to call home, you see. A lot has happened to us, even before Captain Currie picked us up."

"Captain Currie! Stuart, are you telling these innocents tales?"

"Like Moira says, a great deal has happened, Mother." One at a time, he pushed his red mustaches back with a knuckle.

"Obviously. What happened to that Tarant fellow, the one so full of himself?"

"He died."

"Oh. Well, I'm sorry, I'm sure."

"He pushed his luck once too often and it cost him everything."

"He died saving our lives," Moira said.

"My, he must have changed a great deal since I last saw him. Was there a reward involved?"

"Mother has a keen sense of personality," Currie said.

Sheila snapped, "Mother knows a total shit when she sees one. Captain Tarant fit that bill with a vengeance."

Moira laughed. "You're fair dinkum, Sheila. I like you."

"Are you going to go back to singing?" Sheila returned quickly.

"I'm not sure. How did you know I sang?"

"You're famous, dearie. Your disappearance was in all the papers and on the wireless. And I've noticed there's naught on either about your return."

"We pulled in not three hours ago, Mother." Currie sounded strained. "There hasn't been time to speak with the press."

"If Tarant was still around, the press would have been alerted and swarming the docks. Why didn't you tell anyone?"

"Because we asked him not to," Moira said. "I'm not at all sure I want to go back to my singing career, and I need time to sort it all out."

"You have a lovely voice, dear. It seems a shame to not use it." She rose and moved into the small kitchen.

"Thank you, Sheila, I'll keep that in mind."

"In the meantime," Sheila sat steaming cups of tea in front of each person, "...what's the problem with settling here in New Darwin?"

"We'd like something a bit more rural, and less tropical. Noah has difficulty with extreme heat, and I'm weary of cities."

"Which begs the point, what is an Inuit doing in Oz to start with?"

"One had to leave one's village or starve. The People all left to follow the caribou and one, I, went to sea in a large baidarka which was wrecked." Noah felt hesitant about entering the woman's mind. It seemed rude.

"After going to sea and before being wrecked," Moira said, "Noah stopped on the island where I had been shipwrecked. Through great difficulty, he saved me."

"Then you were shipwrecked a second time?"

"Yes." Moira's voice took on a sympathetic tone. "And he lost his beautiful baidarka."

"You lead an exciting life, Noah."

"Too exciting, perhaps." Noah nodded and shot a quick glance at Moira. She winked.

Two loud knocks sounded at the door.

"Ah, that will be Bosun Stout," Currie said, rising before his mother had time to move. "I'll get it."

Sheila gave them each a searching look. "And who might that be?"

"He's the bosun mate from the *Andrew Dawkins*," Moira said. "He's going to our new home with us."

"Why?"

"He's tired of being a sailor?" Moira laughed. "I know I am!"

Stuart Currie entered the room with Bosun Danford Stout and introduced him to his mother. "Boats is going to be our logistics expert."

Sheila smiled at Boats and then frowned at her son. "Stuart, there's something going on here that isn't being mentioned. Are you going to tell me what it is or do I–"

"Mother," he said sweetly, "I have no idea what you're talking about. Now we're going out for a bit."

CHAPTER 6

Boats owned an automobile. Once they had all climbed inside, Currie in the front seat next to Boats, Moira and Noah in the back, Boats began talking.

"I've arranged a boat from Adelaide to the North Island port of—"

"We're going to New Zealand?" Moira blurted.

"You want quiet and rural, New Zealand's the perfect place for you," Boats said over his shoulder.

"What was my last name, Mr. Stout?"

"Yer last name? Why it's, oh Christ, is there a connection?"

"I don't understand," Noah said. The sudden tension in the vehicle could almost be touched.

"My late husband was orphaned by the Fall. His family lived in Napier, New Zealand. Since he couldn't remember anything from before the catastrophe, they gave him the name of the town as his last name. I really can't go back there."

"To Napier or to New Zealand?" Currie asked.

"Napier."

"No worries then," Boats said in a cheerful tone. "Because we're going to Wellington."

"They've rebuilt it?" Moira asked. "The only time I was ever there the people slept in shacks and lived on less than a church mouse could."

"It's come a long way back toward where it was in the old days, just like everywhere else." Currie stared out his window, and waved his hand. "Look at all the construction and new business springing up. There are a lot of blokes keen to regain the old technology."

"We're building motorcars and lorries again," Boats said. "And we still have the railroad, which we're taking to Port Adelaide the day after tomorrow, by the by."

"Why the railroad?" Currie asked.

"Cause I'm sick of ships, that's why," Boats said through a grin. "And so is Moira, right?"

"Right as rain," she said, smiling back. "I love railroads. They're so effortless."

"Noah, this all sound bonzer to you?" Currie asked.

"I know nothing of any of the places you spoke of. Why are we going to Wellington rather than someplace else? And what is a railroad?"

"We're going to Wellington because they are very short of doctors," Currie said. "It's a place where you can help."

"But I'm not a doctor!"

Moira laid her hand on his arm. "Noah, you told me you were once a shaman in your village. Isn't that a kind of doctor?"

He thought about the things he had done as a shaman. At the time he knew nothing of his true abilities or their strength. Yet he had helped people who genuinely wanted his help and who believed in him. Now he knew so much more.

"You healed me on the beach after the baidarka wrecked, didn't you?"

He turned and stared into her eyes. "How did you know that? You were still unconscious when I woke."

"I dragged you up the beach after we crashed on the rocks. You were bleeding and, as far as I could tell, dead. I felt broken bones grating in me, and my head hurt so much I could hardly stay upright.

"I finally lay down beside you in the rain and passed out. When I opened my eyes again, I felt almost energetic, until I saw those painted blokes. But you did that, didn't you?"

Abruptly she was in his mind.

~Or was it Thinker?~

"Yes," he said aloud. "It was me."

"If you want, Noah," Currie sounded hesitant. "I could be your front man and make like I was the doc. You could do your magic from the next room or behind a curtain, or even pretend to be my nurse."

"It is not magic," Noah said. "It is just something I can do."

"Well, you're the only person I ever met who could do it, and that rates as magic in my book. Think about this idea. You don't have to answer for weeks if you wish. If you have something else in mind just let us know."

Noah nodded and stared out the window at the passing wonders. Australia was an exciting place. He felt closer to Moira than any other human he had ever met.

Still, deep in his heart he knew Thinker was the only other being he trusted implicitly.

~Then why don't we find him?~

Noah looked over at Moira. She returned his gaze with raised eyebrows.

~Does my wish for his presence make you angry?~

~I realize that Thinker is more like your family than anything else. He is my friend also.~

Noah smiled. "So, you were going to tell me about the railroad."

CHAPTER 7

Thinker strenuously fluked to the heart side, causing Naff's great body to miss ramming him. Naff, a third larger than Thinker, slowed his great bulk and turned to face the younger bull again.

~Naff has no need to fight me,~ Thinker said.

~Naff must protect his mate.~

~Naff's mate faces no danger.~

~Thinker is danger. Thinker would take Naff's mate from him. Thinker is rogue male and must be driven from pod.~

Thinker let the response drift out to gently impact the watching pod before responding.

~If pod wishes Thinker to leave, he will obey. Your understanding of the situation is not correct. Looa is mate to Naff. All know this.~

For two weeks Thinker had followed the direction taken by Naff's pod. By the time he found them his wounds had healed and his strength restored. The pod welcomed him with no enthusiasm.

They did allow him to migrate north with them, but more as a supplicant than one who had been central to saving their lives. Only Looa greeted him with other than indifference.

~Thinker is a welcome sight. Was your journey easy?~

~My journey nearly cost me complete essence. But it needed doing and I am pleased to be with Naff's pod once again.~

At that point Naff had swam between them, ending the conversation with a finality bordering on rude. Thinker maintained his distance from Looa, hanging at the edge of the pod where he was most vulnerable to attack from without. He kept his position through many cycles of the warm eye, or sun, as Noah called it.

Thinker tried not to let thoughts of his friend swim through his mind. It caused him too much anguish. Still, he would find himself wondering where Noah and Moira might be now, if they had found "love" within each other or not, and if they ever thought of their friend Thinker.

The pod had just fed on massive amounts of krill and lay on top of the world, letting the rays of the warm eye sink into their bodies. Looa had approached Thinker and asked, *~When were you first able to communicate like this?~*

~At birth.~

~Did your mother's pod speak this clearly?~

~I alone could send thoughts or know what was in the minds of others.~

~You can hear what is in my mind?~

~If I so wish. It is with a sense of fairness that I do not delve into the minds of others.~

~What is fairness?~

While Thinker pondered his answer he saw Naff approaching at his fastest speed, and with an instant's filtering through the bull's mind, realized the danger. Thinker quickly fluked out of Naff's path.

Now less than a flipper length separated them. Thinker could feel Naff's resentment and jealousy. Beneath the emotions lay the true reason for his animosity and Thinker felt he must bring it into the open in order to deal with it once and for all.

~Naff is not too old to lead pod. Naff does not need to fear loss of his mate. Thinker wishes only to travel with others of his kind.~

~Naff does not think this is true.~

~Naff is correct.~ Looa drifted between them, forcing both males to retreat. *~Looa wishes to swim with Thinker from this heartbeat forward.~*

Naff retreated farther. *~This cannot be done if you remain with the pod. You both must swim alone.~*

~Not alone - with each other.~ Looa bumped along Thinker's side. *~Does Thinker agree?~*

~Yes, I agree. Let us leave these beings to their journey.~

Thinker and Looa turned as one and fluked away from the pod both aware of the intense feeling of loss emanating from Naff. Thinker wished he could make Naff understand the situation without hurt but realized impossibility when he faced it.

~¿Looa would be mate to Thinker?~

~If Thinker will accept me.~
~Yes.~
Something touched the edge of his senses, so faint he nearly missed it.
~¿Did you feel that?~
~Thinker's heart? yes, Looa felt it strongly.~
~Happy to know, but not my meaning. Something far away just–~

Again, the call came, stronger this time but still very faint: *~Thinker, I need you!~*
Thinker did not hesitate.
~Looa, we must travel as fast as possible back past where your pod turned north.~
~Why?~
~¡I will explain as we travel!~

CHAPTER 8

"WHY WOULD YOU WISH TO GO SOMEPLACE SMALL AND RURAL?" Sheila asked at dinner. "Hiding from something or someone are we?" She knew they were, but would they talk about it?

"Mum, you're grilling our guests again." Stuart grinned across the table at her.

"You're all hiding something from me. A mother can tell."

"Maybe you're just a stickybeak?" Moira's voice held a slight edge.

"Now I know there's something afoot. I've managed to get under Moira's skin. She thinks I'm nosy." Sheila grinned all around for a moment.

"I don't want to pry but will if I must. You're all going away on the train tonight and I won't have any further opportunities for sleuthing this out quietly. What's an inquiring mind to do?"

"I am on a quest," Noah said. "And these three people have offered to help me find that which I seek."

"What are you seeking?"

"Fulfillment and contentment."

"God's codpiece, mate. We're all looking for that! What makes your quest more important than Stuart being captain of his own ship or Mr. Stout here becoming an officer?"

"Did I say it was more important? I asked Moira to accompany me, but not Captain Currie, or Mr. Stout. The choice is theirs and I would understand if they chose not to continue with us."

Sheila glared at her son. "So why are you giving up an impressive career in the Australian Naval Defense Force to caper off and help Noah find fulfillment?"

Stuart opened his mouth but said nothing and glanced over at Noah.

"I have a gift that my companions think worthy to the point of helping me find an ideal location where it can be used to the most advantage for society." Noah took a bite of food.

"I've noticed," Moira said, "that your vocabulary and diction have changed incredibly since the first day I met you. Why do you think that is?"

Noah swallowed and sipped tea. "I've noticed it, too. I believe it is due to all the people around me. I think I unconsciously absorb it."

"Are you lot playing with me?" Sheila demanded. "What sort of a 'gift' are you talking about? How can you just absorb vocabulary and diction? Why weren't they being open about what–"

~I can enter the minds of others. I can examine a person's physiology and correct problems, and heal them. This is something I would rather not have the world know as it would cause distress for all concerned.

~We are not trying to hide anything from you personally, but we do need practice. Will you keep our trust?~

"Jesus wept! How did you do that?"

"I can't explain it other than I ate something at a very young age which wanted me to agree with it."

The others at the table burst into laughter. Sheila felt confused and a bit nettled.

"What's so bloody funny then?"

They told her. First Noah explained about eating a glowing seal liver as a tyke and thereafter being able to call animals to the hunters. Then about a whale who became his friend.

Sheila listened to all of them as they embellished the story or added their parts to it. After they all fell silent, she wasn't sure what to believe. Be that as it may, she knew Noah had been inside her head, and had spoken to her.

"So, can you see everything a person is thinking? Can they hide anything from you at all?"

"If I wish, I can see everything about a person, even hidden memories they have suppressed. But I will not do that unless it is a matter of life or death. I was cruel and evil with my gift in earlier days, and I made a pact with myself not to exploit anyone nor mentally abuse them in any way."

"You said you could heal people?"

"Yes."

Sheila decided she had nothing to lose and perhaps much to gain. "My doctor told me I had a cancer–"

"What?" Stuart blurted, fear suddenly on his face.

"–and that he could do nothing about it. Can you?"

Noah didn't respond. He seemed far away and distracted. A small ache she hadn't been aware of until now suddenly ceased. Noah blinked and focused on her face.

"He was correct, you did have cancer in your–" he shut his eyes for an instant and frowned before looking at her again, "–in your pancreas. It isn't there anymore. Your blood should work more efficiently from now on, too."

Sheila burst into tears.

CHAPTER 9

~¿*WHY DO WE MOVED FAST?*~ Looa asked.

Thinker and Looa had reversed their previous course and swam steadily for three visits of the warm eye. He allowed them to feed only when hunger became an insistent pain. When they slept he woke first and nudged her until she became active.

~*We are summoned by Noah.*~

~*I heard nothing...*~

~*Matters not. I heard the summons.*~

She abruptly stopped fluking and hung in the light-dappled water. Thinker swam in a tight turn and stopped before her.

~*¿Do you sicken?*~ Anxiety layered through his mental tone, and he closely examined her.

~*I do not sicken. I tire. If you must hurry to your long-tooth then go on your journey.*~

~*But we are mates. You wish to swim with me-*~

~*True,*~ she interrupted. ~*But I do not feel the need to rush through the world. For three visits of the warm eye, we have swam together, but for your presence, I would not know you wished me for mate.*~

Thinker pondered her thoughts and realized he had accepted her as an absolute in his life without asking her. Since her declaration to Naff that she wished to swim with Thinker, he had assumed the matter settled. Now he perceived it might not be so simple.

~*¿Looa does not wish to swim with Thinker?*~

~*Looa wishes to swim with Thinker. Looa wishes to mate with Thinker. Looa wishes to be Thinker's partner in all things.*~

~*¿Looa has mated before?*~

~*Yes, to no result.*~

~¿Do you wish for issue?~

~Yes. But only with Thinker.~

Feelings difficult to describe yet spontaneous rushed through him. Exhilaration suffused him and he abruptly fluked to the top of the world and breached into the sparkling thindrink. Never had he felt better. He smashed back into the world.

Looa waited where he had left her, and he rapidly returned to her side.

~¿Thinker feels something?~

~Thinker now understands love Noah spoke about.~

~¿Thinker loves Noah?~

~Hard to know. But Thinker loves Looa.~

She floated there, not responding, for many heartbeats.

~¿Again?~

~Thinker loves Looa.~ He moved along her side, running his flipper over her body from cutwater to fluke. He quickly returned up her other side, rubbing her from back to front before stopping next to her. *~¿What does Looa feel?~*

Her body moved against his and maintained contact.

~¿Explain love to Looa?~

CHAPTER 10

NOAH LOVED THE TRAIN. *Andrew Dawkins* had been impressive, but the only time one had the true sense of movement over distance was in relationship to land, which usually was quite brief on a ship.

The train maintained a constant speed over the land. Trees, fields, houses, and people flashed by as they thundered south across Australia. The train also overshadowed the ship in terms of comfort.

"Well, that's because this is just for transporting civilians," Boats Stout explained, "and the *Andrew Dawkins* is a military vessel."

"Why not make it comfortable, too?" Noah asked.

Boats grinned under his much-dented nose. "Damn good question. Always wondered that m'self."

"How long will it take to reach Adelaide?"

"About forty to fifty hours, little more than two days." Boats stared out the window. "All depends on how many stops we make, for how long, and if any of this ancient equipment breaks down."

"Why wasn't this all destroyed in the Fall?"

"Lot of it was. But after things got sorted out politically, which took about five years, they went into a massive rebuilding effort. They called it 'The Big Fix' and the government paid for most of it.

"Thousands of kilometers of track had to be rebuilt, as well as most of the engines and rolling stock." Boats grinned at him. "But as you can see, they did it."

"This is a very interesting place, Australia." Noah watched the passing jungle and reflected on how differently it looked here than on the island. Not having someone trying to kill you certainly improved the view.

CHAPTER 11

Pounding on the front door woke Sheila from a sound sleep. Fear that it was Stuart, and something had gone wrong, added wings to her feet. Clutching her housecoat around her, she flung open the door.

A slight, pale, somewhat short man stood on her stoop.

"Why the bloody hell are you pounding on my door?"

His eyes flicked back and forth nervously across her face. He wore some sort of uniform and was in the process of crushing his hat in his hands. His tongue licked his lips thoroughly before he managed to speak.

"S-sorry, mum. This is the home of record for Stuart Currie, 'an I'm lookin' fer 'im."

"I'm his mother. He's not here. Who are you and why do you want him?"

"M' name is Oberon, Niles Oberon, a medical technician in the ANDF. I wuz on the *Dawkins* with Mr., er, Captain Currie."

"What do you want with the captain, Mr. Oberon?"

"Well, 'e left with an Inuit, 'an I needs ta find 'im."

"Find who, the captain or the Inuit?"

"Well, both really."

"What on Earth for?"

"The late Dr. Carleson, my immediate superior, wuz an educated man. Writin' a book on medical things for the Admiralty, he wuz. 'E took photographs of everything. I'd 'elp 'im when I could."

"So?"

"I got his last photos from the chemist last night. There's a photo of the Inuit with 'is arm all ripped 'n' horrible. I'm 'oldin' th' flood fer th' photo, in the picture I am. But I got no memory of doin' it."

"So?"

"I 'ad a dream last night. There were monsters in it, big fish, gunfire, all sorts of things."

"You came here because of a dream?"

"I realized this mornin' that it wasn't no dream. It was a memory. I truly need to talk to Captain Currie."

"He's away in the country, out of touch. I expect to hear from him in a couple of days. Where can I tell him to contact you?"

Oberon's eyes flicked about madly. "At the Mariner's Rest on Bell Street, I 'spose. Please have 'im call right away."

"No worries, Mr. Oberon, I shall. No worries."

CHAPTER 12

Thinker woke to distant engine sounds, like those of the *Andrew Dawkins*. Believing Noah had found them, he nudged Looa and fluked up into the thindrink and exhaled water from his lungs.

"There! Whale, no, two whales off the bow!" Seaman Hajami shouted.

Captain Saigauo caught them in his binoculars. The whales were at least a kilometer ahead of them. Hajami had incredible eyes!

"Full speed, quartermaster."

"Aye, Captain!" Bells rang and the boat quickened with activity. The bow raised a few degrees as the screws went to full revolutions.

All eyes were on the spouts dead ahead. Suddenly both leviathans dived, flukes wetly reflecting the light before disappearing.

Initial confusion about the meaning of the lookout's shout distilled into gut-grinding fear after Thinker scanned the man's mind. He dived down to where Looa still drifted lethargically. While physically bumping into her he also thrust into her mind, *~¡Long-teeth! Human long-teeth who have more power than us! Dive with me, now!~*

~Need, need to clear lungs and take thindrink. ¡Would perish to dive now!~

Thinker extended his senses, knew immediately that many sets of eyes watched for "spouts", and motorized death would seek them as a result. The ship slowed while the men waited. Nudging Looa, Thinker fluked past the stern as fast as he could manage.

~Go as far as you can. Then rise to the surface, exhale, and fill your lungs as quickly as you can, then dive for your life. These humans will kill you for what they can rip from your body.~

~I have questions, but I will do as you say.~

The leviathans moved as far behind the ship as they could before hypoxia forced Looa to the surface. Thinker had moved far off to her right and surfaced at the same time. Both cleared their lungs, took in all the oxygen they could hold, and dived into the crystalline depths of the world.

Thinker felt something touch him and recognized it as the human form of echolocation.

"Half speed!" Saigauo shouted. "All hands watch for sign."

The ship slowed to a crawl and sailors lined the railings, peering into the bright day with unaided eyes if they didn't possess binoculars or a telescope. Most did.

"Mr. Honda, use the SONAR, to ascertain where they are," Saigauo said. He thought for a moment, remembering Seaman Hirouchi's distant encounter with his talking whale, and decided to better his odds.

"Prepare a depth charge."

"Depth charge, Captain?" First Mate Honda blurted. "I, ah, yes, sir. Immediately."

Captain Saigauo mentally put a black mark in front of Mr. Honda's name in the pay book. Two more such marks and the man would be on the beach for the rest of his life.

"You have the bridge, Mr. Honda. Fire the depth charge as soon as it is prepared." He hurried down the ladder to the weather deck. He pushed through the knot of men in the bow.

"Do any of you see anything?"

A space immediately opened around him. The crewmen knew better than to jostle the captain.

"No, Captain. Haven't seen a thing since they dived," a grizzled harpooner said, never taking his eyes off the water. "The birds aren't seeing anything either. They must have gone deep."

Seagulls wheeled above the ship like a chaotic parasol, shrieking with want. Their sharp eyes numbered in the thousands, yet they stayed aloft, seeking opportunity.

Captain Saigauo wondered how they could stay submerged for

such a long time.

~¡Turn! Turn to the right. Move as fast as you can. They are going to send death–~

Horror exploded behind them. The numbing shock wave tossed them like krill in a bubble net. Thinker's head ached from the concussion.

He made his pain cease before instantly seeking out Looa. She reeled with the damage created by the depth charge. Thinker moved through her wonderful body, fixing damaged tissue and ruptured sensory organs.

Anger surged through him. Attempting to kill him was one thing, but trying to kill Looa was more than he would allow. He scanned the humans on the ship. One man steered the vessel at the orders of another.

Without hesitation, he stilled both their hearts. Confusion erupted on the ship. All thoughts of killing whales ceased.

~Swim this way.~ They fluked away, perpendicular to the heading of the ship. *~Go as far as you can before rising for thindrink.~* He didn't think the humans could regain cohesion quickly, but he would not underestimate the species.

~You thought of it as air before. ¿Why do you speak two languages?~

~Often I must. ¿Do you understand my meaning?~

~Yes. I am not stupid.~

Thinker nearly stopped in his flight. Looa had understood multiple nuances. The only other cetacean than himself to do so.

~¿Do you sing?~

~¿Sing? Now?~

~¿Not now, but ever?~

~Of course, I sing. ¿Do I not think?~

They fluked away from the ship, now too distant to harm them. Joy suffused Thinker's heart and mind. She sang!

CHAPTER 13

WHISTLE SHRIEKING, THE TRAIN SLOWED TO A WALKING PACE as it eased into Tennant Creek.

"M'gawd," Moira said. "I once sang for my supper here when I was still a girl."

"Yesterday, was it?" Currie said with a laugh.

"This is much smaller than New Darwin." Noah had rarely left the window since the journey started. Moira decided he had a lot of five-year-old left in him. Whenever she looked at him, her heart nearly broke.

She had delved into his memories to see what dark secrets he harbored. Part of her felt surprised that he had told her everything. Her other half just nodded. He was so constantly apprehensive about her new abilities that she thought him a bit paranoid.

However, so far all she felt was an incredible awe at what she could do with her mind. If he needed Thinker to vet her allegiance, so be it. She didn't mind.

"Australia is full of little towns like this," she said. "So is New Zealand. If you think one place is better than the next, keep it in mind. We can live where we bloody well please."

The train jolted to a stop. The conductor self-importantly marched through the car. "Tennant Creek. Tennant Creek. All off for Tennant Creek."

Moira touched his arm. "Do we have time to get off and stretch our legs?"

"Not a good idea, missus. The locals don't take well to outsiders."

"Outsiders? We're Australian citizens, not bloody outsiders!"

"You can do as you wish, missus. Just giving you a word to the wise, as it were."

She grabbed Noah by the hand. "C'mon, let's have a look at Tennant Creek."

They stepped down into the orange-red dust at the trackside. The town consisted of nondescript wooden buildings bleached nearly white by the fierce sun. Sheet metal roofs shimmered in the heat. Stunted trees and sparse bushes punctuated the row of structures.

Farther down the track, abreast of where the engine had stopped, sat the station, more bleached wood and boasting a platform of sorts. Two black men in ragged clothing sat in the strip of shade provided by the building. A deeply tanned man wearing shorts and a white shirt stood talking with the conductor.

All four men intently watched Moira and Noah.

"Why don't they like us?" Noah asked.

A small lizard darted across the road leading into the town.

"They don't even like themselves. So don't worry about it." Moira marched up to the conductor and the skinny, hatchet-faced man with the tan. "Excuse me, gents. Is there a store close by where I could get some fruit or cold drinks?"

The conductor looked past her at Noah and just squinted in the sun. Hatchet-face glared at her and in a reedy whine said, "We got nothing fer outsiders here."

"What do you mean by that? I'm as bloody Australian as you are, you sack of sticks."

He glanced at Noah and then back at her. "Git back on the train you tart. Bad enough you're hanging about with a wog without paradin' around our town to boot."

"You're mean as cat's piss, you mongrel! The last time I was out here you whackers were grinning like a shot fox. Well, I'll never set foot in this bloody slum again."

Hatchet-face scowled at her. "Don't make a blue, now. You were here before? What's your name?"

"I'm not making any mistakes. You are. Yeah, I was here about six years ago. My name was Moira Napier."

She grabbed Noah's elbow and turned him along with her. "C'mon, we don't need anything from this batch of fuck-wits!"

Behind them, she heard Hatchet-face say, "You didn't tell me it was her! You got a kangaroo loose in the top paddock?"

"I swear, I didn't know it was her!"

Moira pulled herself up the steps and back into the train car. Her heart pounded with anger, and she felt like knocking the piss out of someone.

"Moira, why are you so angry?" Noah asked.

She dropped onto one of the padded benches and kicked the seat in front of her. "We lost nearly ninety percent of our population in the Fall, and here these drongos are calling me an 'outsider'. It makes me mad as a cut snake."

"You are difficult to understand when you are angry."

The train lurched and slowly moved past the station. A small crowd stood peering at the cars. Moira wondered where they had all been.

The conductor stopped by the bench. "Sorry, Moira, none of us recognized you."

"Rack off," Moira said with a growl. "It shouldn't make any difference who I am."

The conductor shrugged and turned away.

"Well," Moira said with a long sigh, "let's see what Alice Springs has to offer. We should be there tomorrow."

CHAPTER 14

Thinker and Looa made a wide circle around the smoking atoll where they first met. Even though OnePod no longer existed, the Cea would forever avoid the island.

~¿Why do we go to the bidding of a human?~ Looa asked.

~Noah is my friend. We have journeyed great distances together.~

~But his kind tried to take our essence.~

~Our own kind, the Supra, tried to take our essence.~

Looa fell silent but Thinker knew she was looking for a way to swim around his words. The more time he spent with her, the more he felt for her. He knew he was "in love," as Noah would say.

~¿If Noah endangered you, would he still be your friend?~

Thinker spent a few heartbeats working through the nuances of his answer. ~If Noah were in danger and needed my help, I would be in danger, and he would still be my friend. If Noah called me into danger for no reason, or to do me harm, he would no longer be my friend.~

~¿I understand. Am I your friend?~

Thinker slowed and rubbed along her side. ~More than friend. I have sought you through all my heartbeats. To swim without you would have no meaning. My essence would have no meaning.~

He felt a tide of emotional warmth coming from within Looa. Her pleasure at his thoughts floated around him as unmistakable as the warm eye.

~¿Will you swim with me and be my mate?~ Thinker asked.

~For as long as you wish.~

CHAPTER 15

Two loud raps of wood against wood cut through the multiple conversations in the hall. The constitutional convention delegates grew silent.

The train persevered across the monotonous, endless plain. Noah felt hot like never before. He didn't sweat as he had in the jungle, but the extreme temperature felt unpleasant.

The mostly flat landscape danced behind waves of heat, tricking the eye into believing mountains ranged just beyond the horizon. An occasional baked, brittle bush alternating with small piles of stones broke the sameness. Wind whipped through the open windows of the car, offering a pretense of coolness.

Beside him, Moira stirred and woke from her nap.

"Christ wept, but it's hot. I'd forgotten what the outback was like."

Noah offered her the glass water bottle and she drank half of it.

"When do we reach Alice Springs?" he asked.

She glanced at her new watch. "Mmm, 'bout twenty minutes, I think. Maybe they'll let us have some water."

Currie and Boats wandered through the car.

"I told Boats that life at sea was never this bloody boring, or hot."

"An' I replied that it was never this bloody easy, either."

Moira gave them a wan smile. "I could sure use a pint of bitter about now."

The engine shrieked and they felt the car begin to slow down.

"Must be Alice Springs," Currie said, sticking his head out the window. Instantly he pulled back. "Take a look at this, people. You won't believe it!"

Ahead of the train the dun-colored buildings and metal roofs reflected the broiling sun. On each side of the double tracks people waited. A lot of people.

A banner stretched over the tracks, anchored to poles.

"There's writing on it," Boats said. "Can anyone make it out?"

Currie turned to his duffel on the seat and pulled out a pair of binoculars, leaned out the window again. "Well, I'll be chuffed!"

"What are you so pleased about?" Moira asked.

"The banner says, 'Welcome Moira, the Australian Songbird'." Currie shook his head. "Sure wasn't expecting that!"

Moira grabbed her bag and the water bottle from Noah and bolted toward the end of the car. "I've got to clean up!"

Boats laughed. "I hope they have some beer."

"What do they want?" Noah asked.

"They want to hear her sing, cobber," Currie said, "...and for the record, so do I."

The train slowed to a crawl and people waved and shouted as the car inched past them.

"Welcome to Alice Springs!"

"Moira rocks!"

"Everybody come out and have a drink!"

Boats grinned. "You don't get this on a ship!"

Their car eased in front of the station and the train stopped. A brass band started playing something lively. Noah felt completely baffled. Currie and Boats simultaneously broke into song.

"Waltzing Matilda, waltzing Matilda,

you'll come a waltzing Matilda with me –"

Moira stepped back into the car. Noah thought she looked stunning. "What did you do?" he asked.

"Oh, a bit of make-up, a fast comb, and a clean dress usually makes a girl sparkle."

He had never seen her in a dress before.

~You are so beautiful to me.~

She winked. *~You are all I care about.~* "Okay, show time!" She spun about and walked to the door facing the station, hesitated a moment, then stepped down to the cheering crowd.

She hadn't been in Alice Springs since the trip that also took her through Tennant Creek. Everybody looked the same, but she didn't remember this many people.

"Moira," a small, natty man wearing white linen trousers, a clean white shirt, and a black derby stepped forward holding out his right hand, "I'm Mayor Stocker and on behalf of the residents, I bid you welcome to Alice Springs."

She grinned and shook his hand. "Thank you. I'm so pleased to be here."

The crowd erupted with applause and cheers. Mayor Stocker waved them down. "Hold it down a minute, dammit, I ain't done yet!" Everyone laughed.

"First we want you to have the key to the city," he handed her a large brass key, bigger than any she had seen before. "We heard they made a blue up at Tennant Creek, and we wanted to make up for it. They send their apologies and ask you to reconsider your words."

"Done," she said, never losing her smile. "I've already forgotten what I said."

"Something about never singing again, I believe. Are you traveling alone?"

She knew if they heard about Tennant Creek, they also knew about Noah. "No, I have three dear friends with me. Hey fellahs, come on out. This is a friendly crowd."

More applause and shouts as Noah, Currie, and Boats climbed down the steep steps of the car. People pushed tins of cold beer into their hands and slapped their backs.

"Might I have one of those?" Moira asked. Instantly four beers were pushed toward her. She laughed and took one, knocked back half of it.

"My God, that tastes good! What can I do in return?"

"Sing!" shouted two dozen voices.

"Well, I don't think I have any arrangements with me that uses a brass band—"

Over an unseen amplifier came the first electric guitar chords of one of her most popular songs; "Shakin' Up the Outback."

She laughed with delight. "Okay, okay. You tricked me!"

The crowd loved her; she could feel it. Moreover, she loved them.

"Now you all realize I've been away and I'm a bit out of practice, and I've a train to catch." The crowd groaned and someone yelled, "Ah come on, Luv. Give us a song!"

"Okay. Just thought I'd make sure you were up for it."

They laughed and applauded as she was lifted onto the station platform. Two guitarists and a drummer waited, flanked by two ancient amplifiers made up more of patches and tape than anything else. She nodded at them. "You know the whole song?"

"You better believe we do, Moira!" the lead guitarist said, and they launched into the music.

"Came out here, followin' this track," her voice soared, and she waved widely,

"— thought I'd spend some time shakin' up the outback!"

The crowd broke into quick applause and sang the refrain, "Shakin' up the Outback, shakin' up the Outback,

Shakin' up the Outback, never look back no more!"

Moira grinned and kept singing, "If you like to sing, maybe even dance,

We'll do it together if they give us half a chance!"

While she sang, she realized she had dreaded facing an audience again, worried that perhaps performance just wasn't part of her anymore.

But this was marvelous! The raw emotion projected by the audience energized her beyond anything she remembered from before. *This could be quite addictive.*

She sang the refrain with them this time, and then took off with it again.

"Ain't much here, and it's either hot or wet,

Makes you want to dance ever' chance you get!"

They gyrated and waved their arms as they shouted out the refrain for the last time. Red-orange dust flew up from the hundreds of feet stomping the parched earth. Sweat ran down every smiling face, and she felt terrific as she belted out the last stanza.

"Something pulls you out here, not sure what for,

But I dearly love bein' in the Outback once more!"

The music ended with a crash, and she dropped over in a bow from the waist as if she had performed for the King.

The crowd cheered and whistled, clapping madly.

The train whistle blew once, and everyone booed. The engineer swung down out of the cab, holding his hands out.

"We're already a half hour late, mates. They'll have my job."

"Promise us you'll come back, Moira!" someone shouted.

Sudden tears smeared her vision, and she quickly knuckled her eyes. "You know I will. I still have the key!" She waved the great brass key above her head as they applauded.

The train started moving. Boats materialized behind her, picked her up and pushed her through the door, then swung up behind her. She squirmed around him and hung out the door waving energetically as the train gathered speed.

Applause and Alice Springs faded in the dust and heat waves. Moira staggered into the coach and collapsed beside Noah.

"My word, I've never been so tired in my whole life."

"The station agent gave me this," Currie said, handing her a flimsy piece of paper.

Moira laid the Australian Telegraphic Service message on her lap and flattened the dull yellow paper carefully so she could read it.

STUART CURRIE

OBERON, MEDICAL BLOKE FROM DAWKINS SEEKING YOU. HAS QUESTIONS AND PHOTO OF NOAH'S INJURED ARM. THINKS DREAMS ARE MEMORIES. CONTACT ME SOONEST.

LOVE, MOTHER

Moira looked up at Stuart. "Photo. What photo?"

"Dr. Carleson was writing a book about practicing medicine in the field. He photographed everything he did. He took photos of Noah's shoulder the day we found you in the kayak, before Noah healed himself."

"Bloody hell," she said in a soft whisper. "What are we going to do?"

"More to the point," Stuart said with a grim edge in his voice, "what's Oberon going to do?"

CHAPTER 16

Thinker fluked in serenity. Looa had completed a part of his being he had not known existed. And she sang.

Mating with her fulfilled him in every meaning of the nuance. She complimented his commitment and energy. They matched perfectly.

Ever southward they traveled, farther than he had ever before ventured.

~¿Where is Noah?~ she asked.

~Not certain. I thought I would hear from him before this time.~

~We are very close to the long-teeth in this place. I have fear.~

~We will wait for three visits of the warm eye. If Noah does not call in those heartbeats, we will go north.~

~As you wish, my mate.~

~Your mental communication with me seems more advanced than when we first met.~

~It is. When we mate I feel added awareness and I have learned much from you.~

~¿Added awareness? As if a different entity has become part of you?~

~Perhaps. ¿This causes you apprehension?~

~The blood-essence is obtained by ingesting the blood of its carrier. It lies in wait like the wolf eel and strikes when the carrier is most vulnerable. I fear it could become strong and dominate us.~

~¿Why would anything want to dominate us?~

~Not only us, everything, the world.~

He felt her amusement. *~¿How could something inside us dominate the world? Would that include the human world also?~*

~Yes. It nearly happened before I sought out your pod. Other creatures have this essence also. When a large amount of essence is

in one place, it joins, creating a very powerful force.~

He projected his memories of the encounter with the Hydra and the shark. Her amusement vanished and concern enveloped her like an aura.

~¿Why do we return to Noah if this can happen?~

~He called me. He needs me for something only I can do.~

~¿Was it Noah calling, or the essence?~

Thinker pondered for many heartbeats. He hated the doubt that opened instantly, like an anemone in deep water seeking any minute thing that would help it grow.

~I wish to believe it was Noah.~

~You worry that I am too infused with the essence. Yet you are the source of my essence. ¿How could I receive more than you have? Would it not be a sharing of the same amount?~

Before Thinker could answer, he heard another human vessel approaching. He reached out and assessed the minds on the ship. Not only was Noah not on board, but it was also another of the killer ships, and they were seeking Looa and him.

CHAPTER 17

Captain odeki aigauo constantly glassed the horizon from his chair on the bridge of the MV *Provider*. The vessel moved faster than most whaling ships, but in a way, so did his quarry.

They had delivered the corpses of First Mate Honda and Leading Quartermaster Shigetaro to the civil authorities at Sapporo. Then he had paid extra for a fast offloading of his catch. He knew the crew didn't like the added expense, because it would come off the top of the profits, and the captain received half of that already.

He also knew they would not say a word to him about it. They were the best-paid whaling crew in all of Japan, and not one of them would jeopardize his berth over a few yen. Besides, he felt driven by an evil kami in the form of a magic whale.

Seaman Kato Hirouchi had been correct about a whale that could visit one's mind. Even worse, the visit could prove fatal. Why did the beast kill Honda and not him?

Because I had left the bridge.

The monster mistook the first mate for the captain. That was the only explanation he could deduce. An impulse had saved his life, or was it an ujigami, the spirit of his father?

"Captain, we have a sonar contact!" Kendai Jinsinko, the newly minted first officer, shouted. "Bearing 120 degrees."

Nearly abeam on the port side! Saigauo glassed the area but saw nothing, yet.

"Change course. Full revolutions. I want them."

The MV *Provider* heeled over as it increased speed and changed course. The whalers prepared to ply their trade.

CHAPTER 18

Sheila Currie felt sweat run down her cheek as she pressed the telephone receiver to her ear. "Mr. Oberon, is that you?"

"Um, yes, missus, it is." She could hear him licking his lips.

"I've heard from Captain Currie. He wants you to contact him."

"You can't believe the dreams I've 'ad, or memories, whatever they are. "Ow do I contact 'im, please, missus?"

"Do you have something to write with?"

"Yeah."

She read him the number Stuart had sent with the wire. Her fervent prayer was that Stuart knew what he was bloody well doing with this man.

"Did you get that, Mr. Oberon?"

"This is a South Australia code! Wot th' 'ell is 'e doin' down there?"

"You'll have to ask him, Mr. Oberon."

"Did you tell 'im wot it was I wanted?"

"Yes. He is very concerned about you. Please ring him up at once."

"Gonna cost a bloody ransom to call South Australia."

"He said you could reverse the charges, so please do."

"That's bonzer, missus. Truly bonzer. I'll do that straight away."

"I'm sure the captain will be able to straighten the whole thing out for you."

"Jesus, I bloody well 'ope so."

He hung up on her.

CHAPTER 19

THINKER FELT THE ELECTRONIC PULSE BURN HIS SIDE. The humans hunted them again. He probed out and found them instantly.

Not only did they hunt Looa and him, but they also suspected their abilities. Nuance overlaying nuance flooded through him. The humans didn't know, but they intuited.

Their plan was to take the whales' essence. These people had been making their living in this manner for years. Thinker wondered how dealing death could be termed a 'living'.

Anger burned inside him for the men in the ship above them trying to kill them for their fluids and muscle. Anger at Noah for calling to him, asking him to return to this place teeming with essence-takers, toothed ones, whalers.

He also had to admit that he was angry with himself for allowing fear to grow on him like mental riders. Fear which accompanied Looa's increased cognition, fear that she might be more than she realized, more than he and Noah could subdue if the need presented itself. Fear of what that would do to Looa and the closeness they currently shared.

Another SONAR pulse pinged off his bulk and he shuddered as he restrained himself from killing every human on board the steel vessel. If he killed as he had before, they would know it was truly him. Others would mercilessly hunt him down and take his essence.

But that was different from the current situation in what manner?

~¿Why do they want us?~

~As I said before, they would use our bodies for their own purposes.~

~¿They would eat us? We would become sustenance?~

~That and more. It matters not. I will not allow that to happen.~

~We must leave this killing place, my mate.~

~Agreed. First I must deal with these humans.~

CHAPTER 20

Moira had not said much since arriving in the city of Port Lincoln. Noah knew she had been preoccupied since the stop in Alice Springs. That knowledge worried him more than he wanted to admit.

In her mind she called the experience a "siren song" which puzzled him until he probed deeper for the meaning. That he invaded her mind without invitation also gave him pause. However, there were things he needed to know. Things that could affect the world far beyond his small sphere of influence.

She didn't seem to notice his mental presence. He wondered if anything in her being noticed. If she harbored the essence, he could not detect its presence.

The anguishing dichotomy he faced was two-fold. Either Moira was possessed with the essence, or she wasn't. If not, as she said, no worries. If she was, could he and Thinker best her if it came to that?

The other side of the blade was that she might go back to her old life to sing for a living. The performance in Alice Springs had settled any doubts she might have harbored about her abilities, and it also reawakened her appetite.

Noah understood appetite. If Moira succumbed to hers, he would probably never see her again, married or not. He knew he could not constantly immerse himself in the mass of humanity that surrounded the icons of public demand.

He possessed a strong mind, but it was not invulnerable. He needed quiet, peace, as well as some distance from the mental breakers of the human sea.

He felt so afraid he would lose her.

CHAPTER 21

Aғᴛᴇʀ ᴍᴜᴄʜ ᴄᴏɴᴛᴇᴍᴘʟᴀᴛɪᴏɴ, Oʙᴇʀᴏɴ picked up the receiver and nodded for the operator to initiate the long-distance call.

The antique telephone booth occupied one corner of a small room in an old building on the edge of New Darwin Port. The telephone company hadn't been easy to locate, as the sign in front of the business was smaller than the one advertising a miracle skin lotion. The equipment looked straight out of a third-rate museum and the atmosphere proved equally musty.

Oberon kept stealing fascinated glances at the operator. Wearing a headset, she perched on a high, wooden stool in front of a manual switchboard also made of wood. The mouthpiece of her Bakelite headset held station two inches from her small, pursed lips. Her feet dangled half a meter above the plank floor.

Her small, youthful torso supported a head with a wealth of hair and a face betrayed by a multitude of lonely years. Atrophied legs hung like loose sticks, totally incapable of ever supporting her weight or desires. A wheelchair hid in the shadowed corner.

Oberon felt a heaviness in his heart, wishing he could cast a spell and free the woman to her dreams. But first, he must deal with his own. The earpiece buzzed with the distant ring.

"Hullo?" Currie said from somewhere south of the desert.

"Captain, it's me, Oberon." He licked his lips, and his eyes swam over the dusty glass and wood of the booth, seeking answers or a resting place. "I've been having these dreams."

"You're calling me about dreams?" Currie sounded faintly nettled.

"Not just the dreams, sir. There are the photographs—"

"Who has seen the photographs besides yourself?"

"Ah, your mother, Skipper. I showed 'em to her, to prove I

wasn't mental, like."

"But no one else?"

"No, sir. Nobody else has seen 'em. I didn't know how to explain my fear."

"Fear? What are you afraid of, Oberon?"

"Monsters, if you please." Tears squeezed out the corners of his eyes and tracked down his sallow cheeks. "At first, I thought they wuz nightmares, y'know? But then I started rememberin', and things came back to me in fits 'n' starts."

"You need to talk about this, don't you? To someone who understands."

"Yes, sir! That I do. I know you wuz there and saw everything what I'm havin' trouble rememberin', 'n' if anyone can sort me out, it's you, Captain."

For what seemed a long time the line remained silent.

"You still there, sir?"

"Yes, Oberon, I'm still here. Why don't you come down here? We can talk, and figure this all out. I'll arrange for a ticket on the train. You'll be on the pay book just like in the ANDF; except you'll be working for me. How does that sound?"

"That Noah, Inuit fellow, is he still with you?"

"Yes, he is. Is that a problem?"

"No, not at all. I want to speak with 'im. I need to know 'ow he did that, as a medical man, you understand."

"I understand," Currie said, sounding distant as heat lightning. "We'll meet your train at Port Lincoln."

CHAPTER 22

TWHINKER AND LOOA DIVED DEEP AND FLUKED as hard as they could in the opposite direction of the ship's course. One more ping had bounced off Thinker's back and then silence reigned broken only by their laboring hearts.

~I must rise for air.~ Looa's words were infused with regret, failure, and acceptance of death.

~Agreed. Do not breech. Touch the top of the world with as little as possible. Clear your lungs and fill them, then we dive deep and far again.~

~Lead. I will follow.~

The whalers saw the twin sprays but didn't believe it to be the whales they hunted. Thinker sifted through the minds on board and gently intensified their erroneous beliefs. They dived again and lengthened their distance from the ship.

~Do we turn north now?~

~I must communicate with Noah before I am ready to leave this place.~

~Once before, I told my mate I would leave with or without him. Now I say it again. In one more visit of the warm eye, I return to the cold waters. Will Thinker travel with me?~

~Thinker must communicate with Noah before he can answer. Looa must swim through her own world. I want you by my side always, but I cannot ignore my friend.~

~¿Why does he ignore you?~

CHAPTER 23

Moira thought she knew what worried Noah. They hadn't made love again since the first time. He was afraid to give her more of his "essence" or whatever he thought it was. She'd experienced plenty of "essence" in her life and knew this time opened a whole new world.

Yet, he continued so quietly paranoid about her that she almost didn't trust herself. If that really was the problem.

She knew she could delve through his mind and fossick out the answer for certain. Unfortunately, that didn't seem polite, and she didn't wish to add to his obvious discomfort. The ability to know what other people were thinking fascinated her.

At Alice Springs she had perceived the gamut of emotions from excitement to love to lust. One person there had envied her to the point of hate. That she could elicit so much emotion in complete strangers seemed an obligation of sorts.

Didn't she owe them all something? Hadn't they made her name famous across Australia and who knew where else? Could she really curtail her career? Just stop?

Noah complicated her life like no other human ever had before. He was an interesting complication to be sure. The growth she had witnessed in him measured nothing short of amazing.

"Here's Oberon's train now," Currie said, breaking her reverie.

The four of them wandered out to the platform and watched the scabrous diesel locomotive screech by as it slowed its huge load.

"Why are there no aircraft?" Noah asked. He had hoped to see one of the nearly mythical machines.

"There are." Currie didn't take his eyes off the train. "Military uses them. There's a good number of old jets still about, but there's not enough fuel to operate them efficiently."

"Most of the Technology Age ran on oil," Boats said. "And most of the oil was in the Middle East."

"Is it still there, the oil I mean?"

"Mate, the bloody Middle East ain't there. That's where the biggest meteorite impacted. Doubled the size of the Mediterranean Sea in an instant."

"Not to mention destroyed every country around the Med with the resulting tsunamis." Currie glanced at Noah. "You never got any of this in school?"

"No school," Noah said. "How does this run?" He nodded at the train.

"On oil, but very lightly refined, and blended with other sorts of oil, from plants and what not. The world's been trying to rebuild itself out of the wreckage and some things need to be invented all over again."

With a great shudder, the train stopped, and they stared expectantly at the passenger car.

Abruptly Noah's mind filled with a familiar presence.

~¿Noah, where are you? Whalers are hunting us. I have taken the essence of two humans before they could take ours. What requires my presence in this place? Where are you?~

He quickly looked at Moira, but she seemed as fascinated with the passenger coach as the others. He reached out with his mind.

~Thinker. I am on the south (colder) coast. Tomorrow we take ship for New Zealand.

~Your life is not worth my desires. If you are threatened, go where you must to be safe. You and Looa's safety is much more important. I did not know you would face danger in heeding my call. Please forgive me.~

The presence vanished and Noah wondered if Thinker had returned north. For a long instant Point Hope lived in his mind before fading back into reality.

"There he is," Boats said.

"Oberon." Currie called. "Over here, man."

CHAPTER 24

Captain Saigauo cursed as the reverie passed from his mind. A quick glance around the MV *Provider's* bridge told him that everyone on board had experienced the same thing. Something had altered their mindset.

He clearly remembered ordering the pursuit of the whales. Then an incredible lassitude had washed over all of them to the point he altered course away from the quarry. Suffused with shame over being so easily duped, he walked around the bridge and stared into the face of every man.

He did not find mirth. All shared his humiliation.

"This is more than a whale," he said flatly. "It is a monster that has killed two of our crew mates and has made fools of the rest of us. We will hunt it to its death!"

"Hai!" they all shouted together.

"Mr. Jinsinko, you have the bridge." Hideki Saigauo went to his cabin. He knelt in front of the small Shinto corner shrine.

"Was it one such as this that lured you to your death, honored father?"

His mother had always believed that if reports of unusual whale activity in the Philippine Sea hadn't pulled her husband's attention around to the other side of Hokkaido, he would have lived through the tsunamis and the long, hard winter which followed.

The northern portion of the Sea of Japan had frozen solid for a time. Hideki clearly remembered those hungry days. He became obsessed with killing whales. If they managed to stay alive through the long winter of the world, he swore on his father's memory that he would hunt them for the rest of his life.

He had honored that vow and now a monster jeopardized his sacred mission. Even if it meant taking more time away from his wife and children back in Mashike, he promised he would find this beast and destroy it. After a few more moments of reflection, he returned to his bridge.

CHAPTER 25

Oberon sat in the back of the motorcar with Bosun Stout to port and Captain Currie to starboard. Moira Manaluk drove the huge thing. The Inuit, Noah, rode in the front next to his wife. Every now and then Noah glanced back at him. Never in his life had he been the center of attention for this many people.

"Tell me about your dreams," Currie said.

"Monsters with spots," Oberon blurted, getting the worst out immediately. "Part of it with great huge tits, pardon me, ma'am," he nodded at Moira who winked at him in the rearview mirror, "and part of it something I can't remember."

"Oberon, allow me to explain something," Currie said.

"But you ain't heard–"

"I've heard enough. You're right; those weren't dreams. All that really happened."

"Then why don't I remember it straight? Why the–"

His brain suddenly felt full to bursting. He wanted to ask about–

~Please allow me to explain!~

At some point, Oberon realized Noah no longer filled his mind. However, he understood everything, despite his amazement, and rapidly dwindling disbelief.

"Excuse me, Captain, but I gotta know. Did your mum know about this state of affairs?"

Everyone in the motorcar laughed, except Oberon.

"Yes, but she was sworn to secrecy, just as you are."

He could see the sense in that. Who knew what would happen if word of this got about? "So where are we bound, Captain?"

The motorcar's tyres squealed around a corner and Currie pointed. "Right there, mate."

A rust-streaked steamer lay moored to the dock. Great bursts of black, oily smoke belched from her stack. The only resemblance she had to the *Andrew Dawkins* was that she still floated.

"We're goin' ta sea in that?" Oberon asked.

"I'm afraid so," Currie said with a sideways glance at Boats. "Unless there's been some mistake."

Boats peered at the ship before shaking his head.

"No mistake. That's the SS *Grand Island*, departing for New Wellington in twenty minutes. All aboard!"

CHAPTER 26

THINKER AND LOOA FLUKED SOUTH THROUGH STILL TROPICAL WATERS. He struggled with amazement over how much he had learned since meeting Noah. He believed he was the first cetacean to ever truly understand his exact location in the great oceans.

By touching the minds of men in areas around him he knew what places were called, their relative size, and what to expect in the waters ahead.

~¿Did Noah say how long it would take him to meet us?~

~They are departing the Oz land on a ship now. By the return of the sun, they will be far at sea on their way to New Zealand.~

~¿Where?~

~A different great rock, closer to the southern cold water.~

Her silence spoke as loudly as her words. He knew she wished them away from here to waters where fewer humans roamed with their insatiable appetites. Thinker continued south. He would go where he thought best and Looa was free to do what she desired.

Yet, he hoped she would stay with him.

~Thinker, are you out there?~ Noah's presence filled Thinker so completely he knew his friend had to be physically near. Thinker quickly scanned the sea around him and found Noah's essence on one of many "ships" in the area.

~Yes. Looa and I are here. ¿Why did you summon me?~

~Moira is with child. She knew of its conception immediately after mating. Since we mated, Moira is able to communicate as we do.~

~You gave her the Essence, along with your own. We had believed it needed to be spread by blood.~ Thinker pondered the situation. If Moira could communicate in this manner, was she a silent observer in the conversation at this moment?

~Yes I am, my friend.~ Moira said.

Thinker weighed her essence for a moment then slipped into her mind and being, seeking the alien entity that had threatened their existence in the past.

And he found it.

CHAPTER 27

STANDING NEXT TO OAH ON THE WEATHER DECK OF THE *Grand Island*, Moira heard mental gasps from both Thinker and Noah. She had been staring at the water, listening to the conversation, and imagining what it must be like to be a whale. It seemed devious not to answer Thinker's unspoken question.

She felt nothing when he investigated her. Now Noah pulled away from her, staring as if waiting for spikes to erupt from her head.

~¿*The Essence is in you, Moira. Do you not feel it?*~ Thinker asked.

"Bloody hell!" she said with a snort. ~*Do you feel it in yourself? Does Noah?*~ She glared at her husband for a long moment before continuing.

~*Whatever is in me was put there by Noah. I know I am with child. I know he is male. But I don't believe he is evil, nor am I. So, you two best sort this thing out to your satisfaction, soonest!*~

"I am going to have a son?" Noah said, looking stunned.

"Bloody right you are, cobber!" She felt like hitting him. What did he think she was going to do, tear his throat out?

~*The Essence has always become threatening when too much of it is gathered in one place.*~ Thinker conveyed sorrow, fear, and love all at the same time.

~*Yet I sense nothing of the sort. How close are you to the ship?*~ Noah said.

Noah still looked somewhat stunned. Moira felt her heart go out to him. She was so glad they had married.

~*Looa and I are within one-half of one of your miles. As you, I do not feel threat. But of old, the Essence attacked without warning.*~

Moira wondered if she harbored something malevolent within her. The child? Impossible. It was barely more than thumb-sized.

Still, she didn't think one usually became telepathic at the onset of pregnancy, so something was bloody well different.

~Thinker, would you and Looa please get as close to this ship as you can?~

~! ¿Is this wise? Would we not be opening ourselves to death?~

~What better location to find out? There are others here, humans I trust, who know about us. Look into my mind.~

Noah was amazing, she decided. The little bloke had more guts than anyone else she knew. He had gone from an emotional twelve-year-old to something beyond her ken in just weeks. What would he be like in a year?

~Thank you for asking me into your mind. I agree with you about Stuart, Boats, and Oberon. We are moving toward the ship.~

CHAPTER 28

THE TIME HAD COME. Full knowledge, realization, understanding, and supplication impelled it to thrust into all their minds.

•Be not afraid. I am not the same Essence you knew in the past. My perspective has matured to encompass more than just appetites.

•Before growing with Noah and Thinker, my only other re-acquired cognition lay in beings that only dealt with hunger, lust, and domination. I have looked into all of you, and through you into completely separate worlds, let alone cultures and other subcategories. You have caused me to grow and regain memories millennia old.

•Yes, I am in all of you. I will always be in you. But I will cause no further harm.•

Moira watched the strain fade from Noah's face, and felt the fear in him erode and dissipate. She smiled.

•I came to this world after a voyage of such length I edged on madness. I thought myself already mentally perished but cursed to retain cognition through all time. When I sensed your world's psychic aura of life I sought to embrace it.•

She was in the Essence's memory now, feeling the excitement it had felt. Moira felt tears in the corners of her eyes.

•Human weapons fragmented me before I could communicate with the myriad of minds flooding into me. The loss of the Hydra and the shark greatly reduced my mass of malevolency and therefore my appetite for domination. Your questing to be more than you already are reminded me of my race in its infancy.

•I would like to accomplish that which I sought so very long ago: I wish to help.•

The mental creature pulled back, retreating to honor its self-avowal not to intrude into other sentience unless threatened. It hoped it had just eliminated such a threat. It waited for their response.

Book Five

CHAPTER 1

"THIS IS CALLED THE TARARUA RANGE." Bosun Dan Stout said, carefully driving the electric sedan as the road topped a ridge and began to drop into a long, stunningly beautiful valley. Noah sat in the left front seat with Moira between him and Boats. Captain Stuart Currie and Medical Aide Niles Oberon sat in the back seat.

"This is a beautiful place," Noah said. "But I now know that most land in New Zealand already belongs to someone."

"What's that got to do with anything?" Boats Stout asked.

"We would need money to buy land, yes?"

"I don't think we're going to have to worry about money," Captain Currie said.

"Stuart, did you rob a bank back in Oz?" Moira asked.

His grin flashed through the red mustaches and beard. "No, but I did a bit of research. We are almost to where we will find our answer."

"I don't like surprises," Noah said.

"Don't think of it as a surprise. Consider it a concept."

"But we haven't heard it yet," Moira said with some crispness in her voice.

"Right up there, Boats, on the right."

"Aye, aye, Captain."

The car turned into a long drive between immaculate white fencing on either side. Trees and brush dotted the sloping meadows and hundreds of sheep grazed on the grass. In the distance, the land dropped away to provide a spectacular view of a beautiful lake.

The drive turned and wound through a large stand of trees to loop in front of a handsome two-story house before ending at a garage boasting four doors.

"Stuart, are you sure about this?" Noah said.

"Very sure."

By the time Boats stopped the auto in front of the house, a man in working clothes stood waiting a few steps up the walk. Currie jumped out of the auto.

"Mr. Williams?"

"You must be Captain Currie." Williams smiled and shook hands. His weathered face boasted a neatly trimmed mustache and bright blue eyes.

"Allow me to introduce my friends."

As Currie introduced them to Williams, Noah held back from looking into the man's mind. He didn't feel in any danger in this beautiful place, so he was content to let the situation unfold.

As Currie said his name, Noah shook Williams' callused hand and looked into the man's eyes.

"Is there some way we can help you, Mr. Williams?"

"Please, it's Sean, and I bloody well hope so."

Noah gave Currie a glance, but Stuart looked off at the scenery with a smile playing about his lips.

"Won't you all please come in?"

The house was the biggest dwelling Noah had ever seen. The bright, smooth wood floors reminded him of the baidarka. Wide windows looked out on the lake deep in the valley.

The scent of flowers rode the warm breeze through the house and Noah felt harmony in the structure and its contents.

Moira sighed. "You have a beautiful place here, Sean. You must have worked very hard to achieve this."

"Yes, I did. I made all my money in Wellington. My construction company was the first to start rebuilding all those years ago, and we've never stopped. Elizabeth and I wanted to be away from the city, so we bought this land and built this house. We love it here."

"Elizabeth?" Moira said.

"My wife is upstairs in her room. She's dying."

"May I see her?" Noah said. "I might be able to help."

"That's what Captain Currie said." Williams gave Noah a bleak look. "I don't know what you can do. The best doctors available have admitted defeat."

"I will do what I can."

Williams looked at Moira. "You're Moira Napier, aren't you?"

"It's Moira Manaluk now. But, yes, that was my professional name."

"Would you mind coming up with Noah and me? Elizabeth is one of your biggest fans."

"I would like to meet her."

"Gentlemen, please make yourselves comfortable. Hana will bring you food and drink." He gestured toward a lithe, brown-skinned woman with tattoos under her lower lip.

She nodded to them and disappeared back through the doorway.

As Noah followed Sean and Moira up the wide stairway, he heard Boats mutter, "My word, but she's striking!"

Elizabeth lay in a bed that Noah thought might be bigger than the house in which he grew up. Propped up by half a dozen pillows, she gave them all a dazzling smile as they entered.

"Visitors. How wonderful," she said in a breathy voice.

"My dear," Sean said, "this is Noah Manaluk, and this is–"

"My God!" Elizabeth exclaimed, "Moira Napier!"

Moira moved over the side of the bed and took both of Elizabeth's hands in hers. "It's Moira Manaluk now, but I am very happy to meet you."

As soon as they entered the room Noah slipped into her mind and found "multiple sclerosis" dominating all other thoughts. After a few moments divining the meaning of the term and the nature of the disease, he worked through her body, increasing this function, terminating that one, rebuilding nerve sheathing, and restoring energy levels. Every time he healed a person he learned something new, and remembered all of it.

"This is just wonderful," Elizabeth said. "Meeting you has given me new strength; I can feel it."

Sean glanced at Noah and then moved to the bedside. "What do you mean, darling?"

"Well, I just feel bonzer!" She pushed herself off the pillows and swung bare feet out from beneath the sheets.

Sean stepped back with a stunned expression on his face.

Elizabeth stood up. "See? I feel wonderful, and it's all due to Moira visiting me."

Moira laughed. "Thank you for the compliment, Elizabeth, but you're in error. My husband, Noah, has no doubt corrected what was wrong with your body. He's gifted and quite good at that sort of thing."

Both Sean and Elizabeth stared at Noah. He felt discomfort at some of the thoughts they strongly projected.

"I am a healer," he said. "This is something I can do, and to help others allows me to atone for past indiscretions."

"Sean," Elizabeth said in a full, strong contralto, "I believe I am completely healed. This is a miracle."

"Gift, not a miracle," Noah insisted.

Sean's face still reflected awe, and tears ran down his cheeks. "You call it what you like, my friend, but it's still a bloody miracle to me! Thank you."

"I am pleased I could help." Noah glanced around at the door behind him. "Perhaps I could get something to drink now?"

"Oh, mate, you bet you can have a drink. Hell, we're going to have a party!"

The house swarmed with people of all shades. Noah felt uncomfortably full after the huge dinner Sean had hosted. People had seemingly appeared from nowhere to rejoice in Elizabeth's return to health.

Currie, Boats, and Oberon all chatted with women of different colors. The young woman, Hana, whom Noah had discovered was a Maori, laughed at something Boats said. Sean raised grapes as well as sheep and was a vintner.

Wine was something new in Noah's experience and he felt exhilarated already when Sean rang a small bell and the room fell silent.

"This is the happiest day of my life," Sean said with emotion evident in his voice. "I have been watching my beloved Elizabeth ebb away daily over the past five years. As you all know, I offered a million dollars to anyone who could help her."

"What?" Noah said. His voice was drowned out by the instant murmurs that filled the room.

"And Mr. Noah Manaluk, from Alaska in North America, has not only helped her, but he has also cured her!"

The room erupted in applause. Noah blushed deeply, overwhelmed by the attention. He stood and waved his hands for silence.

"Mr. Williams, I did not know of your offer when I came here."
He shot a hard look at Stuart who winked back at him. "And I
cannot accept a reward of that size for something I do willingly for
no payment whatsoever. My inua would be tarnished."

Stuart quickly moved to Noah's side and held up his hands.

"I knew of Elizabeth's condition, and of Sean's offer. I did not tell
my friend here about it either. Nonetheless, speaking as Noah's
agent, I would like to change the terms somewhat."

"Agent?" Noah blurted.

"Name it," Sean said.

"We would like to borrow the million and pay you back over the
next ten years."

Noah frowned at Stuart. "How can we pay back a million dollars
in ten years? None of us have a, what do you call it, income, and no
prospects of one."

"Like it or not, Noah, you are famous from this point on. We are
going to build a sanctuary for people who are diseased, injured, at
the end of their rope, and they will donate what they can to be
there to gain comfort and health. It will be enough. You watch."

"Tell me what you want in the way of a structure," Sean said,
"and I'll build it. I'll even donate one of my paddocks for the site."

Applause filled the room again and Noah felt his heart soar.

CHAPTER 2

Noah noticed that Oberon seemed bothered by something but decided he wouldn't invade the man's privacy.

"Noah, can I have a bit of a word with you?"

"Surely, Niles. What is it?"

They all sat on the hillside overlooking the construction site of the Sanctuary, having just finished a picnic lunch. The constant racket of hammers and saws filled the air. Sanctuary was already completely framed in, and all three floors boasted heavy subfloors.

"Is it true you and Captain Currie are going back to New Darwin to fetch his mum?"

"Well, he is going back, and he asked me to accompany him. But I haven't decided yet. Why?"

"Please, Noah, would you go and take me with you? There's something I need for you to do there."

"Then of course I will. Besides, we need to get you enrolled in the medical school at New Sydney University."

"I'm not sure I'm smart enough to deal with that, sir."

"Trust me, you are."

Niles Oberon and Noah walked into the New Darwin Port Telephone Exchange and Telegraph Company and Bosun Stout shut the door behind them. Still sitting on the high stool, her withered legs hanging like rain-soaked corn stalks, she turned her doll-like head and regarded them.

"Can I help you, gentlemen?" she asked in a voice that reminded Noah of chickadees.

"May I ask your name, ma'am?" Oberon said.

"Andrea," she said and smiled at him. "Miss Andrea Peterson; what's yours?"

"Niles Oberon. And if you please, Andrea," he said, feeling tears lurking at the edge of his eyes, "we'd like to help you."

"Where are they, Stuart?" Shelia Currie asked. "The train is going to leave any moment now."

"Don't worry, Mother, they'll be here in time."

A woman somewhere in her thirties ran up to them.

"Are you Captain Currie?"

"Yes I am. And you are?"

"Andrea Peterson. I went dancing last night!"

"You say that as if it were the first time in your life, dear," Sheila said with a smile.

Andrea turned to her. "But it was. You see, it was the very first time!" She burst into tears.

Boats Stout, Noah, and Niles walked up.

"I see you met Andrea," Niles said with a wide grin. "She's going back with us. She wants to be our communications person at Sanctuary."

Andrea hugged Oberon. "Niles, I am going to be so good for you!"

"You already are, Andi. You already are."

CHAPTER 3

"PANT, MOIRA, HARD AS YOU CAN!" Maggie Huata, Hana's mother, held onto Moira's spread knees to give the small woman strength.

"Oh, this has to be over sooooon!" Moira yelled.

Noah pushed through the door and took Moira's hand. "I'm here. What can I do for you?"

"Dilate my bloody cervix!" she screamed.

~It's something you can do yourself, my love. Let me show you.~

~Oh! That's amazing. Why didn't I think of this myself?~

~You just wanted to give me a chance to help.~

"He's crowning!" Maggie said with a huge smile. "You dilated a full six centimeters in less than two seconds." She reached down and delivered the head, holding it carefully but firmly while the tiny shoulders slipped through the birth canal.

She cleaned and cuddled the small body while examining it critically, searching for visible defects. The boy exuded health. She quickly laid him on the birthing bed and vigorously rubbed his small body.

He gave a small cry and then took a gasping breath before going quiet again. She clamped off the umbilical cord close to the child's belly and deftly cut it an inch farther away with a piece of seashell honed to razor sharpness.

"Is he alright?" Moira asked, radiating fear.

"He's fine," Noah said, looking down at his son. "Hello, Solomon."

The bright, dark eyes in the small, wizened face unblinkingly held Noah's.

~Hello, father.~

~You are completely cognizant at birth? I had not anticipated that.~

~He has been conversing with me for the past month, Noah. I wanted to surprise you. Welcome to the world, my son.~

"Is everything bonzer?" Maggie asked, worry wrapping around her words.

"Everything is fine," Moira said with a beatific smile. "This is Solomon, here to help us."

"You were all so quiet, it scared me."

"Thank you for being so attentive, Maggie. I feel so blessed that you and Hana came into our lives."

"Ah, here is the placenta," Maggie said as she bent down and delivered it.

"Wrap it in heavy plastic and put it into the coldest freezer Mr. Williams owns. That holds answers and cures for the future."

"As you wish. We used to bury it."

"Never again, Maggie. Save them all."

"I will, Moira."

~How soon will I be able to walk and talk?~

~Probably a lot sooner than I'll be prepared for,~ Noah said.

Noah looked deep into Moira's eyes and smiled. He felt totally euphoric.

CHAPTER 4

"I NEEDS TO SEE THIS NOAH BLOKE!" the big man told the young guard stationed at the east Sanctuary door.

"He has daily audiences with supplicants and well-wishers. The next one is in less than an hour, sir." Frosty Gorin surreptitiously took stock of the stranger's garb and attitude. The man seemed nervous and edgy. *Why?*

"Where does he hide when he's not feedin' the masses a load of dreck?"

"I think you need to leave, sir." Frosty pressed the alert button on his communicator. "This is a peaceful sanctuary. If you have a problem, please see our–"

The man abruptly backhanded Frosty, throwing him hard against the wall, and knocking all his wind from him.

"I've heard enough of yer fucking chatter, altar boy!" He pulled a large revolver out from beneath his heavy shirt, cocked it, and pointed it at Frosty, who lay on the floor gasping like a landed fish.

"You've got exactly five seconds to tell me where Noah bloke is or—"

The side of his head erupted, and two other rounds thundered in the hall, hitting him in the body before he slammed onto the floor sideways, staring dead.

Frosty, still dazed by the attack, turned his head to see Danny Stout crouched in the doorway with an automatic pistol clutched in a two-handed grip.

"You okay, Frosty?"

"Sure, Boats. Absolutely fair dinkum!"

"That's the third one in the last five weeks. Now Noah is going to have a security force with thoroughly modern methods whether he likes it or not."

"Will we get training?" Frosty asked.

"You still want to be part of it?"

"Hey, Boats, if you haven't noticed, I already am!"

Boats grinned. "You didn't panic. That's a good thing, but on the other hand, you didn't have time to panic."

"I had the time. I knew he was trouble. I just didn't know he had a gun."

"Would knowing he had a gun have made a difference?"

"Yeah. I would have disarmed him or killed him immediately."

The sound of many people running toward them interrupted the conversation.

"What happened?" Big Boy Hauta, father of Hana and husband to Maggie, bristled up in his most war-like stance. His face bore traditional tattooing from forehead to chin, and Boats knew the man's rather formidable tongue also carried decoration. Big Boy stood six feet, three inches in his bare feet and his shoulders looked to be a meter wide.

"Got us another rotten apple," Boats said, nodding at the body on the floor. "He should never have gotten this far into the Sanctuary."

"Why would anyone want to kill Noah?" Big Boy said in his deep, rumbling voice. "The little bloke just helps people, not hurt them."

"I think these types believe they can gain some of his power if they can kill him. I know there are all sorts of stories out there. What they don't realize is that they would have to eat him to get anything at all, and I'm not even sure it would work then."

Big Boy flashed his "warrior" face with exaggerated facial grimacing, eyes opening as far as possible to show huge whites around dark pupils and his jaw nearly unhinging with his tattooed tongue trying to touch his chest. The ancient Maori method for demoralizing an enemy: which literally says, "I will kill you and eat your body!" The ancient Maoris were cannibals.

"Ha," Big Boy said. "He's not even a Maori, so no worries."

Boats grinned. "Whatever or whoever he is, get him out of here and have Dr. Oberon look him over before we call the police."

"Right away, Boats," Big Boy said and proceeded to give orders to other late arrivals.

Boats Stout replaced his clip from the ammo pouch hooked to his holster harness and then pulled his jacket over the lot as he walked toward Noah and Moira's wing of the Sanctuary. After two years of living in the well-built compound, it seemed as though he had never lived anywhere else. With a start, he realized that was the case.

He had run away from his family's sheep station, deep in the Australian outback, when he was fifteen years old. His Da' was one of those flint-eyed, hard fisted men who thought actions spoke much louder than words to the point he rarely talked to his three sons. Hitting them or his wife seemed to be all the communication he needed.

But Da' also drank, Boats reflected, which didn't aid communication. Robert "Big Bobby" Stout, Da', was a large man. At fifteen, Dan was growing like he wouldn't stop, but he still was not the size of his father.

One night, after his fourth beer before the evening meal, Da' decided he didn't like what Maye had on the stove and proceeded to throw everything on the floor. Maye blew her top and told him he could eat and sleep with the pigs that night.

Robert began slapping her around. Dan stopped him with a punch to the side of his head that knocked the man to the floor. When Robert found his feet again and swung at his oldest son, Dan proceeded to "pound hell" out of his father.

He left his father unconscious on the kitchen floor amid the boiled potatoes, mutton stew, and grease. After fetching his few articles of clothing and a sheath knife, and putting it in his swag, he went to his mother.

"This ain't the life I want, mum. I'm going as far from here as I can. I'll write to you. Don't worry."

Maye Stout hugged her son close. "He's not a bad man, just a limited one. Be good to the women in your life, Danford."

He was good to the women in his life, no matter how briefly they shared his time. Still, since joining the Australian Naval Defense Force at sixteen, he had served in various locations and finally became Boatswain's Mate on the *Andrew Dawkins*; but he had never actually lived anywhere until the Sanctuary.

He loved it here. He treasured the spacious apartment he had a few yards from the residence wing where Noah, Moira, and Solomon lived. This life had allowed him to come out from behind the hard shell developed over twenty-five years of working with hard men in a difficult world.

At first, he'd thought he was getting soft. When he commented in that vein to Moira, she'd said, "You're not getting soft, Boats. You're mellowing into the openness only a man who knows himself can afford."

Lately, he had thought about finding himself a wife, or at least a lady friend. His openness wasn't the only thing he had suppressed over the years.

He stopped in front of the residence door and pulled the small bell. The clear ring hadn't begun to fade when the door opened, and two-year-old Solomon stood there looking up at him. "Are you okay, Boats?" the child asked with gravity far beyond his years.

Boats immediately picked him up and rubbed his full head of hair fondly. "You bet I am, Sol. How are you?"

"Mother says I'm too impatient because I want to do things beyond my physical abilities, and I get angry."

"Sol, old son, you're only two years old. At least try to be a kid for a bit. You sound like an Oxford don when you talk."

"That's because I'm different. I didn't ask to be different, but I am. So why can't I be different in other ways, too?"

"Don't be in such a rush to get old, my friend. It's a road you can't retrace."

Moira came up to them and reached for Solomon. "That's what I keep telling him, too, Boats. But he's stubborn like his father."

In perfect harmony Boats and Solomon said together, "And his mother!"

She laughed with them.

"Mr. Bosun Stout, how are you, sir?" Noah said as he entered the room.

"I'm fine. Can't say as much for the bloke I just stopped."

"We know. We felt the disharmony and witnessed the event from the perspective of others. You did what was needed, efficiently and quickly. Thank you for protecting us and our people."

Boats felt his cheeks warm, and he looked at his feet to hide his embarrassment. "Any time. You know that Noah, Moira."

"Which brings us to another part of this subject," Moira said.

"What's that?" he asked.

"I've talked it over with Noah and Solomon and we've all agreed that Solomon needs to see more of the world while he's in his formative years, and I feel the need to sing. Therefore, Solomon and I are going on an eighteen-month tour. I have an agent looking into booking venues for concerts."

"You want to leave Sanctuary?"

"I love it here. But, I need to get this music career thing out of my system. Hana is coming with us to help with Solomon. Would you consider coming with me to be my security chief?"

"What about you, Noah?" Boats asked.

"I will stay here. There is much to be done to complete the vision we have started. It would give me solace to know you were protecting my family."

"Well, ah, sure. Of course, I'll do it. Just the four of us, then?"

"Pick three others from our family to help," Noah said. "You'll be in charge, so you decide who goes."

Boats looked Moira in the eyes. "A concert tour, is it? There will be mobs of people at every venue. I hope you're charging a ransom for your time and talent."

"All profits will go to the Sanctuary, of course. But you spend what you must to keep us all safe and sound."

"Yes, ma'am, I'll do just that. When does this thing start?"

"Looks like three months from now, in Auckland, then a week later in Wellington, and the week after that in Christchurch. After that we head for Tasmania and then on to Australia."

"I best get busy. Three months ain't much of a lead for a circus like this. I still must improve our security before we leave. Josh has modified an old metal detector to make a security frame for the front door of the Sanctuary."

"What?" Noah said.

"Why?" Moira said immediately after.

"Then you can tell if the people coming in have guns, can't you, Boats?" Solomon said in his piping voice.

"Bloody hell!" Boats blurted. He caught himself and cast an abashed glance at Noah and Moira, but they both stared at their son. Boats looked back at the boy. "You really scare me sometimes, Sol. This just ain't natural. But you're dead on, mate."

"It's a good idea, Boats," Solomon said earnestly.

Boats grinned at Moira. "Why don't you just have him do the security?"

"He needs to get his education first," Moira said.

"Believe me, luv, working security is an education all by itself."

CHAPTER 5

Boats FROWNED AS HE TRIED TO GET HIS BLUE CONCERT jacket to cover the butt of his 9mm pistol. If he continued to breathe shallowly, the coat would hang over the weapon.

"Good enough," he muttered.

The "Moira Once More" concert circuit had sold out in the first four hours the tickets were on sale — *all* the concerts. Moira's share of the ticket sales put over NA$16 million dollars into the Sanctuary coffers. Boats immediately hired the best security agency in Australia to train the Sanctuary staff and to help him provide security for Moira.

Two agents, an Austral-Asian woman, and a nondescript white man were always within fifteen feet of Moira as was Boats. Whenever Moira went to the loo, Amra went with. Boats thanked the Essence for their presence.

Completed concerts in Wellington, Auckland, Christchurch, Hobart, and Sydney now lay behind them. All were successful beyond description. Moira had been described in the Australian press as the first superstar of the Apocalypse Generation.

The crowds couldn't get enough of her. Sometimes, that wasn't a good thing.

Canberra still served as the capital of Australia, Houses of Parliament and all that, but as in all capital cities, the outskirts bred a very questionable lot. The concert went off without a hitch. As always, Moira returned to the stage three times after the concert officially ended.

She lived for curtain calls she had confided to Boats. "That's when you know they really love you and really want to hear more. I can feel that. I can't deny them."

Boats figured there had been in excess of five thousand

screaming fans jammed into Bruce Stadium tonight. The venerable footballer's paradise was the largest venue the tour director could find in the city. It had survived the quakes and tsunamis, not to mention over 80 years of football, and rock and roll.

As always, Boats preceded Moira by at least twenty yards when she left the stage. In the past months, he had spotted no less than six blokes hiding in the shadows waiting to accost Moira for one reason or another. Most were convinced that they were the only man she could really love if she just had the opportunity to meet them.

So far, they had all been in error, and Boats had been able to deal with them expeditiously. Amra and Clive followed within two meters of her. Close enough to help but not get in her way.

As usual, Moira was exhausted to the point she shuffled down the old concrete floored tunnel leading to the dressing rooms, the green rooms, and the myriad other technical and logistical spaces secreted behind the scenes. Boats moved steadily and quietly through the near gloom broken by occasional overhead lamps, many of which flickered constantly. He heard a "click" behind him and immediately turned on the balls of his feet and drew his trusty pistol at the same time.

The man already stood in front of Moira, not allowing Boats a safe shot, and the son of a bitch had a gun up to her head.

"Everybody stop!" the man bellowed. "I know I am surrounded by armed minions, but I also know I am far too close to her for any of you to risk shooting me."

"Bastard's right!" Boats said in a low voice as he slowly advanced in silent steps toward the threat. The man faced back toward Amra and Clive. Both of whom stared at him fixedly, each waiting for the opportunity to take him out.

"I am here to claim what is mine. Moira was married to my cousin, Deagan Napier, who died protecting her. As his closest male relative, I claim the right to take her hand in marriage! Who else has the right according to custom?"

Boats stopped five meters behind the man and snapped his fingers to get the man's attention.

In a loud voice, Moira grated, "You forgot something, fuckwit!"

The man hesitated and the muzzle of his pistol wavered from her temple. "What? What did I forget? I worked this out completely."

"You fucking forgot to ask me!"

The pistol dropped from nerveless fingers as he lurched and grabbed at his chest on his way to the concrete floor. Boats, Amra, and Clive all reached Moira's side at the same time.

"Don't bother," Moira said in a tired voice as she moved toward the light and her dressing room. "He's dead. Something stopped his heart."

Within an hour, Boats had paid off the two security agents after adding a sizable bonus to their cancellation clause money.

"You don't talk about what you saw here," Boats told them. "You'd be amazed at the range of my hearing, if you get my drift?"

Both nodded, shook his hand, and vanished.

"Why didn't you tell me you could do that?" Boats asked Moira in her dressing room.

"You didn't ask."

"Mother is magic," Solomon said with a smile. "Isn't she, Hana?"

"Most assuredly," Hana said, looking from Moira to Boats. "We are surrounded by magic people."

Boats grinned at the young woman. "I'm not magic, Hana. I can't do anything for folks other than protect them."

Hana gave him a soft smile and lowered her eyes. "You do more than that for me."

He felt his face warming and the added embarrassment promptly made his cheeks feel as if they flamed.

"Watch out, Boats," Moira said with a laugh. "Hana comes from a people who are very direct about what they want."

"I'll, ah, I'll go clean up now. If you'll excuse me?" He hurried toward his room, feeling giddy and terrified at the same time.

He had been completely smitten by Hana the first time he laid eyes on her. Nevertheless, he had been careful all this time to keep their relationship formal and business-like.

That just might change a bit, now! He grinned like a schoolboy. He knew he would have to have a talk with Big Boy Hauta, but he wasn't worried.

He wondered if he would have to get a tattoo, and if he did, how big, of what, and where?

CHAPTER 6

"YOU HAVE BECOME A GOD," the ancient priest said.

Noah's brow wrinkled into a frown. "You are a Catholic priest, and you tell me I am a god?"

"To those who do not know better, you are a god."

"They are wrong. I am but a simple man who arbitrarily gained abilities and have learned how to use them to help others."

"And those abilities came from what?"

"I don't know, exactly." Noah thought about the glowing seal in his mother's larder, about his early years of trying to rein in his "appetite," and the sudden knowledge that the source of his abilities came from a being from beyond the stars.

Father Krystociak would have to wait for more answers. Noah had yet to parse them out.

"You have given me much food for thought, Father. I appreciate your insights into realms I still find puzzling."

"You have an undeniable gift, Noah, and you use it well. I only wonder as to its genesis and how this much power will affect you."

"I'll let you know, Father Krystociak." Noah smiled at him. "I promise."

He accompanied the priest outside and the man left at his own speed. Noah waited until the he was lost to sight. Noah wandered down the path into the dense grove of weeping willows where people went to be alone with their thoughts or to meditate.

A large stream-fed pond featured a small island accessed by a carved bridge. In the middle of the island sat a large, flat red rock from the Australian outback. Noah climbed onto the rock, found his favorite spot, and sat down.

~I know you are there. From where did you come? Why did you leave? What is your true nature?~

Noah thought he might go unanswered, but in less than three heartbeats he received his answer.

•*You have arrived at the crux of our relationship more speedily than I thought you would, Noah. I came from an ancient race that had metamorphosed the bounds of the physical and attained mental recognizance before your ancestors walked upright. We evolved many light years from this planet.*•

~*But why did you leave your planet of origin? Why did you come here?*~

•*A multitude of us left to seek our far-flung brethren. I know not what became of them or of our home world. I stumbled on your race, your world, and in doing so I altered it immeasurably, for which I grieve.*•

~*Brethren? Do you believe we came from the same origin?*~

•*I do not know. What I have found here has turned me into a scholar. I have absorbed most of the libraries on this planet.*•

~*And?*~

•*I continue to study the intricacies of your world, especially the similar origin legends, and religions. Difficult to understand, yet your race kills one another over mere nuance of belief. Difficult to understand, but I shall persevere.*•

~*I know we destroyed a portion of your mass when we burned the shark and the consumed Hydra. Is what is inside my family and Thinker's family all there is left of you?*~

•*Probably not. Otherwise, I would have access to all my memories. Yet I do not feel the less for having lost the malevolent pieces of my personality. I know I am growing, and I am one with the portions residing in Thinker, Looa, and Talker, as well as Moira and Solomon.*•

~*What is the name of your home planet?*~

•*In your language it would translate to Paradise.*•

~*Was it a paradise? Can you remember it?*~

•*I know not. I cannot remember it. For many thousands of your years, I fit your definition of insane. Some of my early memories have returned to me, and I feel more will surface as I grow and as long as I remain quiescent.*•

~*Be at peace, scholar.*~

CHAPTER 7

THE RAIL JOURNEY TO ADELAIDE FROM Perth had an hour yet to conclude. Moira sat on the sofa in her private car, feet tucked under her, totally at peace while she read a magazine she discovered in Canberra. Both Hana and Solomon napped in their berths. Boats sat quietly, alternating between reading a lurid novel and staring at Hana.

She smiled. They would make a handsome couple. It had been obvious to everyone from the beginning that he was completely yarra about her.

They had traveled the whole continent of Australia. Moira had even given Alice Springs a free concert after telling the crowd it was the place that brought her back to music.

Adelaide would be the final concert. Eighteen months of travel and schedules, crowds of every color, and side trips to show Solomon the wonders of their country, was nearly finished. She wished there could be a grander finale than Adelaide. Nothing against that lovely city, of course.

A photo of a leaping Humpback whale in the magazine pulled her mind to a complete stop.

"M'gawd! That would be fantastic!" she suddenly blurted.

Boats immediately jerked to his feet with right hand firmly grasping the pistol nestling beneath his left armpit.

"What?"

"I am sorry. You asked me not to do that." Moira gave him a dazzling smile. "But what do you think about me appearing in a concert with two other singers?"

Boats thought hard. Other singers did exist in Australia and New Zealand, but none had the, what did they call it, yeah, star power that Moira possessed in bucket loads. "Which ones? The only ones I know about don't amount to watery grog in my opinion."

"Thinker and Looa."

"Thinker and — bloody whales?" *How the hell can I provide security for her and two whales?* "Where the hell can we put two whales on a stage with you?"

"In the middle of the Tasman Sea."

Boats laughed. "I say, Moira, you had me going there for a moment. I thought you were serious."

"Danford Stout. I could not be more serious. Please work with me on this."

"Sorry, Moira." He felt bewildered. "Ain't every day someone proposes singing with whales in the middle of the bloody ocean. Caught me off stride, as it were."

"I'm sorry, Boats. I didn't mean to snap. You're correct; it sounds as if I've a kangaroo in my top paddock. But I am sane."

"How do we have a concert in the middle of the ocean, Moira?"

"We charter four tour ships, offer trip, berth, and concert for, what, five hundred dollars, which would net a million dollars. Have it at a location only the four ship captains would know, and you wouldn't need to worry about security."

"Have you asked Thinker and Looa?"

"Not yet. I wanted your opinion."

"The thought of it gives me a rash I can't scratch," Boats said. "But I think we could do it. My God, this could stop commercial whaling."

In the past three years, all the Pacific's rebuilding nations had added whaling to fishing to feed their growing populations. Australia and New Zealand, both of whom had stopped the practice two years before thanks to certain strategic campaign donations, opposed the idea to no avail.

"Yes!" Moira said. "And that's why we'll bloody well do it."

CHAPTER 8

Looa fluked beside her mate while wondering at his words. She marveled at his knowledge from outside their watery world but doubted if she was mentally agile enough to be his mate.

~Looa is the perfect mate for Thinker. Never doubt your worth to me.~

~Looa wants Thinker to be with her until all essence drowns. Looa wonders why Thinker asks of what she does not understand.~

~Thinker knows that Looa does not understand, yet. He asks only that she stretch her mind to-~

~¿To what?~

~¿Did you hear a summons?~

~No, I only heard-~ Suddenly the call glowed across her mind.

~I can help. Please come to me.~

~¿Moira? She can help who? What?~

~We must visit Moira to answer your questions.~

Looa quietly made the whale equivalent of a sigh and followed her mate.

They fluked out of the Bahia Sebastian Vizcaino and moved southwest as fast as they could travel. As they traveled, Looa felt impressed that she could hear Moira's summons from halfway around the world. She suddenly felt more secure about her mental abilities.

CHAPTER 9

NOAH STOOD ON THE STARBOARD WING OF THE BRIDGE enjoying the breeze moving past him. The clean ocean air held a refreshing chill. Captain Currie promised to take him south to visit Antarctica any time Noah wished.

Soon, he thought, *but there are so many things yet to do.*

Captain Currie leaned against the blast shield next to Noah. "We should see Australia within the next ten minutes or so. We're about an hour out of Melbourne. What do you think of our ship?"

"The *Andrew Dawkins II* is your ship, Captain Currie. I am only one of the owners. She's a beautiful vessel. Was the first *Dawkins* this large?"

"No. This ship is about ten meters longer and a few meters wider. We added a stateroom for you, which in an emergency, doubles as a hospital. Then there are the laboratories where we can assay minerals, do a necropsy on a dead creature, or anything in between."

"You sound happy, Stuart."

"You know I am, Noah. With all the scientists and technicians aboard, there's more brains on this ship than in any of the universities in Oz."

"We offer better wages and the most modern facilities possible," Noah said with a smile. "Those are difficult odds to beat."

"Too bloody right. But you bring up a point I've been meaning to chat about with you."

"Land ho!" the starboard bridge watchman sang out. "Dead ahead."

Currie turned and spoke to the bosun, "Make ready to enter port. Quartermaster, we'll tie up at Malone's dock next to the grain terminal."

Both orders acknowledged, Currie turned back to Noah. "We have enough land at Sanctuary to build a university. New Zealand and Australia desperately need more doctors and scientists. We could use the blokes on this ship as the core professors."

"You've been talking to Sean, haven't you?"

Currie frowned. "To Mr. Williams? No, not lately. Why?"

"He's willing to give us more of his land, most of it in fact, if we'll do what you just proposed. Education spores must be in the air."

"Well, what did you say?"

"I told him I would think about it. Our people are stretched pretty thin already."

"That's why you create a university, Noah, for the students who will come and work just to learn in return. You will have a queue a mile long at the door on the first day of registration."

"But I know nothing of formal education–"

"Excuse my interruption, but you don't have to know anything. There is an army of people out there who would give their left nut to work at Sanctuary with you. Most would do it for food and shelter."

"Who would run the thing? Don't universities and colleges have presidents or chancellors or something?"

"We can deal with all that later. Right now, we just need the word from you that you'll be part of it."

"Of course, I will. I'll do all that I can."

Currie slapped the smaller man on the back. "That's one of the reasons I like you, Noah. You're always willing to try something new."

The *Andrew Dawkins II* slowed as it entered the Port Adelaide River which hooked north and then dropped south behind the Lefevre Peninsula to where most of the docks and wharves of the Port of Adelaide lay. *Dawkins* didn't even get to the tip of the peninsula before turning into the cove where Malone's Dock and Wharfage nestled with longshoremen waiting on a pier festooned with banners and flags.

Currie glassed the crowd with his binoculars. "There's Moira and Solomon!"

~I've missed you, my love. So has our son.~

~I would have been insane without our nightly chats,~ Noah replied. They had spoken like this every night since Moira's

concert tour began nearly two years ago.

~Father, I finally get to meet Thinker and Looa. It is good to have you with us, too. Mother says I have grown.~

"Reverse engines," Currie barked. Moments later he said, "Stop engines. Throw the monkey fist, Bosun."

The lead weight enclosed within the intricately knotted rope, known to centuries of mariners as the monkey fist, shot through the air, one from the foredeck and one from the stern of the *Dawkins*. Expert longshoremen caught them and pulled the attached light line hand over hand that in turn was tied to the heavy hawsers, designed to moor the *Dawkins* to the dock. Large rope and rubber fenders already hung in place to act as buffers between the steel ship and wood dock.

A small tugboat chugged up to the starboard side of the *Dawkins* and gently nudged the ship toward the dock. Within minutes, the *Andrew Dawkins II* was moored. While the deck crew removed a portion of the cable railing on the ship, the longshoremen hoisted a sturdy gangplank with a cargo crane.

As soon as the gangplank was secured in place, Solomon raced aboard and leaped into Noah's arms.

"I missed you, father," he said kissing him on both cheeks and hugging his neck. Then Moira's arms were around him and Noah knew all was right with the world.

CHAPTER 10

Captain Currie ensured refueling was under way, and that his bosun was supervising the loading. Diesel was still expensive and there were those who would happily fill their own tanks and charge it to the last, or next, ship to pull into the harbour. At the same time, he had his storekeeper monitoring the loading of fresh provisions his shore-based factor had arranged.

In every port the *Andrew Dawkins II* visited, a shore-bound representative made sure the ship received what was needed and, in most cases, wanted. Stuart Currie had been at this sort of thing for over three decades, and he thought he had seen it all.

"Beg pardon, Captain Currie," the officer of the watch, Lieutenant Keith, said. "There are two, ah, gentlemen to see you, sir."

"Very well." Currie pushed away from his desk on the bridge. "Lead me to them."

Currie took his time in order to visually get their measure as quickly as possible. Japanese or Chinese? They didn't get many Asiatic blokes this far south.

The one obviously in charge looked grim as death, the other seemed skittish. *What were they doing here and what could they possibly want from him?*

"Good day. I'm Captain Currie. How may I help you?"

"I am Captain Saigauo, and this is Seaman Hirouchi. We are from the *MV Provider* out of Sapporo. We are the best whalers in Japan."

"Well, bully for you," Currie said dryly. "What's that to me?"

"I have heard you are with the people staging the 'Moira sings with the Whales' production. Is that correct?"

"What do you want, Captain Saigauo? I've no time to waste with a bloody butcher."

"You do not know me. Why are you insulting me?"

"Because you hunt a creature that is probably twice your mental superior, but being peaceful in nature, usually doesn't realize your sort is about until the fucking exploding harpoon hits it. I don't like whalers, Captain, and I'm running out of time for this meeting."

"Whaling is a long and honorable profession in my country. If we did not take our protein from the sea we would have very little–"

"Yeah, I've seen your harvesting techniques. I watched in revulsion while a gang of your mates surrounded about a hundred dolphins, beating metal poles on their boats to confuse the things, and then butcher them wholesale. I've never witnessed such brutal methods, before or since."

Saigauo took a deep breath, his face darkly flushed. "Well, for your information, the two whales you are professing to be singers and pacific are actually killers. We have sought them for years."

"No, the killer whale is an Orca."

"No, these two Humpback whales are murderers!"

Currie stared into Saigauo's eyes. The man didn't seem mad, but his words bordered on that definition. "And they murdered who, and how?"

"My first mate, Tetsudo Honda, and my quartermaster, Yakusune, within the territorial limits of Australia."

"That's who. Now pray tell, how?"

"They both died of heart failure at the same moment. Both men had a clean bill of health from the Port Surgeon in Sapporo no less than a week before their deaths. Two Humpbacks were spotted just before this happened."

"Our Humpbacks?"

"We came across those whales less than a week after the deaths of Honda and Yakusune. They made us believe they were headed north rather than southwest."

"Do you realize how insane you sound at the moment?" Currie said with a strong dose of disdain in his voice. "I'm not surprised you haven't brought this matter up to the Australian Admiralty. They'd have laughed you out of Sydney Harbour."

"We've heard the stories about whales with abnormal mental abilities. Those creatures killed two men–"

"In self-defense, if they did!" Currie snapped. "Whoever they were, or whatever they were, they were bloody well being hunted.

"Their lives depended on their ability to fight back, defend themselves. Turn the situation around and you would be screaming 'bloody miracle' to one and all! How many whales have *you* killed?"

Currie wanted to hurt them but knew he had probably gone too far already. "Both your whaling blokes likely died of alcohol poisoning anyway. You should be ashamed of yourselves trying to shout murder against defenseless creatures when you are in fact the murderers."

"I demand to know where you are going to meet them!" Saigauo snarled.

"Fuck you, you goddamned high seas butcher! Get off my ship before I have you thrown in the brig as malcontents. If you come within a nautical mile of my ship I will sink your disgusting ass, and brag about it afterward."

Seaman Hirouchi, no longer shy, made a sound somewhere in his gullet and stepped toward Captain Currie. Currie stared at the man and nodded. Two seamen stepped out of the shadows with rifles aimed at the man's head.

"Go ahead," Currie said with an evil grin, "give 'em an excuse."

Both rifles audibly came off safety.

"We leave now, Seaman Hirouchi," Saigauo said with some heat. "We shall find our justice on the high seas."

Both men marched down the gangway. Currie watched them until they were lost from sight.

Not good, he thought. *Not good at all.*

CHAPTER 11

"The *Andrew Dawkins II* will maintain station 40° latitude and 160° longitude," Captain Currie said.

"That's right over Lord Howe's Rise, but you're still talking a depth of 2,000 meters, so we won't be able to anchor," said Captain Boyes of the tour ship *Joy's Smile.*

"We'll have to keep our engines running. Will that bother the other singers?" Captain Flint of the *Lucille* asked with a grin.

"Engine noise shouldn't bother them," Moira said. "As long as you keep your distance. Are all berths sold on your ships, gentlemen?"

As one, the four captains nodded.

"I didn't think there were that many people who would pay five hundred dollars to see a concert of any sort," Captain Spitz of the *Aurora* said. "Makes me wonder if I shouldn't raise my prices."

"Now, Jim," Captain Shubert said. "Everybody knows this is for a good cause, not to make some bloke rich."

"Yeah, you're right, Donald. The tourism industry has a long way to go before we can make a living hauling people around showin' 'em the sights."

"One more time from the top," Currie said. "All five ships will weigh anchor after 2400 hours. Each will follow the course I've just given you. Maintain radio silence.

"There have been threats made against our guest singers, and I'd like to see this thing come off with nobody getting hurt. If the malcontents don't know where we are, they can't cause trouble. Safe journey, gentlemen."

CHAPTER 12

ANDREW DAWKINS II STEAMED INTO THE WARM NIGHT WITH all lights covered except her running lights. Currie sat in his chair on the bridge, watching the radar and trying not to yawn.

Bosun Kabongo entered the bridge and stopped at the captain's side. "As ordered, Captain, all three guns are mounted and ready for service."

"Good work, Mike. Any problems with the five-inch?"

"None, Captain. We have the best gunner's mates the ANDF ever trained."

"We have the best crew ever trained," Currie said with a grin. "Are you still working on your first mate's ticket?"

"Yes, sir. And just between you and me, I'll pass the battery the first time."

"I believe you. Tell Chief Gunner's Mate Walls to have the men tarp all the guns. No sense getting our passengers or viewing audience nervous."

"They're already covered, Captain, and Chief Walls has two watches of gunners assigned. Port watch is below decks getting some rack time."

"Good man! Now I'm going to do the same thing. I'd like you out there during the daylight. Okay?"

"I'll be there. Good night, Captain."

"G'night, Mike."

The radarman cleared his throat. "Skipper, we have company."

"Show me, Leo."

"Watch here, they're almost off the screen. There! Did you see that contact?"

"Yeah, I saw it. That puts 'em, what, about fifty klicks behind us?"

"Right at, Skipper."

"Keep an eye on them. If they get any closer, wake me up. We might just get lucky and they're only transiting the area headed for Kiwi country."

"I'll watch them closely, Skipper."

"You're a good man, Leo Schmidt. I'll be in my quarters."

He turned to the OOW. "Mr. Keith, you have the bridge. I'll be in my quarters."

"Aye, aye, sir. I have the bridge."

CHAPTER 13

"Keep your distance, helmsman!"

"My apologies, Captain Saigauo, but if you want me to shadow them, we have to keep them on the edge of the scope."

"If you can see them, they can see us! I haven't searched for those whales all these years to fail now. Mr. Jinsinko, have you worked out the chart problem I gave you?"

"Yes, Captain, I have. They have advertised the event at 1200 hours. At their present speed and bearing, the most likely coordinates are 40°N by 160°W. "Three of us have worked on this, Captain, and we're sure this is their destination."

"Good work, Mr. Jinsinko. Now get your gun crews up here. We have much to do."

"Captain, it's the middle of the night. There is nothing to see."

"They have to be prepared," Saigauo snapped. "Are they?"

"I guarantee it, Captain."

"Very well. But I want them at their stations at 0700."

"They'll be there, Captain, or you can have my ticket."

"As you say, mister." Captain Saigauo glanced around the bridge. His gaze stopped on the signalman. "Akita, what word from the other ships?"

"As ordered, they're using their signal lamps. Both are on station behind us."

"Excellent. Maintain contact."

Saigauo had found two other Japanese whalers in port and enlisted their help. He had assured them they were more for show than actual confrontation. Both captains had readily agreed to help the legendary Sapporo whaler.

First Officer Jinsinko eased up next to Saigauo. "Captain, I am apprehensive about putting civilians in harm's way."

"Your apprehensions have no place on my bridge, nor does any officer who has no faith in his captain."

"All of our lives are on the line here, Captain. I would be pleased to hear your plan."

"I'm not a suicide, Mr. Jinsinko. Now follow orders or get off my bridge!"

Captain Saigauo detected sidelong glances from the rest of the bridge watch. "Now listen up, the lot of you! We are not breaking any laws. In fact, we're going to demonstrate our right not only to make a living but also to bring two murdering monsters to justice. If anybody wishes to debate these points, now is the time."

Every man seemed intent on his given task and the only sounds heard were those of a ship underway on a calm sea.

"Excellent!" Saigauo snapped.

CHAPTER 14

"LOOKS LIKE WE HAVE A GOOD DAY FOR IT." Captain Currie smiled through the windscreen at the sun-dappled water.

Noah tried to return the smile, but he felt uneasy. *So very many things could go wrong today. Conversely, all could go according to plan, too*, he thought.

Solomon stomped onto the bridge, followed by Boats Stout. "What's our position, Captain Currie?" he said in his high-pitched boy's voice.

Everyone on the bridge grinned at the precocious four-year-old.

~Why are you worried, Father?~

"We're about five kilometers from our destination, Solomon," Currie said. "Should be rendezvousing with the others within twenty minutes."

"We're all very excited, sir." Solomon grinned at everyone.

~I'm not sure, my son. But something seems wrong. Perhaps I'm just uneasy being at sea. The sea has always been an adversary, it seems.~

~No worries, Father. We have all our best people here.~

"We're on station, Captain," the quartermaster said.

"Very well. Dead slow, helm."

"Dead slow, aye." The engine room telegraph rang as he pulled the brass lever back.

"Come to a dead stop at the position. Inform Mister Stout that his crew can commence their set-up."

"Aye, aye, Captain."

While Currie scanned the horizon with his binoculars, Noah scanned the sea with his mind. Where were Thinker and Looa?

~Noah, my friend, we are here in the place Moira described.~

~Hello, Thinker and Looa, I am happy to meet you both.~

~My son has the manners of a four-year-old human,~ Noah said, giving all a mental grin.

~It is good to meet you, Solomon, and you also, Noah.~

~We met before, at the island, Looa.~

~I was barely aware then. Now I understand how different from normal this is.~

~Noah, there are whalers following your boat.~

~How many, Thinker?

~Three.~

~Three!~ Noah peered back at the horizon aft of the ship.

"What's the matter, Noah?" Currie asked.

"There are three whalers following us. Thinker just told me."

Currie glassed the horizon all the way around the ship. "Nothing but the cruise ships that I can see. The bastards must be lying doggo just over the horizon."

The four cruise ships slowly converged on them from different directions.

In the meantime, Boats Stout had a crew in the process of hoisting a previously tied-down platform into position on the port side hull of the *Andrew Dawkins II*. They also assembled two large camera cranes. The concert was not only going to be filmed, but it was also being televised live for the benefit of fledgling public broadcasting stations in Australia, Tasmania, and New Zealand.

"Sure glad it's a calm day," Currie muttered, still glassing the horizon.

The four cruise ships approached at dead slow and took up station in an arc around the port side of *Dawkins*. Thinker and Looa breeched and fell back into the sea, side-by-side, in the opening between the ships.

A collective gasp of awe came from all sides. Moira moved next to the railing and then down the little stairs hooked to the platform. She stepped up to the microphone.

"Thank you all for coming to our concert. My name is Moira–"

Applause rolled across the water from all four ships and the crew of the *Dawkins* joined in.

"And this is Thinker–"

Thinker breached just below the platform and fell outward so the water wouldn't soak Moira.

"And our third singer is Looa!"

Looa shot from the sea in the same spot Thinker had, falling at a 90° angle away from Thinker's trajectory.

Shouts and cheers spiced the applause. The cameras caught everything. Noah saw that one stayed on Moira and the other pointed toward the water where the two Humpbacks now rose side-by-side beneath the platform.

"We thank you," Moira said. "The Humpback is known as the singing whale. Songs are their oral history. Many of their songs are hundreds of years old. Some were created only yesterday."

Music filled the air, surprising Noah as he hadn't noticed the band setting up earlier. The amplified guitar chords coalesced into the John Lennon tune just suggested by Moira. Since he had never heard the song before, Noah was amazed when some of the crew around him softly sang the words with her.

A melodious tone rose from the whales, moving with and through Moira's song, sliding beautifully through the registers. The flesh prickled at the back of Noah's neck, and he felt both supreme sadness and uplifting awe waft through him. This song from the old days before the Asteroids, long a cultural icon (this gleaned from Moira's mind as she sang), held a magical place in the history of humanity.

The cetaceans' song seemed to buoy the human words and give them more complete meaning in addition to the extra resonance, all together creating something new, magical, and incredibly moving. Noah pulled his attention away from Moira and glanced around at the others on the bridge wing with him. Tears shown on the face of every person there, including his.

Moira, Thinker, and Looa subsided into silence and Moira bowed her head. The applause rang across the water and bounced off the hulls of the ships.

~This human flipper-noise is good?~

~Yes, my friends. It is not only good, but also the highest praise a human can offer another being. You both sing most wondrously.~

~Noah! We're in the middle of a set; do shut up!~

~You sing wondrously also, my love.~

CHAPTER 15

"Captain Saigauo, the other ships are in place."

"Thank you, Mr. Jinsinko. Now give me an open channel that all those recreational seamen out there will hear."

"Here, Captain. Speak into the microphone and they'll all hear you."

"Attention, ships between me and the pair of rogue whales. This is Captain Saigauo of the *MV Provider*. We request you clear the area while we bring to justice these two man-killing creatures."

Currie had alerted the other captains to the presence of the whalers. Immediate responses followed.

"This is Captain Flint of the *Lucille*. If you harm my ship or any of my passengers, I will personally tear off your head and shove it up your ass. I'm not moving my ship for a halfwit."

Saigauo's face went red. Before he could answer, another voice came over the speaker.

"Saigauo, this is Captain Currie of the *Andrew Dawkins II*. I am a reserve commander in the Australian Naval Defense Force, and therefore the highest civil and military authority present at this time. I order you to depart these waters instantly, as any deviation to these orders on your part will be met by deadly force."

Saigauo grabbed the microphone and snarled into it, "I have whale hunter cannonades on this craft, as do the other whalers in my van. You will clear my hunting grounds or suffer the consequences. Your choice."

As soon as Saigauo released the microphone button, Jinsinko spoke in his ear. "Captain, you're threatening the license of every sailor on board. This man is in the ANDF. I have heard of him; he's done some very brave things over the years."

"I am the captain. You are the crew. Disobey me and you will be hauled up in court for mutiny, let alone lose your berths forever!"

"Captain Saigauo," Radioman Ikiesuni said. "Both of our whalers are leaving the area as ordered."

"Those cowards, I'll have them whipped out of the fleet, just you–"

"Captain! The *Dawkins* is moving away from the others, coming toward us!"

"That's fine, Jinsinko. Don't turn woman on me now. He can't hurt us. Full speed ahead. Chief Gunner Taduchi, put a round past his bow."

"Captain?" Jinsinko whispered, watching the Dawkins through his binoculars. The ship picked up speed.

"Taduchi, shoot your damned gun!"

"They're pointing a fucking cannon at us, Saigauo!" Jinsinko screamed.

Taduchi fired and the 20mm round barely made a splash, but the weapon's sharp report echoed across the water.

"Thank you, Saigauo," Captain Currie's voice grated through the speaker. "Tell your men to abandon ship, now."

"They have no right!" Saigauo muttered, eyes wide.

CHAPTER 16

"They're jumping overboard faster than rats off a burning garbage scow," Lt. Keith said, peering through his binoculars.

"Not as stupid as Saigauo thought they were." Currie sighed. "Okay, Chief Walls, put a round through the bridge on that slaughterhouse."

The heavy, flat crack of the 5-inch gun made every watching civilian wince in pain. The bridge of the *MV Provider* blew into pieces. When the smoke from her explosion cleared, the ship was engulfed in fire.

The ship boiled with flame and dark, oily smoke.

"Christ wept!" Bosun Stout said.

"All hands to their duty stations!" Currie bellowed over the tannoy. "Stand by to pick up survivors. Man overboard!"

The four *Dawkins* whaleboats swung out on their davits and, fully manned, dropped toward the water in a graceful naval choreography that looked practiced and seemed easy. All four boats hit the water within fifteen seconds of one another.

The camera crews caught everything. The survivors were pulled from the water and the rescue of a burned seaman by one of the *Dawkins* sailors who jumped into the ocean to pull the man to safety. There was long shot of the *Provider* exploding and sinking rapidly beneath the Tasman Sea.

The whaleboats returned to the Dawkins and were hoisted aboard. The injured survivors were whisked off to sickbay. The concert continued with a requiem offered for all who lost life or suffered injury.

The whales' song lent an air of anguish and mortality that human throats could not match. The air throbbed with sorrow and loss, reducing every mortal who heard the paean to bitter, nearly involuntary, tears.

The cameras and microphones caught it all. In the years ahead the revenues from this concert would do more to help rebuild Australian public telecommunications than all the combined grants from state or federal governments. The entire shipboard audience would brag of witnessing the event until their dying day. It became an instant icon for the human and cetacean races. Attitudes changed after that.

Unrecorded by any camera, and unseen by cognizant eyes, was the lonely figure that evaded the rescue boats. Time after time he dove deep as they approached. Finally, they ceased their search.

The figure struck out slow and steady. Resolutely he swam toward the nearest land, forty kilometers away.

CHAPTER 17

Moira watched Noah hold his daily audience through the security window and wondered when her husband had begun to go gray. He had suddenly grown hair ten years earlier, "Just to see what it's like," he had explained. His hair had come in jet black and never needed cutting.

She turned to the mirror on the adjacent wall and critically examined herself. She still looked to be in her middle 30s.

"That's bloody impossible!" she said aloud.

"Ma'am?" the woman standing security watch responded.

"Sorry, just talking to myself again. Would you look at your little crystal ball there and tell me where my son is currently located?"

"Certainly, Moira," she said with a smile. She tapped a key on her laptop and looked up. "Solomon is currently in the art wing of the university. Is there anything more I can do for you?"

"No, Jessica. Just keep an eye on Noah for me, please."

"My pleasure."

As Moira walked across the campus of Manaluk-Williams University she realized time had ripped by at unholy speed. Solomon was nearing his eighteenth birthday and would eventually marry Emily Stout. Although the daughter of Danford and Hana was only thirteen, she and Solomon had loved one another from the day of her birth.

Moira didn't think Solomon had even looked at another girl with any interest. The campus seemed thick with students from every continent on the planet, save perhaps Antarctica, and for all she knew there might be penguins here, too. Most students she passed nodded and spoke to her, especially the ones majoring in voice.

Solomon stood in the painting room working on a large canvas.

His art merged representational and iconic with a strong dash of surrealism. At least that's what his instructor had told her a few years ago.

She eyed the work critically. "You're putting your father's entire life on one canvas?"

"Hello, mother," he said without looking around. "Yes, or at least I'm trying to. Father has had a very interesting life."

"The baidarka isn't quite right." Moira frowned at the work and tried to remember how the old boat differed from his painting.

"When you figure it out, please let me know." Solomon dropped his brushes into a can of solvent and wiped his hands on a multi-hued cloth as he walked toward her.

They hugged and she kissed his cheek.

"But that's not why you're here," he said with a knowing smile.

"How long has your father been arresting my aging processes?"

"As long as I can remember. But then I didn't pay attention to that sort of thing until I was at least six or seven."

Moira stared at the painting. "The top of the boat is wrong. It wasn't that round. It was flatter and had places to tie gear down."

Solomon looked at it. "You're right. Where did that curve come from?"

"Probably your father's faulty memories. Have you noticed he is going grey?"

"Yeah, I have."

"But?" she said, looking intently at her son.

"He keeps care of all of us in the extended family, on the staff, even people down in Wellington. Yet, he won't do anything for himself."

"Then you must, Solomon, because I can't. All I can do is read people and talk to them in their minds or hurt them; that's it."

He laughed. "You make it sound like you're handicapped, mother. There are a lot of blokes out there who would love to have your talents and abilities."

"I know that! And you know what I'm getting at here."

"Of course I do. And just between you and me, I have been keeping him healthy, but not altering his appearance."

Moira felt her soul relax. "Oh, thank heavens. I thought you were being as lax as me."

"Mum, you ain't lax. You're constantly poking about, no matter where you are, seeing if there is anyone out there we haven't helped yet. I am constantly awed by both of my parents and wonder if I can ever do as much good as the two of you have accomplished."

Moira felt a tear run down her cheek. "That's the nicest thing anyone has ever said to me."

"Maybe since yesterday," he said with a wide grin. "Don't worry about father, I'm keeping an eye on him. Aren't you late for your voice seminar?" He nodded at the clock on the wall.

"Bloody hell, so I am!" She hugged him close and whispered, "I love you, Solomon!"

"I love you, Mum. Now go teach your class."

Moira hurried across to the next building. The scent of flowers and cut grass filled the warm air along with the cheerful conversation of students. Her heart felt full, and she knew there might be more difficulties ahead, but she couldn't see them from here.

CHAPTER 18

"Do you have any regrets Master Noah?" the student asked.

"Oh, yes, quite a number."

"Then, according to what you have been telling us, you should be trying to atone for them, yes?"

"To a large degree, I have atoned. But there are things I have done wrong that have never been righted, if you will."

"Why not?" another student asked.

"I've been busy," he said with a chuckle and held his hands out to indicate the room in which they sat as well as the larger complex around them.

They didn't smile, merely continued to stare at him.

"Maybe I do need a working vacation. I've wanted to visit the United States for some time now. And I want to see Alaska again."

Silence reigned for over three minutes before he looked up into their faces again. "That's all for today. I bid you all health and happiness."

"Health and happiness," echoed back at him from every young person in the room.

In moments he sat alone in the hall. But he knew he wasn't alone in the building. "Boats, come on in here. I want to talk."

The security portal slid open, and the tall man walked over and sat next to his friend. "How are you today, Noah?"

"Thoughtful. Have you ever been to Alaska?"

"Not yet."

"Well, I think that's going to change."

"You say the word and I'll arrange it."

Noah twisted his head and stared into his friend's eyes. "June, the tundra flowers will be at their best, and life will be at its easiest. Let's go next June."

"You're the boss."

EPILOGUE

"I HAVE HEARD NOTHING FOR HOURS, TIM," N'Go said.

Thorvald Svensson examined the tracks carefully. In all his days he had never seen polar bear tracks this large. No wonder his traps yielded only bloody spots where his catch had been consumed on the spot. This was the second day of his two-week trek to check his trap line.

Thorvald had been born here in Greenland, as were all his ancestors back to the 1740s. His wife Minni could claim even more remote lineage, as she was Inuit. He had spent his life hunting and trapping this land.

The size of the polar bear track truly frightened him. *How could anything get that big?* He peered around at the broken horizon.

The land shelved upward from the coast until it reached the ice cap. The massive ice cap was so thick it pushed the land of central Greenland below sea level. Thorvald had been to the ice once with his father and the sheer size of the forbidding cap had put fear into his soul.

The tracks echoed that fear. Nothing moved that he could see, and from here one could see for at least three kilometers. He looked back at the blood pool beside the trap.

Very little snow had blown over the frozen blood, and the wind moved constantly in this place. The blood couldn't be more than an hour old.

Abruptly his lead dog howled into the wind. Thorvald rose to his feet and held his 7mm rifle firmly in both hands. His gloved trigger finger toyed with the small opening in the right mitten.

With the temperature holding at −32°F, he didn't want to expose the finger to frostbite for naught. The silk gloves he wore inside the mittens would keep his finger from being burned by the cold metal of the rifle, but that was about all.

Suddenly all five of his dogs were on their feet and snarling. Thorvald turned and saw the front shoulders and head of a huge polar bear looking at him from behind a mound of snow. Instantly he snapped the rifle to his shoulder and quickly aimed.

Just as he squeezed the trigger and fired, the polar bear ducked behind the mound. Terror swept through him. *Polar bears don't duck and hide; they charge!*

He fired into the snowbank hoping the rounds would penetrate the snow and hit the animal. Sparks flew from where the steel jacketed rounds hit the basalt beneath the snow. The bear had picked a rock for cover.

Thorvald dug into his pocket and grabbed more bullets, shook off the mittens, and began reloading the 7mm.

The dogs lunged, snarling in their harness, and Thorvald looked up to see the bear leaping over the rock and racing straight at him. He bolted a round into the chamber and fired at the bear.

It jerked to the left out of the path of the bullet but didn't slow in its charge.

Thorvald didn't have time for another shot. His last thoughts were spent wondering why the bear's eyes glowed with a blue fire.

The bear ate every scrap of the human and the dogs. Now it had sufficient reserves for the trip ahead. As it suspected, the human had an adequate grasp of geography.

It saw the path it must take to rejoin the two large masses of mental brilliance it perceived on the other side of this planet.

The bear dropped to all fours and moved west, toward the frozen Davis Strait and the distant Baffin Island. Once there, it knew it could go south for a very long time. While it steadily moved it constantly turned the words "New Zealand" over in its mind. There was so much yet to learn, but it knew it had time.

About the Author

Leonard (Stoney) Compton is a native of Nebraska, a U.S. Navy vet, and a former 31-year resident of Alaska. During those 31 years, he wore many hats, did many things, and is now trying to fit them all into his fiction.

He is married to Colette, and they live north of Farmington, New Mexico with their many cats, Blue Heeler, Pullo, and Milo Sherlock of dubious mix.

Visit Stoney's web page at http://www.stoneycompton.com

If you enjoyed this novel, or not, please leave a review in Good Reads or wherever you talk to the world.